ALSO BY HORTENSIA DE LOS SANTOS

The Noumenon – Shadow of Distant Past

First Exodus – Gone from Earth

Power of the Gods

The Drop of Blood

A Forgotten Love Story

La Otra Historia (In Spanish)

Between Worlds (Poems)

A Través del Velo Rasgado (In Spanish)

Caverna de Cristales Gigantes (In Spanish)

Tras el Velo Rasgado (In Spanish)

The Broken Veil

CHAPTER XVII	138
CHAPTER XVIII	156
CHAPTER XIX	164
CHAPTER XX	174
CHAPTER XXI	186
CHAPTER XXII	193
CHAPTER XXIII	200
CHAPTER XXIV	207
CHAPTER XXV	213
CHAPTER XXVI	217
CHAPTER XXVII	222
CHAPTER XXVIII	230
CHAPTER XXIX	234
CHAPTER XXX	239
ABOUT THE AUTHOR	244

INTRODUCTION

Waves taller than the tallest mountains rose before me and I heard a multitude cry in terror, but I couldn't see them. I knew it was daytime and the darkness that surrounded me made no sense. Hard as I tried I couldn't see the stars in the sky. The only thing visible were the waves, dark as the night and yet still visible because of the strange phosphorescence in their slopes. As much as I craned my neck trying to see their cusps, they were invisible in the dark and the terrible height.

The ship wobbled, like a leaf ready to fall from the tree. Before those huge waves, it looked and felt minute, microscopic, irrelevant. Yes, as irrelevant as I felt in face of this terrible sea.

The wave fell upon us. I thought it was taking an inordinate amount of time to crash on the ship, as if time was slowed so we could experience the coming of death to its depth. And then, suddenly, it crashed. I felt suffocated, flattened, I could not breathe, and I trashed, trashed, trying to rise to the surface, to fill my lungs with precious air.

I woke. My mother was there beside me. Sitting on the side of my small bed she was holding my arms, leaning towards me and I sensed her fear and concern; most of all I felt her love for me.

"It's just a dream, Andrew, just a nightmare." She was whispering, and I knew she had been whispering for a while. "It's just a terrible nightmare, wake up, all is alright!"

All was not alright, however. I knew I had experienced something terrible; I knew I had died.

Sent Back

CHAPTER I

We lived in a big two floor suburban house with a magnificent stair I planned to use as a snowboard slope when I was bigger. It also had a beautiful large garden, full of insects and strange creatures. I was free as a bird and spent much of my day there, playing and hiding in the treehouse my father had built for me. I hadn't reached that age when children lose their freedom and fall under the yoke of society; I mean when they start school. Reading and writing were still a mystery, but I had mother and sometimes father, to read me stories and my imagination flew with their fantastic protagonists.

There came a day, however, when all that changed.

My mother stopped laughing; she was not her usual happy self; my father's expression, though never as cheerful, was now brooding and unapproachable. I could hear them arguing after they had put me to bed and they thought I was asleep, but I wasn't, and I trembled in my little bed awash with uncontrolled fears.

My days were not happy anymore and I would hide in the treehouse not to play, but to escape from an atmosphere that had become intolerable.

Then, one day, my father had come home with the most perfect truck. At first it reminded me of a truck I had seen in a movie, but it had nothing for towing other cars. Mother burst out crying when she saw it and ran into the now almost empty house. Empty because some men had come before and taken most of our furniture, while my father looked at them with anger and my mother hid her tears behind the door.

Father had remained beside the truck, watching her run back to the house with sad eyes, but I was excited beyond belief and ran to it, trying to jump. I felt his anger, when he, unceremoniously, picked me up under his arm and slamming the driver's door, walked into the house.

"You know we must do it, there's no other way. There's nothing else we can do." He said, and I couldn't understand why he sounded so angry.

"I'll start loading." And then, handing me to her, he added: "Here, keep him inside, I don't want him messing up with the truck."

"You are always so hard on him, so stern." Replied my mother.

"He has to grow up a man, and with you coddling him…"

He finished and leaving me with her walked to the living room, now filled with boxes and bags.

Next day, we left the house where my childhood had taken place and rode to the city.

I was full of enthusiasm and stared through the truck's cracked glass windows at the scenery now flowing slowly by us. This was not as when we rode father's new car, which went so fast I could barely look at what sped by the windows; this was a marvelous truck that took its time to show me all that was wonderful outside our home. I loved it.

Then, all changed, green turned to gray and black, pretty to ugly and dirty while hundreds and hundreds of cars passed us.

"Where are we momma?" I asked, worrying about going into one of those terrible places I had seen on parental controlled movies.

"We are going to live in the city from now on, puppet." She had said and added in a low voice I could have almost not heard. "No more carefree country life for us."

I insisted on more explanations, refusing to even admit we were gone from my house for good. "Where are we going?"

"We are going to visit Granuncle Birdie." She replied in such a voice I sat back and remained silent for the rest of the ride.

In my mind, however, the answer turned and turned as an echo to the car's noises, and I kept hearing the words again and again. Granuncle Birdie? What was that? A bird, but why Granuncle? Were we going to the Zoo? But then why were my parents so upset?

After taking so many turns, I had gotten carsick we finally arrived in front of an imposing iron fence. Across the road extended a wide park, full of very tall, very dark, ancient trees. I watched through the window but couldn't find the beginning or end. Then, a gate I had not seen opened and we drove through it into the most perfect garden I had ever seen. I will leave the description for later, as I am eager to tell you about the Granuncle Birdie.

My father stopped the truck before the house's entrance. A few steps led to the wide double door, which was as dark as the surrounding ground. Dead leaves fluttered in the wind, this being already fall and collected in the corners. The door opened even before my parents had knocked and we went in.

An old lady stood beside it and nodded to us.

"Welcome." She said and then. "Come this way."

We followed her while I still wondered where we were. This was no Zoo! How could a bird live here and a bird like the Granuncle, which must

Sent Back

be huge! I was aquiver with curiosity and asked in a whisper: "Mother?"

But she shushed me and grasping my hand gave it a squeeze, a sure sign to behave.

We then followed the woman through a long dark hallway, its walls covered with a reddish wood so smooth it reflected us as a mirror and a ceiling so high I could almost not see it. Then we reached another big dark door, which she opened after knocking and announced.

"They are here, sir!"

When we entered, something rose from a nearby armchair and advanced to meet us. I was all confused; this must be Granuncle Birdie, but it was not in a cage, but sitting.

I stared; it was tall, much taller than father. The wings flapped by his side, long wings that fell to its feet. Thin, long grayish feathers covered its head. Then my eyes focused and showed me I was deceived. What I had imagined wings were not and, on its head... well, on his head those were not feathers, but hair.

True, it had a beak of a nose, and the eyes were as piercing, small and set back as the ones I had once seen in an eagle, but try as I might, I couldn't find wings or feathers, unless they hid beneath the great loose house coat he wore.

He shook hands with my father and embraced my mother. Then, crouching down from his mighty height, he faced me, staring at me with amused eyes.

In my fright, instead of the courteous greeting they had taught me to say when I met a grownup, I blurted.

"Where are your feathers?"

He gazed at me, looking intrigued.

"My feathers?" He repeated and turned a gaze to my parents. "What's he talking about? Is he alright?"

The Birdie returned to crouch before me and gazed into my eyes, trying to discover if I was, indeed, all right.

"What do you mean, child?" He asked.

"You are a Granuncle Birdie, so, where are your feathers and your wings?" I almost shouted, now terrified.

"A Granuncle Birdie!" He cried and laughed so hard he rocked on his feet and fell backwards to the rug.

Mother pulled my arm in anger and ordered me to shut up, I couldn't understand why. The man, which I realized now was not a bird, was laughing. He was not angry or upset, he kept repeating 'Granuncle Birdie' till tears came to his eyes and he lay exhausted.

"Now Marjory, don't chide the child. He has given me the most beneficial laugh I've had in years." He said. He sat cross-legged by my side with uncommon agility and forced me to sit beside him. Even then he towered above me; he was really a tall man.

"You see, child, I am not a bird, but a man. What is your name?"

"I am Andrew Kirkpatrick, sir." I replied, as they had trained me to do, still gazing at him in wonder.

Now that he sat beside me, I could see he was truly a man, though he definitely had birdlike qualities and reminded me now not of an eagle, but of an owl, a skinny owl and his nose was as an owl's beak.

"Well Andrew and what did you think I was?"

"A Birdie. My mother said we were coming to see Granuncle Birdie."

"Ah."

The man looked at me with amusement.

"Who are you?" I ventured to ask, avoiding my mother's eyes.

"Child, you named me and so I'll tell you." He smiled a wonderful smile. "I am your Granuncle Birdie, pleased to meet you." He offered a hand as similar to a bird's leg as might be and shook mine.

And this was how I met the man who would have the greatest influence in my life and my future

.

CHAPTER II

My parents must have agreed with the Granuncle, because after a while he called and the old lady came.

"My niece and her family will be staying from now on with us, Mrs. Urville, as I had previously told you. Please show them to the guests' house." He said and turning back to my mother he added. "Welcome to your new home, dear niece."

Mother stood and turned to follow the lady, extending her hand for me, but I didn't take it. I moved nearer the Granuncle and looked up at him.

"Can I stay with you?" I muttered, almost inaudibly, but the man heard.

"Can you?" He asked, questioning my mother.

"Won't he be a bother?" She replied.

"Oh, no. Not at all." Said the Birdie, extending a long arm to bring me into his wing.

I couldn't shake off the feeling he was an enormous bird whose wings and feathers hid under the ample house coat. The coat's sleeves looked more like large brown wings than anything else and the whole impression it all gave was that of a magnificent bird. I was not scared, however, as the man made me feel safe and welcomed.

"Come, child." He said and then detecting my slight gesture of rebellion. "Come Andrew, sit with me. Let's get to know each other."

"Are we going to live here with you now, sir?" I asked as he lifted me and sat me on an enormous desk in the center of the room.

He pulled a chair over and sat facing me.

"I believe so, my friend. What do you think? Do you like my house?"

I hesitated. From what I had seen, the house was a child's haven, probably full of mysteries and places to explore, but I was reluctant to show my eagerness.

"I think so." I said after a moment.

"You are going to love it." He said. "I have always loved it, ever since

I was as small as you are now."

I looked up, doubting this tall, slender old man had ever been like me. He understood my look and smiled.

"Now, tell me how old are you, Andrew? Are you already going to school? Did you have friends there?"

Being questioned about that which for children is so important; ourselves, I started chatting and did not stop until the return of my parents cut the overflowing torrent of my explanations to zero.

"He's been driving you crazy with his chat!" Exclaimed my mother, running and trying to lift me from the desk.

"No." Said Granuncle. "No, it has been just fine. Your son has brought a ray of joy to my dreary existence, don't you worry. Now tell me, are you settled? Did you find everything agreeable to you?"

"Yes, uncle and we thank you." She replied and father nodded, though he didn't look happy.

Granuncle looked at him and sighed.

"I know it is very difficult, especially for you, Albert; I am sure; however, you will recover."

"Thank you, sir." Said my father. "If I may trouble you more, have you made any enquiries about employment opportunities for me?"

"I have, as I had promised." He turned to my mother. "Marj, why don't you take the child to see his new home? Perhaps show him the garden? This is talk for men, not for children."

"Alright, uncle. and… thanks again." She said.

"Mother," I said as soon as we were out of earshot. "Mother, why are we going to live here? What about our house? Will we go back there soon?"

She continued walking for some steps and then, stopping, knelt by my side.

"No Andrew. We will never return. This is now our home and you must forget all about our previous life. Papa is going to have to work very hard now, more than before and I, too, will need to work. That means you will remain here, alone, a great part of the day. You must promise to obey uncle and Mrs. Urville." She looked at me with that look I knew meant I had to promise, so I did.

"Good. It will not be so terrible." She added and I knew it was terrible for her and that she was talking more to comfort herself than me.

"Can we go to the garden, now?" I asked, she nodded.

We were walking on the leaf covered gravel garden path when I asked, "Mother, who is that man?"

She smiled a sad smile.

"That is my uncle Ferdi," she said. "My uncle on my mother's side."

"Ah."

I mussed for many minutes more.

Sent Back

"And why do you call him Granuncle Birdie?" I asked.

This time she laughed.

"No, my son. I had never called him that. I think you misunderstood me when I said we were coming to see Granduncle Ferdi, it was you who named him thus." She bent and kissed me. "And he liked it." She added.

We were walking toward a smaller building, somewhat separate from the house, when we met another fixture of my Granuncle's house.

He was as gnarled and bent as the old tree we had in our old house's front garden and as brown. His back was bent and he seemed to walk with difficulty, but his eyes were bright blue and he was smiling.

"Hi there!" He said, squinting at my mother. "Why it's little Marj!" He exclaimed and added. "Are you not?"

"Yes, yes, it's me, Gregoire. How have you been?"

"Ah, fairly well, fairly well." He replied. "The years have been good to me, though I am now all bent up, but that makes it easier to reach the ground." He laughed and offered a hand to my mother.

"Andrew." Said my mother. "This is Gregoire, uncle's gardener and keeper of the grounds. You must obey him as you promised to obey Mrs. Urville, you hear?"

"He will, Marj, he seems to be a well-behaved boy. This the only one?"

"The only one, yes." She nodded.

Gregoire nodded, he understood more than what mother had said. He bent more and looked straight into my eyes.

"Do you like my garden, little imp?"

"I am not an imp." I replied, stepping back.

"Naturally you are not, my apologies." He said. "But tell me, do you like it?"

"Yes." I said, hesitating.

"You will find lots of things to do here. Your mother loved it and I am sure you will, too. I want you to promise, though, not to harm the plants or animals you'll find here. Each plant has its place and function, as do each animal and all have as much right as you to be in this place." He stopped and frowned. "Do you understand?"

"Yes sir, yes. I do, I promise."

"Good, see that you do."

At that moment and from the undergrowth, appeared a ball of fluffy golden yarn walking in four legs. A cat.

It brushed against the gardener's legs, mewing softly.

"There you are, Lord Byron!" Sais the man. "Come meet our new family."

He lifted the cat by its underbelly and offered it to me.

"Here, say hi!"

15

I looked at mother. She had never approved of any contact with dogs or cats; didn't want me ever to have a pet. None had been allowed in my house, not even after hours of implorations and crying. Would she let me have this one?

"There's nothing your mother can do about this." Said the old man. "It belongs in the house and its owner is Mr. Ferdinand. Go ahead."

I received the cat in my trembling arms, wondering who this Mr. Ferdinand could be. It was heavy and I felt a grumbling sound; scared, I looked up to the gardener, but without letting go of the animal.

"Is he angry? He's growling."

"No, child, that's how cats show they are happy, it's called a purr." He explained.

I stroked Lord Byron, what weird names people here had and Lord Byron! Well, if that was his name, it was all right with me.

I sat on the ground, the cat on my lap and held him for some minutes. Then, after the animal had allowed himself to be caressed for a while, it jumped and ran back into the undergrowth.

"He is hunting." Explained Gregoire. "Don't take it amiss."

"Will he come back? Can I play with him again?"

"Cats come and go, that's the way they are, but I think he liked you, so I'm sure he will find you again."

Days passed as they usually do when you are not yet 6, amidst games and rules.

Granuncle had taken a hand in some of my affairs and convinced my parents I needed time to adjust, this meaning I need not be enrolled in school for still some time. This arrangement suited me just fine. There was an enormous house to explore, his, not ours and a similarly vast garden to play in.

Little by little I got to know all the trees and bushes, even the different grasses in the garden, under the tutelage of Gregoire, always ready to teach about it. I could even help sometimes and my hands grew accustomed to dirt and worms, tiny spiders and beetles that would have given my mother a fright.

The house, however, was different. Its many rooms were not all open to my explorations, several doors were locked but others looked so gloomy as I opened their doors I closed them immediately, afraid of the ghosts and monsters who could lurk inside.

Granuncle watched me with interested eyes, following my investigations of his own house with amusement mixed with curiosity. It was easy to see he enjoyed having me there and I frequently returned to his study to chat with him while my parents were out working.

One day, when I entered the room, I saw Granuncle bent over his

Sent Back

desk. I approached silently. He was wearing his thick spectacles and looking at something I at first could not identify.

"What's that, Granuncle?"

He was startled and looked up with what I recognized as fear.

"Who?" He muttered. "Ah, it's you. Come, come here, child." He bid me approach and lifted me to his bony knees.

"Look!"

"What is it?" I insisted.

"Can't you see? It's a box!"

"Ah."

"You don't understand, do you?" He inquired. "No, why should you?" I lifted my face to his.

"I am going to let you into a secret Andrew." He said.

I settled better on his lap and waited eagerly for what would follow.

"Boxes are the most appealing of mysteries. Have you heard the story of Pandora?" He asked, his eyes sparkling with merriment.

"No. Who's that?"

"Ah, the tale is not to be told now, my son. Some other time. It requires to be told in the dark nights of winter, by a lighted fireplace. Yes, we can do that soon but not now."

"I was saying boxes are a never-ending source of surprises. Not the ones they now use in the stores, though some of those could be really intriguing. I am talking about the old ones, those that previous generations used, boxes made of different types of woods, or of glass or porcelain."

I looked at him with bewilderment. What was he talking about, a box made of glass? Not unless he was talking about the one the dwarves had made for Snow White.

He smiled, understanding me better than I did myself.

"Wait here." He said and lifting me, sat me on the desk, beside the box he had been considering. I heard as he opened and closed cabinet doors, muttering to himself in a low voice some incomprehensible babble.

He returned; his long scrawny arms filled with boxes which he placed carefully on the desk.

"See!" He ordered and I did, my eyes wide in wonder.

There was a shiny white box, with little pink and red flowers placed on the lid and sides. Garlands of gold surrounded it and formed handles by the sides. The top was also surrounded by these golden garlands, forming a crest with a spread eagle at the center and little legs, also of gold. A key hung from one of the box's handles.

I looked up at Granuncle, not daring to ask.

He understood and taking the key, opened the box. Inside, a little woman danced, as music filled the silent room. I gasped.

"Beautiful, isn't it? Made in Limoges, France, this box of porcelain has almost three hundred years. It is very old and precious. Do you like it?" Asked the man.

I nodded.

"But that's not all. Look what happens when I flip this switch." He did and the place where the ballerina danced lifted, showing a secret hiding place.

"Show me more!" I implored.

He removed the porcelain one and brought forward another box. This one was simpler, nevertheless, most beautiful. It was made of glass encased in a golden frame, but the glass was carved into little perfect squares. Again, handles and top were made of gold, or some similar metal. It was smaller and hid no mystery as all was visible from outside.

"This one is made from rock crystal, my son, which is now a very rare mineral. It is, however, very, very old and it is said to have contained the famous diamonds of Queen Anne of Austria, the French queen."

"How can you know?" I asked, though the name was noise to my ears.

"Collectors, which is what I am, you know? A box collector. We keep a record of these things. It has to do with History and people and time. Do you like it?"

"Yes. Yes." I repeated. "I too, want to be… what you just said." I hesitated, not knowing well the word.

"A collector." He supplied.

"Yes, that." I nodded eagerly.

"To be a good collector Andrew, you have to study about many things. You have to know your history and you have to know of minerals and Geology; that's what studies the ground and its history. You have to know of Botany, to understand the woods used to make the boxes."

"I will learn. Will you teach me?" I asked, eager to become a collector.

"Some of it I could teach you, my son, but others you will need to learn on your own or in school. You want to see the one I was studying?"

"Yes, yes!"

"Here, come and see."

He brought the box; not letting me handle it, but near enough for me to feel the strange aroma that emanated from it.

"Ah, you feel it, don't you?"

"Yes, what is that smell?"

He laid the box back on the desk.

"Look here. This box is made of wood, a very good wood called cedar from a tree called 'Cedrus libani'. It was made many centuries ago, that is hundreds and hundreds of years ago, in a faraway country where the trees that gave this wood grew. The metal is bronze, that can shine as gold if you take the proper care of it. Now, the smell you sense is myrrh, perhaps

Sent Back

frankincense too. Those are substances used in very far away times. Do you know about Jesus Christ?"

"Yes. Mommy has talked to me about him." I would start the long story, but he interrupted me.

"Right, so those substances were used during those times as perfumes and also for healing. I am going to open it and you'll see…"

He lifted the lid. There was no key, no locking mechanism, it simply opened on the bronze hinges. Inside I could see something dark and before he could stop me, I had touched it. It was gluey and dark, like the oil left by cars on the parking lot.

"What is this?" I exclaimed.

He brought out a white piece of cloth from his coat's pocket and cleaned my smeared finger while explaining.

"It's the resin, the remains of the myrrh that was kept here for centuries." He closed the lid and then it was I saw what he had been staring at.

On its top was a polished glass and beneath it a sliver of wood and a little piece of what could have been cloth.

I looked back at him, not wanting him to think me obnoxious, as my mother frequently called me.

"This." He said, pointing at the glass. "This is not glass, or crystal; it is amber. I'll tell you another day what it is and how it is made."

I thought many things were being left for another day but held my peace.

"What it is, is not important. What it protects, that's another matter."

He became silent and stroke his chin for a while.

"I was told when I purchased it… I was told it holds a sliver of the Cross and a piece of Christ's mantle."

Here again was a reference to Christ and I was eager to ask many questions and tell what I knew, but I was sure this was not the moment.

"I am full of doubts Andrew. The man who brought it to me is an honest man and I trust him. But to be in the possession of such relics is truly…" He stopped and passed his index finger slowly and softly over the polished amber.

"Amazing." I offered.

"Yes!" He agreed, startled from his thoughts by my voice. "Yes, amazing. and I don't believe there could be a way to prove it."

"May I touch it?" I asked.

"Softly, softly and carefully."

I extended my finger as he had done and caressed the yellowish glass, I mean amber. It was so smooth and yet warm to the touch.

"It is warm!"

"Yes. Amber is not like glass, or crystal, or gems; amber is made from life and from the Sun. Amber is alive, not dead."

Again, I passed my finger over the amber.

"I like it. Are all your boxes like this?" I said.

"Ah, child, I have so many you couldn't see them in an entire day, but none had I ever found that pulls so at my heart. No, not all my boxes are like this one, but you will see them all, one day."

There again was the reference to a future I didn't think I had patience enough to wait for.

"Why not now?" I ventured.

He looked at me for a while.

"Why not." He said and nodded. "Come with me."

.

CHAPTER III

Hand in hand, we walked down the hallway. I had not been this way before and as I wondered how many more there were, I admired the different trinkets that stood on tables or hung from the walls. There were no boxes, though, but little figurines of men and women, of horses and dogs and other animals. There were portraits of old people, portraits that must have been very old and were darkened by age; and clocks, many clocks going ticking together like music.

The hallway floor was covered by a rug, a rug so plush and thick our steps were silenced in it, though sometimes the creaking of a board beneath reminded me this was a house and not a fantasy place.

"Here we are." Granuncle interrupted my thoughts, stopping before a, for once, white door. He took a ring of keys from his pocket and after searching for the right one, he opened the door.

"Well, go on in." He said.

I was reluctant to do so, the room was dark, perhaps he had brought me here to feed me to his monsters.

As if he had read my mind, he turned the switch on.

"No monsters here Andrew." He said and walked ahead of me into the room.

It was a large, a very large room. The ceiling was so high I had to bend backwards to see it and it was full of statues and carvings and drawings. The walls, too, were decorated, covered by something I after learned was wallpaper. The wallpaper was of a soft shade of green with golden leaves and twigs, but they were almost invisible behind the armoires and shelves that covered them.

"This used to be the dining hall, where my ancestors gathered their friends on important occasions for a banquet." He explained enclosing it with a broad sweep of his arm. "I saw no need to keep such a place and now it holds my collections."

I must explain Granuncle always spoke to me as if he were talking to a grownup and many times I couldn't understand half of what he was saying as he used so many new words. I somehow understood him well and loved his explanations.

I followed the movement and gazed at the armoires and shelves full of boxes of all sizes and shades, of many materials.

I gasped.

"You like it?" He asked.

"So many!" I whispered.

"Yes, many hundreds, but I have been collecting them all my life, you see."

He walked further into the room and lit a fire in the chimney. I had not realized it, but the room was chilly, as we were now at the ends of autumn and the temperatures had been going steadily down.

He then pulled two armchairs nearer to the fire and gestured me to join him.

"You like it here, don't you?" He asked again.

"Oh yes, oh yes, this is lovely!" I replied.

"There are many ways to visit this place, Andrew." He spoke with unexpected seriousness and I sat more erect and attentive than before. "You could walk up and down the room, looking at this and that box and leaving the room with a general but unspecific knowledge of what you have seen."

I shook my head. That was definitely not what I wanted.

"There is another way and it requires many days, patience and understanding."

"I prefer that one." I whispered.

"You prefer that one, that is good. Then we will start with the most distant cabinet because there I keep the first box I ever collected. Are you warm enough now?"

"Yes, yes let's go!" I replied, eager to start.

"Alright, but remember everything here is very fragile, we don't go running, or jumping, or making brusque movements that can bring down an item or, God forbid, a whole shelf or cabinet. You understand?"

"Yes." I replied, serious and contrite. "I will behave, Granuncle."

"Good. Come now."

The first box he took was not interesting. Made of a reddish wood, it had no drawing, no carvings, just a smooth surface. Only on the lid was there some carving, well, not carving, but that's what I thought then. It was an inlay of another darker wood.

Granuncle explained the box was made of mahogany and the inlay was a darker, unknown wood, perhaps ebony.

"What does that mean?" I asked, pointing to the black drawing on the lid.

"This box was made by the primitive people of Honduras."

He saw I didn't understand and added.

"Honduras is a country in Central America where a very important people lived many hundreds of years ago. They were called the Mayans and these people knew a lot of things about the world and the stars. They used a strangely accurate calendar by which they became famous to us. The symbol there is called 'Wayeb' and it was used to name the five dangerous days of the year."

"Why? Why dangerous?" I asked, absorbed in the contemplation of the drawing.

"Wayeb was when the wall between our world and the underworld, the world of those who had died, disappeared. When this happened, evil beings could come to our world and cause disasters." He whispered.

I felt the hairs of my back raise and a shiver ran down my spine. It was marvelous!

"Why would you have such a terrible thing here, Granuncle? Aren't you afraid?" I whispered back.

"Oh no!" He replied with his normal voice. "On the contrary, this box was to aid, to help fight the evil. You see, you would leave the box open and put inside some sweet, a pastry, anything you thought the evil beings would like, they would put the seed of cocoa, but any sweet would work; and then, when the evil ones came smelling and wanting to take it, the box would close and trap them there."

"Does… is one in there now?" I asked, shivering in fear.

"No, dear one, no. There's nothing evil in my collection. I have taken good care of that. Do not be afraid."

I gave a great sigh of relief.

"Show me more."

"This one," he said, bringing a little one that appeared to be made of straw. "This one my father brought from the Caribbean, and it is made, as you can see, of braided straw. He brought it to me from one of his trips and it was full of seashells. It has no other history than that and that it was the first box I ever had."

"Can we open it? Does it still have shells inside?"

"No. I lost the shells many years ago, it's empty. Do you still want to open it?"

"Yes!"

He gave it to me and I carefully opened the lid. It was tied with pieces of what I thought was leather to the box proper and when I opened it, I felt, or I thought I felt, the smell of the sea.

I looked up with wondering eyes. Granuncle nodded.

"Yes. I could never understand it, but it has kept the smell of the sea all these long years."

"Perhaps it's magic?"

"Perhaps." He replied and shrugged.

It was funny when he shrugged, because the eternal housecoat would be lifted by his shoulders, and it always gave the impression the huge bird was getting ready to fly. I used to love it.

In this way we continued for the rest of the afternoon and soon the return of my mother interrupted the wonderful visit.

That night, when we were sitting for evening meal, I told my parents what I had been doing. I talked about the box with the amber and about the large room with Granuncle's collections.

"I used to go there with him when I was little." Said my mother, reminiscing. "I liked to look at the pretty little ones made of porcelain."

"I like them all." I said in an unexplainable rebellious tone.

"And so, you should." She replied, somewhat astonished by my reply. "If uncle is showing you them, it is because you are truly interested. But be very careful never to break one, do you hear?"

I looked at her. Perhaps she had done that when she was little.

"I will be careful, I promise."

"See that you do." Intervened my father now. "I don't want you to do anything to anger the old fellow."

I fidgeted on my seat. When father spoke like that, I remembered the only time he had spanked me, the day I had crossed the highway on my own and almost gotten killed. This was serious.

Day followed day as they do when you are young and carefree, I never paid attention to any of it, only learning a week had ended when my mother remained at home for the weekend. Those were days of joy, when she and I will go to the garden and spend hours playing there, looking at the different insects and birds, watching Lord Byron's stealthy approach and unfruitful attempt to catch the flying creatures. Those two days would pass as swift as lightning, and I would remain alone but for Granuncle Birdie.

Then, my carefree days came to an abrupt stop.

I knew something was wrong when I heard my name. I had been playing in the garden and trying to catch Lord Byron who seemed to play hide and seek with me. He had finally drawn me to the hedge under the study window and sat there, watching me and twitching his bushy golden tail. It was as if he were daring me to listen and I did.

"He is losing time, playing all day and not learning a thing." I heard my father's voice. "He will lag behind the rest of his peers when he starts."

"I don't see why, Albert." Replied my mother. "He's very young!"

"At his age, I had been a year in school already and knew how to read and write." Countered my father. "I tell you, I am not happy about this, playing and gardening and gallivanting all around the property with no aim in view."

I heard the noise of a chair moved and realized my father had come to the window. I crouched, trying to make myself as small as possible. It was

Sent Back

my future being debated in here and I wanted to hear everything.

Then, I heard Granuncle's little cough, the one he used to clear his throat before talking.

"If I may?" He said, in a composed voice.

"What?" My father replied and then, realizing who he was talking to, repeated. "Yes, Ferdi, what do you think?"

"I believe you are right, Albert. It is time Andrew starts learning and has some obligations brought into his life, he's been playing for too long now."

I couldn't understand if Granuncle was serious, he always seemed to encourage my games and investigations.

"Yes, I agree with you, Albert." He continued. "I believe, however, that to enroll the child in school will complicate your lives more than they already are."

I felt him approaching my father, who had remained standing by the window. Now the two men deciding my destiny were an arm's length from where I hid.

"Consider this; Albert, you start working before seven o'clock and you Marj, only a little later. Who is going to take Andrew to school? Who is going to pick him up? Are you going to be paying for after school?"

These questions were followed by an uncomfortable moment of silence.

"No. I have to think about it, but this dawdling is to stop." Father replied.

"I totally agree with you so listen to what I have been thinking. You will leave him here, no school for now. Yes, he will remain as he has all these last months, but order will come to his life. I will not take him to school, but I offer to school him myself. Now, what do you think about that?"

The room was silent. I could imagine mom's and dad's faces.

"Would you?" Asked my mother. "Would you do that for him?"

"Surely."

"But how will you? Are you a teacher? Do you have any experience?" Asked my father.

"In a time, I taught, long ago, yes. Yes, I have experience and I am certainly better prepared than any kindergarten teacher, I'm sure." Replied Granuncle.

My heart was beating rapidly, I was so nervous my hands shook; let's face it, it was my future that was being decided here. Then, the cat mewed and jumped on my lap.

I heard a voice above my head and looked up. It was Granuncle. He winked.

"These windows shouldn't be open, it is freezing and the wind is coming inside, it will chill the room. Let me close them."

He winked again and gave a small nod. I understood. All would be all right.

That night, after the evening meal, my parents conversed with me. I was not expected to reply anything else than, yes father or yes mother.

"Andrew, we have something important to talk about, my son." Said father.

I knew he would talk about the arrangements made with Granuncle and I thought the old man's decision would be to my liking, nevertheless, I was full of apprehension. What if they had decided to send me to school?

"Pay attention Andrew." Ordered my mother.

I looked up and set my face in the 'attention' mode.

"You, my young man, should be learning many things by this time, which you are not. At your age I knew how to read and had read many a book. I also knew how to write and do my numbers."

Mother moaned softly; we had heard this story before. I had never heard her comment anything about it.

"Surely, Marjory!" He exclaimed.

"Alright, alright. Go ahead." She replied.

"So, my son, we have been thinking it is time for you to start school."

My heart fell to my bottom, and I bowed my head, I couldn't help it.

"Uncle..." My mother started but father stopped her.

"Please let me take care of this, my dear." He said and then. "Yes, as your mother was going to say, uncle Ferdi has offered to help with this."

My heart lifted.

"You see, child, he has taken unto himself the task of teaching you your letters and your numbers, too." He coughed slightly. "I expect you to pay very good attention and to apply yourself to it. I will test you by the end of the month. If you show improvement, you will remain here to be taught by Mr. Ferdi. If not, it's boarding school for you, mister. It did a lot of good for me, and you are no different."

Oh, but I would improve, I would learn all I had to and more. Yes, sir, anything but boarding school… I had heard stories about the things that happened there.

"Yes, father. I will apply myself; I will learn everything. I promise." I said.

"Good, I hope so. Now, let's eat."

I could barely, eat I mean, I was so relieved. Oh, I would learn and not only to read and write, not only what he called 'my numbers' though I had not the faintest idea what that was. But I would learn about Geology and History and all Granuncle had told me I needed to know to be a collector, about stones and wood and stuff. I would show him! I would show them all!

Sent Back

With this decision formed in my head, I got back to my food and ate.

Early next day I was awakened by my mother. She had prepared a new set of clothes and they lay in the chair by my side. Also, a small cloth bag was waiting for me, which I later understood to be my school bag.

"Listen to me Andrew." She said, kneeling before me to tie up my shirt and fix my trousers. "This is your first day of school. I know it's not really a school, but with uncle Ferdi; be it as it may, I want you to take it very seriously. Will you?"

I nodded in agreement.

"Right." She stood and inspected me. "Today I helped you, but because of it I will be late for work. Tonight you will leave your clothes ready, as you see them now; your pencils sharpened, your books organized. Tomorrow and every day of the week you will wake up early, dress up, have your breakfast and go to uncle Ferdi, who will wait for you in his study. Go now, breakfast is downstairs and as soon as you finish, go to him. I must leave; I am too late." She fussed for some seconds in the room and after giving a look around to see if she had missed something, left for work.

I did as she had told me though I could barely swallow the milk and toast. I finished, placed the glass and dish in the sink and went out.

The beginning of my learning started then; it has never stopped.

CHAPTER IV

I had been studying with Granuncle now for several months and summer was drawing to an end. I already knew how to read and my father had been amazed by my swift learning. He had tested me, making me read different books, thinking I had them by memory, but I could not have memorized the ones he had. This convinced him and the decision stood; I would continue my classes at home.

I had not only learned quite fast to read, but now I was able to write. True, my handwriting was not as perfect as Granuncle's, the letters jumped here and there, as if they were walking through hilly terrain, but I was improving.

He had taught me Geography. He said that was the first thing I needed to know, about the country and the world we lived in. So, I knew about America and Europe, Africa, Asia, Australia. I had learned about the different countries in America, which were not only the United States, but many others. I had particular interest in Central America and Honduras, perhaps because of that story about the Mayas. So he taught and I learned quickly.

One chilly November night, when father and mother had gone out after the insistence of Granuncle they needed to have some fun, my uncle and I sat beside the library fire, enjoying its warmth.

"Do you remember I told you about Pandora, Andrew?"

He asked, startling me. I had been daydreaming about what I would do when I was a collector and his voice had brought me out of my reveries.

"Yes." I replied, immediately alert. Was now the proper time for the story? I awaited eagerly for him to continue.

"I think now is the proper time to tell you. Listen."

"A long time ago, when people were beginning to learn about themselves, they tried to find an explanation to all the ills that beset them. They didn't know why they were plagued by sickness, nor why did they have to die; they wondered why there was war and fight between themselves, why had they to feel jealousy or hatred, why were they subject to hunger and to all the feelings that made them act so strangely."

Granuncle stopped and looked at me, clearly asking if I was

Sent Back

understanding it all. I nodded, though, as you would imagine, there were many words I didn't know then.

"They didn't know from where they had come, who had made them and the world around them, so they came up with the idea of gods. This was in ancient Greece, you know, and there they had decided there was a huge number of gods taking care of them. These gods were Zeus and Hera and Hermes, Athena, Mars and several more. But Zeus the king of the gods had not wanted men to be as gods, so humankind was struggling, they had no fire and led miserable lives. Then came Prometheus, who was not really a god, but a Titan." He stopped and looked at me, as I had raised my hand. "I will tell you later about it, let me carry on now."

"Prometheus was very sad; he loved humankind and saw they were suffering and unhappy; so he went and stole the fire from the King of Gods, Zeus. Naturally, Zeus was furious, so furious that he punished Prometheus to a kind of prison of which I will tell you other day. Now, Zeus, who was a very violent god, decided he had to punish humans too, so he had this terrible idea. He made a beautiful box, the most splendid thing you could ever imagine and inside he didn't put anything nice, but terrible. He placed there sickness, death, turmoil, strife, jealousy, hatred, famine and passion and gave it to a woman called Pandora. Perhaps you don't understand, but these were all the bad things hurting humans since the beginning. Now, Pandora was very beautiful and had many good traits, but she was also very curious. Now, when Zeus gave her the box, he admonished her never to open it. That was enough to set her curiosity on fire and after many doubts, she finally opened it. As soon as she did, all the evil things came out and the only thing she could keep as she rushed to close the lid, was hope."

"She let all that, death and sickness and the other things out? That's why people die? Because of what she did?" I asked, concerned and worried.

Granuncle, who had been quiet, perhaps considering the story, gasped and looked at me. I believe now he realized the story was not proper for a child of six, because he tried to fix his apparent error.

"Now, child, remember this is a story. I only told you about it because it's a famous story about a box and you told me you wanted to be a collector, too."

"But did she? Did she?"

"No. This is a myth; a story you could also call a fairy tale, something to explain things people could not understand so many hundreds of years ago. Something like the story of the Sleeping Beauty."

"That's not true?" I asked, surprised. I had always thought she existed.

He smiled.

"No Andrew, it is not and neither is Pandora nor Pandora's box. We suffer pain and illnesses and death because that is the nature of our bodies and we have not yet learned how to remain healthy and alive forever. Poor Pandora is not to blame, child."

I sighed. Granuncle was giving me a lot of information I could barely understand and it was truly making me very nervous.

We spoke no more about it that night and as soon as my parents returned, I went to our little house with them and went to bed trying to forget all about the beautiful Pandora and the wicked god and his box.

Next day was a holiday and I spent it with mother playing in the garden. The day was bright, a blue sky and the sun shining as if it had been recently born. The temperature was cold, but mother and I were keeping warm with our sweaters and coats. Lord Byron had joined us and I showed mother how he liked to play hide and seek with me.

Next day came the thunderbolt.

That terrible day I had been studying since early morning and we were getting ready to stop for lunch when someone knocked at the study door.

"Come in." Called Granuncle.

Mrs. Urville opened a crack and motioned for him to come. I should have known something was amiss, she was distraught and her face showed the remains of tears.

Granuncle rose and walked swiftly to the door, closing it behind him. I waited. And waited and waited. Noon came and went and I still waited, not daring to move, not wanting to know but in my inner self knowing something terrible had happened.

Finally, the door opened slowly and Granuncle entered.

He was sad and his eyes looked at me with pity and pain.

"Son, come here." He said, as he sat in the armchair. "Come, son."

I slipped out of my chair beside the desk, where I had been looking at maps and approached him.

"I have very bad news Andrew, terrible." He said.

He pulled me and placed me between his long skinny legs. I looked at his face and shook.

"Mommy?" I whispered.

He nodded.

"There's been an accident, my son, a terrible accident."

"Is she…" I hesitated, saying the horrible words would make them true, so instead I said. "Is she alright?"

"No, son. She's not, she is gone."

"Gone?" I repeated as an echo.

"Gone to Heaven Andrew. She's with God now." He said and as he cried, he pulled me to him and hugged me.

"No!" I cried. "No, mother can't be dead! You are lying!"

I shook myself free and ran, I ran out of the room and the house and didn't stop until I reached the farther end of the garden. There, I crouched and as the sobs and the crying took hold of me, I slumped on the damp freezing earth.

I remember little of these days. I was in a daze and the damp cold had made me sick. In my fever and pain, I kept calling mother, but only Granuncle came. I didn't want him, I wanted mother. Then came the nightmares and I dreamt of her flying away, calling me from high above, from the clouds. Then I saw the evil ones, the ones freed during Wayeb' and they came and pinched me and laughed at me. They mocked me, crying 'your mother is gone', 'she is gone', 'gone', 'gone'.

I sat up in bed with a terrible cry of agony. Father was there, or his shadow. I couldn't recognize him. He had lost lots of weight and his face was dark and sallow. He looked at me with empty eyes which frightened me more than any spanking could ever have.

"Father? Dad?" I whispered.

He raised his head again, but I knew he hadn't heard me.

"Father!" I cried and then Granuncle entered the room.

"It's alright Andrew. He's alright, but he hasn't been sleeping and is exhausted. Come, come with me. Let him rest."

In my sweaty pajamas I followed Granuncle, who threw a big shawl over my shoulders to keep me warm. He took me to the kitchen where a pot of milk had been kept warm on the stove. On the table was a tray with oatmeal cookies, the one with creamy chocolate chips melting inside, the ones I loved.

"Come Andrew, drink some milk. Mrs. Urville made these cookies for you, but I ate some, they are very rich."

I knew he was trying to be helpful and I obeyed and took a sip of milk and bit a morsel of a cookie.

"What has happened? How long… How long was I sick?"

"You've been sick for more than a week; you were very sick my son. You caught pneumonia, you know and that is a very serious sickness. But you pulled through. You feel better now, don't you?"

I didn't answer, my body felt better, yes. The pain in my soul, however, was unbearable.

"Mother?" I whispered.

He bowed his head and shook it.

"I am sorry, child, we buried her two days ago. You were too sick to attend and say your goodbyes."

Tears jumped out of my eyes, but I brushed them away angrily.

"Your father has been through a lot, Andrew, he needs your help now more than ever. He needs you."

"Where was he?" I muttered.

"Eh? What?"

"Where was he? Where was he when mother… when mother had the accident?"

"He was not there Andrew."

"Why? Why wasn't he with her? He should have saved her! He had sworn to protect her, hadn't he?"

Granuncle didn't answer.

I pushed the chair away from the table. I wanted no milk and no cookies from Mrs. Urville; I wanted my mother and I knew nobody, nobody would ever return her to me.

I wrapped the shawl tighter around my shoulders and left the kitchen. I went out and sat in the little wooden bench where my mother and I had so frequently sat in the evenings. It had been snowing and the white sister still clung to the shadows under the trees and under the benches.

My heart hurt so badly I thought I would die and I think in that moment, I would have welcomed death. How was I going to live without my mother? She was the glue that kept us together, my father and I; she was the love that protected me. Why had she been taken from me? I needed her!

I cried again and angrily berated myself. No more tears. I would find her! Somehow I would find her and bring her back. Heaven should not be hard to find, if I used the proper knowledge. Yes, I would learn about Heaven, every story, every legend; all that had ever been written about Heaven and death I would read and then… and then we would be together, again, as it should be.

I went back into the building that had been our home, now empty of life and love and climbed the stairs to my room. Father was still there, sitting on the chair as I had left him, with as vacant a face as he had when I had woken up.

"Father?" I said, prodding him. "Father, are you well?"

"Andrew?" He replied. "Yes, I am well. and you?"

But he was not there. It was as if he followed the motions set by a puppet master. He had no soul.

I left him there and taking some clothes I went to the bathroom. I took a shower and dressed myself with my classroom clothes. I carefully washed my teeth and combed my hair. I inspected my nails and hands, I brushed my shoes and smoothed my shirt. It was a ritual in my mother's name, this is how she had wanted me and I would do all she had wanted me to do.

I looked at myself in the mirror, I was ready.

"Grand uncle Ferdi." I said, presenting myself before him whom I used to call Granuncle.

"Yes?" He replied without looking up and then. "Andrew! What are

Sent Back

you doing here, child?"

"Grand uncle, I want to continue my studies." I said, matter-of-factly. "Please, will you teach me?"

"Sure, child." He gazed at me with attention now and instead said. "Sure Andrew, my son. Is that what you want?"

"Yes." I replied. "I want to learn, I want to know about everything, but mostly I want you to teach me all you know about Heaven and death. I want to read all the legends and stories ever written about people who died and came back to life." I almost sobbed but controlled myself. I would not cry.

"Andrew, son!" He whispered.

"Please, Granuncle." I said, reverting unconsciously to my old appellation. "I need this."

"Alright, but we'll do this differently. Come with me."

He offered his hand, but I was not the little boy anymore, I refused with a swift shake of my head and walked to the door.

Uncle sighed and followed.

He took me to the same hallway where we had walked the first time he showed me his collection, this time we approached a different door.

"This is my library. It has many wondrous books, books that only I have and first editions, too. I want to believe all the knowledge of the world is herein contained Andrew and you are welcome to it."

We entered after he had unlocked the door.

The walls were covered from floor to ceiling with shelves tightly packed with books. I thought there must be thousands, millions of them and gazed at them in awe.

"There is a method here." Said Granuncle. "I organize the books according to subject and time. I will show you how to access the index and how you find each different subject and then the book."

I nodded, intuitively understanding what he meant.

He considered me, mussing his beard which he had let grow after the catastrophe.

"Most of these books use a language you are not accustomed to. Oh, it's English alright, but a grownup person type of English, with many strange words and ideas. You may read any book you want, but I will make a selection for you so your knowledge grows and builds upon the last you read and carries you to the next. Will you like that?"

He was treating me as a grownup, and I felt better for it.

"Yes, Granuncle. I think that will be best. But…"

"But what?"

"If a book appeals to me for some reason, may I read it?"

His eyes roamed the shelves, it was as if he were passing mental review of what the books held, checking if they were appropriate for me.

"I'll tell you what. If any book other than the ones I set apart for you takes your fancy, tell me about it. If I believe it will not harm you, you can read it."

"Will you give me some, now?"

He approached one table set up at the center of the room.

"Come here."

I obeyed.

A huge book lay on the table, opened by the middle. It was almost two feet tall and twice as wide. It must have thousands and thousands of pages, and I saw it was brightly painted with shades of gold and red and green.

"What is it?" I asked.

"This is the Bible Andrew. The book of God and the people of God. It is the first book I want you to read, because it talks mostly about what you want to know, about Heaven and about death; but it is heavy stuff, so you will read only one chapter each day and this is how you will do it. I will give you another book with a shorter, more comprehensible style, one more adapted to your age and this one you can take with you and read it in bed, or outside in the garden. When you have read the chapter in this smaller book, then you will come to this great one here and try to understand it as well as the version you had previously mastered. If you have questions, ask me in the evening at meal. I have decided you and your father should now have your meals with me."

He added little, but I understood papa was not in conditions of taking care of himself, much less taking care of me. I nodded.

"I understand, Granuncle."

"Good, now, when you finish your Bible chapter…" He went walking around the room, apparently searching for books. He pulled one, then another, until he held around ten books in his arms.

"Uff, they are heavy." He commented bringing them to the table. "Here you are. Hmm, I will need to put an order to them and a brief introduction."

He gazed at the books for a while.

"I believe Andrew, it would be better if we…" He didn't finish and, walking to the end of the room he opened something, perhaps a drawer. I heard him rummaging inside and after a while he returned with another book. This one was smaller, but still exquisite, its pages' borders were golden and the cover all painted with figures and leaves and angels.

He gave it to me and I took it carefully. I was sure this was also a valuable book by the looks of it and the cover was made of a strange material.

"What is this, Granuncle?" I said, touching the cover. It was smooth and I felt a strange longing for it.

"That is also a Bible Andrew, but one made for the Queen Victoria of

England. The cover is made with leather, a common practice in that time."

"What?" I cried and almost let it fall. "This belonged to a queen? Isn't it valuable? Aren't you afraid I will damage it, or lose it?"

I was staring at the book as if it were a viper ready to strike, a book made for a queen of England.

Granuncle looked at me with amused eyes.

"I realize you've learnt more than I had thought possible. Yes, it is very valuable, but I am not afraid you could damage it. To be on the safe side, however, do not take it to the garden. Read it when you are here, or with me in any of the other rooms, or in your own bedroom."

He opened a drawer under the desk where the huge Bible lay and brought out a box.

"When you are not reading it," he explained as he opened the lid. "you will put it here."

He showed me and the little book fit perfectly in the box, as snug as me in bed.

"In this way it will be protected." He added. "So we are agreed? When you have mastered a chapter in this one," He pointed to the Queen's little book, "then you start reading this one." He said, pointing to the enormous Bible.

I nodded, yes, I understood that.

"Here, this chair would be tall enough for you to reach the book."

I climbed on the tall stool and gazed at the writing on the ancient bible. It was very strange.

"Granuncle, I cannot understand this." I said and felt slightly ashamed of my admission.

"That's no wonder Andrew, as they used very adorned characters. As soon as you read and know a chapter, it will become easier, you'll see."

I believed him, as I always did and climbing down, went to a chair beside him.

"I will read this one now." I offered, opening the Queen's book.

"Do that and I will sit here and work on a list and explanation of the other books you will read."

"Granuncle, isn't this going to be too much work for you? I know mother would not like me to cause you trouble."

"No, no, my son." He replied, waving his hands. "No. I will love to do this. Now, let's start our work."

I read. At first, I didn't understand a word, then, forcing myself to read the sentence again and again, its meaning opened. After a while I read faster and understood better. Sometimes I had to ask about a word, or the meaning of a phrase, but Granuncle didn't seem bothered about it. I realized he loved to explain everything in the Book. Then, after we had been sitting there for a while, he slapped his forehead.

"I am so dumb!" He cried and standing up practically rushed to an armoire, a dark armoire with glass doors. He opened it and after searching for some minutes, pulled another book out.

"Here it is!" He exclaimed, bringing it to the table. "This Andrew, will probably answer many of your doubts." He said. "It was written by men of extraordinary faith and knowledge. You can trust their explanations. It is organized according to the Bible's chapters, so it will be easy for you to consult. When you do not understand something, first check here."

"Thank you, Granuncle, I'll do that." I said and returned to my reading.

The day passed and soon Mrs. Urville was calling us to dinner. Father had not come, so Granuncle sent Mr. Gregoire to fetch him.

"I am not hungry." Said papa when he finally entered the room.

"You must eat, sir." Said Mrs. Urville, as she filled his dish with meat and potato stew and some vegetables. "If not for yourself, at least for you son."

My father's face crisped in anger, but he soon relaxed. I thought his strange detachment didn't let him hold any emotion for more than a few seconds.

He started mechanically to lift the spoon to his lips and brought it back to the dish still full.

"I am sorry, sir, I cannot eat." He said to Granuncle; he pushed the chair back and left the room.

"But sir!" Cried Mrs. Urville.

"Let him be." Said Granuncle. "He will recover, eventually." Though I realized he was not very convinced.

That night I woke up several times to find him standing in my room, gazing out the window, or looking at me. In the morning he was gone, and we never saw him again.

CHAPTER V

Naturally, after two or three days of my father's absence, we had to inform the authorities.

They came, they came to the house and invaded it, they invaded the garden and our old house. They asked questions and more questions of Mrs. Urville and Gregoire and other servants, but most of all Granuncle. They even asked me questions, but I was too terrorized by the procedures and the fact I had been left alone by my parents; I was of no use to them.

I eavesdropped on most of Granuncle's interviews, though and knew they were asking about my father's state of mind, about my mother's accident, about the family's economic situation and my father's job. It got boring, so I went to the library and resumed my readings.

It was there Granuncle found me. He was followed by a woman, a woman whose only presence sent shivers of fear up and down my spine.

"Andrew, come here." I obeyed promptly and went to his side.

"This lady comes from Legal Services, my son. She's Miss Adams and she wants to know if you are alright and well taken care of."

I nodded and looked at the woman's face. She was serious. Not a hint of a smile crossed her sour face. Her brows were knitted, as if she were reading a difficult text and the mouth was set in a hard line, her thin lips almost disappearing under a big nose. An unappealing face. Again I shivered with apprehension.

"Hello Andrew." She said, with a tone appropriate to her face and demeanor. "Is your uncle taking good care of you?"

"Yes." I replied with the monosyllable, as Granuncle had taught me something of great importance: never offer more information than the one asked of you. So I said nothing more.

"Good." She commented. "And I see you are reading. Do you like that book? Do you understand it?"

"Yes."

"But you are not going to school, are you?"

"No."

She turned to Granuncle.

"Shouldn't he be attending school already? I believe he is almost seven."

"His parents," replied Granuncle. "My niece and nephew agreed to let him study at home. I have been taking care of his teaching."

"Hmm." She said. "That must be considered by the department."

"Why?" Asked Granuncle. "He has learned much more than he could have attending school. He reads and writes with ease and perfect grammar, he has also started his arithmetic and can do sums and multiplications, even of three digits. No school could have given him that."

"As I said, we will need to look into that. Now, sir." She continued, dismissing me as if I had never been there. "Now sir, you told the officer in charge you had the boy's custody? Why?"

"My niece made the necessary arrangements in case something happened to them."

"So there must be a legal document in your possession?"

"Surely."

"I would like to see it."

My uncle hesitated for a second. Perhaps the woman didn't see it, but I did and trembled again.

"I am very sorry, but it is in the hands of my lawyer." He proffered. "I can bring it to you tomorrow."

The woman shot a calculating glance at my uncle.

"No, I will come again tomorrow. Make sure you have it ready for me to inspect." She turned on her heels and without a by your leave or goodbye, she left the room.

I heard her steps going away, the strong forceful steps of someone used to command.

"Granuncle?" I whispered.

"Not now, child, not now." He said placing a hand on my shoulder. "We'll talk later."

He left me and I returned to my book and tried to read but I could understand nothing, my mind drifting to the woman's interview and what I imagined could come. Would they take me away?

That night someone came to share our evening meal. When I arrived at the dining room, a portly elderly man was sitting at the table, talking in a low voice with Granuncle.

"Ah Andrew, there you are." Said my uncle. "Come, meet my friend Mr. Lagerfeld. He is a good man and a good, a very good lawyer, I want you to trust him always."

I dutifully approached and offered my hand, which the man shook with a smile. I liked him instantly, he had a warm, meaty hand and his face was full of love. I felt it.

"Very pleased to meet you, Andrew." He said, shaking my hand softly. "Very glad indeed."

"Thank you, sir. I am glad to meet you, too." I replied and following a

Sent Back

gesture of uncle, went to my seat and sat.

"So how are you doing, my young friend? I heard about your losses; I am sorry about them. I knew your mother, you know?" He continued.

Brought back to the terrible situation of my bereavement, I heaved a sigh, but did not answer, only bowing my head.

"Let's not talk about that now, William." Granuncle said. "Let's eat and then we will go to the study and talk about what concerns me most."

Later in the evening, after our meal was finished, Granuncle sent me to my room. This was unusual as we always kept company for some time before going to bed.

I have not explained that after my mother left, Granuncle had fixed it so I would sleep in his own house. I now had a large room near his own bedroom. It was full of old furniture, heavy and dark, but I was rather happy there and no sad memory came at the sight of anything in the room.

So, as my curiosity was aroused by the unexpected dismissal, after I had said good night and closed the door of the study behind me, I remained listening.

At first, I couldn't hear well what they were talking about, but finding a better place, I followed their conversation.

"… legal. You must understand that." Said the man.

"I know, I know and appreciate it, my friend. No person will ever know about it."

"Surely, because if you do… I can't express the trouble you would be in and regarding the boy…"

"I know I tell you." Said Granuncle and I knew by his voice he was upset, or perhaps afraid.

"The document is legally stamped and signed in the date you told me and all the pertinent information is, as you may see, correctly entered." Said the lawyer.

"Yes, yes. Oh, it's perfect. Thank you, my friend."

The man harrumphed.

"I am only doing this because I know you well, Ferdi and I knew your sister and her daughter. I would not want her grandson to be fostered in who knows whose home. He has a house here and you to teach and protect him, nothing should come between you two."

"That is precisely my wish, William, the poor child has been through hell, losing first his home and then both parents. Everything has been taken from him, I don't want his future to be taken away as well. I will see to it."

"And I applaud you!" Said the lawyer. "Now, if you give me a sip of that excellent brandy you keep for yourself, I will be on my way."

I heard no more and rushed to my bedroom. I had known as soon as I saw that woman something bad was coming. Fostered! If the movies I had seen with mother were right, being fostered was the worst that could happen to anyone. Again, I felt the pain of the loss and curling up on my bed, allowed myself the rare privilege of crying myself to sleep.

I was still in bed when a knock sounded on the door. I thought I had just gone to bed, but already the sun was creeping into my room.

"Yes?" I cried, wondering who could knock, Granuncle never did.

"Andrew," said a voice I recognized as Mrs. Urville's. "Your uncle needs you right away. He is waiting in the study."

"Yes, Mrs. Urville, I will go right now." I said and rushing to splash water in my face and do a quick brushing of teeth and hair, I dressed and went down.

I knocked on the study door and entered.

Granuncle was there and by his side stood the woman of ill omen, but uncle's eyes were not sad or clouded and when he threw me a quick glance, I realized there was no need to fear. At least I hoped so.

"Come here Andrew, Miss Adams wants to ask you some questions."

I approached and stood before the woman who then sat down and gestured for me to come nearer.

She stared into my eyes, trying to read into my soul.

"Do you know what this is Andrew?" She asked, pointing to a paper now lifted in her other hand.

"No." I replied and shook my head.

"Did your mother ever tell you she wanted you to remain here with your grand uncle?"

I stroke my chin as I had seen Granuncle do when considering a difficult question.

"When we came here, she said this was to be our home from then on." I said.

"Nothing more?" Insisted the woman.

"Only that…" I hesitated.

"Yes, only?" She prodded.

"Father told me to obey uncle Ferdi and that he was going to be my teacher from then on and to be good and study well." I added.

"And you like it here? Is your grand uncle good to you?"

"Yes, and I already know how to read and write and do my numbers. You want me to show you?"

"Hmm." She mumbled incomprehensible words and pushing me aside, stood up again.

"Well sir, I believe that settles it. Nevertheless, be aware we will conduct periodic visits to investigate the wellbeing of the child. By the end of the summer holidays, we will send someone to test him in his subjects. If he passes, he may continue home-schooling. If not… But we will cross that bridge then and not earlier. Have a good day."

She didn't address me, as if I were a chair, or even less than that.

Sent Back

Granuncle followed her to the door, and I am sure he didn't do it out of politeness, but to make sure she was gone from our home. Yes, our home, because that was how I already felt about the old family manor.

He soon returned and lifting me over to his chest, with a laugh full of joy, he cried.

"She's gone and you are mine!" He twisted in his heels, and I flew around the room held by his arms.

It was exhilarating and I also laughed.

"And thus," he added, putting me down on the floor. "And thus, today is declared a holiday, we will not study, but wander in the garden and play with Lord Byron and do all kind of mischief and eat naughty unhealthy things."

"Because…"

"Because you are legally in my custody, my son and no one is going to change that now."

Day followed day and month followed month adding up to years. Many times did the lady from Legal Services intrude into our lives, mostly unannounced, but as much as she tried to find a problem, everything was always in order and finally she gave up, the visits became sporadic and soon none.

Men from the education department had come, as she had announced, but I passed all the tests with top grades and they were greatly impressed when I read to them from several books they picked at random from uncle's library and some pages they had brought in their briefcases.

In this way, I could be home schooled, my uncle my official teacher, which was great.

Years passed and my knowledge of Geography and History amazed even Uncle William. I called the lawyer in this way as he had come to dinner frequently and remained with us for a long time in the evenings, chatting with uncle and including me in his conversation, a thing that made me feel all grown up but mostly, cherished.

Naturally I still missed my mother and father and deep in my heart the hope of seeing them again never died. The pain, however, had become numbed and I worked and studied without being distracted by sad thoughts.

Yes, many times I thought I saw my father in the street, when I went out with Granuncle; I even imagined once I had seen my mother and ran after her for a block until I realized the woman was someone unknown. Those instances shook me, and I know they also affected Granuncle, who would strive to hide the tears that came to his eyes, I couldn't say if for my pain or for losing his niece.

Granuncle had been thorough in his teaching and, keeping abreast of the current trends and the official school's curriculum, was convinced I would eventually apply for the university and would manage it wonderfully.

The task, however, rested more and more on my shoulders as I grew up. Sometimes he would give me some brief introduction of what he wanted me to learn that week and then I would be on my own. I had the whole library for myself and rarely needed to ask him questions.

One day, when I had gone with him on one of those visits to the Antiquaries who held his confidence, I saw, in a store window, a new type of appliance. I was intrigued and after my uncle had concluded his dealings with the Antiquarian, I implored him to go into the neighboring store and ask about what had captured my interest.

"That's a computer!" Replied the salesman to our question and I felt he thought it weird we didn't know about it.

"What is it good for?" Asked Granuncle.

"But sir! It is all the rage now! It does everything!"

As my uncle enquired for more details, I wandered about the room, looking at the different models being offered, and I came upon someone demonstrating the machine's capabilities. I was flabbergasted and knew instantly I needed to have one.

After more questions and answers and seeing my interest in the newfangled appliance, Granuncle bought it. It would be sent to our home and then a technician would come to install it, getting it to work and demonstrating to us how to use it.

I could hardly wait for the scheduled arrival and when it came and the technician explained us what it could do, I fell in love.

This was a machine to cherish, the sum of knowledge would be found in here, questions would be swiftly answered, and I could research on even the farthest, most secluded country. If what the man had told us was true.

Granuncle seemed stunned by everything the computer could do and looked at it with suspicion, even with misgivings.

"I don't know if this thing is going to be good or bad at the end Andrew." He said when I questioned him. "You must forgive me, son, but all my life I have searched for knowledge in books and in other person's or my own experiences and studies. To think this computer will replace that, is a bit daunting."

"It will be easier to learn new stuff, Granuncle and research must surely be faster!" I protested.

"Things easily gotten are easily forgotten. Even learning should come the hard way, or it will not benefit you at all. It is here, however and you may use it as you will. Do not, please, throw our books into oblivion; I doubt even that 'thing' has all the knowledge my books carry."

He turned around and left the room, a sad old man. It broke my heart to see him thus and there and then I decided I would continue my work in his library, using the books he cherished and only using the computer when nothing else gave me an answer. It was the least I could do for him, after all he had done for me.

Granuncle, however, had come to another decision and soon we received visits from old friends of his, men and women who had specialized in one or the other branch of science. An old professor of Geology came many nights and talked to us about the Earth and how it had changed over the eons of its history. He brought stones and vials with earth of different colors, textures and origins and I listened in awe to everything he told us.

A famous archaeologist came to visit, too. She had discovered an ancient, amazingly ancient pyramid in Peru, and she talked about it with an enthusiasm and fire it made me eager to follow in her steps. She spoke about the strata and the way to identify the different finds. About the ages of civilization and its beginnings. When she spoke of Egypt and the Pyramids I was hooked.

True, I would still be a collector as Granuncle was, I was being groomed for that, wasn't I? But Egyptology grew in my mind, and I frequently searched for more information on its ancient civilization, or new discoveries, or theories. It became my pet project and Granuncle saw it with approval.

"Uncle," I began one day at dinner. "Granuncle, do you know how I could learn more about the ancient civilization of Egypt?"

He stopped eating and lifted his head to glance at me. A slight smile spread over his lips.

"It's got its hooks in you, hasn't it?" He commented.

I nodded.

"It's no wonder. Egypt is one of the greatest mysteries of humanity and many, oh, a great many have tried to unravel it. What can you do to learn more? I'll tell you, my son."

He paused for a while and passed a white napkin over his mouth. He seemed to withdraw inside himself, and minutes elapsed before he continued.

"You must already know there are two ways of learning about things, one to read what those who have already worked or studied or researched them wrote, or to do it yourself." He looked at me and I nodded. I, too, had stopped eating and was eagerly expecting his responses.

"Much has been written about Egypt, the vast majority by those who consider it their private field of study. You could read their results and spend years of your life learning about what others consider is the History of Egypt. Or you could learn about it yourself."

"But how would I do that, Granuncle?"

"Let me first ask you: do you want to become an archaeologist?"

"No. It's not that, I still want to follow in your steps. But… There is something so appealing… No, not appealing its… It's something I need to know." I felt I wasn't able to express what it felt like.

"Like it holds an answer to your questions?" Suggested Granuncle.

"Yes!" I agreed. "And more than that, it is as if the understanding of something in its development, in the ancient Egyptians development is of such importance it needs to be found… and told."

Now Granuncle nodded.

"I understand." He chuckled. "Well, I believe it's time, you are old enough to spread your wings." He paused.

"Give me some days, my son." He continued. "I think you should begin by learning what is thought as being their language; a language not spoken in millennia, but read, oh yes, definitely read thanks to the efforts of Jean-François Champollion."

I quickly noted the name, ready to search for information on the man. Granuncle smiled as if he had read my mind.

"You go and study about the Frenchie, son. Maybe your path will follow his, I only hope it will go much farther. Your studies in that direction, however, are out of my hands and even not included in my library. You will have to go to university."

Next day, I was making my bed and hadn't come down yet when I heard voices below. At first, I paid little attention but then it hit me. That was uncle's voice, but that was, definitely, not Mrs. Urville. What could someone else be doing at our house at that time of the morning?

Like a flash, the memory of the hateful Miss Adams came to my mind, and I hurriedly finished my toilet and went downstairs.

I was still at the top of the stairs when I heard my uncle's voice again.

"… sixteen."

"Only sixteen!" Exclaimed the other voice.

"But he has been studying all these years very hard, it's all he's done!"

"Even worse, can you imagine what the university environment will do with his innocence?"

I rushed the few remaining steps and with a perfunctory knock, entered the dining room.

A sumptuous breakfast covered the table, something never seen before in the years I had lived there; my uncle and a woman sat at the table barely paying attention to the food making me salivate.

"Oh Andrew, there you are!" Exclaimed Granuncle at my abrupt entrance. "Come, we are talking about your future."

I approached and greeted the woman; the famous archaeologist Granuncle had invited days before and whose talk had triggered my interest in Egypt.

Sent Back

I sat and watched their faces aglow with excitement.

"My future?" I quoted. "What about it?"

"We were…" Started my uncle.

"Do you think you are ready to go to the university? To bring your studies to a higher level?" Interrupted the lady straight out.

I was shocked and didn't know what to say. Was this what Granuncle had said about he taking care of it?

"Well…" I hesitate. "Yes, I would like that." I finally answered at the lady's visible impatience.

"But you are only sixteen!"

"I've heard of others who started even earlier." I countered.

"They were geniuses!" She exclaimed, banging her hand on the table and making the crockery jump. Uncle also jumped.

"Come on, Morley, why are you reacting like this? I can't see how terrible it could be." He exclaimed.

The professor turned to look squarely at him.

"Because I've been there, because…" She repeated with profound feeling. "Because I am there, every single day, well, when I am not in the field. I am there and I see what happens. Specially with young innocent kids."

I moved uncomfortably; the lady was talking about me as if I were a six-year-old.

"Mam, I am sure I can handle it." I said.

"Do you have a girlfriend?" She asked and the question was like lightning out of a blue sky.

"What?"

"Do you have, or have you had, a girlfriend."

"Why, no. Not that it's any of your business." I replied, somewhat upset now.

"You see? You see? He will meet 'her' and then classes will be too boring, time too scarce to be without her, in the case she returns his interest. My God, they will all be older than him! Imagine, just imagine!"

"I don't see why my probable love affairs would have anything to do with you, mam." I said, upset.

My uncle stood and came to stand behind me placing a calming hand on my shoulder, as he had done so long ago.

"Children, children, compose yourselves." He said.

Professor Morley harrumphed and looked at her coffee cup without seeming to understand what it was and how it had come there. Granuncle sighed.

"What's there to lose?" He asked.

"Lose?" Shrieked the woman.

"Shh, calm down and listen to me." Said Granuncle and returned to

45

his place.

"Listen to me." He repeated. "Let us say you help us here and, after passing the required exams Andrew enters the university."

The woman made an indescribable sound but remained quiet after that.

"He enters the university," continued my uncle. "And he finds there the love of his life. He fails in everything and makes a real mess of his classes. So what? How many have gone through that before? I could even say millions!"

"My reputation, they would know I had…"

"Ah," said my uncle smiling. "Now we come to the root of it, your reputation."

"What about it? He would be sponsored by me, wouldn't he? What would my peers, my academic fellows say?"

"Is that so important for you, dear Sarah? More than helping a young man follow his dream?" He continued, with an appealing voice and a sad twist of his face.

She fidgeted and we waited for a while. Then she looked squarely at me, she stared.

"I would like to talk with you in private." She said and stood.

I imitated her and, with a quick glance to Granuncle to get his approval, led her to the door and then to the collections room.

Once there and after we sat on opposite armchairs, she spoke.

"I am going to ask you some questions and from them I will gauge your readiness to start higher studies. This does not, in any way, mean you will not need to pass the official exams; it only means I will consider sponsoring you. Is that clear?"

"Yes, mam." I replied, with tremors of anticipation.

She suddenly spoke in French, asking me questions, then quite as sudden she changed and continued in Spanish. The changes didn't surprise me, as we used to play this game, uncle and I.

She seemed satisfied and now continued in Greek, which I answered though with not as much fluidity as the previous ones.

In that way we continued, and she tested my knowledge in ancient history, scientific method and all the fields of science she could think of. Apparently, she was becoming more and more convinced of my aptitudes because her sour face had become relaxed and sometimes her lips spread in a fleeting smile.

"What do you know about Archeoastronomy?"

The word was strange but I quickly analyzed it. Old astronomy.

"I haven't studied that subject, mam." I replied.

"It is alright." She said. "It is not required but it would be helpful to you if you consider entering my field. It would also be something the board would find a bonus when you apply."

She slapped her thigh and stood looking at me from above, like an angel considering a sinning mortal.

"I think you will do, yes, you will do well." She said offering me a hand, which I rose to accept.

"I only wish," she continued. "I only wish you have the strength of character to withstand the, let's say temptations, you are going to encounter once you walk into the real world."

She left the room, while I remained standing and wondering about her last words. Temptations'?

CHAPTER VI

After a brief conversation with Granuncle and a shake of hands, the professor left. I had followed her to the dining room and witnessed the exchange, though not making much of it, she was careful to keep a low voice.

Granuncle escorted her to the door and then turned to face me.

"I think we've done it!" He exclaimed. "And that only thanks to your dedication to learning, my child."

He reached me and gave me a quick hug.

"Your parents would be proud." He added as an afterthought.

I simply nodded, his pride on what I had accomplished was a comfort. I returned to the study and there, for the first time during my study hours, I opened the computer.

Rightly had my uncle suspected it. The information it returned after I wrote 'Archeoastronomy' in the search engine was amazing. Now I had to clear the shaft from the grain, a daunting task, as I was beginning to see.

Suddenly, a tray with juice and a sandwich appeared by my side.

"You have been working without pause and missed lunch, so I brought you this." Said Granuncle while he gazed at the computer screen.

"Ah, searching for that." He commented and squinting came nearer the display.

"Archeoastronomy was never a subject of interest for me." He muttered, absentmindedly. "Too far and too difficult to prove, unless you live beside an observatory."

"It is very interesting, Granuncle and it seems to be helping archaeologist to confirm the time ancient monuments were built." I replied.

"Yes. It could do that." He nodded. "Did our good friend Sarah insist on you knowing about it?"

"She asked if I knew anything about it and said it would be a bonus, something they would consider during my application." I explained.

"Well, then get on with it." He said, getting ready to leave.

"Granuncle!" I exclaimed and standing ran to him. I grasped his arm and was surprised at how thin it seemed but continued. "Granuncle, if all goes well, when will I need to submit to those exams you spoke about?"

Sent Back

"Though classes never stop, usually the examinations take place throughout the year, except the summer months. Sadly, or perhaps, luckily for us, the next SAT will be in October, so you have some months to get ready. I will do the proper registration, don't worry about that."

"But do you know what they will cover?" I insisted, getting worried.

"If I am correct, they will test you in Literature, and World History, which I am sure you'll ace, Math which would cover algebra, geometry, trigonometry, functions, statistics and other subjects we can find out about later; you will also be tested on Biology, Chemistry and Physics. But don't worry about it, I will find out with detail."

"Do you think I am ready?" I insisted.

He patted my cheek.

"I am positive. I'll leave you to your Archeoastronomy now. Eat something." He added pointing to the sandwich and left.

I spent the remaining of the day learning about the new subject; I printed and took notes as the quest took me through different avenues. A barrage of scientists and their opinions, hypothesis and astronomical facts overwhelmed me.

They were truly marvelous; the possibilities the internet offered were unparalleled. I didn't regret my decision to use only my uncle's library but promised myself I would use more of this repository of knowledge, especially when and if, I entered University.

The moment I had grasped his arm came back to me then and I stood still, as if a giant hammer had suddenly whacked me. He was so thin! I had never paid attention to it, with more reason because of his eternal housecoat, but now I remembered instances, when we had gone to the beach, or done some gardening outside. He hadn't used the housecoat then and I remembered a swift wonder at his diminishing size.

How old was Granuncle? He was my mother's uncle, which made him of the same age my grandmother would have had, more or less. My mother would have been forty-six now, if her mother had given her birth during her twenties, that would make Granuncle at least sixty something. Well, that was not so old, I thought and still he seemed to be, at least much older than that. and a weird idea came to mind. Would uncle be reported on the internet?

I immediately typed his name and sure enough, it came up. I stared in great amazement at the screen and sat straight, unnerved at what I was reading.

A familiar face looked at me from the display and underneath it read:

'Sir Ferdinand Thomas Whittaker, Esq. (22 January 1888 unknown).'

That could not be him, I cried to myself, that would make him what, over one hundred years old! I continued reading, my heart beating uncontrollably inside my chest.

49

'An American amateur archeologist and antiquarian who studied the Mayan ruins on the northern Yucatán Peninsula. He is said to have collected several items from that site now lost, or remain unaccounted for.

Whittaker was born in the Orkney archipelago's largest island: Mainland in the city of Kirkwall. While still very young his family returned to Edinburgh, their city of origin and where Whittaker spent most of his childhood. At his father's death, his mother sought the help of a distant cousin who had emigrated to America at the beginning of the century.'

'Ferdinand Thomas Whittaker and his mother soon moved to the cousin's estate, where the young man began his new life. He was elected a member of the American Antiquarian Society in 1928.'

I sat back, still amazed at my finding. Uncle? Granuncle Birdie? Could this be really him?

I kept on reading until the darkness of the room bothered me.

He had written extensively and traveled the entire world. His opinions on archaeology and ancient trinkets had apparently been considered by several of the most notable scientists and still he proposed an amazing idea: that civilization had originated in Central America, more properly with the Mayan civilization.

This was preposterous. I closed the computer. I wanted no one else looking at this information, I wanted even less for Granuncle to realize I had been looking him up. I still had my doubts, because I was positive he could not, ever, be as old as the Wikipedia website said. There must be an error, perhaps it was not 1888 but 1988. No, that would make him too young. Pondering on the matter, I reached the dining room.

Granuncle was waiting for me and when I approached the table he chuckled.

"You found out?" He said in a low voice, his eyes full of amusement.

"I found out what?" I replied, upset at his cheerfulness when I was so distraught.

"Who I am."

"What do you mean?"

"Come on son, you know what I mean. You found out when I was born, from where I came, all about me. Haven't you?"

"Yes, but how could you know?" I replied, intrigued and a little afraid. How could he, indeed, know what I had been doing? Soon it downed on me, perhaps the computer…

"No Andrew, no. Not through the computer or any new-fangled device I may have brought secretly into my home. I knew because I can do those things."

I waited not knowing what to ask, there were thousands of questions and all seemed outlandish.

"Come, sit." He begged. "We can talk about this while we eat. You didn't have a proper lunch, you know."

I obeyed, still gazing at him with wonder.

He took my dish and filled it with potatoes and gravy, with roast beef and string beans. He added on top a thick slice of bread and handed it to me.

"Eat." He ordered and I, as usual, obeyed.

After a while I broke the silence with the question that would solve all the doubts.

"When were you truly born, Granuncle?" I asked.

He stopped eating and placed the fork and knife carefully at the edge of his dish.

"That's at the heart of it, isn't it?" He replied. "Yes, my son, I was born in 1888."

"How can it be!" I cried. "That's impossible!"

"May I ask why?"

"Well, because that would make you, you would be…"

"I am 129 years old, nephew." He said.

I spluttered and shot up to my feet.

"You are joking!" I cried.

"No. I am not. Sit down." He replied in the calmest manner. "Sit down, sir!"

I sat with alacrity; he had never used that tone with me.

"Now, dear one, let's consider this as the pair of scientists we are. What's so strange about me being almost 130 years of age?"

"No one can live so long, uncle! Everyone knows that!"

"Everyone thinks they know things the scientist knows are wrong. There are even some who have lived more than I have, even to 147 years."

"But… But…"

"It is not so rare Andrew, but I will grant you it's not very common, either. I know you are all awash with questions but there are things I cannot say, not yet. To answer your doubts, yes; whatever information you found about me in that internet of yours I believe it's quite reliable, the place I was born in, when I travelled to the United States, all of that."

"Even about your trips? About the Mayans? Is that how…"

"Yes." He interrupted me. "That's how I got it and other items I will let you study later, not now; not yet."

"But why the mystery? and… and… Then you cannot be my mother's uncle, can you? What is truly your relationship to us?"

"I am your uncle, but many times removed. Let's say your great-great-grandmother was my younger sister, born in 1890."

I gaped.

"Close your mouth, son." He said, chuckling. "So yes, I am related to you and your mother, though not as close as you would have thought."

"And mother knew this?" I said, still trying to digest all the new information.

"No, oh no. I never found the need to tell her, nor did she guess or perform any research, as you just have."

"But my grandmother didn't tell? Any other relative?"

"Listen Andrew: you and your mother have been the only ones I have let into my privacy. No one had lived before you in this manor and my communication with the rest of the family had become inexistent many years ago. Only your mother did I admit here, when she was small, very young in years and I'll tell you another day the reason why I did that. So, my dear great-great-grandnephew, I have answered most of your doubts and I am tired. Go now to your Archeoastronomy, or to whatever thing you are studying now and let me rest."

Never had Granuncle complained of being tired and it worried me, more now because of my previous experience of his thinness. I approached him and bent to kiss him, realizing his cheeks seemed sunken, as the eyes, the bones more marked, his neck's skin hanging in loose folds.

My heart contracted in my chest. Was I going to lose him, too? No, God, please! I prayed; Don't take him away!

Uncle seemed to hear my prayer.

"I won't leave you, my son, not for some time yet. Be at ease." He said and with a gesture insisted on my leaving.

I left.

CHAPTER VII

I was already in my senior year at the University. As the professor had foreseen, my first year had been turbulent and pitiful because my complete ignorance of my peers' habits, practices and rituals placed me at great disadvantage.

I had had bad moments, brightened here and there by a sudden ray of sunlight when I received praise from my teachers, the friendship of a fellow student or a special girl granted me a date. They were few, as almost everyone found me awkward and uninteresting. There was nothing in my conversation to attract them until I learned how to talk in an interesting way and became better at it. Soon many fellows were confiding in me, not even expecting my opinions. Sometimes I felt I was a confessor, but I learned much about human psychology in those days.

Slowly I adapted and by my junior year I had become, at least outwardly, one of them. True, I still had little luck with the ladies, but being a senior had its advantages and that will be all the information I'll give on the theme.

I had decided majoring in Archaeology, considering the broad spectrum of its disciplines and my goal: to become a collector as my granduncle had. Professor Morley had taken me under her wing, and we often met; she wanted to make sure I was taking the proper courses and liked to discuss some subjects of her interest with me, perhaps finding me a more attentive listener than the rest of her students. She had done more excavations on her recent find and the results were staggering, suggesting civilization in the Americas was of an even earlier date than previously suspected, throwing it back to one hundred twenty thousand years ago.

As my electives, I had taken languages, among them Archaic, Old, Middle, and Late Egyptian covering everything written from 2600 BCE to the 7th Century BCE. Naturally, I had to add Coptic and Demotic, but I found these not as hard, as some Coptic is still spoken among the tribes and churches.

It was not an easy task, but with the professor's help I muddled through and finally became proficient in them and in the understanding of the hieroglyphs both Egyptian and Mayan.

So at the end of my Junior year, I had mastered several languages and participated in archaeological excavations in Egypt and Peru. It had been an excruciating time; archaeological investigations took much patience and great attention to detail, not to talk about the physical efforts, but slowly I was becoming an expert and was enjoying it greatly.

I had taken a room near the Campus and during the last year had seen Granuncle only two or three times, my work for my thesis and the excavations taking all my time. So, it was not a surprise I was eventually summoned to him.

I suspected, when the call came through, the old man was tired of waiting for my visit and had forced the thing himself. I was wrong.

I expected to be greeted by him, but when I arrived, Mrs. Urville waited at the door, having been alerted by the security camera at the gate. She had aged, but still was the same severe and yet kind woman I had known since my childhood.

"Mrs. Urville?" I asked instead of answering her warm greeting. "Mrs. Urville, where's uncle?"

She shook her head, her eyes reflecting sadness and my heart fell to my feet.

"What? Is he alright?"

"He is very sick, my son, and in his room." She replied, wiping her always clean hands in an even cleaner apron. "He's not feeling good and has remained in bed for some days now." She added.

I waited for no more and rushed upstairs to his room.

When I opened the door, I was at first startled by the darkness inside, but my eyes quickly adapted and I saw the bed, my uncle and a woman beside him.

"Granuncle!" I cried, rushing to him. The woman turned and gestured for silence.

"Is he… is he…" I couldn't say the awful words, but she shook her head.

"He is asleep." She whispered.

"No, I am not." Came the voice from the bed. "At least not anymore. Come here, my son."

I approached and bent over the bed to see him. He was emaciated and his otherwise large build now practically disappeared below the covers.

"Granuncle!" I whispered, awed by the change. "What happened?"

"Hah." He replied. "Time. Time has happened. Tell that woman to leave us." He added in a very low voice, which, however, was heard by her.

"I am leaving, I am leaving." She said. and in an apart. "Don't let him get up, he's been trying all morning and he shouldn't be walking."

I nodded ushering her to the door while she kept looking back, making certain of my uncle's status.

Sent Back

"I'll take care of him." I promised and closed the door behind her.

"Come, come here." Said my uncle with a stronger voice. "I have much to tell you."

I pulled a chair and sat by his side.

"Only promise you will not over-excite yourself." I said.

"Oh, rubbish, that will not change anything. I know I have still time." He said with a chuckle.

"Then why the urgency on my coming to see you?"

"You are very busy, then?" He asked, grasping for my hand and gazing at me with those beloved eagle eyes of his.

"I am working hard on my thesis, yes." I replied.

"This is important, my son, I wouldn't have asked to see you if not. Yes, yes, I know I said I have still time, but better be sure. There are things you need to know."

"You already said that." I answered, wondering if the old man's mind was going.

"No, I am as clear minded now as I ever was, I am not going gaga or anything like that. I want you to be certain of this, child, because what I am going to tell you will be difficult to accept." He answered my unspoken thought with this uncanny ability of his that had always amazed me.

"I am listening."

He looked again at me with that peculiar twist of his head that always reminded me of a bird looking at the worm it was ready to eat.

"You have always wondered how I have been able to live these many years."

I nodded.

"The reason I brought your mother into my house when she was a child was to prepare conditions to your living with me."

I gasped in amazement. How had he known I would ever exist?

He chuckled.

"Yes, I knew you would exist, and I knew how your abilities would blossom under my teachings. You see Andrew, sometimes, after several generations of irrelevant people, one is born that has extraordinary abilities, even powers."

I was now even more convinced Granuncle had gone off his rocker.

"Listen, listen well Andrew." The old man continued, and he sat and took my hand in his. They were bony and now more than ever they resembled a bird's claw.

"I cannot remember how many were born after me who never amounted to anything. Lives of total anonymity, mediocre and uninteresting followed one after the other until you. I knew of you, my son, as soon as your mother was born. Yes, I had the gift of foreknowledge, among others."

"Then," I exclaimed. "Why didn't you prevent my parent's death?"

I had become angry, though I realized this was a fantasy, the fantasy of a mind now lost by the passage of time, the idea the death of my mother had been known before it would ever happen irritated me.

"You will learn, my dear, that you do not meddle with what is to be. I could do nothing, please don't blame me, don't be angered by my apparent negligence." He gazed at me with what I thought was compassion. "Furthermore, my son, this gift is not like watching a movie, some things you can see, but many are as hidden to me as they would be to any other human being."

I shrugged and stood, ready to leave.

"You must listen!" Said the man and I felt compelled to sit back on the bed by his side.

"As I said, you are one of those who have escaped the silence imposed over the minds of humanity."

"What are you talking about, old man?" I said, full of unexplained disdain and anger. "I have nothing."

"You are born with eyes, but they don't see. Only after days can they focus correctly and just after some time is the information they bring to the brain decoded. In the same way, you were born with several abilities that have not been activated yet."

"Humph."

Suddenly, to my mind's eye came the image of a young couple with their son. They were before me and I heard the little boy ask, 'You are a Granuncle Birdie, so, where are your feathers and your wings?'

I realized I was seeing myself the moment I had arrived in Granuncle's house through my uncle's eyes.

"You are seeing my memory of that moment Andrew and you can see it because in you is the ability to communicate mentally. It is one of those you must work to develop."

"I was seeing your memories?"

"Yes."

"That is impossible." I stated.

"Please keep an open mind! Don't you remember the number of times I was able to know your questions even before you stated them? Don't you remember the time you first searched for my information on the internet and I knew you had?"

It all came back, and I realized the old man was right, he had known before the fact.

"But how can that be possible?" I asked.

"As I said, once every several generations one is born like me, like you. I have searched for the answer to this question all my life, wanting to know why our family differs from the others. The explanation always escapes me."

"What else…"

"Can we do?" He finished my question. "Well, we can prolong our life." He smiled. "Something we have to do to wait for the next one and guide him, or her."

"Is that my function, then? Waiting for one to be born like us and to guide them?"

"No. You have an important destiny, your life should uncover some hidden truth, some secret that those who control the world do not want revealed."

"Who control? What are you talking about?"

He looked around the room with I could only explain as fear and continued.

"Not now and not here, though I doubt they could hear our conversation."

I had been watching him, his lips didn't move and yet I had heard his voice. I looked at him with wide-open eyes. He nodded.

"I am very tired now, my beloved nephew and need to rest for a while. We will continue later. Please don't go back to your apartments, not yet. Your room is ready. Go now."

I was turning to leave when I felt called back by him.

"Andrew, please think about this. I am sure we are capable of more wondrous things I haven't yet discovered."

I nodded and bent over him to give him a kiss as I was used to since my early years.

"I love you, Andrew." He whispered as I left.

Early the next morning, even before breakfast I went to his room. He was awake and motioned me to his side. The nurse was absent, perhaps getting his food from the kitchen and he bade me lock the door.

"I want to talk to you about the prolonging of your life." He said.

"Listen." He continued. "If your mind is correctly attuned, if you train it and strengthen it, you can control your cell's aging. That is what allowed me to live so many years. The electromagnetic field generated by the energy of life can and must be controlled and nurtured. If you can do that, your cells will not age as fast as it does for the rest of the world. Perhaps I will have time to teach you how it is done, but in case I don't, promise you will look into it. Promise you will study this."

"I promise, Granuncle."

"This electromagnetic field can be controlled; you can expand it so it can create an enclosure around you that prevents harm from reaching you. This is what ancients and mystics have called 'aura', perhaps proven by

Kirlian photography. It has been known since the dawn of ages, as Qi and Prana." He paused. "By the way, if ever you have time to learn Sanskrit, promise me you'll read the ancient Hindu science, the Vedas." He looked at me quizzically until I nodded. "Not all the truth therein hidden has been translated to more common languages."

"Good. I believe that ability is the most important you must develop, your mind controlling what is. You can control many things with your mind, not only your body, but I think I am going to have to rest now for a bit. I am strangely tired. Nevertheless, next time we will talk about the origin of our family; remind me in case I forget."

"Wait." I exclaimed. I had a question I needed answered. "Wait, if, if your mind can control everything, or at least everything in your body, what is happening to you now?"

"Everything has to end, my son and there is a time for renewal of all life on Earth which can't be avoided. Being away from the Source for so many years takes a toll." He was whispering now. "I long for the Merging, Oh, how I long for Him!"

I heard him whisper, or was it I heard it on my mind? He was repeating a verse of the Psalms, the songs of King David:

'As the heart pants after the water brooks, so pants my soul after thee, O God. My soul thirsts for God, for the living God! When shall I come and appear before God?'

He reclined deeper into the pillows and closed his eyes.

I leaned forward, he was breathing slowly but deeply, and I knew he was sleeping, only sleeping. I sat back and looked at the old boy with wonder.

Was it true? Did he believe what he had told me? It had always seemed a fantasy, something people had made up to assuage the fear of dissolution. But here was a man who had lived for now almost one hundred and forty years, who had lived through the First and Second World War and on three different centuries. Could it be true? I asked myself again.

I heard a soft knock, and the door opened a crack. The nurse's head appeared.

"Is he sleeping?" She asked.

I nodded. I had been nodding a lot today, perhaps the shock of the call, of his sudden sickness, of his revelations had stunned me.

I went to the door and the nurse came in.

"Is he alright?" She asked, scrutinizing my face and looking to the bed.

"I believe he is, as well as he can be." I replied. "He fell asleep, saying he was tired. I will be in the study, in case he, or you, need me."

This time she nodded as she walked to the bed.

I looked once more at Granuncle and closed the door behind me.

Sent Back

I was bewildered, not only because of what he had been talking about, but by something more down to earth, the sickness of my last remaining relative. The perspective of being left alone in this world was now patently clear and it scared me. It scared me stiff.

CHAPTER VIII

I walked out the room and down the stairs. Mrs. Urville was standing at the bottom, looking up to me.

"How's the master?" She inquired.

"Sleeping. We spoke for a while, but now he is asleep. Tell me, Mrs. Urville, how long has he been in this way?"

I had by now reached her and saw she was nervous and fidgeting.

"Some days now." She said, but her head was bowed, and she didn't look me in the eye.

"How many?" I insisted.

She shook her head, and I heard a stifled sob. I approached her.

"Tell me how long, Mrs. Urville, I need to know!"

"Oh, young master, he has been like this for almost three months now!" She exclaimed and burst out crying like a bereft child.

I passed an arm over her trembling shoulders.

"Now, now, don't be so upset." I muddled and then asked the question I knew she feared. "Why didn't you call me earlier?"

She pulled out of under my arm and walked two or three steps away from me.

"I knew you would ask. I told the master, I told him he was putting me in a very difficult position, but he shrugged. He shrugged and forbade me to call you!" She finished with a wail.

I did nothing to comfort her, I knew she needed the catharsis, the release of her pain and remorse.

"This is not your fault, Mrs. Urville, you obeyed my uncle's wishes, as you have always done. I understand. Don't be so hard on yourself." I said after some minutes and patted her hand, a hand crossed by veins and now full of liver spots, a hand that had fed me and guided me through many a street. She was old, too and the realization made me feel even more distraught.

"Mrs. Urville, I am going to the study. I will stay there in case the old boy needs me. Could you bring me something to eat? I had no breakfast."

"Sure, sir, sure. I'll take care of that myself." She replied, bringing up a corner of her apron to dry up her tears. "Anything special?"

Sent Back

"No, just the same breakfast you used to prepare for me, before I left."

She smiled sadly, nodded and rushed off to the kitchen, while I walked toward the study door.

I opened it and stood paralyzed in the threshold. It was a veritable mess! There must have been a break-in, something terrible must have taken place here. I knew well Granuncle would let nothing like this happen to his beloved study.

I rang the bell, I rang it so insistently two or three servants, accompanied by Gregoire and Mrs. Urville rushed to the site.

"What is this?" I cried, severely, pointing a trembling finger to the overturned chairs, the open desk drawers, the books strewn on the floor.

My question was greeted with silence and when I turned to look at them, I saw amazement and terror in their faces.

"You hadn't seen it?" I asked.

A unanimous shaking of the head was my answer.

"But you had not come to this room to clean it? Order it? Nothing?"

Again, the unanimous denial.

I was reluctant to reprove them, these were men and women who had been my helpers, even my playmates during my childhood. I knew them and I also knew they would let nothing like this happen in their master's study.

I gazed intently into their eyes.

"Alright, return to your tasks, but you, Gregoire," I said to the gardener who was more than a gardener, "please stay and help me put this back in order."

The old man nodded and entered the room. He immediately straightened the chairs, picking up the books and papers on the carpet.

"Gregoire, do you have any idea who could have done this?"

"No Andrew." and then, realizing I was not anymore the child who had met him by his mother's side, he added. "No, sir and I can't imagine there could have been a break-in. We have a very special security system; you have seen it yourself." He smiled, remembering awkward situations I have been brought into because of that same security system.

I smiled too, but swiftly my worry returned, wiping the smile from my face.

"Could it..." I hesitate to speak the words. "Could it have been my uncle?"

The old man looked back at me and I would have sworn it was with pity.

"Perhaps, sir. Mr. Ferdinand has been acting strangely lately, even before he took to his bed."

"What do you mean, strangely?"

"Well, sir," continued the man, now looking into the desk drawers as he closed them. "He himself called me two or three times here and after carefully closing the door, insisted on telling me nobody could come in here but you."

I gaped.

"He said that? But then, what is this?"

"My only explanation is he did this himself, sir." Said the gardener and I could see he, too, was bewildered.

"Did he tell you anything else?"

"No, Mr. Andrew, but…"

I could see he was not eager to talk.

"Come on Gregoire this is important and my uncle sickness makes it even more so. What do you know?"

The man looked around, as if expecting someone to be hiding in the shadows; he then came closer.

"You know I sometimes walk the garden and around the house at night, to check if all the windows and doors are closed and everything is alright. I trust the security system but trust more in my eyes."

"Yes, yes." I prodded.

"Well sir, one night, it was past midnight sir, and I was sure your uncle had gone to bed. Be it as it may, Mr. Andrew, I saw a light on that window there." He pointed. It was precisely the window under which I had hidden and heard my parents discuss my future with Granuncle.

"And?"

"Well sir, I was worried, as, who would be in the master's study at that hour? I knew none of us would have dared. So I came and peered through the glass. A shadow crossed before me, sir and I was sure it was your granduncle."

"But you just said he had already retired!"

"I know, I thought so myself. But you know… you know that housecoat he loves to wear at all times, it conceals his body, but is so typically his… I am sure it was him, sir."

"So you are saying it was my uncle who did this mess? But that is preposterous!" I exclaimed and realizing I was getting angry I took a deep breath, as I had been taught precisely by this man.

"Wait, master Andrew." Said the man, returning in his distress to the way he had called me for so many years. "Listen to what I heard then."

"Speak."

"I was so concerned I got to the window and leaned over. It was slightly open, though I was sure it had been closed before and through the crack I could hear the voice of Mr. Ferdinand, muttering something."

"Are you sure it was him?" I asked. "What was he saying? Could you hear him?"

Sent Back

"I heard him quite right, sir. He said: 'He must be able to find it, but how can I hide it from the rest? I must find a place.' That was it, because it was only muttering after that and I couldn't understand any of it."

"He must be able to find it?" I quoted. "Who, me?"

"I don't know sir, but I surmised so."

"And who did he want to hide it from? And what was it? Oh, Gregoire, you've left me now with more questions than answers."

"I know, Mr. Andrew, but that is all I can tell you. I thought then that perhaps he wanted to hide it from us, but what was the use? We would never search or look for anything in the house. As to what he wanted hidden, again I am at a loss; it could be anything!"

I nodded, agreeing with the old servant. Uncle had so many things, so many curiosities, trinkets, collectibles it would be impossible to surmise what he wanted me to find.

We looked again around the room and sighed in unison.

"Look here, Gregoire, you return to your duties, and I will finish organizing the room. If you remember anything else, please tell me immediately, yes?"

"I will do that, sir, surely I will." The old man started toward the door and stopped, as if suddenly taken by an idea.

"You know Andrew?" He said, turning to face me. "The next day..."

"What about the next day?"

"It was the next day that the master took to his bed."

I saw the gardener leave, closing the door softly behind him. I walked to uncle's desk and setting upright the big study chair, sat.

I didn't have time for this. I really didn't have time. My thesis had been taking much of my days and nights and I still had other classes, because I had wanted to take a minor in Geology and those were not yet ended.

The problem was I could never forsake Granuncle, not after everything he had done for me and more important, because of the love I felt for him. I reviewed in my mind our last interview, trying to see if he had seemed unhinged, manic, but all about it seemed right. Try as I might, I couldn't detect a hint of madness in our talk other than what he had said about my special abilities or powers. I remembered his statement about the control of our body by our mind, but this was not the first time I had heard about this idea, it was a widespread theme in many circles, though mostly labeled as pseudoscience.

Why had he overturned everything in the room? What had caused this? and what, in the name of God, would he want me to find?

I stood and got back to placing the books in their places, stacking up the papers strewn all over, straightening the chairs. I was putting back three remaining books, books that all belonged in the same shelf, because as I have previously explained, every book in my uncle's study was carefully placed according to subject, time of printing and author. I was, I say, going to the corresponding shelf to place the three books when I observed the back of the armoire was not made of the same wood. It was of a different color and shape, being white and with squares carved in it. It looked more like a door than the back of the cabinet. I wondered at that moment how weird it was I had never observed it but shrugged and let the question pass.

I took out the remaining books in that shelf and placed them on a table. The strange fixture extended all along and seemed to continue behind the other armoire.

I eagerly removed the books in the other library and found the door, or whatever it could be, ended just halfway. I touched the wood, it was warm. I stepped back and contemplated the whole thing. I was almost sure now it was a door, a concealed door. I wondered if it was an accident, if the door could have been condemned to place the library there, or, the other possibility, that the libraries had been placed in front of the door to hide it.

I looked at the floor, there were no marks there, nothing to hint at the movement of the furniture over it. How could the door be accessed?

I passed my hands over the surface, checking for a hidden release, a latch, something that could show how to open; how to reach the door, but my search was unsuccessful and finally I went back to sit on the chair, still gazing at the strange door.

That it was a door I was now sure, as I had removed all the remaining books and could see its contour. Curiously, I had not found a lock or a handle, only the big, square, six by eight slab of carved wood. The raised blocks adorned it from top to bottom and between them cords or…

I stood and approached the door again. No those were not cords, those were snakes. I could now distinctly see their heads and… were those their eyes?

Tiny, almost invisible stones stood in the place of eyes. I extended my hand and touched one with my index finger. I felt a movement.

Was it the door? Was it, in a strange way, reacting to my touch?

I swept my hand down, caressing the carved snake's body and then I came to another head. The snakes entwined together and bending down, I could see each snake held the other by its tail. Mouth to tail, tail to mouth, the snakes were linked around the door and their skin-like carved squares wavered in the light. They had glittering little jewels or pieces of glass instead of eyes.

Suddenly an idea hit me, and I pressed between index and thumb the snake's head, being careful to touch only the stones. Nothing happened. Then I tried another and another, I had done so to almost all when I saw, above and crowning the door a two-headed snake apparently the one who gave origin to all the other ones.

Sent Back

It was beyond my reach, as I was hampered by the library's shelves, so I went back and took a chair to climb upon.

This time I realized I would need to use my two hands, one to press the eyes on one head, the other on the other head. I did so and I heard a soft rumble and a hiss, then I felt a tremor on the door and the top central square moved; it rotated and then moved aside.

The position of the shelves had, miraculously, allowed this movement, or perhaps they had been placed in such a way for precisely this purpose.

The block moved and now I could see it had covered a hole, well, not really a hole, but a shallow chamber carved in the wood. In the farther wall of this chamber was imprinted the contour of a key. It must be a key, though it was so ornate and different from what we commonly expect of a key, only a few would have realized what it was at first glance.

So, a key must have been hidden there, that was obvious now, but where was it? The imprint was there, in fact there was a carved-out space to put the key in, but the key was missing. Was this what my uncle had been trying to hide with such urgency it must have gotten him sick?

Why not leave it there? Who could have found the place? I couldn't even explain to myself the steps that had led me to find it. A key to what? The door had no lock and if the key was not for this door, what would it unlock then? The mystery was making me hungry and just then I heard a knock on the door.

I swiftly placed the books on the shelves, without order, just to cover the white door. Then moved the chair I had used to reach the serpent's head.

I went to the door. It was Mrs. Urville with a tray; I could smell the refreshing smell of freshly brewed coffee, hot pancakes and maple syrup.

"Thank you, Mrs. Urville." I said, taking the tray and preventing her from coming in.

I think she understood my need for privacy, because without trying to enter the room, she nodded.

"Will there be anything else, Mr. Andrew?" She asked.

"No, Mrs. Urville, this is perfect. Any news from upstairs?"

"No. The nurse called to ask for something to eat for herself and the master, but she explained he was still sleeping."

"Good, let me know if he wakes up."

"I will, sir." She closed the door, and I took the tray to the desk and sat to eat while I pondered on the mystery laid before me.

After more time spent considering the mystery, I gave up. I knew by experience how often the answers come when you leave your brain alone and allow it time to search its innumerable archive files.

So getting my laptop, I returned to work on my thesis.

Hours passed and Mrs. Urville called me to table for dinner. I ate, a sad lonely meal, swiftly finished, returning to the refuge of my work.

It was late when I retired and I was tired, exhausted by all the emotions of the day. Then, from a deep slumber, the voice of Granuncle woke me. I was still befuddled by sleep and in that region of mindfulness when dreams are reality and reality a dream, I was again a child and Granuncle was beside me.

"Andrew." I heard again, realizing this was what had woken me up. Now truly awake, I looked around the room. I was, naturally, alone, but I was sure I had heard my uncle calling me.

"Andrew."

I twisted my head, I would have sworn the voice came from behind me, but again nobody was there.

I threw my old robe over my shoulders and walked into the hallway. There was no light anywhere, even Granuncle's room seemed darkened, so I went back to my room and took the old flashlight that had helped me in so many escapades.

I walked cautiously down the hallway and reached Granuncle's door. Something cautioned me, telling me there was danger beyond the door.

Nonsense, it was Granuncle's room! I said to myself and entered. I shone the light instinctively towards uncle's bed and it was then I saw it, a black shadow leaning over the bed, over uncle.

I cried. I can't remember what, but the cry was one of terror.

The male nurse, who had relieved the day nurse, jumped to his feet throwing the side table and everything on it to the floor. I heard below the cries and calls of the servants, but my attention was on the shadow.

It did not seem alarmed by being discovered but had straightened up and seemed to look at me. A shiver of terror ran up and down my spine and all my hairs stood on end as, though terrified, I ran to my uncle's side.

He was there, his eyes wide open and staring at the thing beside him. He seemed unable to talk and still I heard his voice calling my name, calling in my head.

I grasped his hand and challenged the shadow with eyes and posture, it lifted. Yes, it rose high above the bed, and I thought it was coming for me. Then, it exploded in little puffs of darkness that swiftly disappeared.

"Granuncle!" I exclaimed, leaning over him. "Granuncle are you alright? What was that?"

His eyes searched mine and I knew he was dying, but I still heard his voice in my head.

"Andrew!" and then. "They don't want you to know, but part of the answer hides in the house. Search for it, son, search for what I hid."

I heard him gasp for air and I saw his throat crushed by an invisible fist.

Sent Back

"Search!"

At that last moment, a sudden image came to my mind, that of the burial of the old cat, of Lord Byron, whom we had buried in the garden. Then, the image, the memory disappeared from my mind, all the voices quieted and there was absolute silence after that.

CHAPTER IX

I barely remember what happened next. I suppose the doctor was called in, as I remember talking to him. He considered my uncle's death something natural because of his recent ailment and his very old age.

I said nothing, I told no one about the black shadow and the hand crushing my uncle's throat. I kept silent about uncle's call; who would believe it? They would think it was the product of my distress; perhaps prescribe some pills as was the usual response to these things.

The nurses were recalled and questioned to make their statement. I thought it very strange that the night nurse didn't speak about the shadow but thought perhaps he didn't want to attract attention to himself. Could it be the shadow had been visible only to me?

The doctor prepared the death certificate using his newfangled laptop with printer attached and the preliminaries of death were taken care of.

Mrs. Urville was devastated, and the rest of the servants were also very distraught, but I managed, in my affliction, to order them back to work. and then I sat beside the bed, beside the corpse of my last remaining family.

I felt numb, unable to understand his death, in a weird way expecting him to laugh and sit up, making fun of all the fuss. Naturally it didn't happen and as the minutes ticked away, I accepted his death. I remembered vividly when my mother died and the disappearance of my father; the pain surged as alive and strong as during the first moments of my bereavement.

A knock on the door brought me back to the present and I went to open; it was an unknown man, but behind him I saw the bowed head of Mrs. Urville.

"He is here to take care of the funeral, Mr. Andrew." She whispered.

I nodded and made the man come in.

He offered his condolences and, in a silent, solemn way explained my granduncle had done all the arrangements years before and everything was prepared.

"Wait." I said, worried. "I know nothing of his wishes in this matter, he never talked about it. What will happen now?"

"Oh, it's very simple, a Christian ceremony, a few words and then the burial. We will take care of everything and call you when it's ready, do not worry."

I didn't know why, but I was becoming suspicious of the man. I rose my eyes to him, he was tall, much more than me and I am considered above average. So I looked up at him and tried to read his truth there.

"Don't worry, sir." He said, apparently understanding my misgivings. "Here is my card and here you have the documents your granduncle signed. Everything is in order."

I took the papers and swiftly read them, then I inspected the man's card, all seemed right. I returned the documents, and the man placed them back in the briefcase from where he had taken them out.

"Is it alright then?" He asked, matter-of-factly.

I nodded.

"I will send my men in. Perhaps you'll wait outside?"

Understanding this was more an order than a request, I went to the door. But as I reached it, I heard a strange sound and turned.

The door to the terrace that had remained closed during all this time was wide open and the man from the funerary, extending wide black wings, was taking my uncle's body in its claws. He flew away.

My cry of terror brought the servants running, but only Gregoire was in time to see what I was pointing at. He had sense enough to forbid the rest of the servants from coming in and closed the door in their faces. I was terribly distraught but still my mind kept thinking about the silly little things, like what would they think of me now, with all my screaming and weird actions.

We gazed at the disappearing black bird for a while until it became a distant dot and then turning, we looked at each other in terror and awe.

"You saw it." I affirmed.

"Yes, sir, I did. But I wouldn't be telling anyone about it, not if you don't want to be put in the madhouse."

"How am I going to explain uncle's body disappearance then? What am I to do?"

"Mr. Andrew, you have to call the lawyer, Mr. William Lagerfeld, sir; you must call him now." Whispered the good man. "I am sure he is the only one who can help in this dilemma."

"I don't know his phone number and it is very early!" I protested.

"The master surely has it somewhere here and I am sure the man will not care for the time."

As he spoke, Gregoire searched the drawers in the night table and, sure enough he found a little black notebook which he immediately opened and offered. He was pointing at a page with his gnarled finger.

I saw the name and number and picking up the phone, dialed, expecting an answering service, or perhaps a voice mail. But I heard my uncle's friend voice.

"Mr. Lagerfeld," I tried to speak, but the voice came as a croak. Then, I coughed and repeated: Mr. Lagerfeld this is Andrew.

"Is he dead?" He asked and his foresight shocked me, I couldn't reply, so he repeated the question.

"Yes, just a while ago. I need to talk to you urgently, sir. Could you come to the house?"

"I will be there as fast as I can Andrew." He hung up and I remained there, standing with the phone in my hand and looking at it as if it were a serpent ready to strike.

"What did he say?" Asked Gregoire, gently taking the thing from my hand and setting it back on the table.

"He knew. He knew why I was calling. How is that possible?"

"Well, sir, the master had been sick for some time now and we all knew he was very old; I think it was just an educated guess, you know."

"Perhaps." I muttered, but the strange phenomena happening around me were frightening me. Was there something else about uncle I knew not of? Something otherworldly? Mysterious?

I shook my head to dislodge the disloyal ideas. Uncle was uncle, he loved me, and he was simply a very old man, nothing more.

"Yes," said something in my head. "And what about that thing that took him away? Is that normal? Or his very old age? Or have you forgotten how he read your mind?"

I again shook my head. Gregoire had meanwhile gone to the terrace door and closed it, pulling the curtains over.

"Come now, Mr. Andrew, let's lock the room and then go downstairs. Nobody should come in here until the lawyer arrives. Come, come, you must drink something."

I obeyed as under a spell and waited beside him until he had turned the key in the lock. Gregoire then offered it and I pocketed it while I followed the man downstairs.

I entered the kitchen, looking for Mrs. Urville and unconsciously sat at the servants' table, as I used to do when I was a little boy. The table was in the center of the kitchen and the servants had gathered in a corner.

Mrs. Urville had prepared a pot of tea and though I was not partial to the beverage, I drank some. At least she would stop pestering me about it. I did, however, eat one or two of the chocolate chip cookies uncle had liked so much, the memory closing my throat and tightening my heart.

I realized that I had not cried and remembered how long it had taken me to find this relief after my mother's death. Was it hardness of heart? No, I didn't think so, because my heart had been and was now, full of pain.

I shrugged and drank more tea while I listened to the servants' low voices and a sob or two, quickly suppressed, whispering about their loss. That brought to my mind it was not only my future in question here but

Sent Back

also theirs. What had my uncle ordered in his last dispositions? Had he made a Last Will?

The bell for the gate rang and Mrs. Urville glanced at the screen, pushing the button that opened the door.

"It's Mr. Lagerfeld." She offered.

"Show him to the dining room, Mrs. Urville, I don't want to use the study and the dining room is the most appropriate place now, I believe."

She nodded and rushed up the stretch of stairs to the entrance hall. I heard her speaking and then the low bass of the lawyer.

We met, as I had told Mrs. Urville, in the dining room.

"I had surmised we were going to the study." Said the man who was well aware of the way things were run in the house.

"No, Mr. Lagerfeld, we will have to do with this room, I'll explain later."

"As you wish, my son." He accepted and sat at the table, placing a large leather briefcase on it. "I also thought we would be going to see him, so I could say goodbye."

"That is the first matter we should address, sir."

He shot me a quizzical glance but remained in silence.

"Sir, I do not know how well you knew my uncle." I started.

"I think I knew him pretty well." He replied. "And if you are talking about his incredibly long life, I know about that, too."

I breathed with relief.

"There is something, I want to…" I couldn't bring myself to telling him all about the previous night.

"Go ahead, son. I am now your lawyer and everything you may say to me is totally confidential."

I talked for a long time, telling him everything. I told him about my last conversation with my uncle and about the unexplainable disorder in the study. I explained my search and what I had found and then I told him about his voice in my head.

"Telepathy." Said the man.

"Eh?" I muttered, not understanding him.

"I say he was using telepathy. Oh, don't look at me like that, it is a recognized ability; not that many would have it." He shrugged. "We have experimented with it, your uncle and I and I know for certain he was quite expert at projecting his thoughts."

"So you won't think me crazy?"

"Not at all, not at all. Was that why you were so eager to see me?"

"No. My uncle's body has disappeared." I proffered bluntly, tired of hiding what worried me most.

I expected an exclamation, a comment of doubt, amazement, but there was nothing. The lawyer sat with total leisure, looking at me expectantly.

"Did you hear me?" I asked.

"Quite well, my hearing is perfect. I assume you have an explanation?"

"You will not believe it."

"Try me."

"A man came, a very tall man, saying he came from the funerary and that my uncle had taken care of everything regarding his funeral some time ago. He even produced some papers which I reviewed and thought them to be in order."

"Yes?"

"The man asked me to leave, so he and his men could take care of uncle and I was nearing the door when a sound caught my attention. When I turned, the man was…" I hesitated, now that I would say it in a loud voice it seemed even more outlandish.

"The man was turning into a gigantic bird; a huge black bird or eagle and this thing took my uncle's body in its claws and flew away with it through a door that had been well closed before."

I had said all this with a single breath and when I stopped, I was almost panting with nervousness and lack of air.

"A falcon." Said the old man matter-of-factly but in such a low voice I barely heard him.

"Did someone else see this?" Mr. Lagerfeld asked, while he bent to open the briefcase, so I couldn't see his face.

"Gregoire, the gardener. He was the first to arrive at my shouts and had the presence of mind to close the door before the other servants could see anything."

"Ah, yes, Gregoire. Don't worry, he's an old and trusted friend of you uncle, not just a gardener."

"He was who told me I needed to call you." I added.

"Stands to reason. So, tell me then, what's your worry?" He was taking papers from the briefcase and after setting them carefully on the table and placing a pen straight beside them, he lifted his eyes.

"My worry!?" I cried, standing in amazement.

He lifted his brows, and I sat down.

"Yes."

"How am I going to explain it? There is no body! It flew out the window! Come on, it sounds like a joke, though I have no wish to laugh, none at all."

"First, I need you to sign some documents. I had them prepared in advance, knowing Ferdi had not much long to live."

"Do you think this is the moment for papers?" I asked, bewildered.

"Yes. The appropriate moment. By signing here you enter in a contract with me and henceforward I will be your lawyer, constricted by all

Sent Back

the laws that favor client lawyer relationship. It needs to be done before another word is crossed between us. Do you understand?"

I nodded and bending over the papers, I swiftly signed them, perusing them with a fast look.

"Now that it has been taken care of, let's go to your uncle's bedroom. I want to see by myself."

I was feeling numb, but I rose and guided him out of the dining room, up the stairs and to my uncle's room. The door was locked and I pulled the key out of my pocket and opened it. I let the old man go in first.

"By all that's holy, young man!" He exclaimed, stepping in front of me and with an angry and exasperated expression in his face. "Why did you lie to me?"

I couldn't understand what he was saying and only when he pointed with his hand to the bed did I realize. The bed was not empty and on it, my dead uncle gazed at me with half-opened eyes.

I was frightened, terrified. I had seen it, I was sure of it, I had seen him dead and taken by the bird but now he lay there and, if I was seeing right, he was alive. I realized I was shaking and wondered if all had been a dream, a terrible nightmare.

The lawyer approached the bed and leaned over uncle. He touched his forehead and then reached for the wrist and checked for a heartbeat.

I saw my uncle lift his now so skinny arm and pull the man toward him. He lifted from the bed and whispered in Mr. Lagerfeld ear. The man nodded.

"Come Andrew. He wants to talk to you." His anger had left him, and his face expressed a sense of awe almost like the one I felt.

I approached the bed and, like in a dream, sat by my previously dead uncle. The lawyer retreated to a corner and remained there, as if he were keeping watch.

"I scared you." Whispered uncle with coarse voice. "I am sorry."

"How?" I muttered. "How is it possible? I saw you die, I saw you taken away! Gregoire too. I am not crazy!"

"No, you are not. Listen, I have little time. There is a mystery about us, specially about you and I of which I have left hints in the Testament, be sure to read it slowly and carefully, they will lead you to the answer to your questions. I was taken by the enemy before I could tell you, so I was given this opportunity to talk to you. The falcon you saw taking my body... it, he belongs to something very special and, thanks to it I am here. It took me to a place where my life was given back, but only for minutes. You must be always alert, because now that I am gone, no one will stand between you and those who want to keep the secret. All my life I have searched for it with no result but I believe you will succeed where I failed. As I said, search for it, my son. Search for the truth, believe nothing but for you own experience. Even facts held true for millennia could be completely wrong." He stopped and then with his last breath he whispered. "Look in Byron."

The hand that had been holding mine relaxed and fell to the covers. He was, again, dead. I turned to look at the lawyer who at my silent call came toward me.

He again bent over uncle. This time he found no heartbeat, however. There was no warmth of life on the forehead.

"I do not understand this." He said, mostly to himself. "But he was always a weird one."

He harrumphed and straightened, looking at me.

"Well, the problem of his disappearance is resolved, and you only need to talk to Gregoire so he keeps silent about what you two saw. The funeral can go on now without any complication." He seemed sad and worried.

"I thought you had lied to me, I am sorry." He added.

I shook my head, it was unimportant.

"What will I do now?" I asked him.

"If you want, I can take care of all the formalities." He offered and I nodded.

CHAPTER X

Finally, on a sad and rainy October day, my uncle was put to rest in the safety of a private mausoleum. I was alone with the company of the lawyer and the house help. No other friend came, no other family, of which naturally he had none. I wondered why I hadn't heard from my tutor, Dr. Morley, but imagined she would be out of the country in this or that dig. So, when everything was finished and I had said my last goodbye to Granuncle, we returned home.

This sad event reminded me of the memory I had seen in my mind, an image I was sure had been sent by my uncle; the one of Lord Byron's burial. I went and searched for the place in the garden. I went up and down the paths that crisscrossed the place but couldn't find the burial site. The insistence of the memory, however, pushed me to ask Gregoire; the man should remember well.

I finally found the gardener working the patch near the house where I had used to live when my mother and father were alive. I had never been back there and returning there after my grand uncle's burial was an amazing coincidence.

"Gregoire," I said, crouching beside him and helping him with the stubborn lump of earth. "Gregoire, do you remember where it was we buried the old cat?"

He straightened and looked at me in surprise.

"Why would you need to know that now Andrew?" He replied.

"Please, Gregoire, is something I need to check on." I said, not wanting to let the man into the mystery, at least not yet.

"Oh, alright, I'll take you there."

He stood, brushing his hands clean with the ever-present handkerchief.

We walked for a while and he kept glancing at me, wondering about the strangeness of the request.

"Here it is." He said at last, when we reached a part of the garden nearest to the surrounding walls.

What I saw surprised me. A tiny chapel had been built at the site, a most marvelous thing. It was made of carved marble and resembled in all details the St. Mary Magdalene Church, where the poet lord was buried.

"This is very weird, Gregoire." I said, pointing to the tiny monument. "Who did it?"

"The master ordered it done some years after. He used to have so many quirks and strange ideas I didn't ask, just found people to do it."

"This is very strange." I commented. "Do you…"

I was interrupted by one servant calling him.

"If you would excuse me, sir?"

I allowed him to leave and sat in a nearby bench, considering this strange development. Why had uncle ordered such a memorial built for a simple cat? Sure, we loved the animal, but was this necessary?

I knelt on the ground before the tiny church's front; even door and windows seemed real and had I taken a photograph, nobody could have discerned any difference between the real St. Mary Magdalene Church at Hucknall Torkard, Nottinghamshire and this one.

I tried the door and, lo-and-behold, it opened. In that same moment, a ray of the setting sun at my back struck the monument's façade and I saw something glimmer inside. My curiosity afire, I groped for the object and pulled. It was a curiously formed key, a golden key that would fit, snugly and precisely in the carved hole on the white door. I returned to the house with the object tightly clasped in my hand, hidden in my coat pocket.

Mrs. Urville and the others had gathered in the kitchen for some food and remembrances of the master, while the lawyer rested in the dining room in front of a bottle of brandy. I went in his search and guided him to the study.

I hadn't returned to it after that fateful night and the disorder that faced us when I opened the door was a sad reminder of what had come to pass.

Mr. Lagerfeld gave a short exclamation of surprise, suppressed quickly and glanced at me.

"I don't know." I replied to his unspoken question. "I found it like this the first night I returned, before he…" I couldn't say the ominous word.

The lawyer nodded and went in, gazing at the room in wonder.

"Did he speak about this?"

"No." I said. "Only vague references of searching and hiding, I couldn't understand most of it."

Oh, yes, I was dissembling, but something was telling me I shouldn't repeat all Granuncle had told me.

"Perhaps it's in the Testament." He offered.

I nodded while I picked up the papers and books nearer me; those I hadn't had time to organize that night.

Mr. Lagerfeld pulled the armchair he used when visiting Granuncle

Sent Back

and sat, placing his hands in a steeple, and watching me from above his spectacles.

"Well Andrew, what are your plans now?"

"Plans?" I repeated. "What are you talking about? My plans remain the same, I must finish my thesis and my remaining courses."

The man harrumphed and moved in the chair as if trying to find a comfortable position.

"First," said the lawyer. "First, I want you to learn some of your uncle's Last Testament and Will."

"Do you think that is what must be done now?" I asked, in the cusp of amazement.

"Yes Andrew, because things must be done in a precise order, and you need to know how to proceed from here on. Perhaps something will be written here that will help you understand what troubles you so much. Please sit."

I obeyed, spellbound.

"I will not read the whole thing, because it is tedious, long and full of legal terms and in fact they are just for the benefit of the authorities. The important thing is he leaves you as sole inheritor of all his properties except for several beneficiaries." He looked at me and I nodded, yes, yes, I was following.

He carried on, explaining the different gifts uncle had left for the household and the special requisites to be followed. Gregoire and Mrs. Urville, for example, were to remain in this house as they had until now, if they were willing but receiving a very generous monetary compensation.

As the lawyer rambled on, I was growing more and more amazed at the huge amount of bequests left. Finally, he stopped and gave a little cough, taking off his eyeglasses and squinting as he did so.

"But, Mr. Lagerfeld, if I know my numbers, up to now we have more than forty thousand dollars in gifts! How much...?"

I was interrupted by the lawyer lifting a hand.

"Wait, I am not finished. He leaves one thousand, heh, heh, only one thousand to his medical doctor. I am sure he was not thrilled with the man. He leaves five hundred to any nurse who could have taken care of him, if only, in case he needed any." He paused with a little laugh and clasped his hands.

I was wondering if that was all when he unexpectedly stood and paced around the room while I remained sitting, twisting my head like an owl to follow him. I was tired of asking, every time I did he stopped me to add this or that commentary.

After a while, the man returned to his chair and placing arms and hands over the document in the table, peered at me with curiosity.

"Apart from that, all belongs to you." He said in a low voice I almost did not hear.

I asked what the 'all' meant, I couldn't believe it would be a lot after all the gifts.

"My son, your uncle was a very wealthy man. You must understand he lived for many, many years, enough to make a good fortune for himself. His family, though seemingly Scottish, really originated in Egypt and there was amazing wealth in their power. Now, he had no family but you; naturally you inherit the house with everything in it. He, however, had other properties around the world, small houses or apartments where he had previously lived or that he owned so he could go, for example, to Paris without having to go to a hotel. The quaint old man had already put everything under your name, you know?" He chuckled. "I must say it was an underhanded way to cheat authorities and taxes, but I helped him, I did."

He chuckled again.

"How many of those…" I asked, at the cusp of amazement at all I was hearing.

"Oh, several, several. It is all written here, you can see it later." He nodded, satisfied. "He invested wisely, and his liquid assets are… Let me tell you, my son, you will be very well set, yes, very well."

I sighed with desperation. Would the garrulous man tell me if I had any money left?

"Oh!" Again, the weird man seemed to read my mind. "Do not worry, there's enough money for you and your descendants to be well off as soon as you don't squander it. You are among the five hundred Andrew. Your fortune rivals with that of Rothschild and that newcomer, JK Rowling."

I gasped and felt overwhelmed. It was too much. I didn't need all that.

"You don't want it?" Asked the perceptive man.

"Is it true?" I asked back.

"Oh yes, I wouldn't, couldn't lie about such a thing. Yes, it is true."

"But why? and… and what am I going to do with all that money?" I almost shouted.

"Well, whatever you want. Or perhaps you can do as your uncle did and just use what you need while the rest grows." He chuckled, slapped his thigh, and rose.

"Well's that's all I had to inform you but let me tell you something I consider of importance: you must now study your uncle's testament."

"Didn't you read it to me just now?"

"No, as I told you, I have not read everything. There are several pages I could not read as they are written in a language I do not know. I believe your uncle wanted to keep that information secret, even from me."

I insisted I saw no need for the urgency, as he had read all the relevant information; reading the will could wait, because the thesis would not.

Again, he looked at me. It was irritating me, this way he had of staring

Sent Back

as if he knew something important about me, something I knew not of, but now he nodded.

"Well, read it in your own time, my boy. I will naturally leave it in your possession but please keep it safe. Is there any place here where it could be secure?" He looked around and I could see by his expression he doubted anything could be safe here after the obvious search that had taken place by persons unknown.

I shook my head. I would not leave the precious document anywhere and as soon as I had it, I would always keep it with me. At least it would be something from him who had been mother and father to me most my life.

He understood my silent answer and stood.

"Alright then, here you have it." He offered the briefcase which I took and almost let it fall. It was unexpectedly heavy. He smiled and then pointed to the lock. This, too, differed from all I had ever seen and only because of my studies was I able to decipher it.

The characters were ancient Egyptian hieroglyphs, extremely small in shape and placed in the eight-digit rotary dial of which there were two parallel sets which should, as is the manner of these things, be set in the proper order for the briefcase to open.

"How am I going to use this?" I exclaimed, pointing to the eight-wheeled lock in amazement.

"Well, I assume your uncle knew what he was doing." He replied, shrugging. "He gave me a piece of paper with the code to open it but explained it would be good only for one time. After that, the locks would change and only you could open the briefcase."

"But those are Egyptian Hieroglyphs!" I exclaimed. "Even though I can read them, I wouldn't know what I should select!"

"True, but I imagine he wouldn't have done that if he didn't know you would be able to open it. Now, young man, I need to leave you. You are not my only client, you know?"

He patted me on the shoulder and went to the door. Once there, he turned. "You remember when he was born, don't you?" He exited and closed the door.

Was that a hint? Was there something in my uncle's date of birth that could open the lock? But that was absurd!

I wanted to read my uncle's last will, but I was distraught, and my mind wandered trying to accept the phenomena of his brief resurrection. I was also very concerned about my thesis, I had only two more months before I was expected to present it and had had little time to work on it in the recent days.

The matter of my inheritance, which placed me in such a peculiar position, had not changed my decision to become a Doctor in Archaeology, nor to get my Master in Geology. True, perhaps I wouldn't need to work, ever, but it was not a matter of need, but of will. I then thought about all the digs I would be now able to fund and imagined my dear professor's delight if I told her we could now do those excavations she had been dreaming about.

If I were to read the testament, however, I would need to open the briefcase. Presented with this new puzzle I sat in the recently vacated armchair and placing the briefcase on my lap, gazed at the lock.

Eight wheels, perhaps month, day and year? But how would the Egyptians write that? Then I remembered I had studied this, the Egyptian numerals. Yes, I could do it but immediately, as soon as the memory returned, I also remembered there was no zero in Egypt. So if I wrote Granuncle's date of birth… but wait, that was not it! That was not how they wrote numbers and even though the lawyer had tried to give me a hint, I doubted much my uncle would put such an obvious code to open something he apparently thought very secret.

I continued pondering the dilemma and slowly, slowly fell asleep.

I was again in Granuncle's room watching as a shadowy hand pressed on his throat; I saw his wide-open eyes, straining to transmit what information he could. and then, I saw the man who had taken him becoming a bird. But now the image was frozen in time, and I could distinctly see the man's face, a face where wide eyes were not black or brown but a yellow iris surrounding a large pupil. Eyes without eyelashes, but set under heavy golden brows, yes indubitably eyes appropriate for the falcon he was turning into. Suddenly a name popped into my mind, and I woke with a start. Horus!

How could it have escaped me? Definitely, it must all be related to Egypt, to ancient Egypt. I saw how all made sense now: my introduction to the famous archaeologist Dr. Sarah Morley, our talks about that ancient civilization, his eagerness in my enrolling in university, so many little details guiding me in that direction. Because what took my uncle was definitely a falcon and Granuncle had referred to a place where they resuscitated. Who could have done that? Only the ancient gods, only Osiris and Isis.

Could it be possible? Was I going crazy? First listening to my uncle in my mind, seeing the awful shadow and the hand crushing his throat and finally a bird taking his corpse and his ulterior resurrection. If I shared this with anyone I would be locked up. However, if I allowed myself to continue with this line of reasoning, perhaps there could be a combination of names to set in the locking device.

The more I considered it, the more important it seemed to open it and read my uncle's last words, but I knew, subconsciously, that only the correct code should be entered. I knew it would not allow a second try.

I was sweating with exasperation when Mrs. Urville opened the door

Sent Back

and, putting her head through the door, spoke.

"Mr. Andrew, sir, would you like me to bring you some dinner? It is past your usual hour, sir, and you must be hungry."

I considered the offer and then, without understanding why, I answered her to bring me whatever she had cooked to my uncle's collection room.

She nodded and withdrew while I repeated my own words in my mind repeatedly.

'Bring whatever you have ready to uncle's collection room'. Why had I suggested such a thing? He would have never allowed me to eat there. With a shock I thought he would never again walk into that room, and I could now do whatever I liked. I shook my head, no, I would always protect the place but taking a small meal there would harm nothing.

I stood and taking the briefcase with me, left the study and went to the room where most of my uncle's beloved findings were kept.

Mrs. Urville was waiting by the door with a napkin covered tray and entered as soon as I had unlocked the door. She placed the tray in the large desk where so many times I had sat with Granuncle to study this or that box.

She arranged the dishes, the glass of water, the cup of wine, the bottle, the flatware, the napkin, all with meticulous attention, making me nervous and anxious.

"It will be alright as it is, Mrs. Urville, thank you." I finally said.

She straightened and, passing her hands over her apron, gazed at me.

"I know he would not have liked it, food in this place." She said and hesitated. "But I imagined the dining room would be full of memories tonight and the study..."

Naturally the study was not a place to do anything now, not in the disarranged conditions it was.

"Yes, I believe this is best." I replied.

"I will leave you to it, then. Call me if you need anything else, Mr. Andrew."

"I will ask now." I offered as I sat before the steaming food. "Stop calling me Mr. Andrew. It seems absurd from someone who cared for me as a mother."

She smiled, nodding.

"Yes Andrew."

She left, softly closing the door behind her.

I had finished the roast beef and potatoes and was drinking some red wine she had brought for me, when my phone rang.

At first, I was surprised, the thing was most of the time silent in my pocket, but I brought it out and checked the caller, it was Dr. Morley.

After expressing her condolences and explaining she had been out of the country and had just landed, she asked if I could meet her at the University's Egyptian department.

I frowned, as the hour was late and the woman had arrived from I knew not where but she insisted, so, still attached to the briefcase and after telling Mrs. Urville I would go out for a while, I got into the car and drove to the school's grounds.

Apparently, she had been watching and had seen me arrive, because she stood waiting for me by the department's open door.

I approached and she embraced me, giving me a hug. This was quite an unexpected reaction from her, and I was surprised and trying to disentangle myself from her arms when I heard her whisper in my ear.

"Shush. Do not speak, just follow, and watch."

Maybe I had been experiencing too many surprises, maybe I was tired, but the fact is I wasn't shocked by her admonishment and did as I was told.

We walked to the storage room where the specialists kept the new items that arrived at the university from their different digs around the world.

Again, she gestured for silence. Why not, I felt no need to talk, not here, not now. She led me to one of the stacked metal shelves, full of cardboard boxes, paper wrapped items and other various artifacts.

I still had the briefcase on my hand, but now she extended the hand to hold it, while she pointed to something that stood at the back of the cluttered shelf. It was a round object, well wrapped in brown craft paper and tied with twine. It was not labeled, something strange in this context and place, where everything had to be named.

I lifted it, realizing it was heavy. I looked at her and she gestured what I should do. I pocketed it and she returned the briefcase and guided me out of the room. We shook hands, she nodded and walked into the night.

The whole exchange had taken minutes, silent minutes. She had said nothing else after the strange greeting and I didn't know why she wanted me to take the heavy object. Perhaps it was good it had not been labelled, perhaps its absence would not be noted. I drove home, mystified.

CHAPTER XI

The house was dark and only the security lights greeted me. I assumed the staff had gone to bed as it was already late and went to my room; placing the briefcase on the bed I then inspected the strange item.

The packaging appeared to be of recent preparation, the knots not fused by time and exposure to the elements, so I opened them with no trouble.

It was an almost circular item, the size of the palm of my hand and I suspected it must be of stone, perhaps basaltic in origin because of its weight. When I finally got it unwrapped, I saw it was made of malachite. It had distinctive bands of dark and light green inter-spaced with bands of light blue and was slightly translucent. The object was carved and beautifully polished into a scarab. The sacred scarab of the ancient Egyptians, representing the sun god Ra, who rolls across the sky by day as the dung beetle rolls its dung ball along by day. The scarab was a symbol of rebirth or regeneration. The convex upper side was smooth, while the underside was coarse and slightly concave.

I gasped as the full import of the discovery hit me. Rebirth! The stone had to be related to what had occurred with my uncle, with his coming back to life. Maybe I was wrong, maybe so many strange happenings had affected my brain but something at the back of my mind insisted it had to do with returning to life.

I got my magnifying glass and brought the scarab under the bright reading lamp.

What first struck me was the detail of the carving, the wings, the eyes, antenna and legs were so precise I feared the animal would take wing any moment. The six legs, each with segments well defined, the ridges sharp to the touch, as were the projections on the head, six. I realized the person who had carved this beauty was well acquainted with the sacred insect.

Then, as I moved it sideways to better inspect it, something different caught my eye. When I tried to see it better, it again disappeared, as elusive as the moon's reflection on a dew drop.

I turned the stone in several positions until, by chance, it came to be upside down. I could now see, right in the center of the scarab, a golden flash. I must be wrong, there was no way that the stone had gold inside. I brought it nearer to my eyes and saw, to my utter amazement, the traces of gold were characters, hieroglyphs.

I saw a word, or words, written inside the stone with a golden thread. That was impossible, the scarab had been carved out of a single stone. There was not a line, no fracture, no hole through which the gold could have been inserted there, much less used to write in the ancient Egyptian hieroglyphs.

Giving up on trying to understand the how, I turned instead to the what. What was written inside the scarab?

I took some minutes, as the light's reflection on the golden thread made it impossible to view the hieroglyphs.

Finally, by one serendipitous accident of which the history of discoveries is full of, I realized that, by putting the scarab in upright position on a table and aiming the light just so, the golden characters, by some unknown procedures were projected in the air above it like a holographic image.

I read it now, I read it clearly and perfectly. In the ancient writings of the land of Osiris, the word wavered in a room five thousand years distant from the time it was engraved.

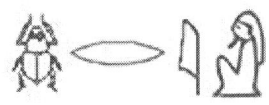

Khephir which in the ancient tongue is Rebirth

Well, I had to agree the whole thing was quite mysterious. The scarab could be a coveted item for an antiquarian, for a collector. Even the way it had been carved and polished was remarkable and it came without saying the golden characters inside it were impossible to have been made, not only in those times, but even now.

Why Dr. Morley's secretiveness? Why not talking? Why the sudden meet me, and now leave swiftness of the encounter? The scarab was amazing, right, but the word inscribed held no hidden message, no special information.

Now I considered; four characters or glyphs. Could it be related to the locked briefcase? But for that I needed sixteen. I moaned in despair. There were millions of combinations I could do using those characters and if I added words like Horus, or Osiris, the number increased exponentially. Could it be so difficult? Could uncle have made it so impossible for me to crack it?

Why would I think something Dr. Morley had found, I knew not where, as she had not explained anything at all, how could I imagine, I say, that it was at all related with my uncle and his last will?

Dawn was coming and still I sat on the bed, pondering the conundrum. I gave up, I stood, stretched mightily, and read the words that had been written in the discarded wrapping paper.

'First comes the one, then comes the middle that was the first, then comes the last and the sacred word.'

What was that?

I had read it, with the common habit of reading everything that comes to the eye, but now I realized what it was and where it was written. I grasped the paper and brought it to my eyes. The message had been written inside a square, as if wanting to contain it.

Contain it? No! This was a box, a box! It all made sense. Then I came back to my senses. This was not from granduncle, it had come from my professor who had it from who knows who, or where. Still, the idea that it was related to my uncle's collection persisted.

First comes the first box, then comes the middle box that was the first box, then the last box and the word! I had it!

My happiness was short-lived. Which was the first, middle and last box? I thought about Granuncle and again it was as if a light bulb had ignited in my brain.

The first box, the one his father had brought and smelled so delightfully of beach and ocean. The middle, which was first, that is the one he was studying when first I saw his collection. I knew the word but, which had been his last box? I slapped my forehead, naturally that must be it, the coffin!

Somehow and I cannot imagine how with all the turmoil in my head, I fell asleep and slept for a few hours. My wakefulness returned sharply, as if I had never been asleep; the course of my enervating thoughts continued without interruptions.

I realized, however, that throughout my brief slumber I had been bothered, prodded by something in the pocket of my trousers. I put my hand in and immediately remember, as I touched it, the golden key I had found in Lord Byron's little chapel.

The number of items that needed understanding had now come up to three, or perhaps four.

First, I remembered, I had found the door with its hidden compartment for the key; key I had then found in the cat's burial chapel. Then I had been presented with the undecipherable code for the briefcase and lastly, I had received, in a mysterious way, the scarab stone and the words written in its packaging. The riddle of the boxes, or what I thought referred to the boxes had been the last of all these incomprehensible events, which I knew could be not related at all.

I knew I had no other option than once again conferring with the lawyer because how in the world would I be able to inspect the box where my granduncle now lay below the ground?

Holding the stone in one hand and the key secured in my breast pocket, I went down the stairs. Perhaps before calling the lawyer, I could check on the other boxes, readily available and at hands' reach.

I entered the room and walked to the distant cabinet where I remembered Granuncle had looked for the item once, so long ago. I didn't need to search much, it was there. True, it was difficult to distinguish among the others if you knew not what you were looking for, mixed with similar ones as if discarded there, but the smell was unforgettable.

Taking it in my hand, once again I allowed my senses to rejoice in the distant memory and in the subliminal feeling of the ocean and the beach. I felt his presence beside me, silent but approving, I felt it so strongly I turned to see if he was, really, there. Naturally he wasn't, nevertheless, I couldn't help thinking he was happy I was searching for the end to the conundrum he had set for me. Was it a conundrum? I double guessed myself. Perhaps it was a way to hide information he wanted to keep safe from other people.

I brought the little box to the desk and gazed at it, trying to understand how a word could be in it hidden and a word that should be written or implied in ancient Egyptian, in hieroglyphs.

I shook my head, let it wait. I then went looking for the second that was first, the one he had shown me with the inlaid symbol on top. Of that one, I had no idea where he could have kept it. Try as I might, nothing came to mind and I gazed overwhelmed at the rows and rows of cabinets that covered the walls.

His words came suddenly to me,

'There is a method here. The books are organized according to subject and time. I will show you how to access the index and how to find each different subject and then the book.'

Perhaps, I thought, perhaps he also had an index for the boxes, it was reasonable enough that a man of such punctiliousness would take time to organize his collection. Where could it be?

I searched cabinet after cabinet, drawer after drawer but nowhere could I find any document, any book he could have used to record his findings. Then, a curious, very unprecedented idea came to my mind and I rushed to the study; there, discarded on the floor amidst the still disorganized objects, as if it were something worthless, was the old computer, the one we had bought that time, so long ago.

I knew this was crazy, Granuncle had never cared for it and I remembered how he eyed it with disgust and suspicion and yet and yet…

It was worth a try.

I hooked it to power and waited as it, slowly as it now seemed started loading data banks.

Sent Back

Finally, the screen lighted and I could see again the screensaver I had used so long ago; a photograph of my mother and I in the garden and holding Lord Byron. I felt a hand squeeze my heart, but it swiftly passed and I logged in and opened the file manager.

Lines and lines of documents listed, as I had used that computer while preparing to enter the university after he had agreed I should use it. I was ready to give up as no file I could see seemed at all related to what I needed when I saw this file: The Particular Life of Lord Byron.

I stared, what? I wrote nothing about Lord Byron, why would I care for his life? and then, like a slap to my cheek I understood. It was not Lord Byron the famous poet, it was the cat!

It had a password, but I swiftly opened it and, sure enough, I read list after list of boxes. Well, I assumed they were boxes as what I read were only numbers and dates. Another mystery.

I sat back and stared at the screen. Now what? I took me only minutes to understand the concept. The dates referred to when he had gotten the box, the numbers should refer to the cabinets, perhaps even the shelf where he had it set. and what about the coded letters? Because now I paid more attention, I saw smaller letters placed at the end of the line for each item. Perhaps that was the label he had used.

That was irrelevant, because now I could find where any box was. I could remember the date; it had been just after we had arrived.

I sat back again and allowed myself to delve in those happy memories. I had been so young and so full of happiness, really a carefree time. I saw Granuncle again, laughing at my questions, 'You are a Granuncle Birdie, so, where are your feathers and your wings?'. He had laughed so hard that time. and that had been during the month of October because I remembered it was autumn already.

I searched then for October of that year and found several entries. They all began with the same number: 1020** which I understood was the month and year. More numbers came after those six but I realized there was a space, so there were two isolated numbers. After a quick review I understood those were the days, they must be the days, as none was above the thirty-one digit. So that was it, month, year and day. What were the other numbers about?

It was curious, they all began with a two and had a set of three, then a period and another three. I slapped my forehead. I knew this, it was the same system he used for his library, the Dewey system, where each subject has a number assigned as for example a branch of Egyptology, I remembered well was 932.

Well, I thought, if this was what he used, things would be easier for me then.

I will not go into details, but in a short time I had identified the place where the box could be and returned to the collection's hall.

There I found the cabinet and the box that had so frightened me in that opportunity.

I gave a sigh of satisfaction. Finally I had three of four… no, wait, I still didn't have the word which should be hidden, written or inferred by the boxes and I still needed to call the lawyer about the investigation of my uncle's coffin. I shook my head. No, I had one word: 'Wayeb'. The word inscribed in this box, the name of the five extra days for the ancient Mayan civilization. Now, a memory came back. I had studied, in Egyptian history, how their calendar also included five extra days, days sometimes held as dangerous. It was a staggering coincidence, one that led to considerations I might include in my thesis.

I had two words 'Wayeb' or its hieroglyph version and rebirth. Two of four, that was not enough.

Lunch time had come and gone and Mrs. Urville had not come to call me, which was strange but immersed in my search I had paid little attention.

I had decided to go to the kitchen and get something to eat when I heard voices in the entrance hall. Realizing one of them was of Mrs. Urville and that she sounded upset, I rushed to the door.

I found her arguing with two men, both dressed in black suits. They were trying to make her take something, to what she was, apparently, strongly refusing.

"What is this, Mrs. Urville? Who are these men?"

She turned and I could see she was both angry and sad.

"These men are from the funerary, Mr. Andrew." She explained, pointing to them with what I knew was a disdainful gesture; I was well used to it.

"Funerary? The one used to bury my uncle?" I asked, surprised. I had never heard of them coming back to the deceased's home.

"Yes, those."

"But what do they want?"

"If you will excuse us, sir." Interrupted the older of the two men. "Are you Mr. Andrew? Are you Mr. Ferdinand's nephew?"

"Yes." I said and it sounded like a question.

"If you would permit us, sir, we have to fulfill a last request from your late uncle, sir."

"A last request?" I repeated and I knew I sounded silly, but this was awkward for me, not to say distressing.

"Sir, when your uncle made his final arrangements for his burial, he insisted on having photographs taken."

"Photographs?" I repeated inanely.

"Yes, sir. Here they are sir."

He offered a small, slender briefcase which I took, still too surprised to react in any other way.

"Will you please sign here?" The other asked now, presenting one of those devices now used to record signatures at delivery.

I obeyed.

"That will be all, sir." They said in unison. "Have a great afternoon."

I returned to the library, my hands shaking, all thought of food erased by the new development. What was I going to see in these macabre photographs? Why did he want them to be taken and then delivered?

It must concern the search he had thrown me into with the need to open the briefcase's lock and yet I dreaded to look at the photographs. With sudden resolve, however, I opened the slender briefcase and found inside an envelope of six by four inches. Here were the photographs, I waited for a second to steady my trembling hands and pulled them out. What I saw there convinced me I was getting deeper and deeper into a mystery.

I saw not my uncle, dressed in his finest clothes, nor did I see his beloved face, dissolving in the chemistry of death. What I saw, what I gaped at was a mummy. I dropped the photographs on the desk, gazed at them with utter disbelief.

Hadn't the men said they were of my uncle's coffin, of his burial? Why was there a mummy? I searched each photo but could find nothing hinting to an answer. The mummy was not old, I was sure it was not an Egyptian mummy, dating from over three thousand years ago. Could it be that my uncle had requested this? Could he be the mummy? How could I know?

Absorbed in the finding, I had not paid attention to the coffin itself, but now my eyes fell on drawings that appeared in the box's interior. They were difficult to see and seemed to have been blurred by the movement of the camera as the photo had been taken.

I opened a drawer, took out a magnifying glass and leaning over the photographs, looked. Helped by the enlargement provided by the lens, I saw the inside of the coffin was decorated as an Egyptian tomb. Images of what I imagined was my uncle in the presence of the gods were now visible. There was Isis, Horus with his falcon head and Hathor and Osiris; farther toward the mommy's feet was Anubis, with his dog's head.

Another photograph, taken apparently from another angle, showed hieroglyphs, which I soon recognized as the Litany of Re.

I went to bed tired of the mysteries, of the deciphering; thinking on the permutations of symbols I could hardly recognize. The recent days had exacted a big price on my emotional energy and saneness. Even now I doubted if all this was only a dream, a nightmare from which I would soon wake and find Granuncle alive and well.

I had secured all the items in my uncle's room. He had built there, some years ago, a false wall which could be opened by a difficult procedure and on which he placed great trust for being secure. So, before going to my bedroom, I placed there the boxes, the briefcase, the computer, photographs and all the pieces of paper I had found and studied. The sacred scarab, however, I kept with me.

Not because I didn't consider it relevant or undervalued its importance. The fact was that it appealed to me in an esthetic manner and I felt a strange attachment for it.

I doubted anyone would covet it, unless in a purely archaeological manner, so I placed it by my side and finally laid down on the bed. I was tired, very tired, but sleep now seemed to evade me as images of the recent days played on my closed eyelids.

By and by the images turned phantasmagorical, my uncle became a large bird of prey trying to lift me by the shoulders to carry me away. My mother held unto me, while my father, in the most ridiculous fashion, fought the bird with a wooden sword.

I felt engulfed by a cloud, a dark cloud of jelly-like consistence that prevented any movement. It had no form, naturally no face and yet, I could feel utter malevolence permeating it. It was evil unmasked and somehow I knew what it was saying: 'you are in my power now'.

Struggling, I knew it was a dream, a nightmare and yet, I could not wake up. The cloud, I hesitate to name it devil, gained more and more control of my body and as it crept upward, I started to asphyxiate. With a resolve born out of desperation and the knowledge I was on the verge of something worse than death, I woke up. For some seconds yet I felt the overpowering of my muscles, I could not move. Slowly, however, it faded and I reached for the lamp switch.

I sat upright as the light flooded the room, sweating and feeling the tremor of lingering fear ran through my now responsive body. What was it? Had it been really a dream? The sensations had been too overpowering, too real. I went to the mirror and searched there for a clue and I found it.

I shiver to recall it, but it must be told, as what had held me in its power had truly been there. On my left hip, where the thigh met the hip, was a mark of a dark hued purple. It reminded me of those birthmarks people have, but this was something new. I never had a birthmark, much less on my hip.

It had a queer shape and bending and twisting I could finally see it better. Truly an evil one had paid me a visit.

Stamped on my skin was the image of one known to Egyptologists as Set or Seth, God of frightening events, of eclipses, thunderstorms and earthquakes, murderer of his own brother Osiris in hate and jealousy.

Sent Back

I shuddered. Was this possible or was I still asleep? I slapped myself, hard, on the cheek. Unless I was experiencing a powerful dream and thusly unable to realize I had not slapped myself, I was awake. Again I shuddered.

All my life I had avoided the thoughts of ghosts, devils and those invisible entities that plague the mind of children and even during my adult years I usually swept the suspicion of these supernatural beings under the rug of rationality. Now, I had no other resource than facing something was truly there, beyond the veil of what I accepted as reality.

I had seen my uncle killed by a shadow, swept away by an eagle or an immense falcon, I had seen him again, alive somehow and talking to me. Wasn't that enough to show me, to convince me there was something else out there? Did it have to come to this, so I would believe?

Suddenly, I remembered the sacred scarab stone and rushed to the bed, fearing somehow it had been stolen by the dark visitor. No. I gave a sigh of relief, no, it was still there. Taking it in my hand, once again I wondered at its perfection, focusing on it, perhaps to avoid thinking of the terrible visitor. I admired the strangely smooth surface which showed no chisel marks, no indentation and as I twisted it around again the curious phenomena of the projecting symbols happened.

Used to it now, I barely paid attention and continued turning it over but then, I froze. What I had seen first, the hieroglyphs for Kephir, rebirth, had changed. I was sure I had seen Kephir; it had sent me on my search. Now, however, I saw not those symbols, but the ones for the name of someone not given a lot of relevance in Egyptian studies: Nebthwt, the Friend of the Dead who brings news of the departed to their living family, Horus mother's sister. She whom the Greeks called Nephthys.

CHAPTER XII

Early the following morning I received a call from my tutor. She was concerned about me, as I had missed two meetings with her to discuss the thesis. She then told me she would expect me that day at noon. I promised to be there and hung up, rushing to get ready and have breakfast. I wanted to employ the two hours left until our meeting in reviewing the last additions to the thesis.

All thought about the Last Will erased from my mind, I dedicated myself to the task at hand and, satisfied of my efforts I set out to the Campus.

It was a beautiful day, only marred by the lingering pain of my loss and the knowledge he who had put me on this path would not be present for my graduation.

I entered my tutor's office and for hours we worked on the document. She seemed satisfied and urged me to come swiftly to its completion.

"What is this note here?" She asked as an afterthought, pointing to some scribbling I had done in the back of the last page.

I looked at what she pointed. 'Wayeb' and the Egyptians birthdays of the gods' it said.

"Oh, that's something I have been considering." I replied, trying to dismiss it but she obviously wanted more explanations than that.

"I find it quite a coincidence," I said. "That the Mayans resolved the issue of the extra one fourth of a day in the calendar creating five extra days, just as the ancient Egyptians had done."

"What is your explanation?" She asked.

"I have none, yet." I said.

"It will be good that you omit any of this from your thesis. It will not help you if there is the smallest hint of that pseudoscience that links the development of the two civilizations." She eyed me with suspicion and preoccupation.

"Do not worry, professor, I am not into that, nor will I have anything to say about those days in my thesis."

"Good. Now go! You have only one week before your presentation is due."

I nodded and left, resolved to do as she had recommended. But there were forces at work here I had not reckoned with.

I had decided to remain in my apartment for the remainder of the week, avoiding the house where the unsolved mysteries jumped at me from every corner.

The night was falling when I arrived. A group was at the building's entrance. Some I knew from sight; others were students at my same school.

"Where have you been, man?" Asked one of the latest.

"At home." I replied, dismissively and trying to go through the crowd.

"We tried to reach you." Said another. "But nobody knew where you were."

"Why?" I asked, somewhat worried now. "Why did you want to find me?"

"Something's happened in your rooms, man." Replied the first. "The police is there. I think you were burglarized."

Without waiting for more, I ran up the stairs to my apartment, which was on the second floor. Sure enough, a pair of policemen were there, standing by the door.

I approached.

"Sorry sir, this is a crime scene, you cannot go in."

"But this is my apartment!" I exclaimed as I saw the terrible disorder inside. "What has happened?"

They consulted in a low voice.

"You are Mr. Andrew Kirkpatrick?"

"Yes."

"Wait a moment, sir."

One went inside, while the other gazed at me with curiosity. I was getting ready to force my way inside when the first policeman came followed by one who seemed in charge.

"Mr. Kirkpatrick?" He enquired.

"Yes sir."

"Please come in, but be careful not to touch anything, we are still dusting for fingerprints."

"Can you tell me what happened? Why are you here and what is this terrible disorder?"

"We hoped you could explain it, sir." He replied. "Where have you been?"

"I was at home, with my uncle." I replied. "I haven't been in for at least four days."

"Well, someone broke in looking for something, apparently, because this is not a common burglary. They even ripped open your mattress."

"What!" I cried. It was an expensive mattress, the only luxury I had allowed myself, hoping for a much-needed restful night.

The man eyed me with curiosity.

"Do you have any idea what they were looking for?" He asked.

"Not in the least." I replied. "I keep nothing of value here and I carry my laptop with me everywhere."

"Hmm." He muttered. "We will need a list of anything stolen." He made a gesture and a young policewoman approached. "She will escort you through the place and help you with anything missing."

I nodded, aghast.

A long time after and satisfied nothing had been stolen, the officers left, insisting I should go to the district office to make a full statement.

Again I nodded and closed the door behind them. I turned and observed my ransacked place.

Who could have been here? and why? Until some hours ago, I was as poor as any other student in the neighborhood. Could they know about my uncle's death and last will? But that was preposterous! Then a flash of understanding hit me. It must be the sacred scarab! That was the only explanation! Perhaps they were looking for it, to sell it, or who knew what. I remembered Dr. Morley's secretiveness when taking me to the storage room; perhaps someone had seen us.

Once again, I looked around the apartment. I would not stay there the night, nor could I remain there for the week before the thesis presentation. I had to return to Granuncle's home and work from there however painful it seemed. I retrieved some papers that lay strung around the floor and after glancing once again at the destroyed place, I exited closing the door securely with my key.

As I did that, I realized the door had not been broken, the lock was undamaged. Either they had a key, or they were expert burglars. I shrugged and went downstairs and to the car.

"Everything alright?" Cried the student who had first appraised me of what was going on.

"Yes, but all is a mess, I cannot stay here. See you!"

"Take care!" Replied the other, with concerned face.

As soon as I was home, I gathered the servants and explained to them the burglary at my university apartment.

"It is clear." I said. "That someone is intent on finding something that belonged to my uncle, I cannot consider any other possibility, so I entreat you to be very aware of any suspicious person or activity and let me, or Gregoire, know immediately about it."

They promised and left, talking in subdued tones among themselves but Gregoire remained.

"I am worried, Mr. Andrew." He commented.

"Yes."

"And I don't think the servants, or our security system would be enough. I am old, I cannot forestall any attack and the women…"

"Why! You think they would dare? Force their entrance here?"

"I don't know what to think, sir. Many strange events have happened, and I am beginning to doubt if the terrible disorder in the master's study was truly created by himself."

He hesitated and then added.

"Perhaps we should get some other security, sir."

"What, like armed guards?" I scoffed.

"No, sir." He paused, fidgeting. "I have a confession to make, Mr. Andrew and I don't know how you are going to take it, but I think you should know."

"What is it?" I replied. I trusted Gregoire with my life, but his words were now worrying me.

"You know the master had given me the small cottage at the southern edge of the property?"

"Yes, that's your home."

"Well, sir, I have also a big yard behind it and I have…" He stopped.

"You have what?"

"I have been breeding dogs, sir."

"You what?" I cried, amazed and amused at the same time.

"I have been breeding Dobermans sir, a great breed, very protective. I have sold some but kept the best of the litter. I have four now, very well trained. I think we could let them free around the property, perhaps one inside, even?"

"A Doberman in the house? You rave! What will the women say! They would be terrified!"

"No, sir, no! The one I'm thinking of is as meek as a kitten with the ones she knows."

"But she will not know us!" I countered. "What if the dog bites anyone here?"

"True, but I will present you to her and she will recognize you as part of my pack. You'll see, Mr. Andrew, you'll see. Let me try it, sir, I would be much relieved if you do."

"Alright, Gregoire, bring your dogs and we will see." I agreed.

The last pet and the only I ever had, had been Lord Byron. The cat had lasted for many years after my arrival, and it had been an added blow to my heart when he finally passed on to cat's heaven. Now, facing the possibility of another four-legged inmate, I had my doubts.

I had heard stories about Doberman's fierceness, I think they were even portrayed in some movies as terrible aggressors, so it was not without apprehension I first met Sachmis. He had pronounced it Sahmis, but I soon understood who he referred to.

When Gregoire brought her to the house and told me her name, I immediately recognized it. Sachmis was a goddess in the ancient Egyptian pantheon; a warrior goddess sometimes manifested as a lioness whose breath formed the desert. She was protector of the pharaohs and led them in war. The coincidence of the name with everything that had befallen me in the past days shocked me and I looked at the dog with renewed interest.

She was well built, strong muscles rippling under the short reddish coat; and very large, she exceeded the height of twenty-eight inches by two or three more. She was not black, and I felt kind of grateful for that, thinking the Dobermans with black coat looked, even if they were not, looked more dangerous than the brown ones. Here again was a memory of the goddess depiction, because she was said to dress in red.

The dog's head was erect, attentive, as were the short cut ears. The eyes, which were now eyeing me with interest, were of a warm golden hue while the wet nose had a tinge of pink over the slightly lighter reddish color.

"Why the name?" I asked Gregoire.

"The master once told me a story about some gods. He spoke about one that was the goddess of war and this one, as a puppy, was nothing else than. She kept her siblings on their toes and ruled all so I gave her that name because I had liked it and remembered it when trying to name this one." He finished pointing to the dog with a head gesture. "Why?"

"Well, she is mostly known to be the protector of justice, called Ma'at. They, the Egyptians, used to call her: The One who loves Ma'at and detests evil. She was also the protector of the Pharaoh."

"Oh." Gregoire looked at the dog with renewed affection. "I like that. Now come here sir, let me introduce you."

The man put his hand over my shoulders and addressed the dog.

"This is mine! My pack. Guard." He repeated it and then added: "Obey."

The dog approached sniffing at me. Gregoire took my hand in his and brought it to the dog's muzzle. She sniffed at it and then gave a quick lick.

"She likes you." Said Gregoire.

"I'm glad." I replied, still slightly anxious about my hand's safety.

He stood there with the dog for some more minutes, letting the animal acquaint herself with me and I finally gathered enough courage to pat her on the head once or twice.

"I will take her to the kitchen now, so the staff knows her and she knows the staff." Gregoire explained as he called the animal to his side.

They left and I gave a sigh of relief. A cat, as fat and big as they could grow, was never comparable to this powerful animal, weighing perhaps 60 or 65 pounds of packed muscles. Knowing how animals can detect fear, I knew I had to control it and become as carefree with the dog as I had been with Lord Byron.

Sent Back

There was a more compelling task at hand, however and I now turned all my efforts to completing my thesis and practicing the presentation. In this way I spent the remainder of the day locked in the study until, tired and hungry, got something to eat. I opened the study's door and a brown shadow leaped to her feet and I looked in the golden eyes of Sachmis.

Ears lifted, mouth slightly opened and the stump of a tail wagging softly, I realized the dog was not in any attack mode. I spoke to her softly.

"Hello Sachmis, good girl." I said and patted her. "Were you guarding me?"

The animal surprised me standing on her two hind legs and putting her paws on my chest. I felt a tinge of fear, that swiftly changed to amusement as the animal licked my face.

"Down girl! Down!" I heard Gregoire exclaim from farther down the hall. "It's alright, Mr. Andrew, she likes you!" He added.

"I can see that. Do not worry, Gregoire, I think Sachmis and I are going to become good friends."

The dog had settled back and was now greeting Gregoire.

"Is she going to follow me always?"

"I think that would be best, sir. Let's see how it works out for you."

"Alright. Come Sachmis, let's go have some food." I said and went toward the stair that led to the kitchen. I heard the clip, clip of the dog's nails in the parquet, understanding she was following me and relaxed.

That night, when I went to my room, Sachmis followed. I was wondering what to do with her, because, as Gregoire had said, the animal was to follow me everywhere. Would she sleep with me?

My mother had never allowed a pet and only when we came to live with Granuncle Birdie did I share one. I was not sure what to do, perhaps I should let her sleep on the rug by my bed.

I took a shower and returning to the bedroom, jumped into bed, arranging the pillows to read before falling asleep. I heard a whimper and looking down I saw Sachmis' beautiful head lying on the mattress. Her eyes were fixed on me with such a sad expression it pulled at my heartstrings.

"What girl?" I asked. "What's the matter?"

She lifted her ears and straightened, the tail wagging uncertainly.

She whined again.

"What?"

She barked.

"Go to sleep, Sachmis, sleep! There!"

She obeyed but looking at me with such eyes I could barely hold my composure. I wanted to laugh and cry simultaneously. But she had obeyed and lay on the rug, her head on her crossed front paws, but still eyeing me with unwavering attention.

I read some papers about my thesis and became absorbed in them.

However, a change of pressure in the bed startled me and I looked down and saw Sachmis, curled at my feet. Her expression was as easily understood as if she had spoken.

"I know this is not what you want, but I think it would be best if I sleep here with you. Please don't shove me down. I'll be good."

I laughed and she rose her head, perking up her ears.

"Alright, you can sleep there." I said. "Lie down now. Lie down!"

She sighed, she really sighed! and laying down her head, she closed her eyes

CHAPTER XIII

I woke up early, having set the alarm for 7 o'clock. I needed all the time I could get to finish my work.

I had forgotten about the dog and was startled when something moved under the blanket. A reddish muzzle appeared, shoving the sheets back and Sachmis' head became visible.

"Woof!"

"Ah, good morning to you, too." I said, remembering immediately the previous day.

We went downstairs and to the kitchen, as my breakfast was not ready, it being too early for my usual hours.

"Good morning, Mrs. Urville." I greeted her.

"Good morning, sir." She said and looking down gasped, bringing her hand to her mouth. "Oh, my!"

"You had forgotten all about the dog, right?" I asked, smiling.

"Why, yes sir. She slept in your room?"

"Yes, and under the covers. I got a fright when I saw her, as I, too, had forgotten all about her. Can we have some breakfast now?"

"Gregoire brought her dishes and food, I'll give her food to her now. Will you want eggs, bacon and pancake as usual?"

"Yes, but some coffee now, please."

I went out into the garden with the cup of coffee, aiming for the terrace. I had not counted on the other three dogs; in fact I had not met them as Gregoire only introduced me to Schools. Now they came charging, barking furiously.

My dog instantly placed herself before me, with fierce attitude, stiff legs, hackles raised. She growled and the other three stopped. Then they approached and sniffed her. She growled again, but more softly and then gave a bark.

The three males laid down on the floor, slowly wagging their tails at the alpha dog, Sachmis.

Gregoire had come running, but by the time he reached us the confrontation was settled.

"Oh my! I had totally forgotten, worried only about Sachmis in the house." He then stood beside me and placed a hand on Sachmis' head. Again he followed the same procedure, telling the dogs I was part of the pack and to guard. He then walked away with the three males.

"So, you are the boss here, are you not?" I asked of the dog as I sat at the white glass and iron table.

She laid her heavy head on my thigh. Somehow, I understood this was a sign of possession, I belonged to her. I smiled.

Overwhelmed by the recent events, I had forgotten, again, about the golden key, but somehow it now came to my awareness, perhaps by the brushing of the coat over my chest.

I took it and gazed at it. It shone brilliantly under the rising sun's rays. Sachmis whined and sniffed at it.

"It's a strange thing, yes." I said to the dog. "And even stranger is where…" I stopped.

How was it possible I hadn't tried it against the carving on the white door? Why did I constantly forget about its existence?

Deciding not to let another minute pass before I brought it to its place in the study, I entered the house.

Gregoire and then Mrs. Urville called out at me, but for once I was decided nothing would distract me from my objective. I opened the study door and went inside, Sachmis following.

I took the books from the shelves, placing them without order on top of the desk and tables. Finally, the top part of the door was free and again I pressed on the snakes' eyes.

Once again, I heard the soft rumble and the hiss and the top central square moved; rotated and moved aside. I took the key from my pocket and pressed it inside the hollowed space. It fit and remained there even after I removed my hand.

I had only time to step down from the chair, when the shelves moved silently to one side leaving the door free. Still, it didn't open.

I studied it carefully and couldn't find a way to open it, but in the center, there was an almost invisible, very narrow grove. I looked into it but could see nothing, then I cautiously put my little finger into it.

With a cry I brought it out and into my mouth, something had prickled it and it was bleeding. Thoughts of venomous snakes crossed my mind before I became aware the door was now effectively moving, opening inwards.

I waited.

There obviously was a room behind, though so dark I could see nothing inside. I waited some more, the air had that feel typical of some places we had excavated during our archaeological digs. Dead and

Sent Back

dangerous.

Finally my curiosity took the better of myself and I crossed the threshold. Immediately a dim light begun to shine, becoming brighter as I walked further into the room.

A museum's storeroom had fewer items than the ones I saw there. Objects from Summer and the Indus Civilization, from ancient China, the Mayas and Incas, even a monstrous head from the Toltecs was there. Shamanistic masks from Siberia and Tibet, samurai's swords, stones from places I couldn't, at that moment, pinpoint. All this was thrown there, with no apparent organization. It had been accumulated through many years and apparently my uncle had felt no need to give it the merest sense of order. Something that seemed very strange considering how persnickety he was about those things.

Farther into the room I walked and now I saw there was a space dedicated only to objects from Ancient Egypt. Burial masks and even two mummies were most visible, but then I discerned something behind them, almost hidden by the innumerable pieces there collected.

I saw it and I felt my heart stop.

Someone was slapping my face and I realized I was back in the study and Gregoire was kneeling beside me. He it was who had slapped me and who now helped me to sit.

"Are you feeling alright Andrew?" He asked.

I shook my head, not because I felt badly, but to dispel the fog that seemed to fill my brain.

"Andrew? Sir?" He insisted.

"I'm alright, yes." I answered. "What happened? Why am I here?"

"I don't know." He answered and I knew he was both worried and afraid. "The dog's barks brought me here and I found you on the floor. Did you faint?"

I stood up with a jump and had to hold on to the old man as I wavered on my feet.

"You found me here?" I asked.

"Just here, yes."

I looked toward the wall where the white door was. The books were back on the shelves, nicely ordered and the door as invisible as always. The only explanation, well one explanation and the most logical was that I had fainted and that the opening of the door and all I had seen inside was just a hallucination. The second possibility that the dog, somehow, had brought me out. But how then could the books be back in their places, the door closed, the bookshelf on its place?

Again I shook my head.

"Can I bring you something, Mr. Andrew?" Said Mrs. Urville now from the door.

I nodded. "Yes, please, some strong coffee."

"And the bottle of brandy, Mrs. Urville." Added Gregoire.

He guided me to the armchair where uncle had sat so many times and helped me down. He remained there, gazing at me, evaluating me.

"Yes, it was due to happen." He muttered, apparently to himself. "I knew something was going to; he was due to break."

"What are you talking about, man?" I tried to growl, but my voice came out week and shaky.

"Too much for you, even for me and I have lived to bury many. Yes, I suppose it was the straw that broke the camel's back."

I understood what he meant but did not dissuade him. Something even stranger had happened here and only if the dog could talk could I make head or tail of it.

I was now sure I had been in that room. I was sure I had seen what I had seen, it was not a dream nor a hallucination. All was possible because of the key and realizing I didn't have it then I checked my pockets. Where had it gone to? Had it been left behind in the secret room?

There was a knock at the door and Gregoire went to open. Immediately and as if she had been waiting for this, Sachmis lifted her paw and I saw the key there, under it. She laid down immediately after, just as Gregoire came back into the room followed by Mrs. Urville, covering the key now with her whole body.

The strangeness of the events in my uncle's study, the hoard there secreted and above all the active participation of the dog in all of it had me wondering.

I couldn't remember everything I had seen in there my only memory was of my amazement at the size of the place and the variety of treasures there hidden. I found this also very strange, because I have always had a good memory, even a photographic memory, that has helped me much not only in my studies but in the digs.

I wanted to go back, open the door to the room once again, but something held me back. I had recovered the key from the dog's protection and once again I kept it in my chest pocket, as close to me as possible.

Then, while examining the room for further evidence of my discovery and the dog's intervention on it, I found, tucked under the bookshelf edge, a piece of ancient papyrus. It had been rent and the characters were difficult to read, so I had put it away in the box with the Wayeb' symbol on top until I had time to decipher it.

I slept fitfully that night, images of what I must have seen in the room coming to my mind and fleetingly leaving it and an indescribable sense of foreboding permeating it all.

Sent Back

The next day and quite unexpectedly, I received the lawyer's visit. After enquiring about my health and looking at me with questioning eyes, he sat in his usual armchair. He had only given a perfunctory look at the dog who had barely raised her head at his entrance.

I had been working on the thesis and this interruption wasn't at all welcomed but I couldn't deny the old fellow this visit.

After some moments in silence, he rose and walked around the study, toying with this and that, taking up little statuettes and putting them back. I knew something was troubling him, so decided to wait. Finally, and standing before me, he spoke.

"Gregoire called me." He said.

I nodded.

"You were found unconscious in your uncle's library, I mean, your library." He harrumphed. "Are you alright now? Do you have any idea why you fainted?"

"Not in the least."

"Hmm."

Again walking around the study and this time he stood by the window, looking outside in a brooding attitude I found kind of endearing.

"I am alright, Mr. Lagerfeld, nothing is wrong. Gregoire thinks it was due to everything I have been going through. Do you know my apartment was burglarized?"

He turned quickly and I realized, by the expression of his face this was news to him.

"Someone tried to rob you? Who? Did they take anything?"

"Naturally I don't know who and no, they took nothing, but they did look everywhere for whatever they thought was kept there." I finished and eyed him with interest. What would be his reply to this?

He walked back to the armchair, sat down again, placing his hands in the habitual steeple.

"Have you been able to read the documents your uncle left for you?"

This non sequitur surprised me. Hadn't the man heard me?

"No, the lock's combination still evades me." I said.

"Listen to me Andrew, this is very important. There are mysteries here, things that apparently someone outside your family wants to discover, or perhaps take. It is imperative you put your brilliant mind to opening the briefcase. It amazes me, truly amazes me you haven't done it yet. Aren't you interested in what Ferdinand wanted to tell you?"

Put in that way, I felt embarrassment. Truly I should have been more eager to read my uncle's last message.

"It is not that." I replied, trying to justify myself. "I am trying to finish the thesis, I have almost no time before my presentation is due!"

He gazed at me in silence, but this silence said it all.

"Alright." He said and stood. "I'll leave you to it, then. I hope all goes according to your wishes. Good day Andrew."

I was standing to escort him to the door, but he waved me away. After all, he was like family in that house.

I sat down and his words seemed to echo in my head, 'aren't you interested in what Ferdinand wanted to tell you'.

No, I said to myself, no, it's not that. I had tried, I had spent lots of time trying to discover the password. I had tried everything!

Ashamed, I realized I was again trying to justify myself.

The idea of Wayeb' then came, brought on by the professor's commentary when she saw it in my scribbled notes.

Wayeb'. I couldn't remember how those days were called in Egypt, so I stood and went in search of some books where I thought I had seen it before. It didn't take me long to find it in one of them, as I remembered I had seen it.

Which meant 'those upon the year'. But there was another version:

'The five upon the year'

If I assumed the reference to the box with the Wayeb' sign should be considered for the lock, I had two options now. Somehow, Mr. Lagerfeld's cryptic comment that first day came now to my mind. 'You do remember when he was born, don't you?'

Uncle's birthdate, how would it be relevant? A crazy notion came to my head. What if I related all this? What if I added, not my uncle's real birthdate, but Horus? Horus the falcon, who had taken him and returned him alive.

I know it seems illogical, I know it's farfetched, but the idea came, and I couldn't think of anything but.

I will not bother you with more analysis, or the permutations I did, coming up with several words, or with a set of hieroglyphs which, in the order I used them, made no sense.

I was feeling a headache coming when, somehow, the characters rearranged themselves in my mind. What they now spelt, was, I was sure, the answer that had for so long evaded me. I ran to my uncle's bedroom and after several tries to open the false wall, I finally took the briefcase in

Sent Back

my hands.

Not bothering to close the compartment, nor to go back to the study, I selected, one by one, the hieroglyphs that formed the sentence in my mind. The lock clicked and the briefcase opened. I looked inside. It was full of papers, papers clipped together, forming a book, a manuscript.

At that crucial moment, I heard the house phone ring. Uncle had never taken to the cellular and all conversations took place over the line phone. Its peculiar ring associated in my mind to bad news.

"It's for you sir." Called Mrs. Urville from downstairs. "It's Professor Morley. It seems urgent." She added.

Tucking the briefcase under my arm, I ran down and took the phone.

"Good morning, Professor!" I said.

"Andrew? Is this you?" I heard her voice as if she were far from the phone.

"Yes, mam, it's me. I can barely hear you! Where are you?"

"I'm in Egypt Andrew, in Egypt! I need you here, please come as soon as possible!"

"But, I have my thesis presentation next week! I cannot leave now!" I cried. "Where are you?"

"In Egypt, please, please come and meet me!" She cried and the line went dead.

I stared at the handset in amazement. I was certain the Professor would not, ever, have such disregard for my presentation, as she considered it part of her success. Why would she ask me to leave everything and go to her? And where was she? Egypt is a very, very big country, she could be anywhere.

I took out my cellular and dialed her phone. No answer. I then called her office and one of her assistants answered.

"Good morning, this is Andrew Kirkpatrick; I need to talk with the Professor, is she in?" I asked.

"Why no, we haven't seen her in the last two days."

"Do you know if she was going to Peru?"

"No, no I don't." A pause. "But if she left for any of the digs we should know. I cannot explain what's going on." She sounded worried.

"Will you have her call me if you hear from her?" I asked. "She has my number."

"I will let her, sure."

"Thanks. Goodbye."

So they hadn't seen her and didn't know of any trip. That was strange as she never went on any expedition without one or two of her student assistants.

Could there be a relation between the burglary, the Professor's absence and the sacred scarab stone? I pondered the matter, confused.

Meanwhile, Mrs. Urville had set up the table and served lunch. I stared distractedly at the food and sat down, only half aware of what I was doing.

I felt something on my thigh and saw Sachmis, a paw touching me, as if bringing me back to this world. Apparently, some time had elapsed, because the food was now cold and, breaking all rules of good dog training, I offered her the slices of roast beef.

Amazed at the unexpected treat, she gobbled them.

"Do you want me to prepare some more, Mr. Andrew?" Asked Mrs. Urville, coming into the room

"No. I have lost my appetite. Thank you, Mrs. Urville." I said and walked slowly toward the stairs to return to uncle's room.

I had left the wall opened and that thought made me rush upstairs. This time, however, nothing untoward had happened and all was as I had left it. I locked the false wall, keeping the briefcase with me and went to the study.

It was still disorganized, but Gregoire had been helping me and now, at least, the floor was free of papers, books and other stuff. I went to the desk and sat in my uncle's grand old chair.

What was I to do? I had worked so hard at my doctorate! Should I drop it all to run at the Professor's biding? A memory flashed before my eyes, the day she had questioned me, trying to understand if I were ready for university. She had made a gamble then and throughout those years she had always been there for me. Then another doubt arose: perhaps it was not she who had called? Perhaps someone wanted me out of my house to search for whatever they had been searching for in my apartment?

I decided I needed to go back to town. In my mind I considered I needed to talk to my thesis counselor, explore the possibility of postponing the presentation, perhaps even ask of any news about Professor Morley. I then remembered that the officer investigating the burglary wanted me to make a full statement.

As I was opening the car's door, Sachmis jumped in.

"What is this?" I exclaimed. "Are you planning on coming?"

"I think you should let her go with you, sir." Interjected the ever-present Gregoire. "I would rather have you protected."

"Gregoire, please! This is not a mystery movie!"

"No? I would rather say many mysterious things have been happening." He replied. "Take her, she will behave."

"Oh, alright!" I said, slamming the door and looking at Sachmis, who sat, very erect on the passenger's seat.

"You better behave, dog!" I muttered. "I have lots to do and don't want any mess, ok?"

She barely moved, only the slightest twist of the head in my direction acknowledged the order.

Sent Back

I started the car and drove out of the house. I had decided to go to the police station first.

I arrived and found a parking space nearby. As I was leaving the car and the dog, a policeman came and asked, pointing at the animal.

"You are not planning on leaving the dog in the car, sir, are you?"

"Why, yes. Is that a problem?"

"It is. It is not allowed."

"But I have to go see officer Adamson." I moaned.

"Is the animal trained?" He asked.

"Yes."

"Well then, take it in!"

"Is it allowed?"

"Try it."

He left, smiling as if he had made a joke and I made Sachmis jump out of the car. She followed me as I walked up the steps that led to the police station.

Amazingly, nobody stopped us, as if bringing into the place a Doberman was the most common of things. I shrugged, adding it to the unexplained events I seemed to be collecting and asked for officer Adamson.

I had finished my statement when an idea came to my mind.

"I wonder if you could help me, officer." I said.

"In what respect?"

"My university sponsor, Professor Sarah Morley is apparently missing. I say apparently because I just received a call from her." I explained the call, my suspicions, the fact her student assistants knew nothing about her or any scheduled trip.

"I don't see how I can help you. Has she been missing for at least forty-eight hours?" Replied the man, who had listened attentively to my report.

"Well, I want to say I have the suspicion her absence is somehow related to my apartment's burglary."

The man lifted an eyebrow and suddenly seemed more interested in what I was saying.

"You think there's a correlation?"

"Yes. You see, some days ago, my uncle's study was also ransacked and left in a terrible mess. He has since passed away."

He stared.

"Oh, he was very old, almost ninety, there was nothing suspicious about his death." I explained ashamed of my duplicity but knowing I couldn't say more than this. "But his study was thoroughly searched by someone, and we haven't been able to find who. We didn't think anything was missing and yet…"

"There's more." He affirmed.

"Yes. A day or perhaps two after this, Professor Morley called me, very secretive and asked me to meet her at the department of Archaeology. It was already late night, which made it extraordinary, but she didn't speak a word. It was all very strange."

"What did she want then, if she didn't talk to you?"

"She gave me an object, a stone from Egypt, only that."

"And that was all?'

"All. I have been wondering if, perhaps, those people could be looking for the stone and have taken her because of it."

He laughed.

"My friend, I think you have been reading too many mystery novels. Surely your professor is alive and well. I have heard they can become obsessed with their digs."

I remained silent.

"If that's all…" He added, standing and in this way letting me know the interview was at its end.

"No. I have another favor to ask."

He sat.

"I received this call at my house's phone. Is there any way you could trace it? I dialed *69 but got no result."

"We can do that. Follow me."

He took me to another, nearby office.

"This is Mr. Andrew Kirkpatrick, case no. 3492845. He received a call we think is of interest to trace." He told the young policeman at the desk and then he turned to speak to me. "He will do what he can. Let me know if anything else happens."

He left.

"Your number?" Asked the young man. "And at what time did you receive the call?"

I gave the required information and waited patiently. Finally, he explained.

"The call appears to have been made in Cairo, but all we can see is that it was made from a public phone, probably at the airport. I cannot tell you more."

I don't know what I had expected, but somehow this information depressed me.

"Thank you." I said.

As I returned to the car, I wondered why nobody had commented about the dog. I had walked around the police station's hallways, gone into offices and it had felt as if I were on my own. I touched Sachmis, to convince myself she was really there. She was, naturally. Still, it did seem strange, her apparent invisibility.

I called my professor and when I asked for an appointment, she told me to go directly to see her, as she had time to talk then. However, I decided this time to leave the dog in the car. The temperature was cool enough, and I had parked under a tree which gave enough shade.

The conversation with the professor was difficult, as she couldn't understand my needed to postpone the presentation. She got quite angry and threatened to drop me. I finally convinced her to ask for a later date from the examination board.

She spoke for a while on the phone, becoming quite flustered at the end.

"I hope your presentation is more than excellent when you finally do it Andrew because I will not accept anything but. You have made me pass through a bad moment and I won't forget it anytime soon. Your postponement is granted. They are giving you six months. I hope you use them well. Goodbye."

She left me in the room and I understood how angry she was by the careful way she closed the door, trying not to slam it with fury.

I also left and, not seeing her anywhere, not in the front office, not in the corridors, I shrugged and went to the car.

If I had I lost her support, there was nothing I could do and would have to bear the consequences. Before her, or even myself, I had a responsibility with Professor Morley. She had asked for me and I would respond.

CHAPTER XIV

I had arrived in Egypt the previous night. Once again, the unfathomable enchantment of the place had gripped me, and a shiver of emotion ran through my back.

It had taken me days to get ready to travel, as Gregoire was adamant I should bring the dog with me and there were many procedures and documents needed for that to happen. I had come to this country before, only the matter of a ticket and a visa, which the professor usually applied for, as our trips were considered study trips and required a special type of visa and a permit. But this time I had to request a tourist visa and I had the complication of the dog. I knew it would not be easy, as the authorities find it easy to deny access for any simple reason.

Luckily and perhaps because of Gregoire's breeding interests, the dog had all her vaccines current. I was told she would need to go into quarantine and wondered why should I bring her if she would not be with me for the majority of my trip's time. Then, as if receiving a message from the grave, I remembered uncle's admonitions; my mind had the power to control. I wondered. Was it something I needed to practice for years before I got to manage it? Was it ethical, controlling other people's will? I thought it wasn't so and yet…

I suddenly remembered Sachmis' strange invisibility when we went to the police station. Could I have been using it? Or was there something or someone else guiding my steps

To make a long story short, I was now in the hotel room with my dog. Apparently, something had worked in my favor, though I would hesitate to ascribe it to any supernatural power. Now I needed to make enquiries about my professor's whereabouts. I didn't want to be too obvious about my search, something in her last call had alarmed me. There was, however, the possibility of contacting one of the dig's aids she had employed before.

I was still trying to recover get some rest, though it was already over eight o'clock in the morning, when I heard a knock on the door. Sachmis stood, her hackles raised, her fangs bared but in total silence, no growl, no bark. Bemused by the dog's attitude I went to the door and when I looked through the peephole, I saw a turbaned man standing outside. It took me a

Sent Back

while to recognize him, but then, with extreme urgency I opened the door.

"I can't believe it, Saher! You are here! How did you find me? How did you know I was here?" I exclaimed without even closing the door.

He brought a finger to his lips, cautioning silence and closed the door after looking at both sides of the hallway. All was silent; he sighed satisfied and silently closed the door. He went then to the window and after the same inspection, pulled the curtains closed. The room became darkened, but he lit no lights.

During all this time, Sachmis had been watching him, but she seemed now more relaxed. That was strange, as she was so protective of me and didn't know this man.

Saher went to an armchair, placed it in the center of the room, then took a chair from the desk, placed it in front of the armchair and sat in it, gesturing for me to occupy the other place.

Only because I knew him from several previous digs did I obey him. His attitude was strange enough to raise my alarm.

Once I sat, he began talking in a subdued voice. It was very difficult for me to hear him, so I leaned toward him. He grasped my wrist and forced me even nearer. Now his lips moved touching my ear.

"Lady professor is in trouble. I believe you know."

"Yes, I came because of that. Do you know where she is?"

He looked around and I realized he feared being overheard. Again, he leaned toward me with such apparent urgency I was even more alarmed.

"We must leave right now." He whispered. "I will explain on the road."

"Now?"

He nodded and stood up.

"What about the dog?" He added in a normal tone of voice.

"She comes."

"I don't think that is advisable." He countered.

"She comes." I repeated.

"As you wish. Come now."

I was stretching my hand to get my bag when he stopped me.

"No. You carry nothing. I have the whole setup for you downstairs."

I shrugged and followed him, Sachmis following me.

We didn't take the elevator, instead going down the service stairway. He took me through the kitchen, greeting some cooks and aids there and then to a room where the cooks changed clothes. He opened a bag hidden under a table and took out a loose-fitting ankle-length robe and a turban. He made me take off my pants, shirt and jacket and put these on. I had hidden the scarab in a jacket's inner pocket and had no idea where I could hide it in the new outfit. I had with me, also, those mysterious, unread papers uncle had left for me.

I had not wanted to leave them behind and had separated those which were only legal babble from the ones written in hieroglyphs. Thus reduced to less than half its size the 'book', protected in a plastic sheet, could be hidden under my shirt. Now, the need to conceal them arose again as, not only the stone, but the document needed to be safe.

However, Saher at that moment was offering me something else, a coat of large sleeves where I found several pockets. I placed the stone in one of them and then tied the coat around the waist with a cord, keeping the document close to my chest. He also gave me a long strip of white or beige cloth and told me to wrap it loosely around my neck. He then inspected me. Still concerned about the dog, he was looking at it when he gave a start.

"Magic!" He muttered.

"What is?"

"The dog, the dog!" He cried in muffled tones. "Don't you see? It disappeared."

"No, it didn't. Sachmis' right here." I replied and then something seemed to click in my brain. "It is something I do when I don't want people to see her."

He looked up at me, a very bewildered man.

"You can do that?" He whispered and bowed low before me. "Forgive me, lord, I didn't know who you were."

Now it was me who was bewildered.

"Now, Saher, who do you think I am? Stop this foolishness." I added as I saw he intended to fall flat on the floor.

"You are my lord, the lord of the pharaohs, the master healer who can change nature, you are Immutef!"

"No I am not. I am a man just like you. Come on, Saher! Shouldn't we be leaving now?"

He shook himself as a dog coming out of water. I saw he was trembling and avoiding my eyes. He nodded and taking hold of the cord fastened to my waist, lead the way out of the room, the kitchen and the building.

He kept looking around and I assumed he was checking to see if we were followed, then he leaned toward me and whispered.

"Is the dog with us?"

Sachmis was scampering before us, so I nodded.

He shivered and bowed his head. I heard him whisper something, perhaps a prayer, perhaps a charm against witchcraft.

We had been walking for more than an hour when we reached one of those places I had been warned never to go to. Here the modern city of Cairo ended, and we entered in a labyrinth of huts and hovels, where the streets were part of the dwellings.

Sent Back

I felt Sachmis and looking down saw she was pushing against my leg. I stooped to caress her head, reassuring her all was all right.

"Why are we here, Saher?" I asked.

He jumped in fright and turned angrily but his anger changed immediately as he remembered who he thought I was.

"The camels, my lord." He whispered. "The camels are waiting here for us, but, let me implore you and don't be angry with me; please, don't speak that language again. They will hear and thinking you are a tourist they could attack us to rob you."

I nodded, as I understood very well what he feared.

The camels he had referred to were waiting in a lateral lane, under a tavern's tattered canopy. A small child guarded the tethered animals, and I was amazed such a little tike controlled such powerful and skittish animals.

Saher took the ropes from the child, dropping some coins in his hand. Apparently, the reward was unexpected in its largesse, as the urchin ran away without even thanking my guide.

I had previously learned the imposing art of riding a camel, so soon Saher was guiding us, still through narrow and twisted streets, out of the city.

Sachmis was running after us and she seemed all right; I was worried, however, on how she would fare once we reached open dessert. We were still in the city of Moqattam, that lies to the East of Cairo and the Nile River.

The sun was reaching its zenith when we finally got to an unpopulated zone. Before us spread the dessert. I had been checking the sun's position and something did not seem right.

"Saher" I said in a normal voice, knowing nobody was around to hear us. "Saher, where are we going?"

He reigned his camel in and waited for me to reach him.

"We cannot go directly to where we are needed." He explained.

"Well," I continued. "But we are going south by south-east and if I remember correctly, there's nothing out there."

"Not there, yes, you are right. But this is the only way we can follow to get to the ancient city." He explained.

"Which city, Saher? Stop talking in riddles and tell me everything. Who's going to listen now?"

He pondered for some minutes.

"The lady professor was taken to Avaris, lord." He said. "To the ancient and buried city of the Hyksos."

"Ah!" I said and it was as if a new light shone over the recent events.

We spoke no more, though I was worried about going into the dessert without provisions and basically water. I shouldn't have worried. The guide knew his world. It was almost noon and the sun had been pounding on my head for a while now when I saw we were nearing some trees. I gazed, amazed.

"Saher? Are those trees I see ahead?" I asked.

"Yes. There is a small oasis there. We will find water and perhaps a group of Bedouins or two. Please remember not to speak English." He looked at me, worried.

"I won't. But my Arabic sounds quite foreign."

"Do not speak, then." He shrugged.

I found it strange, all this mystery, but accepted the man's request. Perhaps no one would be there, and the rule of silence would not need enforcement.

However, when we arrived, I saw the place was already almost full, camels and men sharing the scarce shadow the date palms and dwarfed trees I didn't recognize, were offering.

Saher advanced, crying the usual greeting. Some men stood and looking at him, replied in the same manner. We were then accepted into the gathering and took our camels to the mesmerizing water. It was a small lake, the water oozing from the aquifers that run under the dessert. Around it flourished tall grasses, unknown to me and other small shrubs, mostly acacias.

Saher watered the camels first. It amazes me how these people, even though they are in the throes of agonizing thirst, will take care first of their animals and only after will they provide for themselves. Thus it was this time and when we finished, we were invited by the other Arabs to their place, where they offered us the already brewed tea prepared with spearmint leaves and sugar.

I have always admired the ritual these people follow in their gatherings. The praise to Allah, the bowing, the raising of the cups, it all held a mystery that spoke of ancient times. I imitated Saher and finally we sat around a small fire, though how they wanted a fire in this extreme heat was unexplainable. We drank and Saher offered some of our provisions, which I hadn't known we had, dried fruits and the always present flat bread.

While Saher spoke with the others, I sat somewhat separated from them, counting the beads of the misbahah, the Muslim prayer beads. I had learnt, some time ago, that the best way to avoid conversation in a Muslim environment was to seem occupied in prayer. I knew I would have the help from Saher, who most probably would explain I was a religious fanatic or something of that sort.

Meanwhile, Sachmis, after drinking to her heart's content, had approached me and lay now at my feet. Amazingly, she was still invisible to the others, something imperative in a world where dogs are considered unclean.

How and why was the animal invisible to these people was

Sent Back

unexplainable, but it was a relief, however it was happening. and after all I had seen, after the affair with Granuncle, I seemed impervious to amazement.

It seems I had dozed off because suddenly I was brought out of my slumber by a hand shaking my shoulder and a whisper in my ear to remain in silence and wake up.

I opened my eyes to see Saher right in front of me his face almost touching mine.

"Time to go." He whispered in English.

I nodded and was going to rise when he placed a new cup of tea in my hand.

"Drink!" He ordered now in Arabic. "Then we go."

I obeyed.

Now we were walking toward the East, the Sun, though high in the firmament, already falling towards the faraway sands.

Saher was not pushing the camels and they were going at an easy trot of eight to nine miles per hour. I knew they could run really fast, but apparently Saher wanted them to save their energy.

I was musing, head bowed and eyes almost shut when I felt darkness coming. I looked up, it was too early for the sun to be setting. The camel seemed nervous and I searched around for Saher. He had stopped some paces behind me and his face showed something more than terror.

I made the camel go back toward him.

"What is it, Saher? What's this darkness?"

"Haboob." He replied in a whisper. "Sandstorm." He added. "We are dead." He finished.

I had never experienced a sandstorm, not in the many times I had come to the digs, but by stories I knew how terrible they could be. If I had any doubt Saher's face expression made it clear even he, an experienced dessert dweller, was terrified.

"What do we do?" I cried, as the storm's roar increased.

He did not answer, instead, he wrapped his face in a long shawl like the one he had given me and dropping to the ground, forced his camel to lie down. He gestured to me to imitate him, so I did as he had, the camel needing no coaxing to follow his mate. I saw Saher covering the camel's head with another cloth, but I had none.

I cried to him and finally made him aware of my predicament. He gestured to the saddlebag, and I hurriedly searched them and found a similar piece of cloth, immediately wrapping it around the camel's head. Then a tarp, which I threw over me. But Sachmis, what would I do with my dog?

She had returned to visibility as soon as we had left the group of nomads in the oasis and I could see how fearful she was of the oncoming storm. I pulled her toward me and made her go under my garments, which I spread to cover her and then tucked them under our bodies. I was lying, as was Saher, on the leeward side of the incoming storm, so the fierce wind, carrying almost lethal grains of sand would not hit us directly. I had been told, some time ago, how camels were adapted to the desert storms, but still I worried for the animal, exposed to the brunt of the haboob winds.

It was turning so dark I could see nothing, the proverbial phrase of 'couldn't see the hand in front of my eyes' haunted me with an insistence that was driving me insane.

I felt the cloth around my head was being pulled away, as if a gigantic hand insisted on taking it up; simultaneously I could feel the weight of the sand collecting above and around us. Sometimes a heavier particle hit me, perhaps a small stone, or a clump of sand and each time I crouched lower, trying to hide under the camel's side.

The roar was deafening and Sachmis hugged me her snout lying on my chest. I thought she would be terrorized, because, to tell the truth, so was I. It was not only the terrible wind, nor the sand and pieces of rocks hitting us, nor the high-pitched scream of the wind. Now, I saw, through my closed eyes, flashes of bluish light.

I cracked them open and saw, even on the surface of my scarf, tiny electrical discharges, probably of static electricity. I felt my hair was standing on end and I could feel Sachmis' hair, all of it raised and discharging tiny volts of the same static electricity.

I heard the crack of thunder nearby and crouched even lower, hugging Sachmis' head even nearer and both nearer to the camel that was braying in terror. Apparently, I thought in a crazy moment of irony, apparently, they are not so adapted to a dessert storm. Mercifully, the storm had started when we were not, I insist, not on a high rise. I remembered stories of people being hit by lightning during a haboob because they had been on top of a dune.

Time seemed to pause, as the wind buffeted us, and we were buried deeper and deeper by sand and dust.

At last and after so long I though a whole day had elapsed, the storm began to abate, light crept through the lingering clouds and the terrible sound stopped.

I was buried almost to my shoulders, Sachmis' head lying near my neck so she could breathe. The camel, whose reins and shawl I had held so firmly, now shock himself and, with what I thought was desperation, stood up.

As I was still clinging to the reins, I was pulled up after him and Sachmis and I stood on top of the recently blown sand, gazing at a

Sent Back

landscape very different to what we had seen last. I couldn't find my guide and a feeling of despair was gaining on me when I felt a hand touch my arm. Thinking it was Saher, I turned.

The hand gripped me tightly and I looked down at it, not believing my eyes. Probably I had died in the storm, or was unconscious, maybe for the lack of air, because it was a beautiful hand, the hand of a woman.

Where had she come from? How was she there, with us?

Movement in a nearby dune attracted my attention and I saw Saher's camel, followed by Saher, pull out of the sand.

I felt a wave of relief, swiftly changed to worry. Who was this woman and where was my dog?

The woman laughed.

"I am she." She said with a voice so sweet and crystalline I shivered with delight and fear, too.

"I am Sachmis." She added, seeing I hadn't understood her meaning.

"Sachmis is a dog, my dog, a Doberman bitch." I replied.

She frowned.

"Such a naughty word to apply to a female. I have always wondered why." She commented and the smile left her face for an instant.

"Am I dead? Are you a hallucination?" I asked, unable to accept what she was saying.

"You are not; I am not. Come on Andrew, after so many supernatural things happening to you, after seeing your grandfather taken by a giant falcon… What else do you need to be convinced you live in a world full of magic?"

I had been so intent in this conversation I had not thought about Saher, but now I felt him and turning saw him gazing with open mouth at the, I cannot say other thing than apparition.

"Master?" He whispered. "What is this? Is it a genie? A spirit from the dessert?"

The woman laughed, her laugh like tiny crystal bells on the wind.

Saher did strange gestures with his hands and muttering something in Arabic.

"Stop it!" Said she who called herself Sachmis. "I am no demon, nor a spirit, Saher! How can you not recognize me? Don't you know who I am?" The woman spoke angrily to my guide.

Saher stopped but I could see he was panicking.

I grasped his arm and brought him closer holding him tight in case, in his terror, he could flee and leave me all by myself in this desolation.

"You say you are Sachmis, my dog. If that is true, tell me something only she could know."

"What? Like when I jumped on your bed the first day I met you? Or how I walked with you into the police station and nobody was able to see

117

me? Or when the other dogs came out at you and I stood before you? You want more?"

I gasped. Only if this was truly my dog could she know all that. Well, unless she was a spirit or a goddess.

She smiled.

"Remember my name, you silly man." She said.

I was not very clear about this. My mind was still in turmoil after the shock of the storm, but I seemed to remember that Sachmis, or Sekhmet, was a goddess associated with war and death. Suddenly the scary part came; a myth about the end of Ra's rule on the earth when Sachmis, aroused against the mortals who conspired against Ra, destroys most of humanity.

"Are we dead?" I asked again the most important question; all else could be elicited afterward.

"No."

"No?"

"I'll say it only once more Andrew. You are not dead, none of you are, nor having hallucinations. I have come, I have brought you across the sands of time to when you need to be."

"The middle of the dessert?" I asked in scorn.

"No little man, not to the where, but to the when."

I stared, unable to understand her.

"Has the storm dulled your wits, Andrew?" She asked and I saw she was upset. "Come on, you are an archaeologist, you study 'old'. You have been digging where?"

"Well, last time we tried to go to Avaris, near Pi Rameses."

"Aha, because…"

"Dr. Morley wanted to learn more about its origins."

"Oh Gods, do I have to spell it all for you? And who was she interested in, in Avaris?"

"Joseph." I replied, understanding her drive. "Joseph of Egypt, vizier to the Pharaoh, son of Jacob."

She smiled, relaxed.

"There you are. It was not so difficult, was it? Yes, you've come to the times of Djuseff and perhaps you'll be even able to meet him."

I stared, my eyes almost out of their sockets; by my side, Saher trembled.

I conferred with Saher and we agreed we would make the woman ride my camel, while the two of us would walk beside it. It was not the best of solutions, but I would allow nothing else.

Saher looked subdued, even sad. His shoulders hunched, his head bowed, but now and then he would straighten and look back at the woman-

Sent Back

goddess, then he would shiver and return to his brooding.

He had asked me, in an almost inaudible whisper, if I knew who she was, if I knew about the goddess of ancient Egypt. I had nodded and he had gazed at me as if I were mad.

The storm had hit us a while after noon and the sun was now swiftly dipping into the western sands. As I walked beside the camel, I pondered on the possibility of this trip through time being real. I mean, there was a woman in the place of my dog, that alone merited a trip to a psychiatrist, what she had said, that we had been brought several thousand years into the past was even more unbelievable. However, in case it was true, the danger we faced had increased by a hundred-fold.

Perhaps it was true the Egyptians of that time took no prisoners, or more precisely, they didn't take the Jews as slaves as had been stated by some Egyptian archaeologists. But that time, or the time we were in now, was a time of wars, a time where there was no Declaration of Human Rights. Pharaohs, kings, soldiers, priests all those in power, did not accept that humans are born free and equal in dignity and rights and should act towards one another in a spirit of brotherhood.

They did not consider possible that everyone was entitled any right to freedom, whoever they were, or from wherever. It never crossed their minds that everyone has the right to life, liberty, and security of person nor that no one would be held in slavery or servitude. A life was worthless here, unless you were the pharaoh and even they had been murdered.

What would be our future here? What dangers would we face?

My own face proclaimed I was a stranger in the land, even if I spoke not a syllable. All these considerations were making me angry, as is usual in the face of fear. Why had this damned woman, or goddess, or whatever, brought us here? With what objective? I could think of nothing good coming out of this... this temporal displacement. Then I remembered she was Sekhmet, goddess of war and retribution. Perhaps we would be safe in her company.

I was brought out of my musings by Saher, who, pulling at my sleeve, pointed to a place in the dessert.

I strained my eyes and saw, not too distant from us, the greenery that proclaimed an oasis.

We needed water, we urgently needed water and food, but I was worried about the people we could encounter there. There could even be soldiers of the pharaoh protecting it.

I turned to Sachmis.

"Is it possible for you to know if it will be safe for us to go there?" I asked. Well, I thought, if she is truly a goddess she should know.

She looked at me as if she had understood my thoughts and I blushed.

"Yes, it is safe." She replied. "No one will harm you there Andrew, remember I am with you."

She turned her head away, clearly upset with me and my skepticism, but I couldn't help it.

Saher had waited impatiently for her answer and as soon as he heard, he immediately pulled at the camels' reins, changing directions and aiming for the oasis.

The haboob had spoiled our water, it had somehow filtered through the cap and now instead of water what the containers held was an undrinkable muddy paste; water was sorely needed.

We reached the border of the oasis as the sun reached the horizon, just in time.

Sachmis stopped the camel and climbed down. As soon as the animal felt free, it went to the lake and drank, followed by his mate. We followed and finding a place far from where the animals drank their full, we drank.

I would have thrown off my clothes and jumped naked into the water, the need to cleanse my skin of the dust was unbearable, but the fear of crocodiles lurking, and Sachmis' presence prevented me. This last was silly, I had bathed frequently in the presence of the dog and an insistent voice at the back of my mind kept telling me they were the same. I couldn't, though, so I threw water only over face and arms, promising to take a real bath the next day.

Saher had swiftly done what I was taking a while to finish and when I returned to the place we had elected for our campsite, he was already boiling water for a much-needed tea.

Sachmis had followed me back and she looked clean and refreshed, though I suspected she had not gotten into the lake. I thought now about the absurdity of my acceptance of her transformation. If she was my dog, then how did she have such magnificent dressing? Because the dress she wore was beautiful, as would befit a goddess.

I snorted. This would take me a while to accept.

Saher offered me a steaming cup, which I passed to Sachmis and then he gave me another for myself. In this way we sat and drank in silence. I was sure Saher was considering the same questions I was and the swift concealed glances he shot at the woman confirmed it.

She paid no heed and I thought she had dismissed our incredulity as something that would be, soon enough, taken care off and was enjoying her return to her own body.

As I looked at her, I realized I hadn't looked at her as a woman and the more I looked the more I liked. Her proud lifting of the head on the long and slender neck; the strong chin, the full red lips, so well defined they could have been painted by a master, the ebony black long hair, falling over her back. The eyebrows, that resembled the wings of the raven, lifted in flight and the eyes!

Sent Back

I started, the eyes were looking at me and a smile spread on the perfect lips.

"Are you admiring me 'master'?" She mocked. "Do you like what you see?"

I stuttered, went red on the face and bowed my head avoiding her eyes. Silly, I know, but you would understand if you were in my place and, I was never in the presence of such a perfect woman. That said in my favor.

"You wouldn't be the first and not the last to fall in love with a goddess, or with me. I would advise you, however, not to do so. My presence here with you will not last long and goddesses and mortals do not mix well."

I didn't answer, ashamed by her perspicacity. Well, she was a goddess, wasn't she? They are supposed to know what we think.

Saher had taken some flat bread and on it he had spread a paste, made of vegetables or some such. He offered a piece to Sachmis and one to me. I had thought he had been oblivious of our conversation, but he gave me a look that showed he was aware of everything happening around him.

"Djinns and men... not a good combination." He whispered.

Sachmis' laugh startled us.

"Let me make something clear." She said. "My presence here has been brought about by someone whom I protect and defend."

I straightened, full of stupid pride and she stopped and smiled, looking at me with what I would call compassion. It was clear she had read my mind, or at least understood my gestures.

"Not you Andrew. No. Humans come and go, I have seen thousands of your generations pass before me. Your existence is so fleeting I don't really have time to see you pass. I don't know if you recall anything about me from your so-called studies but let me help you saying that I am the arbiter for Ma'at, divine justice and balance. I have come to fix what was made wrong, to recover what was lost and, through you, to make it known to the world. Have it clear in your mind, it is not I who is here to help you, it is you who are here to help Me!"

On hearing this, Saher bowed low, even to the ground, beating his head upon the sands and whispering words in Arabic from which I could understand 'powerful', 'evil trembles before you', 'mistress of dread'. and then he would utter the prayer of the faithful.

"Oh!" Cried the goddess. "Spare me your platitudes. You are afraid of me and properly so, but I am not here to harm you, Saher Zaghloul ibn Sirin! Once your task here is completed, once I return what is lost to where it belongs and what I came to fix is fixed, you will be back in your own time and city, maybe wiser and maybe wealthier, who knows?"

At these words, Saher seemed to relax and I could see how hope infused him with new strength. Not that he had, suddenly, become a valorous warrior, no, but he at least was not groveling or trembling anymore.

For me, however, everything Sekhmet had said had brought on more worries and questions. Was she referring to the professor's abduction? She had said recover what was lost. What did she mean? I doubted that such a mighty entity would appear in this world for a simple, unimportant professor, if I took her dismissal of me as a standard.

"Your professor was the means I used to bring you to the land where my influence and the influence of the gods is more powerful. I will not speak about the contention raging now between the gods of your world, it is not important for our task. You will find her, unharmed, soon enough and perhaps she can help you. I'll say no more. Sleep now, we have much to do in the morning."

It was late when I finally fell asleep. Of all the things that troubled me and believe me there were many, the one foremost in my mind was a question. How were we going to reach Avaris?

I grant you that having a goddess by my side or being brought thousands of years into the past were enough to drive anyone crazy, but here I was, wondering about the common day traveling possibilities.

I had calculated, even before leaving Cairo, that the distance we had to travel was nothing else than eighty miles and that as the crow flies. Imagine reaching the place going across the sands of the terrible dessert. Would the goddess be able to transport us there, magically? That would be a great solution. Thinking about it, I relaxed and finally fell asleep.

I knew it was too early when Saher woke me up, the birds were only now beginning their songs to the rising sun.

"Wake up Andrew. She wants to talk to you." He said.

With my brain still clouded by sleep, I wondered who he was referring to. I brushed my face roughly, trying in this way to gain some wakefulness and then I saw her. Immediately everything that had befallen us came back. I jumped to my feet.

"A moment, please." I said, rushing to the lake.

After splashing some water on my face and taking care of other matters, I returned to where she had been patiently waiting.

She sat on some rugs that had been previously under the camels' saddles, but it seemed as I approached her, that she sat on a throne, waiting for her servants.

She smiled at me and, without a greeting, spoke.

"I cannot." She said.

"Huh?" Perhaps I was still asleep.

"The answer to your question last night before you fell asleep. I cannot 'magically' take you there, it is not in my purview."

Sent Back

"Oh!" It took me a while again to accept she could know my thoughts. Nothing was private with her. I saw her smile; yes, again reading my mind.

"Alright, then, how are we going to get there? It is very far." Wondering, if she had been able to bring us across time, why couldn't she take us just a few miles north?

"I know. Who better than I? And a very weary journey. So what I propose is to go west and find the great river." She replied. I didn't know if she had seen my doubts about her powers or not. She made no reference to them this time.

"The Nile!" I cried. "What for? We cannot… we have no…"

"When we get there, everything will be taken care of." She said.

"Are you sure? I fear the Pharaoh's guards."

"I cannot use magic to get us there, but I am a feared goddess in my own right. We will be safe."

I shrugged, what else could I do? She was a goddess.

After having a hurried breakfast and saddling the camels, we began our journey. This time I had decided to ride the other camel and Saher, who at first walked by our side, soon joined me.

It would not matter a lot to the camel, I thought; my friend was slender enough and I though he didn't weigh over a hundred twenty pounds.

Now we could move faster and soon the camels were riding at their usual twenty miles an hour gait. It didn't take us much time to get within reach of the river, the greenery a welcome sight to our tired eyes. I could even feel the change on my skin, brought about by the moist air near the famous waterway.

The camels had increased their gait, sensing the water, but Saher restrained them. This was a forbidding territory we were approaching, not only because of the possible encounter with Pharaonic agents, but because of the fauna. I was fully aware, as surely Saher was too, of the existence of hippopotamuses and crocodiles in the Nile, much more abundant in the time we were than they are at present.

The hippopotamus is really a dangerous animal, though you would not think so by its appearance, and no one needs to talk about the sly and ferocious crocodiles.

We approached the river's bank through a land already covered by papyrus plants and date palms. From this height we could see an island bathed by the waters and I thought it should be the Gezira Island.

Some small boats crisscrossed the river and on the other side I could see people working, tiling the land. It was only then that I realized I was in another time, before it had been speculation, not interiorized and I had doubted of all that was occurring to us. As water rushes from a collapsed dam, the many dangers we were facing were making me panic.

The woman, I refuse to call her goddess, grabbed my arm.

"Do not dismay now! Yes, there is danger, your path will be full of obstacles you will need to surmount, but there's a reason why you were brought here. You must be strong!"

She shook me and her otherworldly strength was such that I felt like a leaf in the wind.

I liberated myself from her grasp and stepped away from her.

"Should I enumerate all that is against me doing anything in this world?" I said and pointed, encompassing the river, the land, the boats with an open hand. "The language? My person? My total ignorance off all that is important for these people?"

"That is why I will remain with you." She said. "However, we have something more urgent to take care of."

I shrugged. Everything for me, at that moment, was most urgent.

"I have to dispose of your guide and his animals."

I looked at her in amazement.

"I cannot have him blundering around here and most probably he will be considered mad and who knows what they would do to him."

"He can come with us." I protested.

"No, no he can't."

"Then, what will you do? Will you kill him?"

Now she shrugged.

"I could, but it is not what I mean to do. You see, even his animals."

"What? What about…" I stopped, because suddenly I understood. The camels were not domesticated at that time, the only beast of burden were the donkey and the cattle, perhaps horses, but not camels. Their presence would raise more questions even than my aspect.

I nodded, acquiescing.

Suddenly, without a sound, Saher and the animals were gone.

"Where?" I whispered, awed.

"Back to his time, with no memory of this, be content. He will be alright. Now, as for you, let's go to the river, my barge approaches."

CHAPTER XV

It was true, a beautiful boat was approaching the rise where we were standing and Sachmis walked toward the water, motioning for me to follow.

The barge, as she had called it, was splendidly covered with rugs and sheets of colored cloth. The sail was brilliant white and at the moment, the sailors were pulling it down and fastening it to the horizontal mast. On the last portion of the deck stood a cabin, also covered by rugs, perhaps to grant some protection from the sun.

Besides the sailors, several women, in loose white garments, stood bowing and amidst them stood a man, a tall strong man with shaven head, his powerful arms showing from under the white sleeveless tunic and crossed over his chest.

"Ah, the priest comes! Good!" Whispered the goddess.

The barge touched land and a plank was set to allow Sachmis to board the boat. She took hold of my hand and led me onto it while everyone there, even the priest, bowed with the tips of their fingers touching the floor.

The goddess approached the priest, who now stood before her, erect but with bowed head. She placed a hand on his shoulder and spoke softly in his ear. He nodded and then, turning to the sailors spoke swift commands while Sachmis, the goddess Sekhmet, led me to the center of the barge toward the small cabin.

"Sit here." She said and returned to talk with her priestesses? Servants? Worshipers? Maids? I knew not what they were, nor did I ever learn who they were. Silent, unobtrusive, and obedient, they remained like that throughout our trip toward the Nile delta.

The women brought dishes covered with napkins made of white linen. Under them I found dates, flat bread that seemed recently baked and pieces of some fish, cut in slender strips and probably dried by the sun. A cup with what came to be beer was placed at my side and while I ate, one of these women remained constantly beside me. I cared not, I was hungry and thirsty and enjoyed the meal with all my heart, careless then of what the future could bring.

Sachmis returned and, sitting at my side was served by the women. I do not know what she ate, but I am sure it was not what they had given me. I would hazard a guess and say she drank some beverage prepared with honey; that I could smell. As for eating, if I said she was eating manna, perhaps I wouldn't be too wrong.

After a while, she turned to talk.

"We will reach the delta in two or three days. I have spoken to the priest, so if anyone dares to ask, he will know what to say. He will also spread the word that Sekhmet travels the River, that will help you remain hidden. No one wants to see me in person."

"What year is this?" I asked, as, for me, this was the most important fact of my presence there. "Which Pharaoh rules?"

She smiled and I thought she was satisfied with the question.

"Yes, that is the proper question to ask, young one. I will tell you. It is Amenemhat III. Amenemhat III, of the. We have come more than three thousand eight hundred years back from your time to the golden age of Egypt.

An image popped into my mind's eye, that of the statue of a pharaoh who, differently from all other statues of pharaohs except Akhenaten, had been portrayed as worried, concerned, and sad. I stared at her with an expression that must have seemed stupid to her, because she laughed uproariously.

"By the sacred Ma'at, you made me laugh! I know, you want to know what year according to your records, I think it would fall roughly in the eighteen hundred and sixty before the birth of your god."

So many questions arouse at this answer I had barely time to pay attention to each one. Did she know about Jesus? How could she? Were the ancient gods still alive, I mean were they real? How could they? Then, laying those unanswerable questions by the side, I considered her answer. Amenemhat the Third, yes, ruler of Egypt from 1860 to 1814 BC. He was powerful, yes, but maybe because of Joseph's help in the lean years. Who could know? Was I here to uncover the truth of the Jews sojourn in Egypt?

Inadvertently I gazed into the goddess eyes, while I continued pondering her answer. If so, how was I to talk to them, to Joseph, or even to the people who would surround him? I knew no Hebrew and I doubted very much the one spoken in my time would be the same used almost four thousand years before that time.

And regarding what the Egyptians at this time spoke, I read the hieroglyphs, but from that to speak the language, there was a long strait. Languages came fast to me as soon as I lived in the place; perhaps I could learn it, but did I have the time?

I became aware then of my stare and lowered my eyes, ashamed.

"You seem to have forgotten many things, my young friend." She said.

I looked back to her, with questioning eyes.

Sent Back

"You have forgotten your family comes from here, from the land of Kemet; in your mind lies the key to ancient words. You have forgotten your uncle's words in his last hours, regarding your undiscovered abilities. I know in a few hours you will be able to talk and understand my people, that doesn't worry me much. Something that does, however, is that you have forgotten, and I am to blame for it, you have forgotten what you saw in the hidden chamber at your uncle's house."

"You? You made me forget? But what?"

She nodded and smiled softly.

"I made you forget, because you could not talk to anyone about what was there and I feared you would at that moment."

I remained silent, though all my body cried for an explanation.

"What you saw there was the copy of something your civilization has been searching for during millennia, the place where the Law and Science were kept."

At her words, the veil fell from the eyes of memory, and I saw it, behind piles of boxes, statues, columns and masks, the two golden seraphim, kneeling and facing each other, wings extended over the sacred locus.

"How could it be possible?" I mumbled, awed. "My uncle had the Ark of the Covenant?"

"No, no Andrew!" Countered the goddess. "I said 'copy'."

She was silent for a moment and then continued.

"The origins of your family, Andrew, come back to my land and to the time before time was measured. They lived by the wide reed sea, hunting gazelles, other small creatures, and fishing. The reed sea then was full of living things that thrived among the water plants and further in, where the sea was deeper and the reeds few, very big animals similar to fish grew. You have seen their remains, have you not?"

An image popped into my mind and I remembered the place, yes, Wadi al-Hitan, or the Valley of the Whales; the Basilosaurus and the smaller Dorudon. It had been a great experience to go there, though it did not relate at all to our archaeological investigations, to find the bones of whales' distant ancestors, yet the visit had been very interesting to all of us.

"Yes."

"Some people came then, travelers from farther south whose lands had been destroyed in the big cataclysm. They came and lived among my people by the shores of the sea. They were used to another way of living and though for some time they did abide there in company of the ancient ones in conformity to their primitive and simple way of living, finally they began teaching their own ways from the lost lands."

"Ah!" I whispered, here was confirmation of our suspicions.

She smiled and nodded.

"Yes, it was like that; some of your learned people have been right about it, though many don't want to accept the idea. The newcomers had few women, as they had escaped the destruction only because they had been sailing, so many found wives among the tribe. One of such is from whom you descend."

I listened in rapt attention. What she was saying answered so many questions archaeologists had been wondering about I couldn't miss one word of it.

"The Teachers suffered; a terrible despondency would settle upon them now and again and to those around them it seemed as if a thunderstorm was gathering. Deep was the suffering of the teachers, for they had lost all who were like them in experience, life and education; they had lost their families, their towns, their whole civilization. Can you even imagine the pain of losing your world?" She added, looking curiously at me.

"These people, whom I call the teachers, taught my people how to grow wheat and other food so they would not need to go from place-to-place hunting and gathering whatever grew in the neighborhood. They taught them many arts, how to build better huts, how to care for their own health, what to eat during the different seasons, when it was hot and rained, when it was colder and dry. The teachers were long lived, and it came to pass that the inland sea began to dry up and crops began to fail so they guided the tribe to the East, where they knew flowed a large river which would let my people grow and multiply and be satiated."

"Is all that true? Was it that way that it happened?" I interrupted because what she was saying went against what was publicly acknowledged among archaeologists.

"Why would I tell you lies?" She shrugged and continued. "Yes, that is how it was. So, when the people reached the great river, the teachers taught them how to know when the flooding would happen and many other sciences, those that told of the sky, or of the world. However, they didn't teach this to everyone, but only to those who had the wakened mind."

She saw my face and explained.

"Those who descended from them and others with whom the teachers had done their magic had a different way of thinking, their minds had been awakened to knowledge."

I nodded though the questions were now multiplying by hundreds.

"So the teachers gathered these ones, they made them a group apart and they taught them. They taught them secret things, the science they had known in their lost worlds; how the mind could control the forces of the universe and allow magnificent buildings to be created. They taught the priests how the sky moves and how the different spheres interact among themselves and with this world. Oh yes, they taught the priests all they could, everything they remembered, because they were few and did not

Sent Back

possess the whole lost knowledge. But what they knew was enough to change the course of history in this land. Yes, the priests learnt swiftly and secretly, because none of this knowledge could be made public among the people. And then, because many years had passed, many more than what people live in your time, because they were old and tired and sad missing their lost lands, the remaining teachers set out in a boat, they drifted on the Great River to where it met the sea and were gone never to be seen again."

I was so amazed I couldn't say a word and for the first time, the goddess smiled warmly at me and her warmth was as a refreshing shower, a bath in your mother's arms.

"It was then that the great Master came. He had been traveling the other lands, lands very far to the West of the Great River, across the dark and terrible waters. He had been teaching those who had survived the cataclysm. Teaching them how to lead a perfect life. He worked miracles, healed the sick and returned sight to the blind. He asked of them only to stop the bloody sacrifices, not to kill, and to love one another. He also taught them how to build great pyramids, how to grow the best crops and in general forge a great civilization. He had left them, He and his followers and helpers had then traveled eastward across the ocean, as if by magic, and had arrived here."

"Who was he? I've never heard or read anything about a great Master." I interrupted.

She looked startled; I had broken her revery.

"In the land He had been He was called Viracocha, a lean, white man with a beard, not as our people were. Do you know Him now?"

"Viracocha? That was the god of the American Indians, wasn't he?"

"They called Him that, how else would they? They, however, didn't know who in truth He was, and why He had come to teach them the Way after so great a catastrophe. Now let me continue."

I bowed my head, trying to understand her explanations. Intrigue and mystery were adding up, and I would need a long time to make sense of it all.

She continued.

"As I said, the great Master came to this land, and all those who met Him knew in their hearts who He was. They obeyed his orders without a question, and when finally they decided to leave the land of Kemet, He commanded the priests to build a place that would be the sacred repository of all the knowledge they had brought to the land, in case the priests, by some unforetold disaster would lose the teachings. Under the Master's directions they built it, with the power they build it, just as the Master wanted: 480 feet tall with a base side of 755 feet long. The teachers selected the place and placed it according to their calculations. All their knowledge was imprinted there and inside, hidden to the people, what you call books in their repository."

"Books?" I exclaimed. "But... No book has ever been found from that time!"

"Naturally not. Let me continue. Yes, so they left the teachings to the priests and left. They wanted to return to die in the place where their ancient city had lain before the disaster. But for memory's sake, they made a copy of the repository. Of gold they made it and of acacia wood forty-five inches long and one and twenty-seven inches wide and high. And know Andrew, that I am giving the size in your own system, so you understand me well."

Again I nodded. What else was I to do? All this was so incredible I could only listen and try to remember every single detail of what she spoke.

"Inside and outside it was covered by gold, which the Teachers had taught them how to work, so the acacia wood was as enclosed in gold. and they told the priests how to make wheels, as for a carriage and to place them at the bottom of the repository and to make four rings at the sides, so the heavy thing could be lifted using rods of wood."

"But... But, you are describing the Ark, the Ark of the Covenant!" I cried.

"That's how your people first knew of it, yes."

"Do you mean, then, that the Ark was... That it was made by those teachers? Not by the Israelites? Not by Moses?"

"What I am saying is that what you know as the 'Ark' was built under the command of one who was higher than all, the one the teachers obeyed and revered, the Master."

I sat amazed and pondered on the terrible implications of this knowledge, terrible to me and to all the world.

"Yes, it changes everything you thought you knew, but do you want to know more? Or shall I stop here?" She asked with irony.

To tell you my true feelings, at that moment I wanted to stoop my ears, hide my head between my knees and forget all she had said. But curiosity is one of the most compelling forces in our mind.

"Please do continue."

"Last, the priests were ordered to make two images of the teachers, facing each other, just as they had done many times before in memory of their lost city and to place them atop a board covered also in gold, one at each end of the repository."

Was I hearing right? Was she referring to that which we have been calling throughout four thousand years 'cherubim'? I did not want to make a fool of myself and I realized I had expressed too many times my amazement and incredulity, so I asked, matter-of-factly:

"So the images on top the Ark are in fact images of the teachers?"

"Yes."

Sent Back

"They had wings?"

"Yes and no." She replied. "Do you remember what happened to your uncle the first time he died?"

More nodding.

"He was taken then by Horus, but Horus was a man also, didn't he? You met him."

Nodding. I didn't seem able to do anything but.

"That's why, in that sense, were the wings placed; those ancient ones could, on some occasions, fly."

"Ah!" I gasped. Things were beginning, in her tortuous way, to make sense. "So, the teachers were not really human?"

"Human?" She repeated.

"Like us, like me, like the people of the whole world." I explained.

"Like you, yes; like them….No."

At that crucial moment, before I could ask more, the priest approached, and Sekhmet left me to talk to him. I was left alone to digest the last statement. Yes, she had said it, I was like them, like the ancient teachers. Was that what my uncle implied when he spoke of my family?

It all matched, then. The ancient myths, the winged figures in Mexico, Mesopotamia, India; the stories of the flood and the survivors, of ancient sages and teachers, yes, all made sense, but was it true?

If it were, the incredible accuracy of the Great Pyramid would be explained, and many other archaeological issues not yet resolved. Perhaps other groups of teachers had reached Turkey and created Göbekli Tepe; others, perhaps even the sage known as Manu had helped the tribes along the Indus Valley and the Feathered Serpent, Quetzalcoatl had landed in America. My mind reeled at the implications of what the goddess had told me. I could finally put at rest all the doubts.

Suddenly, the concept of the great Master hit me. The great Master? Could he have been…?

I stopped, couldn't bring myself to accept the idea that was overwhelming me. He had come before? At the end of the cataclysm that brought the old civilization down? After the Flood?

Then I laughed idiotically, I laughed so hard I fell to the barge's floor and remained there, holding my stomach, tears of hysteric merriment running down my cheeks.

I had envisioned myself addressing a gathering of specialists and answering when they asked from whence my knowledge "The goddess Sekhmet told me".

I convulsed and gasped for air until someone splashed water on my face. It was one of the goddess' servants and she was looking at me with anger mingled with concern.

"My Lady is most alarmed by your attitude. Please contain yourself."

She whispered at my ear.

I nodded.

"Sorry." I answered. And the woman stood and left me.

Yes, I had understood her and she had understood me.

Sekhmet was standing on the barge's prow, her priest waiting obediently some paces behind her with bowed head and talking in a low voice. And yes, I could understand what he was saying.

Alerted somehow to my presence, he stopped and turned to look at me.

"Please leave us, Ay." Said the goddess. "I must talk to this one."

The man bowed and retreated, not without giving me a look of pure hatred. Why? What had I done to anger him?

"So it's come to you finally?" She asked.

"What do you mean?"

"You are talking and definitely understanding our language." She said.

"Yes, I am, though it seems incomprehensible that I can. I never heard it pronounced, I knew nothing of it and yet, here I am and…"

"Do not worry about it, young friend. I said you would be able to speak it; it was in your mind, though locked up. Now, why were you laughing so hard?"

The image that had previously made me convulse came again to my mind and I had to make a supreme effort not to laugh again.

"Ah, I see." Said Sekhmet. She smiled mischievously. "You should have realized before this."

"Realized? What?"

"Dear child, there is no way you can ever talk about any of this, nor about anything that I discovered to you, to your fellow archaeologists, not even to your teacher friend. The doors are closed, the masters of life and death would never let you open them."

"Then, why am I here, why did you tell me all that before?"

She looked briefly at me and then turned her gaze to the river's bank that passed slowly beside us.

"You see all this?" She asked and her beautiful arm performed a sweeping arch that seemed to enclose all the land. "This is Kemet, the land I love, the people who belong to me. I want them righted; their history completed. When the knowledge was lost, they descended into their former selves, as they were before the teachers. They tried to do what their grandfathers had done, but the knowing of the science was lost and not as the teachers had though it would, by some climatic or earthly catastrophe, but by the agency of men."

"What can I do? You told me I was here to help you but you are a goddess; what can I do you can't?"

She remained silent and as dusk gathered, I looked upwards to the sky.

Sent Back

Never had I seen a sky like this, yes, it was already dark, but the sky was lighted by millions and millions of stars and the Milky Way was a broad highway extending across it. The beauty of it filled me with awe. No wonder the ancients were enthralled by the sky. How many questions they must have asked themselves then. What were those brilliant points of light? Were they gods? Why did they move? And where did they go when they disappeared at the edge of the world? Did the stars die as humans did?

I was enchanted, absorbed in the dark abyss when a hand touched my shoulder. I shuddered, awakening from what seemed to have been a dream and turned. The servant, or priestess who had previously spoken gestured for me to follow.

"The Lady has left. You must sleep now. Come, I'll show you where."

CHAPTER XVI

I woke up in the water, splashing and terrified. I was aware of where I was, and this made be able to grasp hold of the border of the barge. I expected a crocodile to tear me up at any moment, but what I felt was a hand reaching to mine and lifting.

I crawled on deck, spluttering and shivering, not for the cold but for the terror I had suddenly experienced. I was also drenched and terrified I had lost the manuscript or the stone, I checked. Everything was there and luckily the water had not penetrated the protective sheet. I took it out and carefully dried it with a piece of cloth that appeared before me. I didn't look up until I had taken care of that urgent matter and when I did, I saw the priestess who had been taking care of me.

"You fell into the river. That was very silly of you." She said without a trace of emotion.

"I fell?" I almost shrieked. "How may I have done that?"

She shrugged.

"You mean to say that I, asleep, went from the center of the barge to its raised board and from there threw myself into the dangerous river?" I asked with scorn.

She shrugged again.

I looked at my surroundings, everyone was busy attending to their duties, the priest, however, sat on the prow, apparently absorbed in the barge's navigation. It was absurd to suspect him, but I remembered the look of hate he had given me before. Again I wondered why and if it could have been him who pushed me overboard. It made no sense.

"Where is the Lady." I asked, while drying myself with another, much bigger piece of cloth the same woman had now offered.

"She is not here." She replied and looking at me, perhaps checking if I was all right, she left me.

I had dried myself and was considering the need to find a safer place for my two treasures, when Sekhmet came before me.

"I hear you fell into the river. You were lucky."

I almost screamed 'Lucky?'.

"Yes, that my servant was watching and she saw you fall. You could have died."

I looked at her in amazement. Did she believe I could have thrown myself into the river? Even sleepwalkers know well where and what to do, the sense of self-preservation is too well ingrained in our consciousness to permit anything else.

Most probably my expression revealed my thoughts, as she added.

"You are alright now Andrew, but you should be very wary, things are not all as they seem." She continued gazing at me in silence for a while, which I didn't care to interrupt. If she believed that story, there was nothing I could add.

"You have some writings there, I see. It is important you finally read what it says. This time they were saved, perhaps there won't be another. I will leave you now."

How did she? I asked myself, but promptly remembered she had been the dog and it was in the dog's presence I had finally opened the briefcase. However, she was right. I shouldn't postpone reading my uncle's message anymore.

This is what I read.

Hail Lord of Earth, creator of heaven and of all things.

Lord of all, Father of truth; you created men and beasts and herbs.

you made all things above and below.

You who love the sufferer and oppressed, judging the poor and delivering him.

Lord of loving mercy in whose goodness we rejoice,

Thou whose name is hidden.

Thou art the one, maker of all that is, the one; the only one; maker of gods and men; giving food to all.

Hail to the sleepless who watches when all others sleep,

Hail to thee from all creatures from every land, from the height of heaven, from the depth of the sea.

You have made the spirits mediating betwixt men and You, who say welcome to the Father of the fathers.

Our love and reverence to Thee, the unnamed one!

Seven hundred generations have passed since we began counting time, five hundred have passed while in exile. A few know, only a few remember of what was and is no more.

As it says in the Sacred Book, so it was:

... that the sons of God saw the daughters of men, that they were fair; and they took for themselves wives of all whom they chose. and the Lord said, "My Spirit shall not always strive with man, for he also is flesh; yet his days shall be a hundred and twenty years."

Yes, we were giants on the earth in those days; and after that, when the sons of God came unto the daughters of men and they bore children to them, the same became mighty men who were of old, men of renown.

Yes, so it was, because we were the sons of God, we were giants but not in size, though we were tall of five cubits, or as we now know it, as tall as seven feet or more. We were giants for our knowledge and the sciences we mastered.

Our great civilization, our own country, encompassed five million miles, mostly of coast, but our lands had high mountains and deserts, lowlands and highlands and rivers that washed them. and on them we lived happily. The cities were large and our buildings made with terraces full of trees and plants of all types and flowers bloomed lavishly upon them.

The rulers were sages, elected by their character and most had been reluctant to take the rule of office, but the wellbeing of the community was paramount, and they obeyed. And they ruled with justice and compassion.

We had a large fleet which traveled the world north and east, and sometimes on their ships, that were very large and ocean worthy, scientists traveled to learn about other lands, about their flora and fauna, about the medicinal plants they could use and to make friends among other cities.

They mapped the lands of the world, the lands to the east and to the west, the great frozen lands and ocean to the north. They went to other countries, both to the north of ours and to the west, lands where people like us lived also in peace and harmony. Safe was the world that God had created, safe and happy.

The destruction came one day.

Why were we punished so badly? What had we done to anger God? We were chastised with the terrible destruction that has remained forever in the mind of this humanity among which we now live.

When those who studied the skies first saw it, they were intrigued by its strange movement. It did not follow the movement of the stars, nor that of the ten planets, instead treading a different path. So they studied and they watched and soon found the answer, the terrible answer.

The star was aiming at us, at our world. The encounter was inescapable and now the only thing left was to calculate the magnitude of the disaster.

When the scientists came to the rulers, they were sad, overwhelmed by what they had learnt. In a short time the collision would take place and nothing could save us.

In every city, in every town, everywhere; the news were told. Our people learned of our impending doom and were told to do what they could to save themselves.

Some lands were able to build subterranean cities, where their population could hide, hoping they would be saved. Others created huge megalithic cities at the top of the mountains, where they hoped the ocean

Sent Back

would not reach after the impact.

They had time for this, because they had the technology to create that has been lost since then, a technology unimagined by today's science. They also built strange monoliths, and carvings and statues, hoping by igniting the survivors' curiosity, one day they would learn what had happened to their doomed ancestors. Some of those megaliths had carvings, relating about our civilization and the impending cataclysm, so future generations could know.

We had been well trained, no panic ensued, those who could traveled to the mountains and found refuge in the megalithic cities, others hid in the deep caves, or wherever they thought would be safe. But there were those who, unaware of our peril, still sailed the oceans.

Ships were sent to find them and many other people from the lands they were visiting tried to board them, believing they would be safe upon the ocean waters.

And one day, the star was upon us, traveling at such a tremendous speed it was like a ray of lightning, it appeared and disappeared over the horizon, to be followed by the most horrendous noise ever heard by living men.

It all ended. The sky burned with unquenchable fires and people gasped for air, a thin mist began to fall, and it burned the skin and the hair fell, and the nails. People lost their sight and wandered aimlessly for the few days they remained alive.

The seas took over and wave after wave washed up the land. No building was safe, no city was left as we, ill-advised and believing ourselves safe from any danger, had built our cities on the oceans' coasts.

We, who were on the ships, saw the waves, waves as high as mountains, and we knew we would be crushed by them. Somehow, we weren't, we couldn't explain it.

We knew not then the meteorite was followed by several others. We didn't know that due to the impacts, the lands would move, slipping over the molten center, and lands to the east would move to south, lands in the equator would move to the poles. Earth crust had become unhooked, and the lands moved over it as a ship on the seas.

It was only when we reached land that we saw changes in the skies not explicable even by the changes in latitude we suspected we were in.

Over the waters floated the debris of what had been and the waters were hot and deadly. Poisoned was the water, as was the air. Poisoned was what remained of the land and now the mountains erupted in fire and threw out molten stone. The land quivered and shook, all the world was in turmoil and thus it was for months.

How did some survive? Had God taken compassion of those who lived? Or was living in this moment the worst punishment.

But some did, those who had been far in the south ocean, where the killer cloud had not reached. They had survived in the ships, hiding behind closed doors and windows, leaving the ships to their fate while they waited below decks and trembled. Some survived in the underground cities, a few at the tops of mountains, where the rows of megalithic walls had fought the waves and the terrible earthquakes caused by the continents' displacement.

When they came out, when the atmosphere cleaned a little and they could breeze the outside air, they looked upon an agitated sea, where long waves of deep slopes flowed up and down.

Famished, terrified, horror stricken, the ocean farers set toward their ports, to the cities where they lived. They reached the places, but the cities were not there, the ports were gone and over the land they had cherished a mountain of ice loomed, higher than any mountain there before.

Overwhelmed, many wanted to give up, to end it all at that moment. They had lost their families, their friends, their fellow citizens, how could they now live, bereft?

But others praised the Lord and gave thanks for their deliverance and set out to find other lands, searching, searching for a remnant of their now seemingly lost civilization.

They found nothing. They were alone.

On one of such ships came our ancestor, a sage of great knowledge. He, too, had lost everything as his family had stayed at home. As the rest in the ship, they were crazed with pain and didn't care to steer here or there.

The ocean currents, however, had been destabilized and new ones created. One day, when they came out of their cabins, where they had locked themselves in their despondency, one day, I say, they saw land surrounding them.

It was a land unknown to them. To the south and for as far as they could see a sea of green extended. Plants not suffocated by the fire flourished in this sea and they felt their hearts lifting. To their left, to the north, a barren land, still smoking, impossible to tread.

Their ships could not navigate the sea of green, as they had found it was of a shallow depth, but they followed it, traveling on the ocean waters until they found land much farther to the east. There they landed because these lands had been forgiven, they had been protected and though barren and dry, were not smoking.

Three ships had come together, but one of them did not settle, one continued and left the others behind. We never again heard from them., but we landed and traveled searching for the coast of the shallow sea, the sea we called 'Sea of Reeds' and it was there we found them, the primitive ones, the little brothers and sisters who had been miraculously saved.

They had no cities, no science, no knowledge. They walked the land, killing animals to eat, gathering fruits and roots. Later we learned they had

Sent Back

come from the far south, because they had seen the meteor and wanted to find it to make arrowheads, lances and other things with it, as they had previously done with what they called 'sky stones'. They couldn't have known that 'sky stone' had brought about the destruction of the greatest civilization on Earth and the death of millions of our people. They couldn't have known that they could never reach the place where it had landed, because it was across oceans, buried deep inside the land.

They received us with fear and awe and called us gods, but we were welcomed at the end and lived with them. We settled, those who had come in those two ships and created a town where we recreated what we could of our destroyed lives.

Suddenly, a shadow fell over me and lifting my head saw, leaning toward me, the ominous face of the priest. He spoke, but in my betuddled state, aroused from reading something that seemed unbelievable, I couldn't understand his words.

I saw, however, that he was becoming even more irritated.

"Stand! Stand you fool and bow before the High Priest!" Whispered a feminine voice, the one of her who had been in charge of me.

I obeyed, though I hardly knew why I should, but I knew, somehow, that Sekhmet was not there to protect me and I should be careful with this Ay.

In my mind I heard his words, as an echo.

"Know you will pay, miserable worm, for what your family did to my land and to me. The goddess will not always protect you and then, you will rue the day!"

He gave me another look of pure hate and turned his back on me, shouting orders to the rowers.

A shiver ran along my back, here was an enemy to recon with, even though I had no idea for the reason for his hate. Maybe there was something in the manuscript that could answer my question, so, impelled by self-preservation, I returned to my reading making sure my back was well protected and everyone was within sight.

My eyes ran down the document, skipping long lines full of descriptions of the lives the survivors led. I would read those later but now I was searching, searching for explanations

INTERMEZZO

She stood beside the river, watching from a distance the mountain-like constructions that were then very new and shone with bright light reflected from the white limestone casing stones. Sekhmet was troubled and from her chest escaped a deep sigh. Would she be able to complete her plans? She knew she was going against the interdiction. No god ever had been allowed to change the future, no, not even the great Ra, and yet, this is what she wanted, this was the reason she had gone through all the trouble of finding the young man and bringing him to Kemet. Was she wrong?

Sekhmet felt a presence behind her and turning was blinded by a light so strong, so vibrant she could hardly stand before it. What was this? Ra had never been so bright!

"Before Me, none was. When you are all gone, I Am!" She heard a voice like thunder proclaim and she, the mighty goddess Sekhmet fell to the ground, stretched flat before the Great Creator.

"Beware, goddess, because the people I called mine when they lived in this land will not be hurt! Much in this world depends on the accepted truths and you are nobody to change what I ordained! Your existence has been allowed only because through you, these people will grow and be prepared for My coming. You are all like fleas in My universes, beware I don't squash you as such!"

The voice stopped, the sun-like light grew dim and was extinguished while the goddess shook in uncontrollable terror.

CHAPTER XVII

I awoke suddenly, wondering at the noise I seemed to have heard and realized it was a cacophony of bird songs; birds singing to the rising sun, celebrating the beginning of a new day; birds in such a large quantity that, when they rose in flight, they covered the whole sky.

The air was humid and fresh; somehow, I didn't think I was floating on the river barge, in fact, I realized I had been sleeping on some rough mats haphazardly spread on a rocky, sandy beach.

I sat up, startled. Where was I? Where was the large barge and the goddess' servants? Where Sekhmet and the priest?

I searched for uncle's last will, but it was gone, the stone, however, remained well hidden. The last will! Gone! And I hadn't finished reading it, I was only halfway when I had fallen strangely asleep. I now remembered it all. Sekhmet had disappeared and I had felt suddenly very sleepy.

I remembered also the venomous look the priest had shot at me. This must be his doing! And where was I now? What was this place?

I stood and looked around. Before me, an immense stretch of water extended to the horizon, green and blue. Then my eyes focused and I saw the sea or lake was full of reeds, that was what gave it that green soothing color. Millions of birds floated, flew, swam among the reeds in this virgin land, but far away along the coast I could see smoke rising. Probably there was a settlement there, people who would mayhap help me.

I took the stone out of my pocket. Strange how it had followed me through all this time-traveling. I had it in the palm of my hand when it was hit by a peculiar ray of the sun. I know this is going to sound pretty amazing, but I am telling you it did happen. As soon as the sun hit the stone, above it an image appeared like a hologram, projected in the air. It took me some minutes to understand what I was seeing, so amazed was I of this new development. A map, really a map was being cast by the stone, and it didn't take me much time to understand I was looking at the northern coast of Africa, but a coast much different than it is usually depicted in our maps. I could identify it because of the River Nile and its characteristic delta, also by the Red Sea position. But that was all similarity, as instead of the Sahara, there was a very large lake, perhaps a sea.

Yes, this was the sea by which shore I had wakened, the Sea of Reeds, a sea that had disappeared thousands of years before my time. How could this stone reflect it? Something like this was not even possible by the most modern technology of my time. Had my professor known? Was this the reason for all the mystery in giving it to me? I really doubted that.

I felt very thirsty and had a terrible headache, perhaps the priest had drugged me. Then I saw, by my side, a jug carefully stoppered and a small bundle. Taking the jug and pulling out the stoop, I poured some of the liquid on my hand, carefully sniffing and then tasting it. It was beer, or what passed as beer in that time and didn't seem drugged. I took a large sip and waited. When nothing untoward happened, I drank more and unwrapped the bundle where I saw some flat breads and dried fish.

Apparently, for some strange reason, the priest hadn't wanted me to die of inanition. Weird man.

I ate sparsely, as I didn't know how long I had until finding human habitation. I knew I could not stay there, so I made a large bundle with the mats and the food and throwing it across my shoulders, started toward the place where I saw the smoke, carrying the jug in my hand.

To my right, the sea extended almost without end. I knew I would have many hours to walk before reaching the place from where smoke had risen; and this if I was right and it was a sign of people cooking and not a natural phenomenon.

I walked for long hours, sometimes stopping to put a small morsel of fish wrapped in flat bread in my mouth, or to take a sip of beer. It was during one of these stops when I met the stranger. I had sat on a mound beside the water, reclining on a small date palm to catch at least a bit of shade and protection from the smoldering sun when I saw something strange moving in the water.

At first, I thought it was a hippopotamus, or a crocodile, but soon realized it was a man, a man covered with something that looked more like an armor than cloth.

I shrank back, trying to remain undetected until I could understand if this was to be friend or foe, but I was not counting with the alert senses of the stranger.

The man straightened and came out of the water, walking briskly in my direction. He was tall, much taller than I and well built, very muscular. The hair and beard were of a reddish color, and both were long, so the only visible part of his face were his eyes, of steely gray.

The man approached and with a swift gesture removed what had seemed an armor, placing it carefully on the ground before him.

He peered at me with scrutinizing eyes for a while. None spoke. Then, with a smile that seemed the most welcoming smile I had ever seen, the man bowed.

Sent Back

"Welcome, my brother." Said the man. "I am Arinjay, from the land of Ost."

I couldn't understand how I knew what the man was saying. Was he talking English? Then, when in the world had I come to?

Arinjay peered at me again and bent forward so his face was only inches away from mine.

"This is amazing indeed!" He exclaimed, straightening. "A real miracle!"

I remained silent, not knowing what would be better to answer.

"It is alright, brother." Said Arinjay. "Or maybe I should say son many times removed." He laughed and continued. "They will not believe it, no they won't! But when they see you, ah, then they will have to!"

"I don't understand you, sir." I said. "And forgive me but, how do you know my language?"

"Your language? You mean, how can we talk?"

"No, sir. I mean, how do you know English?"

"English? What's that?" Replied the newcomer.

"English, the language we are talking!" I cried, exasperated.

"Son, we are talking our language, the language of the world that's gone. We are talking Ostish."

I stared in the most bemused way. What was this man saying? Then, like a hammer, it hit me. This was one of the teachers, this was the Sea of Reeds and I had come, by the malefic arts of the priest, several thousand years farther back than when I last saw Sekhmet.

Arinjay was gazing at me, smiling; and I thought that, somehow, he was following all my reasoning.

"You are understanding now, I see; though I can't understand why this seems so strange to you. Was not this your intent in 'traveling'?"

He said the last word 'traveling' as if it meant something different from what I knew.

"My being here is, was, not my wish, though now I am really thrilled to. I believe a priest from your future sent me to the here and now." I explained.

"Please tell me more." Requested Arinjay.

"It is a very long story and there will be many things to explain to you. Do you live around here? Is there a town, a city, nearby?"

The man laughed.

"No, there is no city, nor town. All was lost in the cataclysm." He added, suddenly serious, almost sad. "But I know what you want. Come, let's walk and go to where my brothers and sisters live. It is not what you would call a town, but we have many comforts and water and food. Come!"

He picked up the armor, I couldn't give it any other name and walked at a brisk pace.

"What is that?" I asked, pointing.

"This?" He quoted. "It is what we use to swim underwater. Don't you have them? Though I know not whence you come, everyone near the sea uses it."

"It lets you breath underwater?" I asked. "Then, yes, yes we have them in the place where I came from. I didn't know you could have it, though."

"And why is that? Naturally we do." He shrugged and dismissing my doubts with a wave of his hand, plowed ahead.

After an hour or so, we reached a place full of large mounds, all covered by lush vegetation. Here and there, on the mound slopes, the reflection of light on glass brightened the place. But surely there was no glass in this time, maybe ten thousand years before Christ or perhaps more!

Arinjay directed his steps to one mound and it was then I realized the mounds were houses, or better perhaps, huts.

Arinjay shoved apart a slab of wood and went inside, stooping to pass under the low threshold. I followed.

The room was spacious and high. I had thought we would have to crouch, but the ceiling seemed to be a good two feet higher than Arinjay's head. The walls were not of earth, but of carefully set stones which reminded me of Puma Punku in Bolivia or Sacsayhuamán in Peru, though not as large as those. The floor was also stone, and nicely carved chairs and benches stood against the wall.

Arinjay told me to sit and putting my bundle on a table, he went into another room from where he returned with pottery cups, dishes, food and water.

"Here, eat some and wait for me, I am going to call my brothers and sisters to come and meet you. It will be only a moment." He said, exiting the room.

I took the cups and dishes and examined them. They were well made, smooth and decorated. I saw some had been glazed with some material that added colors to the pot. The material, the perfect form, the colors and glazing did not agree with the time I suspected I was in.

I was still pondering when I heard voices and soon the entrance was darkened by several men following my new acquaintance.

"Here he is!" Exclaimed Arinjay, as a magician showing the rabbit he pulled from the hat.

The men, as tall as Arinjay but with different coloring, stared at me. I could feel the hundreds of questions in their minds and waited with some trepidation for them to start. The group parted, however, making an opening for the oldest man I had ever seen. True, his old age was visible, but his whole appearance was of a strong man, perhaps still in the middle of his life, I knew intuitively, however, that he was well over one hundred

Sent Back

years old.

The man approached me, eyeing me with curiosity.

"I am Yudhishtra, but they call me Yud." He said.

I bowed in acknowledgment and answered with my name, while I stood from the chair I had been sitting on.

"That is an unfamiliar name." He commented. "But by what Arinjay tells us, that's not the only intriguing thing about you. He said you wanted to tell us how you came to us?"

"Yes, venerable sir." I replied and all there laughed, commenting on the venerable in different voices.

"I am old, yes, but from that to be venerable…" Added the man with a wink. "Alright, tell us!" He added.

They all sat on the floor, with the great ease born of habit. A few women had entered now, and they also sat there, among the men.

"It's much to explain and I don't know if all would be comprehensible to you. You see, I believe I come from ten or twelve thousand years into the future."

I heard the murmur of awe and the swift silence at a word from Yudhishtra.

"Twelve thousand years!" He exclaimed, addressing me. "Are you sure, my son? It seems too many for 'traveling'." Here was the word again with its weird connotation. He became silent and I got the distinct idea there was something he didn't want to say.

"I think I am correct, sir." I thought about what we knew of the Sea of Reeds in my time; it had not existed for thousands of years. In its place a terrible desert remained.

"I am not confused about the time from which I come from," I explained. "And I suppose I am right about the time this is, but I am very confused about who you are."

"If you really don't know who we are, that is very bad news for us. I see you want to know more. About us, all will be explained in a while; from you there are millions of questions we would like to ask. Would you be willing to let me examine you?"

I shivered, imagining terrible tests.

"No, nothing terrible or hurtful." Said the ancient. "I just want you to let me see inside your mind."

I gazed at him, bemusedly, and not understanding.

"I can see your thoughts; I can read your memories." Explained Yudhishtra and I knew again he wondered about my ignorance. "It does no damage to you, no hurt at all, but if it's true more than ten thousand years have elapsed, I will be able to see what you know in a fraction of the time you would need to explain it and more completely, too."

"Can you really do that?" I asked.

The man nodded.

"I see much has been lost, yes." He commented as to himself. "Yes Andrew, we can do it, but I am the most experienced among my people."

"If you say it will be alright and no damage done…"

"None whatsoever." He said.

"Oh, alright." I answered with resignation, a new thing to experience.

"Come, let's seat here." He said and we went farther away into the room, leaving the others talking in low voices.

"It is true. He comes from the far future."

The 'reading' had finished. It had taken more than an hour and somehow, I had sensed the impatience of the other men and women, and the ancient's awe.

"Awful, terrible things have happened in this world, events so horrible I dread to tell you, but you all must know."

He went toward where the others waited, and they made a circle around him. They again sat on the ground, an arm's length from Yudhishtra and now they extended their right arm, the hand touching the ancient's shoulder.

Silence descended while I gazed in awe at the marvelous thing men had always desired without getting, mind reading, telepathy.

The process was faster now, maybe extricating my thoughts from all the historical facts had taken more time, but it was only half an hour or so when their contact with the ancient was finished and they stood, turning to look at me.

"Is what you hold in your mind, true? Is it not a fiction?" Said Arinjay.

"To the best of my knowledge, all you saw there happened, though maybe a great part of it, what I learned from the past and never experienced could be different to what really occurred." I replied, nodding and somehow ashamed. Ashamed for what we had done.

"It is truly terrible. Not even in the cusp of our civilization did we damage the world as you have done. Never did we commit genocide or extinguish the millions of other species that coexisted with us." Yudhishtra commented. "And yet, we were thoroughly punished. I wonder."

I could see how the knowledge had affected him. The other ones present, after looking at me in a way I could not understand, left the place, muttering among themselves. Only Yudhishtra and Arinjay remained with me.

"We have learned much from you, and it is not a happy knowledge, but I see you, too, have many questions. What is it that intrigues you so?" Asked Arinjay.

"Oh, so many things!" I exclaimed. "Who are you? From where do you come? How can you read my mind, or in fact each other's mind? Why are you here?" Arinjay stopped me, raising a hand. He smiled.

"I see the story of the cataclysm has been shrouded in the cloth of myth, though some of it remains in your sacred books. Ours was a great civilization destroyed by a meteor impact and its consequences. Only a small group of us survived. The Creator punished, some with death, others with survival." He sighed and his eyes became clouded. "We lost everything, we had lost even hope of life when we found this place, not so badly scorched by the meteor's conflagration."

"I read something about it in my granduncle's will." I said. "But where was this land of yours? Is there anything you can tell me that would help me realize from where you came?"

"Ours was a huge continent; it covered more than forty-three million square stadia." He stopped, and I could see he was trying to say that using my system of measurement.

"I don't know if this is correct, if what I saw in your mind will help." He looked doubtful. "Maybe I am wrong but I think in your system of measurement this will be more than five million square miles. This land of ours lay in the southern hemisphere, some hundreds of stadia to the south of Kumari Kandam."

I didn't recall that place, though the name seemed familiar and thought he was perhaps referring to Australia, but again their strange ability to see my mind allowed him to correct my thoughts.

"No, Andrew, no." Said Yudhishtra "If what I saw in your mind is correct, I am talking about the land you now call Antarctica. Tomorrow, I could show you some maps that were saved from the disaster, and you will see."

He stopped, perhaps remembering, perhaps organizing his mind on what to tell me.

"For hundreds of years we had dwelt there, our origins lost in the many eons that had passed. A few generations before my time, a change began. Our ancestors didn't pay much attention to it, perhaps thinking it was just a slight change in the world's temperature. It was not, however. For decades the ice to the south of our cities had been increasing, never melting even when summer came. Soon there were mountains of ice, and they saw how it was encroaching in our otherwise fertile lands. We didn't understand, then, that this was heralding the beginning of our end, but some started emigrating then, going to the lands to the north, those we knew were free of ice."

Now this was something I could have never imagined, and I thought, if by any miracle I could tell my contemporaries, I would be laughed at, and considered crazy.

"My uncle never explained, not even in his testament, which I seem to have lost." I said.

"Yes, we saw it in your mind, and we realize he, too, was one of us. As are you." Arinjay commented, nodding.

It came as a shock, though the goddess had already said that; in truth I hadn't believed her. I hadn't even believed Granuncle when he had said it in his deathbed.

"But you have lost much in the passing of generations. I see your scientists still ponder about the origins of civilization in the southern hemisphere. It is amazing you still master our language, but I see you knew nothing of mind sharing and most probably you know not how to fly."

"My uncle tried to tell me, perhaps to teach me, but I was too stubborn, too immersed in what I though science." I explained. "Sekhmet was able to somehow help me to regain the languages I had lost, but nothing else."

"You talk about Sekhmet, is that the goddess who took you to what would have been four thousand years before your own time?"

"Yes." I said, nodding.

"But why? Why did she do that?" Insisted Yudhishtra.

"If I understood correctly, something your people will do in the future to preserve your knowledge was stolen, she wanted to right the wrong."

"Ah, yes, what you call the Ark. The Ark… of the Covenant was it?" Said the old man.

"Yes. The Ark is considered a sacred object, where the pact with God was kept, with the books of the Law. It was a pact between the Israelites and Yahve."

They looked at me with uncomprehending eyes.

"Explain!"

"Do you believe in God?" I asked instead.

"God?"

"A supreme being, Creator of the Universe, of all that exists."

"Ah, naturally, yes." Replied Yudhishtra while Arinjay nodded.

The answer amazed me, but I continued.

"It is said in our sacred book that God commanded the Israelites to build the Ark and then the books of the Covenant were kept there. But Sekhmet told me it had been made by you, or your people and in fact it belonged to the 'remetch en Kermet' the people of the Black Land, what we now know as Egypt."

Arinjay and Yudhishtra remained silent. I could see how they were pondering on this.

"He works in inscrutable ways." Said the older man, bowing his head.

I jumped in hearing words so casually said in my time.

"What amazes you so?" He asked.

"Those words, that phrase, we use it, just like that. It sounded weird coming from you and here."

Sent Back

"Though some in our world rebelled against Him, the majority didn't and, those who survived..." He paused. "Yes, we who survived worshipped Him always, at least the ones I know were saved. What was His objective? Why were we left when so many, oh so many, were taken? I don't know, I can't explain it, but perhaps we were saved for this, to fulfill this destiny, not for us, but for the world. I am tired. I am very tired and distraught for all I have heard from you. I will leave you now, stay here with Arinjay, he will answer all your questions and perhaps you can tell him more we didn't gather in the mind reading."

He stood and walked to the door. His more than a hundred years seemed to have fallen on him suddenly and he looked very old, yes, and very sad.

Early next day I woke up. At first I didn't understand where I was, but soon the impact of my situation hit me and I sat up with a jump.

I looked around with eyes still somewhat veiled by sleep. The room I was in couldn't correspond to the place and time I knew I was in. The walls were made of crafted stone, some with carvings of birds, fishes, and strange figures I could not identify; the roof, though made of wooden beams had the same solid, artistic look. A window let in the light and at first I didn't realize, as my previous life experiences told me to accept it matter-of-factly, the light that came in through the glass was tinted a greenish-blue color and it was only after some seconds I saw what it was and approached it.

The window was made by fragments of glass, some the size of my hand, others slightly smaller. How could these people have glass? However, when I looked closer, I understood. Those were the remnants of a meteorite impact or similar conflagration that had melted and fused the sand of the desert thousands of years ago. Probably these people, these ancients had found them and immediately understood how they could be used. If every house had it, the amount found would have been enormous. I shook my head, which seemed ready to burst with so many changes to my previous paradigm.

"Is it all well with you, friend?" Said a voice behind me.

Turning with a start, I saw Arinjay, a slightly mocking smile on his lips.

"Oh, good morning, Arinjay!" I replied. "Yes, all is well, though I find so many unexpected things in this world my brain sometimes refuses to accept them. This glass, for example, how come you to have it, or to use it?"

"I imagine you already know it was made by a meteorite impact, a long time ago?"

"Yes, I surmised so." I replied.

"Well, when we found it in one of our expeditions down south, we immediately realized how we could use it to improve our homes' conditions."

I nodded.

"Do you have something similar in your time?" He enquired.

"Yes, but thinner and more elaborate. It is produced in factories." I answered.

"I would love to see it." He replied. "Perhaps you can show me some time. Now, however, it's time to break your fast." He said, beckoning me to follow.

I did and we entered another room, where a large wooden table was set with pots and crockery full of something with an appetizing meal. A shy woman who had been placing slices of what I imagined was bread, retreated to a corner, trying to hide.

Arinjay laughed.

"This is my wife." He explained, placing an arm around her shoulders, forcing her out of hiding. "She is shy and fearful of you." He added.

The woman turned to him and slapped his hand.

"I am not afraid." She countered and I could see the language she spoke was not her own.

Arinjay somehow understood my unuttered question.

"Ira is not from my people but belongs to those who lived here before we came. My first wife died in the cataclysm." He explained and his face turned sad for an instant. "But that is not important now. She accepted me and now I am a married man."

Again, she slapped his hand and turned to go away.

"Where are you going?" He asked.

"Food is still cooking! You want it burnt?" She replied with a shrug and left.

"She's a good woman, but sometimes it is difficult." He whispered. "It is difficult to understand each other even when you come from the same place and time, even if you have experienced similar situations. Imagine understanding someone from totally different conditions and upbringing, you know?"

I nodded.

"Come, let's eat." He added, sitting and pointing to a chair beside him. "It is good food, you'll enjoy it."

I obeyed. The meal was very good, the seasoning excellent, though I couldn't identify the spices used. Halfway into the meal I felt better, my spirits were uplifted with a sense of hope and satisfaction. I even looked forward to this adventure, and the inexplicable fear I had been feeling disappeared, washed away.

Arinjay laughed.

"You see how a good meal makes you see life with different eyes, eh?"

"Yes, this meal is really fabulous. What, how…?"

Sent Back

"Ira's people have shown us substances, some from plants, others from animals, an even from the earth, stones and the like, that add taste to food and sometimes have another special effect." He looked at me with squinting eyes. "They are mood changers." He added, smiling.

"Drugs!" I cried, pushing away from the table.

He was startled by my reaction.

"What is wrong? What is that 'drug' word that seems to bring fear and disgust to you?" He asked and I could tell he was not happy.

"I am sorry." I explained, contrite. "You see, in my world some people use these mood changers, we call them drugs. These people get in too deep, cannot live without them, become addicted and lose control of their lives. Others exploit them, charging amazing prizes for the drug those others become addicted to. They live only for the drug and waste their lives. I have never been one for it." I explained. My whole attitude expressing my disgust.

"I see." He muttered. "You have lost that, too."

"What? What have we lost?" I asked, still upset.

"Self-control and awareness."

"What?"

"The world, perhaps I should say God, gave us these substances to help us through life. They were never meant to be abused, but used sparsely and never as an escapism, an alienation from life's reality. They fulfill another objective, as some of them can let you pass to another level of awareness where you become closer to the divine. In fact, there are some in Ira's family who are called 'sangoma', and they are quite expert on traveling to the other dimension, if you could call it that. Through the use of some of these 'drugs', as you call them, they receive advise on coming dangers, or teachings for the tribe. I am sorry for your world, my friend." He concluded, commiseration in his eyes and sadness.

"So, you know how to handle these… these mood changers?"

"Definitely. These are not the same as the ones we had in our city, or its sister cities, but I believe they have the same active substances. They are not dangerous Andrew, much less in the small amount we use. Relax!"

I sighed; how many things had gone wrong in our so-called advanced civilization.

"You mean to tell me there has been not one to abuse it? To become dependent on them?"

Arinjay pondered, stroking his beard.

"I don't think so, not to my knowledge, but maybe among Ira's people it has happened. Though I know their sages teach them well." He said and continued. "Now, won't you finish your meal?"

"I will, sorry for my reaction and it's a very good meal, let me tell you."

"I know." He answered, laughing.

Ira came to join us then, with something that appeared to be a pot of coffee or something that smelled similarly. She poured some in a small cup and offered it with a slight bow.

I accepted and brought it to my lips, smelling carefully. It was definitely coffee! How could they have coffee in this place! In this time?

"It is coffee!" I exclaimed. "But how?"

"We call it 'qahwah' and it is brought from a place much to the southeast of where we live. It is a red fruit that grows on bushes, but once it is dried, toasted and grounded we use it to brew this beverage. It is very uplifting, so we also use the name 'quwwa' meaning energy or power giving."

"Yes, yes we drink it, we drink a lot of it, but I never knew it was used from such an early date." I said and sipped carefully. It had a new nutty flavor, not disagreeable at all and I enjoyed the beloved drink, so much missed during the previous days.

The meal finished, Arinjay showed me where I could go to wash and do other particulars. The small room, added to the outside of the house, had a stone floor and walls, with a constant stream of water running from a pipe, midway the wall, into a puddle. I realized I could use it to wash and more to the side there was what seemed a privy. It amazed me how these people, in such old and primitive times were so advanced.

I returned to meet Arinjay at the house's entrance.

"You are ready? Everything satisfactory?"

"Yes, yes, thank you. Your bathroom is magnificent."

"Bathroom?" He uttered the strange word in doubt.

"Yes, there, where I just was. How do you call it?"

"Oh, the hygienic. I see. Yes, we like it to be comfortable. Now come, the ancients want to talk to you again."

I felt a shiver of apprehension. More questioning and now I knew how it was done, I realized I would be very uncomfortable answering about our civilization's wrongdoings.

It had been a long morning, long and sad. I was questioned through and through by the ancients and facts that had escaped me, submerged in my subconscious, came out, elicited by their mental powers.

I felt depleted and ashamed. The damage we had done in our so-called advanced civilization corresponded more to savages than what we called ourselves: 'civilized'. Hah, if I ever returned to my times, I would have much to tell and face.

I was pondering on the effect my new knowledge could have on my own civilization when Arinjay, who had remained with the sages after they had finished with me, came out and spoke.

Sent Back

"I see you are deflated and pessimistic." He said. "I am sorry, but there is nothing you can do about it. Not even He who came to your world was able to change people, even though it is such an amazing happening I cannot understand how your civilization has continued the evil ways. If He had come to us…But He did, though not to us…" He left the phrase unfinished, and I understood how he wished it had happened within his time.

"He changed many people, even now, I mean in my time, millions follow Him." I said, trying to present a better image of my world than I had shown them.

"His name, His teachings were used to cause more death and suffering anyone could envision. How could God tolerate this?"

"I don't know, everyone asks the same question. I have no answer to give you." I replied, more saddened now than I had been after questioning.

Arinjay looked at me, his appraising eyes realizing my state of mind.

"Let us leave that for now, my poor friend and let's talk about things you want to learn from us. There are many, I can see that."

"I would like that so much!" I exclaimed. "I have so much to ask you!"

"Alright, let us go to the coast, there's a place there I like. Come,"

We walked and all around the village I could see people working, talking and children playing. All in all a happy community.

"Arinjay, I have to know."

"Yes?"

"I took it as normal, because it is in my world, in my time, but you have light! You have light in all your houses, artificial light! How is that possible? I thought electricity was a very recent development, from our nineteenth or twentieth century?"

He stopped and he seemed very amazed.

"You mean to say you have only recently started to use the power?"

"The electric power you mean, yes, only during the last two hundred years or so." I answered.

"But how could people live before? How did they work, I mean, you told me you had factories? What did they use then?"

"What we study of history, first our ancestors used burning wood, and candles, or oil; that at the earlier times. Centuries after, when the industrial revolution we started using power obtained by the movement of water, like in watermills, or by vapor produced by burning of coal or other fossil fuels. Presently we use gas oil, petroleum." I stopped because I could see he understood not.

"Deep under the earth there are pockets, very large pockets of a liquid that was originated millions of years ago, produced by dead organisms that underwent a process of very high heating and pressure. When it is burnt it produces great amounts of energy."

"And why did you need that?"

"Why, for everything! To power the cars, I mean our vehicles of transportation, or the machines in the factories and naturally so the machines that produce electricity for all could work."

"You pulled that from underground? But…"

"But what?" I insisted.

"There is energy all around us, right here where we are!"

"Well, yes, I know energy is all around us, it's the frequency of it that differentiates matter, but to be able to channel it into light, that's another thing."

"I cannot explain how it is done Andrew." Said Arinjay. "Sadly, the manner of how it's done was lost with our civilization. We still have a basic knowledge and the instruments we inherited from our fathers and those that were in the ships that were saved. Those are the ones we use to power our village. You are welcome to see them if you think that could help your world somehow."

"I very much doubt both my abilities to understand and the possibility of helping my civilization. There was a guy, someone named Tesla, who I think tried to do it, but those who wanted to get rich exploiting the private use of energy hindered his project, it is said they even killed him. It is not easy in my world to fight against what we call 'the powers that be'; those in control of everything."

He nodded.

"Yes, I seem to understand how all works in that future time. But now I remember about something our people have been working on for some time now!"

"What?"

Arinjay was all exited, I could see he could barely contain himself.

"We have to go back to the ancients; I have to tell them!"

He exclaimed and, as a schoolchild he got hold of my hand and forced me to run back to the village.

When we arrived, most villagers were gathered in the huge room where I had been questioned. What the meeting was about, I never knew, because just entering, Arinjay exclaimed with loud voice:

"I have the most unexpected news to share with you!"

Everyone gathered turned to look at us and Yudhishtra who seemed to be the leader, gestured to Arinjay to come beside him.

"What have you learnt, my dear friend?" He said.

Arinjay breathed deeply, trying to settle himself. After some minutes, he began.

"Those who were present when you queried our visitor remember the images. Far to the East, in the borders of the black river, we saw huge buildings, incredibly tall and brilliant." He looked around, question in his eyes.

Many nodded, yes, they remembered those images.

"And now I want you to force your memories back, back to when we still lived in our own cities." He looked at them, expectantly.

"Don't you see?" He almost cried. "Don't you see them? They are almost the same! That is how they did it! We can do it, too. We can do it for them!"

I had no idea of what he was talking about, or which were the buildings he referred to. The audience, however, was electrified and they all talked simultaneously causing such a turmoil it sounded like a great fight going on.

Finally, a gong sounded and Yudhishtra was heard, asking for silence.

"Will you all, please, calm down!" He said, in a voice louder and sterner than I had ever heard from him. "This is a great discovery, friend Arinjay, and it needs to be deeply studied and analyzed. But if it's true," he paused. "If it's true, then we tried and failed."

A deep silence covered the room, like a blanket of depression. Nothing hurts more deeply than the knowledge of failure.

"We can still try it!" Said a voice from the back of the room. "Who knows, maybe it will change their future."

Yudhishtra shook his head, looking sad.

"You know that is forbidden." He replied in a voice so low it would not have been heard if the silence had not been so deep.

"But we did it." Countered Arinjay. "They are there, in Andrew's mind!"

"Yes, that is true." Replied Yudhishtra. "Well, maybe… We need to think, yes, because that land is far from here and we don't know it well."

"Yet, we know it is in that direction that this land's energy node lies. We've been using the difference between that one and the one here to create light and power." Arinjay's pleading voice made Andrew smile, it was like a little boy asking for a candy without hope of getting it.

"It is true, it is true." Said many voices in the crowd.

"We should try, Yudhishtra!" Said others.

"As I said, we need to think about this very carefully." Replied the ancient. "And I would need to learn more from Andrew." He added, looking squarely at me. I knew he knew how I disliked that mind probing. I shrugged, if it had to be done, who was I to refuse?

I was so tired after all that had happened that day, that I went to bed as soon as I had eaten. My dreams gave me no surcease, plagued by images of what had happened in the future. Scenes I had seen of war and genocide kept coming up and I believe I tossed and turned all night, as the bed was a right mess when I woke up. I also felt very tired, bone tired, as if I had been running all night.

I sat on the bed and took some water Arinjay had placed nearby, perhaps during the night. I splashed some on my face and neck and that brought me back to the here and now. What will the day bring me? I hopped no more mind reading, it was an extenuating process.

I went to what I insisted on calling bathroom and took a quick bath. I had found clean clothes, like the ones the men of the village used, on a chair in my room and decided to wear them. My own were dirty and barely hanging together. I took the stone from its hiding place, weighing it in my hand and looking at it absentmindedly. Where could I keep it? These robes had no pockets and I refused to leave it lying anywhere.

With it in my hand I went toward the room where we had our meals. Ira was there, but not Arinjay.

"Good morning." I said, bowing.

"Good morning, Andrew. Are you looking for Arinjay?" She said.

"Yes, I had some questions for him."

"He went early to a meeting with the ancients, told me he would be back before the noon meal." She stopped and looked curiously at the stone. "What is that?" She asked, pointing.

"Something I brought from my world." I said and offered it to her.

"It is beautiful, such color!" She said, admiring it. "And what is that, inside?"

"I really do not know, Ira. It is a mystery to me. I wanted to see Arinjay about it and because I do not know where to keep it. These clothes don't have pockets."

She didn't understand the word, I am sure, but understood the meaning because she turned and went to another room, asking me to wait.

"Here, you can put it here. It is strong enough to keep it safe." She explained, returning and handing me something like a messenger bag, made of a soft animal skin.

"This is perfect!" I exclaimed. "Thank you, Ira."

"For nothing." She smiled. "Do you want something to break your fast?"

"Oh, yes." I replied. "If it's not too much trouble, I am famished."

"No trouble, Arinjay already had his meal and I was going to eat mine. We'll eat together."

We ate in silence, obviously Ira was not one of those talkative women I used to know, so I had time to savor the rich flavor of the meal while wondering about how I could return to my time and place.

Not that I didn't like it there, nothing could be further than that. I loved life here and the people I was meeting, more enjoyable was all I was learning about a past so distant from my time and one of which we knew practically nothing. However, my time seemed to pull at me.

I had remained sitting at the table while Ira cleaned up and began cooking for the midday meal. I could hear her in the kitchen, singing a soft song with a peculiar rhythm, it was a sad melody and somehow it brought tears to my eyes. What was the woman singing about? Silly me! I brushed the tears away and opened my eyes to see Arinjay staring at me.

"Are you alright?" He asked.

"Yes, oh yes!" I exclaimed, laughing and bashful at the same time. "It's that song Ira was singing, somehow it made me sad."

"Hmm." He uttered and sat on the chair across the table. "It is a song about our loss, a song of remembrance and sadness. I am sure it resonates in your genes somehow."

We sat in silence for a while; he, maybe remembering his lost world and family; I, wondering on how something like that could still be locked in my genes.

"You were out early, today." I said after some time, a question hidden in my statement.

"Yes, we were discussing about the building of the pyramid and all you have told us about it... them." He explained.

"Oh, those were the buildings you were referring to?"

"Yes, they are identical to the ones we used to have in some places of our cities."

The answer provoked more questions than it had meant to, but I was very interested in the result. I was sure now that the ancient pyramids had been built by these people or maybe their near descendants. The conspiracy theory buffs were right in this.

"Did you come to an agreement? Are you going to build them?"

"It is still being considered. You see, we would have to move to the river, abandon all this." He enclosed the village with a movement of his arm. "We are not eager to go voyaging again, in search of another place to call home. You see, one gets tired of leaving their homes again and again."

I gave him a quick look. Didn't they know this land, even this sea with its rivers, would all turn into desert?

"What is it?" He asked, sensing my thoughts.

"Well, Arinjay, I don't know if... I mean..."

"Please tell me what you know, friend." He pleaded.

"You see, Arinjay, I am not sure when it happens, if it's going to be during your lifetime or not, but..."

"Yes...?"

"We know all this became a desert, a huge desert extending through all the north of this continent. No one would be able to live here, only some nomad tribes. The only place that will be able to house civilization is precisely the one on the banks of the river."

He gazed at me with wonder and distrust.

"Is this true? How can it be?" He stood up and went to look out through the window. "The sea there, the many rivers that flow into it." He pointed. "Is all going to disappear? Why?"

"I think it is because the weather, the climate changes and the rains that have been falling regularly will stop, the sea will dry up. I believe it has to do with periodic cycles of the monsoon." I stopped as I realized this word meant nothing to him.

"We call monsoon to a change in the weather, when very strong winds blow from the south bringing torrential rains. Sometimes, the place where monsoon happens changes, and then terrible draughts ensue. I believe that it was one of those changes in the cycle, when the monsoon stopped bringing rain to this land, that it happened. I am sure of it; I have walked this land with my teacher when we were doing archaeological investigations and it is a terrible desert full of bones of animals thousands of years dead."

Though I am sure he knew not this other term, archaeological, he questioned me not. That this fruitful land would turn into desert had apparently overwhelmed him.

"Why didn't you tell us this?" He said and he was angry.

"I thought about it, when I was talking about the time I thought I was in. However, it didn't seem important at the moment, and your people know so many things… I though you knew." I ended.

"We didn't know!" He exclaimed, anger and frustration in face and voice. "We cannot see the future, silly man!"

He walked up and down the room. Ira popped her head out from the kitchen, worry written all over her face.

I shook my head at her, bringing my finger to my lips requesting silence. I knew Arinjay should not be intruded upon now.

"This news changes all." He said, stopping before me. "This changes all. You must come with me and explain it to Yudhishtra. If the land will dry up…"

He didn't finish but I could hear the silent muttering: "A desert? A desert! Oh my!"

CHAPTER XVIII

My hosts had come up with a resolution. Yes, they would move to the banks of the Nile with any tribe that inhabited this region and they were able to convince to move. Yes, they would start working on the great task of building the pyramid. Because they only saw the need to build one, that would be enough to create the difference in energy potential to supply the whole city with what we call electricity.

They were not in a rush, however. I could not tell them precisely when the change would come, they even surmised it would not be a sudden thing. Weather, or climate, rarely changes suddenly unless it results from a cataclysm and I hadn't been able to tell them if a cataclysm had happened, or not.

But I witnessed how the work had already started one day, when following Arinjay into one of the larger habitations, I saw tables covered in documents.

Those of my hosts who had been more related to science before they came to this land had started their calculations. They constantly consulted old maps they had from trips and explorations. Measuring implements and intricate formulas on paper, or what seemed paper, covered the tables. Other instruments of which I couldn't guess the use lay on the maps while the men around argued constantly.

I could see the discussions were about energy points over the land and they had different opinions on how to finetune their instruments to measure them and their location. What were these energy points they were talking about? And then I remembered many years ago, when in the future, I had gone to a place in the United States that was recognized as having maybe these same energy points.

One guide had explained these vortices had different characteristics, some energizing, others calming, but the other guide had said that in some places, the energy form the vortex surges up from within the earth, while in others it does, instead, funnel into the earth, thusly causing different effects in humans and even in animals and plants.

I had never been one to fall easily asleep during an outdoor trip, but it had happened to me then. It had been explained to me latter in the day that

I had been precisely near one of those spots, where the energy was, to use the term they had used: Ying, relaxing; contrary to the Yang, energizing.

Maybe this was what they were talking about, maybe in this continent there were these vortices and that is what had been used for energy.

I went looking for Arinjay and found him in an argument with an old man, though not as old as Yudhishtra and if I understood correctly this was precisely the reason of their argument. I waited for a while, listening.

"It was found a short time before the cataclysm!" The older man was saying and I saw he had been arguing the same thing for a while and was upset. "I am telling you it was found by one of the last expeditions to the north. and I do not think something of that magnitude could have been destroyed, or even affected in any way by the conflagration."

"There were earthquakes, Yamir, and tsunamis, who knows what could have happened to it!" Countered Arinjay. "We cannot base our calculations on something we don't know is there!"

"Our instruments point to a place of power in that direction." Replied the other.

"But we don't know how far, or where!"

I interrupted, guessing I could help.

"I am sorry but, what are you arguing about?"

The two men jumped as if they had been caught doing something bad. Then Arinjay smiled.

"This is Yamir; Yamir, this is Andrew, our guest from the future."

"Yes, yes, I know." Said the other, turning his back to us and leaning over one table, eyes squinting over the maps.

"Arinjay, I don't know what you were talking about, but maybe I can help?" He eyed me with doubt. "Perhaps that thing you want to find is something known by me, by my time?" I added.

Yamir straightened up suddenly, turning to look at me with new interest.

"The youngster is right." He said, in a low mussing voice. "Maybe it is still there, in the future."

"What is it? Tell me and maybe…" I insisted.

"There is a place, far to the west of us where Earth's energies dip and are swallowed, like a throat drinking water. It causes like a vortex of energy. Do you know about anything like this?" Said Yamir.

"I am not sure in this part of the world, but I remember that, in a continent that lies very far to the west and across a large ocean where I once went that something like this happens. They also called it vortex and the guide explained something similar, that some places the earth's energies would go into the ground, while in others they would surge out of the land. Is this what you mean?"

"Yes, but nothing so far and across water would help us." Said Yamir, disappointed. "We need a place in this same land."

"Maybe if you describe it, or what your people found?"

Yamir pondered and hesitated.

"He's alright, Yamir, he is very knowledgeable and remember he is also a descendant of ours." Said Arinjay.

"I know, I know. I was just thinking, we are giving him information that… I don't know how that could affect the future."

"It will affect it more if we don't tell him." Countered my friend.

"Oh, alright. Listen, young man, what we need to find is a vortex, yes, a structure so gigantic it could not be seen when walking the land."

"Then? How do you find it?" I asked.

Yamir and Arinjay exchanged looks.

"You must know Andrew," said Arinjay, "that before the cataclysm that destroyed our civilization, we had something like what you told us you had, airplanes is what I think you called them."

I nodded.

"Yes."

"As I said, we had those and some could fly very, very high in the sky, almost to where there is no more air to breath, and you can see this world almost complete." He continued, but I could see he hesitated, maybe thinking I wouldn't accept such a possibility. Naturally, he didn't know about our spacecrafts reaching other planets.

"I understand." I replied.

"Well, on one of those flies, one of our people found a great circle on the land, a huge circle, surrounded by more circles. It seemed to his crew like an eye. Then he saw how some instruments in the flying craft started to change, as if he were flying at much higher altitude. He knew it was not that and recognized it for what it was, a vortex."

Something of what he was telling me sounded familiar and I asked for a moment to think about it. I concentrated on photographs of Earth that had been taken by our astronauts. Sure enough, there it was and the memory surged vividly in my mind's eye. Precisely an eye and it was called 'the Eye of Africa'. It must be this what they were talking about.

I described it to them, and both were amazed and happy.

"It is still there!" Exclaimed Yamir exhilarated and he shook hands with Arinjay, who seemed also to be extremely happy. "It is still there, so we can use it!"

"I don't understand." I said. "I think that place is really very far from here, even more from the banks of the river. How could it be of use to you?"

"You don't understand!" Exclaimed Yamir. "We don't need to be near, but on the line connecting them, I mean, connecting two vortices. If that place still exists, then we can find the currents, the flow of energy that goes toward it."

"That is not going to be easy, I think." I commented.

"No, not easy, but we have people who have the power to find those currents, those veins through which the energy of the planet moves. It will take time, but the result is certain."

I left them, realizing their work now, after knowing the Eye of Africa still existed, had been pushed ahead, gathered impulse to construct the Great Pyramid.

I had read a lot about the different theories explaining how this monument of antiquity had been built. Theories that considered ancient Egyptians working like slaves for the love of their Pharaoh, or real slaves, which was denied by some of the Egyptian archaeologists of my time saying there were no slaves in that time in Egypt. There were also theories stating they had been made by extraterrestrial beings, or giants with superior knowledge, a knowledge still unknown by present science.

Some, however, mentioned the existence of people surviving a cataclysmic meteorite crash, people with an advanced civilization and a knowledge that permitted them to build such an amazing structure as the pyramid with practically no effort. In the presence of what I was witnessing, I thought this last theory would result the most accurate, but I wondered how such a small group of men, or even all the village including young and old, men and women, would build what the specialists considered was built by over twenty thousand men in many years, I think as much as twenty.

This, I had to see, and I hoped this time traveling of mine would stop for long enough to see it done, or at least started.

The whole village was in what I would call a state of uproar. Men were entering the large building which I now knew they called assembly hall. Others, coming out of it, rushed away carrying notes, or what I thought could be orders. People I had never seen around before and whom I thought were from the tribes that had survived the cataclysm, were entering the hall, many apparently escorting their chiefs or principal people. Then, suddenly all stopped.

Those rushing in or out became still and their faces turned toward the south. I thought maybe someone was calling, but I had heard nothing. Now, those in the hall came out, also looking to the south. The chieftains and villagers, more awed than the others, fell to their knees, with their faces in their hands, almost cowering.

What was happening? I heard nothing, I saw nothing and yet, everyone else seemed to listen to an important message. The ancients turned around, looking for something, or someone and their eyes settled on me.

A shiver ran through my back. What was happening? Unconsciously I

Sent Back

took some steps back.

"HE calls you." Said Arinjay approaching and putting a heavy hand on my shoulder, preventing me from escape. His face was stony with not a flicker of emotion I could understand and again I shivered.

Stories of sacrifices, of monsters devouring humans rushed through my mind; product of all the scary movies I had watched in other times.

"No, nothing like that!" Exclaimed Arinjay. "What? How can you think something as horrible as that?"

I shrugged.

"Who is calling me? I heard nothing and yet all of you, even the villagers seem to have heard."

"Maybe you are not yet attuned." He said, passing a hand over his forehead. "Sometimes the eye is blind, blinded by our own fears. Come, HE doesn't like to wait."

"But who?"

"You'll see."

We walked in a southward direction and a corridor opened before us, all who had come out and listened to the message stared at me and my guide as we walked down the corridor. Another shiver, this was eerie.

Out of the village we walked and into the woods, Arinjay increased his speed forcing me to run after him. When we had walked, or run, more than two miles, we came to a place where large stones, really megaliths, stood among the trees. I was reminded of the Puma Punku, Ollantaytambo and Sacsayhuaman ruins in South America, but these were new, I could see they were new.

A depression, formed as a door, faced me. However, it was only a carving, a hole without opening, the insinuation of a door.

"What are we doing here?" I asked of Arinjay as he advanced toward the stone.

"Here is the door to His place." He said, turning. "You must go alone from here on, I haven't been called."

"Go where?" I almost cried. "This is stone, only stone! How can I go anywhere from here?"

As you can imagine, I was angry with fear and couldn't reason logically. Arinjay and his people had been good to me; they were sensible, quiet people, however, some primeval fear, instilled in me since the womb, rebelled before the inexplicable.

He came before me and placed his two hands on my shoulders, looking at me squarely in the eye.

"Don't be afraid, my friend." He said compassionately. "You are being granted a great honor, a fantastic experience awaits you and you will be enhanced by it. Go now, He awaits!"

Ashamed of my cowardice and of the ridiculous fears that crowded in my mind, I nodded.

"What shall I do?"

"Just go into the door. It will open for you."

Still doubting but remembering something I had heard about a similar door, I couldn't remember in which of the South American ruins, which opened a way into another dimension, I approached the megalith.

I stepped on the threshold and there was no stone in front of me there was nothing in front of me.

I felt a fresh breeze, a breeze with smell of some flower I couldn't remember, but that caused my heart to lift and a sense of happiness pervaded me. Something impelled me ahead, I gave a step, two and I was in a huge room.

How could I describe it? There are no words, no images in our world or our experience to define it.

That it was huge, yes, I can say that and very bright, almost too bright for my eyes. Things affected my eyes I couldn't identify and yet I knew they were colors, colors I had never seen or imagined. Then, I felt a presence and all coalesced, the strangeness of the place disappeared, and I was in a room, large, yes, but a common room, with normal furniture and colors. A man, a tall man, sat before me, almost naked. His nakedness, however, seemed the finest finery, the best brocade. His skin had a faint bluish tint, very faint, in truth. Arms and legs were powerfully built, muscular but slender, his torso proportionate to arms and legs, was thin at the waist.

His face was radiant, glowing with that faint bluish color of his skin, arched eyebrows over large eyes, dark eyes and when I looked into them; I thought I saw the darkness of the cosmos, the emptiness of space, but I felt no fear. Now, his dark blue lips opened, but I heard no words, instead, my mind resounded with his speech.

"I am Thoth,
in eons my life is counted,
multiple civilizations have known my name
and invoked me as they passed.
I am Thoth, the teacher
Elected by the Father of ALL,
Taught by His might I was
To be myself a teacher
To guide civilizations
As they surge and die.
I am Thoth,
My words will be left to guide
The civilization that is to grow
Listen well and keep them

To pass them on.
I am Thoth."

The words stopped, while I stood in awe. So many questions came to my mind I couldn't even select one to utter. Thoth? The god Thoth of ancient Egypt? He who helped Isis bring Osiris back from the dead? He who saved Horus, their son? He whom Ra, the mightiest of the Egyptian gods, left in his place as he left Earth? The 'light' after death?

"I am He, but not he.
Names pour away as water in cascades
As leaves when cold comes.
I am but a guide
A teacher I said."

I braced myself and asked what I thought was the most important question.

"Will you teach me, then?"
"No, child. You already know too much.
Of this, your trip to the past of your world
Some good will come, yes,
But you'll forget most."
"Why then, have you called me?"
"Child, you have been marked by a one full of malice and despair."
"The priest Ai, you mean?"
"No, not by that puny thing. By something more powerful and more eternal."

By I don't know what way, I was again in my bedroom, looking at the mark left in my thigh by the impossible nightmare.

"Yes! That is what I mean." Said the teacher.
"Who was it? Why did this mark come upon me?"
"It is malignant, evil. I know not the depth of its danger to you, but I know it was set there to prevent you from knowledge. Not that knowledge." He added, aware of my thoughts of university. "The deep true knowledge of the universe."

I stood silent for a while, pondering his words and the implications for my search. Then, I asked.

"Can you take it away?"
"Yes, that is one of the reasons you are here. You need to be cleansed of it."
"But how? It is engraved deep into my skin and muscles!"

I looked into his eyes again, and again I saw the deep black sky, full of points of light, the Universe rushed at me, and I travelled, at the speed of light from sun to sun, from galaxy to galaxy. The Cosmos embraced me, the solar wind of millions of stars covered me, penetrated through skin, muscle and bone. I felt a tug, a burning sensation where the mark was and then it was no more and I thought, I understood everything. I knew then the origin of all that is, all that was and will ever be. Exhilarated I laughed, I laughed in the un-void of the Cosmos, free in HE WHO IS.

It lasted but a second and I was back, facing Thoth.

"You saw and you knew." He said. "You'll forever experience the pain of losing what you felt, but you will not remember what it was. Thus it was with me, until by the mercy of the ALL, I am now. Now, when the cataclysm finished your friends' civilization; Now, when this world was made; Now, even when it ends. Past, present and future I am, by the mercy of ALL, I am. I know what will come to pass, how things will be lost and found. I know of you and your uncle and of Sekhmet. She went against my wishes, against the wish of ALL in bringing you to her time. Even worse did the priest connive, sending you even further back. He will pay."

I shuddered; the finality of the judgment was terrible.

"No human can open the doors, but I and the One who taught me. Ai dared and will pay. The ALL already saw to the goddess, I won't dwell in that, but for you, this is what I intend: I approve of what you've done, because it is in the course of things to be. This people will now move to the Black River, what you know as Nile, and they will leave a token of their knowledge for the world to come. As you had surmised, so it is ordered. However, something will be stolen and that has to be prevented."

I thought: 'the ark' and somehow, he knew. I wasn't surprised by it.

"Yes and no, as that which you call the ark is but the canvas where the painting was done."

"No", said Thoth again, reading in my mind the idea there planted by Sekhmet. "No. Your task is not to find the Ark of the Covenant, at least not now and much less to return it to the Black Land. When it is found and believe it will be found, it will herald the beginning of the end, when the coming of Him who has been announced finally arrives. Fear the time, because terrible things will happen, and humans will suffer incredible troubles. But it is not this that I want to tell you. I will send you even farther back, to the place and time this wheel began. May you have joy in it."

Thoth continued talking for a long time. He poured in my mind knowledge of the past, that what he called his Now. The succession of multiple civilizations, their rise and demise, by fire, or by water, by land or sky and some by their own wicked minds. He talked about HE who would come and I felt the love and adoration Thoth felt for Him. In no other time had this come to pass and I realized Thoth was not as omniscient as I had thought.

Then, I was back, back before the stone door, with Arinjay. Time had

Sent Back

not passed, not an instant had passed from when I heard the words of Arinjay: 'just go into the door. It will open for you'.

No time had passed, but I had met Thoth and he had told me.

CHAPTER XIX

I realized Arinjay was eager for information, to learn what Thoth had said, but his integrity prevented him from asking.

Naturally, I couldn't tell him; with Thoth monologue had come, implicit, the admonition I was not to talk about anything I heard. He hadn't said so, but I knew I couldn't; there was something, however, which needed saying.

"Arinjay", I started. "Even though I wanted to tell you what has happened while I was with Thoth, you know I can't divulge it."

"Do not worry, my friend, it has always been like that when someone is called within, I understand." He replied.

"Yes, but there is something I have to tell you, something he wants me to tell you."

Arinjay stopped in the path and turned to look at me, curiosity and fear mingled in his expression.

"What?" He whispered, amazed.

"I am going to leave you, he will send me to where I will complete my task, a task he assigned me. However, he wants me to tell you, all of you, that you must proceed with your plans to move to the lands of the Black River and build all you saw in my mind. It is very important, and no amount of difficulty should prevent you from completing this project."

"We will do it, naturally." He replied. "Naturally we will do it, much more now that I have heard. But Andrew, how will you leave us? Are you going to walk there, all on you own? It is impossible! Or perhaps will you 'travel'?"

"No, my friend, no." I said, with a smile. "Thoth himself will take care of this. He only allowed me to come talk to you, say goodbye and transmit his request, because it didn't sound as an order, to you. I do not know when or how I will leave, but that I will, I am positive. If I don't have time to say my farewells to your wife and the others I met in the village, please do that for my sake."

Arinjay stretched his hand and grasped mine.

"I will Andrew. It was a blessed day when I met you and all my good wishes…"

Sent Back

I heard no more, there was blackness and a sense of absolute vacuum. I felt air was being squeezed out of my lungs, as by a gigantic hand. It lasted a fraction of a second, but I will never forget that feeling and the terrible fear I then experienced.

In a rush, air entered my lungs again, I could breathe, and sense of touch returned. I felt hard ground under my feet and my skin softened in the presence of humidity, I could see nothing, but I knew I was not in that horrible vacuum anymore. Then, slowly, the place got brighter, illuminated by an unseen source and I could see I was in a large chamber, walls formed by megalithic stone boulders.

In the center was what looked like a sepulcher; from its borders came the light that brightened the darkness. It all glimmered. The light now reflected on the chamber's walls, walls of polished quartz.

The air around me crackled under the effect of what I assumed must be an electric field.

Where was I? Was this the inside of the Great Pyramid? Was this the King's chamber? And was I in truth, before what many had theorized was the Ark of the Covenant? What was the source of the light filtering through the cracks?

It was said, in the sacred books of the Hebrews, that only select men could approach and carry the Ark; as for example in 2 Samuel 6:1-7 and 1 Chronicles 13:9-12 where Uzzah, who didn't belong to the selected priests, touched the Ark to prevent it from toppling and was stricken dead.

I remembered more, because when the Ark was stolen by the Philistine, it caused death, devastation, and tumors.

It had been written that God had said: "After Aaron and his sons have finished covering the holy furnishings and all the holy articles and when the camp is ready to move, the Kohathites are to come to do the carrying. But they must not touch the holy things, or they will die." (Numbers 4:15).

When I had been a young boy and read the Bible with my darling uncle, it had always seemed strange to me that God would so act with his people and thought, instead, that the Ark of the Covenant must carry radioactive materials, or electricity. What I understood now, and I know not how, was that the living word of God would have that effect. Our limited minds cannot even imagine what the Creator is, but Moses, after facing Him on Mount Sinai, returned with a face that shone as the sun. Imagine what it could have been.

The so-called sarcophagus was now shining with a stronger light, so I could clearly observe the details and it amazed me that the lid was not a simple slab of stone covered in gold. On the top, beautifully sculpted or forged in gold, were the cherubim, as I had seen in the copy kept in my uncle's hidden treasure room. How was it possible that something supposed to have been forged after the Exodus from Egypt could be here, before me now?

What was this? Wasn't time linear? Didn't ten thousand years ago come after the Younger Dryas period? Wasn't Egypt's origin much later, or at least that old, perhaps as old as Göbekli Tepe?

I had not thought about Arinjay's people's morphology. The concept that beings could be simultaneously human-like and bird-like had seemed entirely natural at that time. Only now, when I was far from their town and in this secluded place, did I see them from another perspective. A group of them was moving around the chamber. They were like those I had met at the shore of the Sea of Reeds, but sometimes, like the flicker of something fading and coming back, the trace of their wings materialized, large wings as those of swans. Out there I had not realized how their bodies shone with light of their own; here, in the semi-darkness of the room, it was obvious.

These shinning beings were moving around, apparently immersed in a task I could not, at that moment, discern. I realized they must be the descendants of those I had met at the shores of the lake, so long ago.

One of them, becoming aware of my presence there, approached me.

"Welcome brother, we have known of you for a long time, ever since you visited us in the shores of the green sea, the sea of reeds. Here we are, as Thoth ordered through your mouth. Come and see the result of your and our endeavors. But do not come too near, the thing is deadly."

As obeying an invisible gesture or order, they parted, and I saw the most incredible sight.

Yes, it was the Ark of the Covenant. Covered in gold, with the so-called cherubim, really the representation of the ancients, on top. Now I knew they were not angels in the sense we understand angels, but the reflection of those who had preceded us in the world, those of whom I was one of the remaining descendants.

The light emanating from it was, I knew instinctively, mortal. Encased in golden planks was something producing an unimaginable energy. This was the energy at the beginning when the Universes came into being. This was the energy of The Word. The glow was like a dark cobalt blue in color, even purplish. I could feel the hairs on my arms and face rise, and from my fingers emerged tiny sparks.

"Yes, this is what we were told to build and leave here. Not only this, but you also know; one of our tasks was to create and leave for our descendants a source of energy that would power their cities. Little did we know what we were talking about. We were to build something that would contain the Word of God, the Living Word. How could we imagine it would be possible? But to Him, all is possible."

He bowed his head, whispering something I couldn't hear. Then, he continued; "The other task was to place and protect here our knowledge,

Sent Back

the knowledge of the worlds that were, of the great cataclysm, of our history. We should include all the scientific knowledge survivors of the cataclysm were able to keep. Everything will be housed here, so that when the appointed time comes and the ones who can read our writings find them all would be made public. But most important of all, by the grace of He Who Is, will be the Covenant with the Word of God."

"There are stories," I replied "Stories about how perilous this thing is, how people who approached it were killed, how when it was taken by another conquering nation, their own people began dying, of what I now know was radiation sickness. How come you are working so near it? Won't you be killed?"

"Our physiology is slightly different from humans, we can survive a higher dose of radiation, you can, too. Still, for those who have been working directly with the Ancient of Times, there will be no future. They know and willingly sacrifice themselves to leave His power here, for your civilization's future."

I stared at him and then at those working in so deep contact with this source of power, unimaginable even in the most advanced civilization. My thoughts returned to Arinjay, had he known of this?

"I see you have questions. Ask and I'll try to answer." Said the

"I... I was wondering about those I met there, at the shores of the lake. Is, is Arinjay well and the ancient?"

"Their lives are spent." He said. "Now, don't be saddened, remember when you were born, they had already perished thousands of years before. You are a time-traveler, dear friend, time-traveling is difficult because you experience the loss of those you love many more times than a normal human being. Arinjay, his wife, the ancient, they died happy knowing their efforts would permit some of our history to be passed on. Their lives were fruitful, and they also had at last surcease from the losses in the cataclysm."

I had felt my heart constricting when he said that, but I understood well what he meant, so I tried to return to the present, at least that present.

They explained how the power source that would reside in the Pyramid would work, how they were almost finishing and how their tasks would be completed, the Ark would be finished at what my contemporaries called the Pharaoh's chamber, while they would leave the library of knowledge in the Sphynx subterranean.

"I believe we are in what, in my time, was called the Pharaoh's chamber." I asked. "Am I right?"

"You are, but I have no idea why they gave it that name. It is the great engine room, and it has been constructed in the way needed to increase the energy output. Those resonance chambers above will amplify a hundredfold the vibrant energy the engine will produce. Come, let me take you outside to show you more."

The thought of crawling through the famed tunnels of so difficult access worried me; it shouldn't have. My new friend took me by the arm and suddenly we were outside, in the bright, burning sun of Egypt's Giza Plateau. Only knowing I was there reconciled me with the idea, because this was not a dry arid dessert. The land around me was covered by lush vegetation, trees, palm trees, bushes of every kind, especially those beautiful date palm trees that abound so much in the paintings done in future pharaohs tombs.

How could it be so fertile then and how had it become such an arid place in my time? I remembered the recent discoveries by the geologist I had met in one conference I assisted, where he had stated, categorically, that the erosion on the Sphinx was due to huge amounts of rain falling on the Giza plateau over ten thousand years ago in my time.

Forcing myself to look at the site my new friend was pointing at, I saw before me a large construction of stones upon stones, not at all resembling the Pyramid, it was just a heap, well, an organized heap of stones. I could distinguish at the center, a square block of a material that reflected the sun in a particular way, more as if it were of lead than of stone.

My friend nodded.

"Yes, that's where the power is housed."

"I don't understand. You talk of the power as we would talk of one produced by electricity, or even atomic energy. Is that what you mean?"

"I don't know what you call by those names, but I'll explain. What we now know is that, when the universe was made, and this world in particular, the Purpose was to grant the use of His power to those He had created. After the 'Fall', that power was withdrawn, and humanity had to work hard to survive. Once again He wants to make that Power, His Power, available once more, but those who will live here after us, after we have completed our task they will know not how to use it."

"Why then…"

"The Power will be on its own, creating light for them, but they will not know how it is. It is His will it'll happen and through His word, the Word of Creation, set in the place you saw, the Power will be for all."

"So what we call the Ark of the Covenant is really that, but it refers to a Covenant much older than we thought it was."

"Yes."

"And you'll house it there? Inside the pyramid?"

"Yes, in the chamber you see there."

"Oh, it was built before!"

"Naturally!" He exclaimed, "Would we carve it after all was done? No, no, first we did the foundation and the chamber, then we will finish the covering."

Something called my attention at that moment, and I saw huge stones moving as by themselves. A group of men below were using instruments to produce some harmonic sound while another, who seemed in control, guided the stones with a very large tuning fork. The stones dropped one after the other, side by side in an organized way.

I was so shocked I could barely breath. I was finally understanding how the pyramid had been constructed. No thousands of slaves, or 'voluntary constructors' pulling the stones up a sandy slope, no movement using trunks of trees or palm trees. It was as it had been surmised by the craziest of the alien civilization theorists' supporters, stone moved as by magic with the power of sound and harmonics.

"Why are you so shocked?" He asked.

"We never knew how it had been done! The raising of the stones so high, as heavy as they are. The whole construction has been a source of hundreds of theories, from the simplest and hard to accomplish, to magic."

"You seem, I mean, your civilization, seems to have lost much of the information we left for you. We didn't know it would happen like that."

"Yes, you told me about a library of knowledge. We have searched. Several years before my birth there was a man, he was called 'the sleeping prophet' who said we would be finding it soon, but we've never did."

He remained silent, digesting the news and his face was not only sad, but concerned.

"I don't know what the designs of God are, nor of Thoth who by His word commanded us to do this, but please do not tell anyone else about it. The least we need now is discouragement."

"Don't worry, I won't. But tell me," I continued, "How is the pyramid supposed to work once it is finished?"

"It will be covered in quartz crystal," he replied eying me with curiosity, "the Power, what I see in your mind you are calling nuclear power erroneously, will produce on the pyramids wall such a radiance that night will be vanished when it is turned on; during the day, the energy will be channeled through the descending passage and it will be distributed around the city to power different machines and instruments. You didn't know this?"

"No, and I am sorry to tell you that even this is lost. The covering stones, which you say were of crystal quartz, were stollen to build temples and buildings, but we were told they were really polished limestone. I do not understand what happened, as it was so many hundred years ago in my time."

Everything I uttered seemed to crush him more, like weight added again and again on his shoulders. I felt sorry for him and realized I didn't know his name. I turned to face him and asked.

"I was called Im by my parents, but as I ascended in knowledge and responsibility, they added Hotep. I am Im Hotep." He replied.

I gasped. It couldn't be! Imhotep 'the one who comes in peace' was supposed to have lived during 2630 - 2611 BCE, the reign of pharaoh Djoser and was vizier, sage, architect and astrologer. Surely this was not him. But then, maybe his name had been kept in the memory of the ancients and bestowed upon someone who, thousands of years later, reminded them of the legends about this one standing before me.

"It seems you are full of secrets, my friend." He said. "Keep them, I do not want to share in your knowledge, bad enough is knowing our past, remembering our doomed civilization and having a slight inkling of the future. Keep them, please.

I remained silent for a while, considering the import of his plea. Then, still plagued by curiosity, I asked:

"You talked about the machines and instruments that will be powered by that energy source. Can you show them to me? Some drawings and strange artefacts have been found, but the truth is nobody has been able to understand them."

"The more you tell me, the harder it becomes for me, Andrew. It seems all our work here will be for naught."

"No, Im Hotep, do not think that. For centuries the quest to understand the mystery of this country has fueled our imagination and spurred on the study of the past. Thanks to what you are doing here was civilization awakened to our own history. I have thought many times if the sole importance of these constructions, the ones here and the ones scattered all around the world for example in Central and South America, were to ignite curiosity in the minds of men so that we would search for the explanations of such marvels and in that way arrive to the knowledge of the cataclysm."

"You say so, I'll have to believe you. Come, I'll show you one of the multiple centers of energy we are creating."

He guided me to a central avenue and from there we walked towards the great river. I saw it was much nearer to the base of the pyramid than during my time. As we approached, I saw multitude of barges pullulating the river, some loaded with stones and materials, others returning empty, or with people. Im Hotep gestured to one barge just leaving the shore and they pulled back to allow us to board.

Memories of my trip on Sekhmet's barge swamped my mind and I hesitated. My host, however, did not seem aware of this and I had to follow him running before the barge left me on ground.

"Where are we going?" I asked, sitting on a low-lying bench and looking worriedly at the near level of the water.

"Far to the south some two hours against the flow of the river. We are constructing something there that will contain enough power to light the whole country. You'll see."

Sent Back

I realized my guide was not in a talking mood, probably trying to digest the disheartening information I had provided, so I remained silent, watching the land pass by and very conscious of the life abundant in and around the river. There were ibises and other beautiful birds whose species I couldn't identify and in the river hippopotamuses and most probably crocodiles hidden under the water level, waiting for an unsuspecting prey. Why were we taking the barge, instead of their strange ability to move through space, I had no idea. Maybe he needed time to digest the news I've given him, maybe there was another reason I couldn't fathom.

As we traveled up the river, I could see no difference with the river I had traveled on with the goddess, but probably the river had already moved westwards when I was there with Sekmeth, I couldn't calculate how many hundreds or even thousands of years in the future.

Sometime after, which in my opinion was a long time to float in that river, the barge approached a small quay and Im Hotep urged me to disembark. He guided me through a verdant garden, flanked by bushes and date palm trees. A stone road led west, and I saw pieces of stone and granite fallen by the side.

"They are being careless," he commented in a low voice. "I'll have to address this."

I knew I was not meant to hear, so I said nothing.

Soon we arrived at a low building, not anything like the wonderful temples done in a later age, it seemed something mostly functional. A large stair led to the underground and we walked there until we reached a large tunnel, brightly illuminated by what I could only call electric light.

We walked further along the tunnel, and I saw openings to right and left, in an alternate way. In these openings stood huge boxes, I hesitate to call them sepulchers, but that's what they seemed at first glance. They were huge and reflected light as a polished mirror, though I saw they were carved from granite.

Suddenly an idea hit me, and I would have cried if I had not been warned not to talk but in whispers. I knew where I was, I knew it! This was what was called the Serapeum of Saqqara in our books of history, where traditional Egyptologists maintained that the ancients had kept the mummified remains of the god Apis.

"What is this place?" I whispered, leaning towards my guide.

"This is where the Power of the Word, generated back there will be made available to humankind, and stored. Those huge stone containers are full of a substance that will keep the energy until it is needed."

He eyed me quizzically and maybe worriedly.

"Don't you have this in your world?"

"Oh, yes, yes. We have something similar, perfected it so much that in my time one that could give power for days would be as small as my fingernail."

He sighed and I saw that at least in this regard, I was giving him good news.

"Well, that's good to know. These power cells would keep enough energy to light the towns and the temples when they are finished."

"But this is far from the pyramid and according to my knowledge, more than twenty-five kilometers away, though I know that kind of measurement is unknown to you."

"Remember when you talked to Arinjay about the Eye of Africa? Do you remember they were talking about lines on the Earth that naturally conduct energy? We are using that here, too."

"Oh!" I had not known if the Eye of the Africa had served them or not. "Were they able to use the Eye?"

"Not only did they use it, but we are also still using the huge potential between the two to help our work here and at the power source place. That was great help you gave us, so much was lost after the cataclysm, even our flying machines."

He looked at me again with a queer eye and I understood he was wondering, again, if flying was known in my world.

"Yes, I know, and it was thanks to machines that now fly far above the world's atmosphere that I was able to remember the existence of the Eye of Africa. Arinjay told me how all that had been lost. The agony of losing a civilization and all its developments must be a terrible pain."

"I knew it not directly, but the memories passed from my ancestors are pungent in my mind, so the pain is there, too. I hope you never experience anything like it."

"I hope so too. These boxes will power the new cities built by the river?"

"Yes, that's our aim. Now you know, will you remember?"

"I will. If you are now completing the pyramid and the source of that awesome energy inside it, what am I supposed to do now?"

"Yours is not to protect it, as you had surmised. At least not now, not yet. It will run untouched for centuries, I think millennia, before any attempt of damage or of stealing comes to it."

I had so many questions, but one seemed at that moment the most important.

"Im Hotep, can I ask you something?"

"Sure, if I know the answer, I will tell you."

"I have always wondered about the huge constructions of the world, and specially here, in what we know as Egypt. Why was it that stones, and stones of such incredible size and weight were used? Why not smaller stones, why not any other materials? I imagine in your cities, in the old civilization, you had buildings of something else than stone?"

Sent Back

He pondered on the answer for a while, and then said:

"As you know, I was but born after the cataclysm. The stories from the old ones, however, explain it. Also remember we can share our memories and see what the old ones saw. Yes, we had beautiful buildings with walls that let the sun in and kept the heat out. The buildings were tall, very tall, and slender and graceful. We used substances elaborated by our scientists and produced in factories, and with these we made all type of implements, and furniture, and means for transportation. Yes, we had all those. When the scientists realized we were doomed, when they saw the asteroid coming towards us, they knew not one of our cities would remain. All our beautiful buildings, bridges, parks, everything would be destroyed. Only stone could remain. Only the biggest blocks of stone would remain. Yes, some of our people were commanded to build, as we now build what you call pyramids. Only those buildings would remain after the crash."

I nodded. That agreed with what I had thought.

"Andrew?" He asked, bringing me back from my thoughts.

"Andrew, I need to tell you: I, too, was summoned by Thoth and through me you are to be sent even farther back in time, my friend. He wants you to experience life before the cataclysm, he wants you to know firsthand how people of our time used to live before the multiple comets struck us."

"Here, in this place? Or somewhere else?" I asked, fearing all the unexpected dangers and encounters.

"You'll go to Kumari Kandam."

CHAPTER XX

I was still mulling over the name of the place Im Hotep had given me. I knew I had heard it before but couldn't remember where or regarding what.

I felt the now familiar excruciating pain of all air being squeezed out of my body, total darkness, emptiness and then, I stood on a populated street, flanked by high temples, or buildings, with elaborate statues and images.

The street was made of perfectly shaped bricks of a red material, probably baked clay, all the same size and form, and by the side of the road there were graceful culverts or sewers made with terra-cotta, or perhaps some reddish stone where clear water, maybe of a recent rain, flowed. Above me, a myriad of birds and butterflies covered the sky, and I could hear the buzzing sound of bees, probably visiting the flowers that abounded there.

At the end of what I thought to call 'block' there were large and round stones, maybe a meter diameter and on top a depression where I saw some oily substance. A vague memory of lightning at night crossed my mind at that moment. With this idea in mind, I now saw many smaller spheres, placed in or around the buildings.

By my side, on the road, traffic moved orderly, as it could have moved in the most civilized city of my time while pedestrians, all nicely attired walked on what I could only call sidewalks.

Far away, I saw tall buildings, probably castles, perhaps temples. Some glittered as if made of gold, and I could see, at intervals, brief sparkles of green, red and yellowish white. I learned later those came from precious stones inlaid on the walls of the buildings.

My sudden appearance had not been noticed, people continued walking by me, occupied in their daily tasks. It hit me, as I saw them and their buildings, that I had come to some part of India, maybe ancient India.

Men and women wore elaborate dressings and shawls, some went barefoot, others wore slender leather sandals with bells and little jewels. They wore bracelets on wrists and ankles, necklaces, and earrings, indistinctly from men or women. Their skin was of a slightly dark color but not as dark as the Tamil of my time, their hair was very dark, black, almost

Sent Back

blue in its dark shades and all I saw were strangely beautiful.

They had large brown or black eyes, strong nose, and wide and generous mouth, generally a long neck, though I saw some whose necks were really short. Most had long graceful arms and legs. I saw only a few relatively fat people, but obesity was not common, at least among the ones I saw.

The streets seemed clean, and I saw groups of women sweeping while other groups, this time of men, were brushing the multitude of statues on the buildings or bordering the streets, cleaning them of dust, leaves, and bird droppings.

There were carts, mostly pulled by zebu bullocks with their typical neck hump. From some of these carts people were getting, most surely buying, tasty confections for lunch. I was not hungry, but the smell escaping from these ambulatory restaurants was enough to make a stone hungry. Not having any money, or any means to purchase one of the tasty items, I walked away, salivating.

I thought it was somewhat after noontime, the sun was high in the sky and the temperature slightly hot. My dressing, though not like the ones they wore, was enough to pass muster, a long tunic covering wide pants. Grant it, they were not beautiful as the ones they wore, nor colorful, but the difference was not abysmal.

I continued walking and reached a place like a plaza. A statue, several times the height of a man stood there, surrounded by a crowd. The well-known smell of incense wafted towards me and I understood the crowd's movements. They were worshipping whomever this statue represented.

I walked some steps more to get nearer to the statue so I could identify it. Somehow my brain offered the answer, not that I had been good in the study of ancient India. This was Lord Krishna, Lord Krsna, the eighth avatar of the god Vishnu. The statue was painted with vivid colors, and the Lord's skin had a bluish tint. In his hands he held a flute.

I was well aware what the man from the pyramid, Im Hotep, had said Kumari Kandam, and this seemed to be a city in India, grant it, clean, very beautiful and I could see no poverty, hovels, or any of those appalling situations you could find nowadays. This seemed to be a rich and prosperous place. Why had he said Kumari Kandam, had I been misplaced? I smiled, scoffing at my own ideas. Doubtful.

I realized then that a woman had been watching me from the crowd nearest to Krishna, I retreated, afraid of having committed a crime of disrespect, but the woman's face was not angry, there was no censure in her attitude and as I moved back some steps, she followed.

She was approaching me now and I could do nothing more than wait; it would have seemed silly to avoid her when she was so determined to talk. I saw now that she was young, maybe in her early twenties, her hair was braided and combed in the most intricate manner, with strands of tiny pearls and brilliant stones intertwined. Her skin was somewhat of a clearer hue than the ones around her, and she was as beautiful as most of her fellow citizens. Her dressing, the semitransparent golden tunic covering a short bodice and tight brocade leggings hid and revealed her fine body. She walked barefoot, with a daintiness that most surely was innate, nobody could learn to walk like that. A golden chain hung from her waistline, above the low-cut pants and from it a stone, which could have been a small diamond fell on her navel.

I was so absorbed admiring her I missed her words. She spoke again.

"Are you a visitor?" She said and I took some time to understand her.

I knew what she meant, but how? Was she talking English, or mayhap that language I had learned to speak when in Arinjay's village? I stared into her eyes in what could have seemed greatly improper manner.

"Yes, you are a visitor." She said, nodding. "Don't wonder about being able to understand me, the ability to understand our language is in your genetic code."

I gasped; how could she be talking about genetic code? That was unknown, more so at the time I thought I had gone to.

She smiled, as if understanding my mental process.

"It's alright, a group of us was alerted about your visit. You are Andrew, are you not? You belong to the family of Osiris' sons."

I had never heard that reference, so I looked at her with an expression that obviously made her laugh.

"You belong to the family of Sir Ferdinand Thomas Whittaker, Esq.; in fact, you are his descendant, are you not?" She pronounced the words correctly, but it was clear they were unfamiliar to her.

More flabbergasted than I could ever say at hearing this woman from an ancient past mention my beloved uncle, I only nodded.

"Yes, yes, I knew that. Well, the gods have given me the honor to be the one to great you, so please follow me. We have much to discuss, much to explain and you have much telling to do. We cannot do that in the middle of the plaza, nor are you properly dressed, sooner or later you'll start drawing attention to yourself. Come, come, follow me."

It was only at that moment that I became aware of the messenger bag, still strapped across my chest and back. I weighed it, and yes, the stone was still there. Would it tell me where I was? Or was that incredible information only for the lands near the Nile.

I wanted to take it out, but was reluctant to, imagine the people around me seeing that image in the air above the stone. I don't know what they would do, to me or the stone. So I decided to keep it hidden until a proper moment arose when I could expose it to the sun.

I saw the young woman was impatient, so I obeyed and followed her.

Sent Back

Was there anything else I could do? My twenty first century independence had been lost the moment I encountered Sekhmet.

We went through identically perfect streets, but with somewhat smaller buildings, fewer statues, fewer temples. I realized we were entering a residential section of the city.

After a while walking, we reached a two-story dwelling. Flanking the door were again the huge stones, the depression on top full of the oily substance I had observed. We entered.

She had preceded me, and I saw her now turn to her right and pressing palm to palm, bow low. An image of Lord Krishna was there, illuminated by candlelight. She muttered something I could not hear and then turned expecting, I supposed, for me to do the same thing, I did.

Then, farther into the passageway we came to a small pool of running water, she stepped into it, motioning for me to do the same. It was at this moment she paid attention to my shoes and stared in wonder.

"I'll take them off, don't worry." I said, pronouncing what came to my mind with difficulty, but knowing they were correct.

I did as I said and then immersed my feet, up to my ankles into the warm running water. It felt incredibly relaxing and cleansing.

There was a towel, or rug on the floor at the other side of the pool and she stepped out into it. I followed. Without taking a moment to dry her feet, she walked into the house. The hallway opened into a room where light entered through shadowed windows. There were seats around the walls, seats apparently part of the walls, covered with cushions and blankets of various colors. In the middle was a low wooden table surrounded by more cushions lying on the floor.

"Wait for me here." She said, as she left through a door hidden under some draperies.

I heard her talking and other voices answering, but so fast I couldn't recognize a single word said. Maybe my ability to understand her language had not developed enough.

I was trying to look out the window when I sensed someone coming into the room, I turned, expecting to see her. It was not. This was an older woman, a much older woman. She had hair as white as snow and she carried it loose. It reached much below her waist. Her face was full of wrinkles, but I don't know how, she seemed young. At least it was a face full of life and maybe that's what made her look young. She was slightly chubby, but not exceedingly so and it looked good on her. Multiple shawls of gauze hung from her shoulders.

I bowed, thinking I could not go wrong with that salutation, but she pressed palm to palm and bowed, so I did the same and she seemed satisfied.

"I brought you some clothes like the ones we wear in this town. Don't be offended but we think it would be better for you to change into these ones." She explained, offering a stack of what I assumed were pants and tunic. "You can change here, if you will." She added, moving a curtain that led into what I guessed was a very small chamber.

I naturally followed her suggestion. If I was going to be there for a while, I should attract the least possible attention. The pants and tunic were well worn, but still much better than what I had been using. I changed quickly and came out of that chamber holding my old clothes, as I didn't know what to do with them.

I said before that I had realized the bag Ira had given me had traveled in time with me, and the stone was still there. I hung the bag on my shoulder and came out.

At the moment the old woman had pulled at her so white hair and was braiding it. She lifted her head and smiled, nodding approval.

"Much better." She said.

The curtain moved apart again and now several people came in, I will not describe them all. They were of different ages, men and women and all as beautiful as the ones I had seen on the streets before. They all bowed before me and I answered in the same manner and then they sat.

At last, my guide came back, bringing on a tray several small dishes with such a smell my hunger awoke with a vengeance.

She made me sit at the central table, placing the tray before me and urged me to eat. I was reluctant to begin, though the smell of the food was driving me crazy, because I knew how in ancient India everything was preceded always by a ritual involving one or another god. I did not want to begin my stay here offending my hosts. But my guide understood.

"We will dispense with formalities. They all know you are a visitor and not familiar with our rituals. Please eat, I know you are famished."

I had eaten under the scrutiny of all gathered there, though they had tried to appear uninterested. My guide had sat by my side and conversed with me while I enjoyed the rich flavor of the different plates set before me.

Her name was Aashritha and she told me it meant somebody who gave shelter. I then tried to pronounce her name, making a total mess of it. She laughed and told me to call her Ritha, that's how the family shortened her name. She continued to explain these ones here were all part of her family, uncles and aunts, cousins, brothers and sisters. The old woman was the matriarch, her grandmother and the ruler of the family. Her grandfather had gone to the gods.

She explained that, among the families of the city, hers was a renowned one, because in them the memories of the beginning were stronger. There were many families like hers, but not all in the city remembered.

Sent Back

I enquired what was so important that they remembered.

"This is not the first world, nor will it be the last; this is not the first universe, nor will it be the last. Four billion years and a bit more, is what the universe existence will last, four billion and a bit more years the dissolution and destruction will last. But when all is destroyed, in the night of Brahma, he, at the end, wakes up to a new day and another universe is begun. His day is called a kalpa."

She looked at me with curiosity, I imagine she was wondering if I understood any of it, so I nodded.

"We are at the end of the Dwapara Yuga, soon the sad yuga of Kali will begin. During our yuga, the Dwapara Yuga, spirituality declined, and sin began to increase, becoming almost as great as virtue. We know this, we cannot prevent it. But worse is to come, the next yuga, the Kali Yuga when you were born. I cannot understand the suffering of this age. During it, civilization will degenerate, and people will separate more and more from the divine; veneration of evil will become fashionable, and wicked rulers will obtain power. It was during the Satya Yuga, the first yuga, that Matsya came, He came as a fish to save Manu. We remember, because Manu was our ancestor, with Ida the miraculous maiden. It was then the lands disappeared under the waves and only Manu and the seven sages were saved on a ship led by Matsya, Lord Vishnu's first avatar. We know this, we remember, and our sacred writings say it."

"Do you know more about what will happen during Kali Yuga?" I asked, curious to see if they knew anything about what had happened.

"No, we know only what I said, and that at the end, when wickedness is rampant on the lands, Lord Shiva will come in his last avatar to cleanse the world. Every bit of creation will cease to exist, the universes will vanish. After a time we call the Night of Brahma, the universe will begin anew."

"Yes, many in my time know this, too." I agreed. "Though I did not study about it."

She did not comment on it but was silent for a while.

I had eaten and felt relaxed and at ease. There was a small bowl on the table to my right and she gestured at it, doing a movement as if she was washing her fingers. I understood and did. She then offered me a small piece of white cloth, with which I dried my hands.

"Now, if you feel comforted and all tiredness has escaped your bones, tell us about what is." Said a man who resembled Aashritha so much she must be his daughter. Apparently, he understood my questioning look so he continued. "I am Aashritha's father and my name is Mahendra."

I bowed in recognition.

"What should I tell you, Mahendra? There is much I do not know and there is much more I don't know if I should tell you." I replied, knowing how the news of what had gone on in the world had shocked Arinjay and his people, remembering how saddened Im Hotep had been when learning of the ignorance we were in regarding to the Great Pyramid.

"We were selected by the great Lord, he who lives forever, to be your greeters. Whatever he wants us to know, he will allow you to tell, whatever he wants kept secret, you'll either forget or won't be able to express. That is how he works."

"First please tell me, because I think I know where and when I am, but it is all guessing. Can you tell me?" I asked.

They looked at each other, I imagined they were trying to find a point in common with me regarding time and place, then Mahendra continued.

"We live in a very large land situated in the southern world. To our west extends a dark continent, full of beasts and fierce animals. The people there are very, very dark and live in forests. There are there some cities, but not as many as we have here, nor as great and with so many temples. But they are very rich, their land has gold, precious stones and their animals have ebony and beautiful skins. Farther to the west that land ends in a huge ocean and their beaches are of white sands."

He looked at me, it was clear he wanted to know I was understanding this.

"Yes, I think you are referring to Africa and the Atlantic Ocean." I said.

"Perhaps that's how you name them. To our East, another land extends, not as large but made of many large islands, all close together and separated from us by a smaller sea and to the southeast there's another large land, where the most amazing animals live, animals who carry their young in a pouch in their belly."

He stopped, maybe expecting me to express incredulity. Naturally, I wouldn't, as he was talking about marsupials, basically Kangaroos and such.

"Yes, I know of those, I know the land you mean, we call it Australia."

"Some distance farther to the south, across a large sea, is a great land. It's a land of riches, and beauty. The people there are the most advanced. They have machines that fly in the sky." He looked at me curiously, maybe doubting I would accept that. I nodded.

"They also have large ships that travel around our world. They come to this city and other cities of my country, trading and teaching us new things."

Here was something I could not identify. He had told me about Africa and the Atlantic Ocean, and of Australia, to their east was what we would call Indonesia, with Cambodia, Vietnam and so many others. But to the south? A huge continent to the south?

Then I understood and would have slapped by head. Was he talking about the Antarctic continent? That civilization destroyed by the cataclysm, the people of Arinjay, were they from the southernmost continent? But it

Sent Back

was a frozen land! One to two miles of ice covered it! How could…

I stood transfixed, pondering in my mind the implication of this information. Theories, theories considered crazy by most scientists but inexplicably supported by the scientist Einstein, considered this possibility. Perhaps…Perhaps at this time the Antarctic continent was not at the South Pole, perhaps it was nearer to the Equator. Could it be?

I remembered another geologist explaining how Australia and Antarctica had been together eons ago. I shook my head trying to organize my thoughts and realized they were all looking at me expectantly.

"Yes, I understand." I said. "However, there is a way I can be certain of it. I have brought with me a stone that was able to show me the place I was before coming here. I would like to confirm my understanding of your explanations with it, but I would need to go out into the sun."

They looked at each other, and I heard whispers of amazement or doubt. Mahendra, however, nodded and, gesturing for me to follow, took me through another opening and across some rooms to an inner patio. It was surrounded by walls with doors opening into it. Doors I assumed gave way to more rooms in the house.

"Is this place good?" He asked.

I looked up, yes, the sun was there. It had fallen from the zenith, perhaps it was now two or three in the afternoon. A portion of the patio was still receiving sunlight, so I went there and pulling the stone from the bag, I exposed it to the sun.

I hadn't expected it to work. I had thought, I don't know why, that it would only work in northern Africa. The image rose in the air, just as it had done by the side of the Sea of Reeds. Mahendra and also Ritha, who had followed us, gasped in amazement. Yes, the image rose, and I stared intently at it.

Northern Africa I knew well; and had been able to identify the place where I was then. The image before us now was something else. Forcing my mind to remember world maps of my time and those that depicted how the land masses could have been before the cataclysm; it was with immense difficulty I identified the eastern coast of Africa, and following this landmark, what would later be the Saudi Peninsula. But where India would be with its characteristic triangular shape what I saw in the image was different, more like a trapezoid than a triangle, and much larger in breadth and length.

Something peculiar was happening to the image above the stone, the lands surrounding what I assumed to be India were disappearing, while the western coast of the subcontinent became brighter for a while. Then the image vanished. Following this development, suddenly the stone became opaque, thin lines appeared on its surface, and very very slowly it started to break. I gazed in horror and amazement at the pieces it was breaking into became dust in my hand, leaving only the center, the gold inscription that had so awed me at the beginning.

The characters turned to light, shinning above my hand, and now they spelt: Consumatum Est.

I stared amazed. These wear the last words the Mesiah, Jesus Christ is said to have uttered at the end of his crucifixion. What was this all about?

The light extinguished gradually, and soon, nothing was left from that stone that had been with me for so many adventures and times of the Earth.

Ritha and Mahendra had been staring to this unexpected process.

"That is magical indeed." Whispered Mahendra, awed. "Was it from the gods? What was the meaning of those characters at the end?"

"It said 'Consummatum Est'. The last words the Son of God said at the end."

Both looked at me, expecting more information, but I was not in the mood, So I answered his first question.

"I don't know, Mahendra, maybe it was from the gods. It was given to me by my professor, back in the time from when I came. She was very mysterious about it so maybe yes, maybe it is something from the gods."

"And now, do you understand where it is that we live? Has the stone given you understanding?"

"Yes, I believe I know where this city is." I replied.

Mahendra continued then.

"Good, so now you know where we are, this is the land we inhabit and we call it Kumarinatu. Farther to the north, the land is still in constant turmoil. Molten stone surges from the earth, and it has done so for as long as we have been. Nobody can travel there, the air is poisonous, even if you could walk on the burning ground. The old ones say mountains like stairs have grown there, farther to the north, where none were before. Now, to tell you about the time we are in, I imagine that is going to be more difficult, as I don't know what you know."

"I will tell you, however." He continued "Our sages tell us this yuga, this era we live in, called the Dwapara Yuga will only last seven thousand and seven hundred years more, that is of human years. Once we reach that end, our lord Krishna will leave Earth and Kali Yuga will begin."

I tried to do a mental calculation, but it was difficult. I had no idea how the different yugas of Hinduism were measured, nor of when each had begun. However, if this was Kumari Kandam, I knew it was supposed to have gone under the waves, or maybe even under India some thirteen thousand years ago. When in that lapse was I, I had no idea.

"I do not think I am going to be able to understand in what times, regarding to my civilization's time, I am. Maybe when I've been here for some time, maybe if I can talk to your sages…" I left the idea unfinished,

Sent Back

there were, as I knew, so many imponderables.

"Yes, and I don't think it is relevant." Inserted Ritha, "You are here now, and we want to learn from you."

While we had been talking, we had returned to the room where the rest of the family had remained, waiting for us.

"So please," she continued. "Tell us about your time, and what happens in our future."

I heard a chorus of muted accord and the faces of all present turned toward me. I was overwhelmed. Yudhishtra and the other sages by the Sea of Reeds had drained me, but it had been an almost effortlessly draining, as they had read my memories. If here, on the other hand, I was expected to verbally tell them about the story of my civilization, I could talk for years without finishing. Furthermore, was I supposed to tell them their land had perished under the seas? Should I tell them that their civilization had disappeared and even the descendants of the Kumari Kandam's civilization, the Indus Valley Civilization, had also disappeared and been lost from human knowledge for millennia?

It had been a debated point in historical and archaeological circles. The white hegemonistic groups that had conquered India in and after the eighteenth century couldn't accept the fact of India's high philosophical developments. They attributed the Vedas, the books of sciences, to a mythical 'aryan' invasion from the north, that had brought the 'white' development to the Indian subcontinent. Only after the discovery of the cities of Mohenjo Daro, Harappa, Mehrgarh and a thousand more could the ancient history of the Indus Valley be proven.

I was interrupted in my thoughts my loud voices coming from the entrance of the house. In my agony, I was at first grateful from any interruption, then, apprehensive. Had this tumult anything to do with my presence there?

The draperies covering the entrance were pulled aside; at the door appeared a majestic old man, very tall, with long white beard. His eyes were like steel, his brow knitted in anger, on his right hand he held a large staff, either of gold or covered in gold and his clothes were so rich and beautifully decorated I assumed he must be the king of that place. I was wrong.

Ritha's family immediately fell to their knees, bowing to the newcomer and she pulled at my side to do the same. I was reluctant, why should I bow, I belonged not to this people, I bowed slightly, however, as I had done when I met the old woman.

The man addressed Ritha's father and I could hear suppressed anger in his voice. I understood some words, 'alone', 'first', 'traveler' and to my surprise, my own uncle's name.

I saw Ritha, she rose and stood proudly facing the man. Tall she seemed among the bowing relatives and her face was flushed with passion.

"It is mine to answer, Sri Kashyapa, not my father's. Mine is the blame."

The man whom she had addressed as Kashyapa and whose name seemed to bring a memory in my mind, stared at her.

"You are proud, child, proud and insolent. You stand there, as if you had any right to talk in the presence of your elders. Not only that, but how have you dared to bring the visitor to your house?"

Ritha flushed even a darker red, and I saw drops of sweat appearing on her brow. She stood her ground, refusing obeyance and answered.

"Reverend father, we were all told to expect the traveler, I understood the responsibility of greeting him would fall on whoever found him first."

"You were wrong in that and so many other things, child; how many times have you gone against my wishes?" He said and hit the ground with the staff, emphasizing the point. "You were wrong! He should have been brought to the temple, to me. I am the one who knows what to do, what to ask and what to answer. Do you think you know everything the priests know? He should be at the temple, there we would all have received him and heard him."

Ritha bowed but I could see she still didn't accept the man's rule. Kashyapa turned to me.

"Andrew, glorious Ferdinand Thomas Whittaker's descendant, Osiris' son, you will come with us and you will be shown to the people at the great temple."

I didn't know why but the fact he had omitted my uncle's titles upset me a little, that is how proud silly things make us, but I saw there was no object to refuse, as all those presents clearly recognized this man, this Kashyapa's power over them.

He turned and went out through the same hallway and door as Ritha and I had entered, so long ago as it now seemed. I gazed at Ritha's family, still bowing. Only Ritha stood there, proud and angry, and yes, also the grandmother.

I stared at the old woman, amazed at the emotions on her face. It was not anger, as her granddaughter was showing. I believed at that moment she was making fun of the old man, as if she knew something about him that caused her to despise him, perhaps I could be exaggerating my impression of her. Also, I thought I felt a sense of vengeful expectancy. Did she know something about the future of this Kashyapa?

I shook my head and followed the man; enough questions had arisen with his unexpected arrival.

Outside we were greeted by a crowd who was amazingly in silence and surrounding a large carriage. Kashyapa entered it and then gestured for me to follow; when Ritha would follow, he stopped her with an abrupt gesture.

"No. You may come to the temple, but by your own means."

Sent Back

He then turned and gestured a seat in front of him.

"Sit."

I obeyed.

He remained silent, watching me.

"So Andrew," he said, pronouncing my name with accentuation on the last syllable. "Do you know where you are?"

"Yes, sir, I think I understand that."

"And when?" He insisted.

"That's been harder to comprehend." I said, feeling a childish rebellion growing and I refused to be submissive though I knew to be respectful.

"Hmm," he muttered. "From this age to the age when you'll be born there will elapse no less than some fourteen thousand of human years."

He looked at me with a cryptic expression. I couldn't understand if he was enjoying this, or in fact worried.

"How do you know about the future when I'll be born? Ritha's family could not explain it."

He harrumphed and moved on the seat, accommodating himself better.

"That's why you should have been brought to me before anyone else. We, the priests, and I above them all have been trained to receive guests as yourself. Not all are prepared to handle the yugas and it's only those versed in the life of Vishnu who should receive you."

He turned his face to watch the streets passing by the carriage windows and remained silent for the rest of the trip.

We arrived at a huge temple. I couldn't accept such a great construction could have been done over twelve thousand years ago and stared with gaping mouth at the ornate façade. Gods and goddesses were carved in the walls, that were already darkened by the passage of time and I wondered when had this building being built. The priest had been waiting for me and finally brought me back from my musings with a loud harrumph.

"I am sorry, but this building looks so old I was wondering when it was built. Do you know?"

"It was made by the gods and it has lasted for the last two cycles. Lord Krishna made it His abode. Come in, now. Don't delay!"

I followed him and stepped through the magnificent doors.

CHAPTER XXI

The temple was huge; the large hall where I stood could have been two hundred feet long, and I was unable to see the ceiling.

I was still frozen in awe when someone came before me. My hair stood on end, as if a source of powerful electric force had come near me. I bowed, as I understood this must be a god.

"Do not be afraid, my son." Said the shinning figure, whose white clothes were as shiny as His face and body. "There is a pattern here that was set up before this earth was made. You are here now by command of My Father, He who created all that is, was and will be."

I was so shocked I stuttered.

"You, You are Jesus? The Mesiah?"

"That name was given to me in time, yes. Stop your linear thinking and know that time revolves, becomes a spiral, like a snake it bites its tail. Do not, however, try to fathom how it all works, you'll go mad."

I bowed my head. Yes, surely, I would go crazy if I tried to imagine the mind of God.

"Yes, you would. Now, regarding your visit here, many things hinge on the survival or not of this city and its sister cities. I will make your heart strong and fearless, so the task that will come to you is done. I will come again, Andrew, once again will I walk this Earth to bring the childish humanity to the path of my Father, but this visit of mine today, should be kept secret."

I nodded, still dumbstruck by the fact I was in the presence of the Son of God.

"Remember, Andrew, all this has happened and will happen again. Try not to limit your understanding with the blocked thoughts of your own flesh. Instead, commune with the Sacred Archive, where some of the infinite knowledge is kept. Now, be strong before this proud priest."

Still bowing very low, because I couldn't stand the brilliance of his apparition, I nodded and by some ancient atavism, I brought my hands together in the classic gesture of devotion.

"Listen to me, then, because this is the reason we are here. I have come to show you what will happen if you don't help these people."

The surrounding buildings disappeared, the temple was gone, and I

Sent Back

saw fierce arrows of red flames cover the skies, while thunder pealed, and mountains shook. Suddenly the day turned into night and none could see the blue lit heavens. I saw then a strange rain of brilliant stars, of meteors falling to the world that struck with force the groaning ground and gusts of wind with fierce force shattered trees and walls of nearby cities. Then I saw the high waves rise from within the ocean's depths and swiftly flow upon the shore, and land, and forest. I had seen these waves, I remembered then, when I was a child in my parents' house. I had seen these waves and had been crushed by them. A chill ran through my back, and again I felt the need to breath as I was suffocating.

Once and twice and thrice the huge waves rose, until nothing stood against their force while from above the rain continued of deadly missiles.

Awed, I wished to gaze no more upon the images I was shown but could not withdraw my eyes fastened to the vision.

Then, as the waves receded leaving behind a shattered world, from above I saw hurling to the ground a bigger object. And as the object flew most nearer, its size increased manifold, as big as any Indus city. Just then, inflamed by unknown fire, the meteor exploded with a mighty sound. A wave of wind shattered the world, the river waters dried while the remaining trees and city walls burned with instantaneous flame, consumed before my eyes. A gargantuan mushroom rose from where it burned and once again the day was night, the ground covered with blazing ashes falling from the skies.

Above the land I flew, observing what was left behind. There were no cities left, not one; no helmet, town or house had stood against the overwhelming fire and wind. Far away I flew and saw, floating over the waves, the corpses of those who tried to flee. They were like carvings done on pumice stone and showed the horror of a sudden burning death. All around the dead lay floating over the dirty waters. Far and wide disaster showed. The waters emptied, the rivers dried and the ocean far behind swaying still with mighty waves, burned with flames of deep red glare.

I felt how tears ran down my cheeks. My chest heaved with broken groans of unabated sorrow.

"Stop! Stop this, I can't watch no more!"

The images disappeared as suddenly as they had started, and once again, I saw Him before me.

"That will come to pass, dear one, if you don't do your task. I will be with you, but these people's survival depends on you!"

I felt a powerful struggle inside of me, I didn't want... I didn't want to... To... Then, with sudden realization felt his power inside me.

"You have showed me the conflagration, so is their destiny set?" I replied. "In this world, are they doomed to disappearance and death? Their cities will be ruins, unknown for centuries to come, this I know. Nobody will remember them, nor the words they spoke, nor the tales they told."

"It has not to be so." He replied. "They can still be saved."

"What do you mean!" I replied.

"You must guide them to another land, one where the cataclysm will not strike so devastatingly. A land protected by my Father."

"Will then nothing remain in this land? What about the abandoned cities? I know knowledge about all this will be gone, as will their history." I replied. "For many eons the remains of their cities will be buried before they can be found. No one will know they were the forebears of the world's new civilization. It will be hidden for several millennia."

"You cannot know my Father's designs, suffice it to you to fulfill the task I am imposing upon you."

I bowed again in acceptance, who was I to argue with the Creator's Son?

Then He disappeared, and I once again stood at the temple's entrance, facing the dark inside where statues of different gods sat.

I looked around, fear and awe growing in my chest.

"You are one among an infinite number, just one more." I heard a voice in my head say. "But in you the Spirit will be stronger so the mighty task of saving these people can be carried out. Now go, do not delay! All the towns must be roused and should be on their way before the new full moon rises."

Time must have been stopped for the priest, because when I turned around, I saw him in the same attitude he had as before my vision. I saw him now with another eyes, my perspective of the situation had shifted, and he was not the awesome personality that had impressed me in Ritha's home, but a pitiful individual who thought he had control of life and people.

However, as he had not experienced what I had, he continued in the same forceful manner, expecting me to proceed to the inside of the temple. I obeyed, to gain some time and think how best to proceed in this situation.

Approaching the center of the temple, I saw before me a statue so big, so high, so massive it was a wonder the ground could sustain it. With awe I gazed at its face, until the priest hit me in the back of my head, forcing me to lower my head and eyes.

"Infidel and unrespectful being!" He exclaimed. "How dare you face the god with such insolence and disregard? Bow! Bow before the God of All!"

I bowed, in fact I did more than that, I lay flat on the floor, my arms extended to my side. Naturally I was not bowing to an image of one of these gods, but to Him who was in all of us. Somehow, the priest was forced to do the same, and I could see, with the corner of my eye, his face,

Sent Back

stricken in fear.

After a while and having forced him to remain thus by my side, I stood up.

"Do you think, Priest, that you were put in a position of power to have control over me?" I asked. "Weren't you told enough about me and where I came from to know it is the other way around?"

I stood there, watching his face contorted in anger and fear.

"Yours is to aid, not to command." I continued "And aid is needed if we are to save your world."

"What do you know about anything, you young idolater? What do you fear about my world? It is protected by God, and nothing will happen to it! Ever!"

"How wrong you are." I replied, and rising a hand to forestall his reply, I continued. "Your world is domed; it has been doomed since the beginnings of time. It is its Dharma. Even Indra will not prevent it from happening."

The priest huffed and puffed and tried to turn and give me his back. I held unto him, forcing him to stay facing me.

"The Gods cannot prevent it, but they have devised a way to save your people. That's why I have come, that's why I was sent here, so many, many thousands of years before my time."

"So now you pretend the Gods sent you? You miserable worm? Who do you think you are?" He replied, insolent and prideful.

I took him by both his shoulders, and bringing him toward me, I locked my eyes in his. He shivered, trying to close his eyes, then he cried in agony trying to shake himself away from me. I realized he was in pain and let him go. He crumpled to the ground, while blood flowed from his eyes.

With a shock I realized I had not known the strength of the power that now imbued me. I bent towards him and lifted him, holding to his shoulder. His eyes were bloodshot, though blood had stopped pouring out of them.

"Are you alright?" I asked. "Can you see?"

"Yes, almighty one, though through a veil of blood. I can see. Please pardon my offense, I didn't know." He replied, with meek voice and lowered head.

"You will not tell." I commanded. "This that has happened between you and I is never to be said. Do you hear me?"

"I will not say, I will not talk about it even with myself in the dark of night." He muttered. "What will happen now? Are you to become the supreme priest in my place?"

I laughed.

"No, man. I have no interest in your position, but I'm going to need the help of all priesthood if we are to achieve what I have been sent to do.

First, however, I am going to need Aashritha by my side."

"I will immediately send for her." He replied, and with a slight bow. He retreated, walking backwards, to a door I had not seen at first and I was left alone in the temple's central square, before Indra.

"Well," I said mostly to myself but hoping the god would hear and respond. "Here we go, then. And how I am going to manage such huge operation, I have no idea."

Like a whisper of leaves, or a flutter of wings, there was an answer.

"By the will of God it will be done, the path is there, you just need to show the way."

I shivered. It was all right to know everything in my previous life was just a learning experience leading to this task, to know the fate of civilization lay on my shoulders, that was another different thing altogether.

In my mind's eye I saw paths. I saw people, countless number of them, walking through the plains of the mighty sub-continent, their shades to the East forming a crawling serpent hundreds of miles long. I saw the ocean covered in ships of all sizes and full of people, and cattle.

This was how it was supposed to be, then, I said to myself.

Meanwhile, the priest had returned.

"I gave orders so the young woman be brought to you." Sri Kashyapa said. "Will you stay here?"

"Where can I wait for her?" I asked. "I don't know where else could I wait in your temple."

"I will show you to the place where we study, where all the writings are kept and our apprentices work. Follow me."

I did follow him; I was so astounded, pondering on his words. Writings? Writings over thirteen thousand years before Christ? This would change even more the history of civilization. I smiled inwardly. Talk about cuneiform from Mesopotamia, or hieroglyphs from Egypt, or Phoenician alphabet, all was wrong.

The priest led me through dark passages, mostly lighted by oil lamps, some by candles. I shuddered. If the man wanted to do away with me, this was the perfect setting. Then I controlled my thoughts and shrugged; he would not go in such a way against the designs of the gods.

We reached a vast hall then, greatly illuminated by high windows. There were tables, dozens of tables spread around, most with two or three men assiduously working. Many of these tables had oil lamps to brighten even more their work, a transparent lamp shade protecting the documents from oil or burning. I was later to learn these transparent shades were done with the finest, most refined alabaster or shale.

Not one of the apprentices lifted their heads at our entrance, and only one priest, who seemed to be the one in charge there, stood and came to us.

He bowed low before Sri Kashyapa, and then stood, hands folded

Sent Back

before his chest, waiting.

"This is Andrew, Ferdinand Thomas Whittaker's descendant, Osiris' son. He is also Shri Indra's, may His name be revered forever, elect." Kashyapa said, and I saw the other priest's eyes widen in wonder. He bowed to me then. "He will remain here for a while, waiting for a woman who is to help him in his task."

He smirked, as if the thought of a woman helper, or perhaps me having a task were amusing to him.

"Make him comfortable. I will return when she arrives." He ordered, and turning he added. "I hope this is satisfactory?"

"It is, I thank you." I replied.

Kashyapa gave a slight bow, addressed to no one in particular, and withdrew.

"May I ask what you do here, sir? Forgive me as I know not your name or how to address you." I asked.

"In my infant days I was Ritvij, I have no name now. I renounced my name, I renounced my self. I am only the instrument of Shri Indra, nothing more." He said.

"How then may I address you?" I enquired.

"Some say 'brother', these ones here call me 'teacher'. Though I am no teacher, only God is teacher. I would like it if you called me brother. We are all brothers, are we not?" Then he pronounced this word.

'Jyeṣṭhabhrātā'.

I thought I could never get my tongue around it. He saw my worry and smiled.

"Just call me 'jyeṣṭha'" He said, and with a gesture indicated the place where he had been sitting when we came in.

It was a type of alcove inside the temple wall. All the walls were covered with racks of shelves where rolls of writings were kept. I was even more amazed at this than at the fact the other priests and apprentices were writing. To have amassed such a large amount of written documents meant this civilization had at least several hundred years of development.

Inside the alcove lay a flat cushion, apparently much used and I thought, as I looked at it, it must be incredibly uncomfortable.

The priest understood my expression, smiling again.

"Come with me." He almost whispered. I understood he didn't want to disturb those working around him, so I nodded and followed.

He brought me to a corner of the large hall, where, behind a very low table I saw a wooden bank, maybe one foot high.

"Very old priests who cannot bend their knees anymore sometimes sit here when they need to work in the knowledge hall. You may sit here."

I blushed. I was neither very old, nor inflexible, but I knew I could not sit in his alcove for over two or three minutes before becoming cramped.

"Thank you." I said and gave the little bow with hands pressed before me that was usual. "This will be a good place to wait."

"I will leave you and return to my work." He said, and was turning to leave when, holding to his trailing robe, I prevented him.

"Wait." I said. And he raised his eyebrows at my loud voice. "Wait." I repeated in a whisper.

"Can I look at some of the documents you are working at right now? I am very interested." I added.

"Do you think you'll be able to understand?" He queried, but immediately realizing he shouldn't be asking that of an elect of Indra, he bowed and went to a nearby table. He talked with one young man who was there working and took several long and narrow strips of something that could have been paper.

He brought them to me. I saw they were held together lengthwise and looked like a small book or notebook. They were maybe three inches wide by five or six long, and exquisitely written in Vedic characters. I was thrilled to hold such thing in my hand. Not a single one item had survived the eons passed between this now and the so-called historic times. Who would have guessed there was an ancient civilization that thousands of years before Egypt, or Mesopotamia and Summer already had literature and a written form of it. I shook with emotion, and some minutes passed before I could focus on the text.

CHAPTER XXII

In my hands rested a treasure and it broke my heart to know that it and thousands like it would disappear and would never again be found, never again the records it kept would be read. The mere idea of anything being written at that time would cause men to mock and laugh, and any scientist who propounded the idea would be anathemized.

And yet, here it was, here they were, kept by the thousands in this version of a library.

I focused on the one in my hands. I took a while to make sense of the characters. Beautiful they were, curves and lines, squares and semicircles, all carefully drawn by a skilled brush. Then, the first lines hit me.

"Agnimīḷe purohitam yajñasya devamṛtvijam, hotāram ratnadhātamam."

Naturally they were not written in our alphabet, the characters were unknown to me, no language I knew used them, and yet, I understood them, and I knew the invocation. This was what was written, I could understand it.

"Agni I adore, who stands before the Lord, the god who seeth Truth, the warrior, strong disposer of delight."

I am an archaeologist, and of that discipline I have studied about ancient Egypt, and some of the ancient civilizations of Central and South America. My knowledge, however, is lacking about the other civilizations. Little do I know about the creators of Göbekli Tepe, Mesopotamia, Sumer. I am not ashamed of this. I know I'm at the beginning of my career, and I hoped I would have time to broaden my knowledge. Of ancient India, however, my knowledge was even less, so it amazed me I recognized this verse as the beginning of the Rigveda, the first Veda recognized by scholars to have been written.

An invocation to Agni, the god of fire who was probably the first god worshipped by humanity, because it brought warmth, and ability to cook food, perhaps even the source of protection from wild beasts.

So here in my hands I had, apparently, a first version of the Rigveda. It had been said the Vedas were not written until maybe one thousand years before Christ Era. Some had tried to push it further back, two or even three thousand BC, here I was finding them sixteen thousand years ago.

I went to the table from where the teacher had gotten it and stood behind the writer. He soon realized my presence and turned.

"Is there anything you need, Master?" He asked.

"Please tell me about this." I replied. "Is this the first time you wrote these lines? Where did they come from?"

He smiled.

"Oh, no! I have copied them again and again. I do not know how many times, and my brothers that went before had copied them many times, too." He stopped and seeing my unbelief he continued.

"We copy it from copies made of the First Book long time ago. No one can see the First Book now, it is kept in the sacred place, protected from damage. But the copies of the copies have been passed on, and we make more and more so that in never dies."

"I thought the law was that the Science the Vedas could not be written, because then it would be changed, its meaning misunderstood. I thought only the priests knew the words, and would know them by heart, committing to memory the verses through a long apprenticeship."

"The priests do know it by heart. I am a priest, too. We are supposed to learn the Vedas as our first task, and we learn to recite them as our ancestors did. However, keeping the sacred word is paramount. What would happen if all the priests died? Then the Sacred Word would disappear. We cannot let that happen."

He seemed restless and kept shooting glances to the door. I suspected the head priest, or even the teacher would not be happy by his talking to me, so I thanked him and returned to my place.

I needed time to think, too. All that had been said in my time was wrong. There was no prohibition to write the Vedas, there was no law that said only by transference from master to pupil was it to be known or learned. In fact, at the beginning of time, it had been written, written by the hundreds or perhaps thousands of times.

I kept reading, and before me the lines spread, turning to words in my mind which slowly begun a song I knew was recited by the priests of my time.

Hours went by, unfelt by me in my absorption of the reading. I was brought out by a hand laid softly on my shoulder. I looked up. Ritha was there.

"You asked for me?" She whispered near my ear.

I nodded.

"Yes." I replied in the same way. "But we cannot talk here. Is there any place where we can, without bothering these priests?"

"Let's go to the temple gardens." She whispered. "Follow me."

I rose and gathering the 'books' went to the writer's table and gave them to him, bowing and thanking him. I then followed Ritha who was halfway to the door already and waiting for me.

She took my hand and guided me through passages which apparently she knew well, until we reached a wide gate, a door of incredible height and width that let in the setting sun rays.

"Come, we can talk in the garden."

"But the sun is setting, it will soon be night." I complained.

"There will be light, do not worry. Come." She insisted, pulling at my hand again.

We walked through narrow paths, flanked by bushes of all types, some with flowers of wonderful aromas and colors, others with leaves of the most varied shades. There were small palm trees, and large palm trees, and trees of different types unknown to me. Farther into the garden we walked until we reached a fountain from where a thin spray of water misted the air. Around the fountain were several trees and small benches to one of which she went.

"Tell me then, what do you need of me? How can I help?"

I gazed at her, thinking of a way to explain what had happened at the temple's entrance. How could I tell her that the Only Son of God, of whom nobody knew about in her time, nor would know in more than thirteen thousand years, had appeared to me and that God had charged me to save her people? In my time, I would be locked up in an asylum or in times before I would be burnt at the stake.

"Do you know why I came to this land and this time?" I asked, searching for a way to start.

"We were told your coming was very important to our city, and that we should help you in any way you needed." She said.

"But why?"

"I don't know. That was not told." She replied.

"Who told you this?" I insisted.

"Some of us are nearer the gods than others. To some, the gods speak, sometimes in dreams, sometimes in our waking hours. My family, specially my grandmother and myself, we hear them at all hours."

A flickering thought of hereditary madness passed across my mind, swiftly discarded. If there was madness here, I was part of it since the beginning.

"So if I were to tell you a God appeared before me and showed me something, you would accept it?"

"Naturally I would. It is so with us, too."

"Vasudeva?" I whispered, and immediately wondered why I had said that name.

Her eyes grew large, and she flushed. Then nodded.

"You know of him?" I insisted.

"Naturally. He is the father of Lord Krishna. He came to you?"

I nodded.

She folded her hands and bowed, whispering an almost inaudible prayer.

"And then?" She asked, and I could see she was awed by this development.

I looked at her, and stood, taking some steps away and then back. How do you tell anyone that her city will be destroyed and erased from the face of the Earth?

I took a grip of myself. If I would do this, explaining it to a young woman would be the least of the problems. Imagine moving a whole civilization. Who was I to do that? But I had my orders.

"Ritha," I started. "Let me tell you a story."

She moved, making herself more comfortable, and lifted her face. She was beautiful. Would she perish in the conflagration? In my time she had been dead for millennia before I was even born. I vanquished the thoughts from my mind and sat by her side.

"You know I come from a very far away future, don't you?"

"Yes, it was explained."

"In that very distant future…" I hesitated.

"Go ahead, I know something awful happens to my city."

I didn't wonder how she knew and started again.

"Not only your city, Ritha, your whole civilization disappeared from history, there was no record of it for thousands of years. Only about a hundred years before I was born were the remnants of your cities found, and only those further inland, near the sacred Saraswati River."

She stifled a moan, taking her hands to hide her face, bowing her head.

"I knew it was bad but didn't imagine how bad it was." She said in a whisper. "Please tell me all."

"Perhaps only some hundred years into the future, or perhaps sooner than that, a huge rock, in fact several huge rocks will crash against this world. They will cause fires, floods, earthquakes, and other disasters. This land will be submerged by the rising ocean as will hundreds of other cities now thriving around the world. This civilization will perish. Not only yours, but every city in the world, far into other continents and island will be destroyed."

Ritha brought her hands to her chest, as if trying to protect her heart from such terrible news.

"Do you want me to stop?" I asked.

"No." She shook her head. "No, there must be a reason you are telling me. Please, continue."

I sighed, this was harder than I had thought.

"Some people survived this cataclysm, saved by the will of God. They spread around the world, and slowly, very slowly, humanity tried to regain what had been lost. It took thousands of years, and in those elapsed years, the memory of what had been was lost. Some stories were called myths by those who thought theirs was the only real and right knowledge."

A look of doubt passed over her face.

"Myths are like stories for children, not really true."

"Oh."

"Those stories spoke about a gigantic flood, a flood that covered all the Earth, and from which only selected ones were saved. But nothing was said about the hundreds of cities, of the great knowledge kept in their libraries, of the science and development they had achieved. And if anyone tried to talk about it, they were mocked and ridiculed."

"Why? Didn't they trust the elders? The priests?"

"No. Humanity had become so self-centered, proud and conceited they thought they knew everything. Even the Sacred Book was put in doubt."

"They couldn't" Ritha gasped "Didn't the gods strike them dead?"

"No." I replied, shaking my head. "God had already punished the civilization of which you are part because of their wickedness, and He had promised He would not do that again."

I waited, but she didn't comment on that, even though my calling her civilization 'wicked' should have hurt.

"Alright, you are telling me these countries, all these people in so many hundreds of cities who coexist with us in this world, will perish. Why do I need to know it? Is it going to happen now?"

"No, I don't think it is immediate, because if I understood the orders I was given, it's going to take some time to prevent your civilization from following that destruction. But it will happen soon, so we need to act swiftly."

Ritha stood, her body reflected incredulity and fear simultaneously. She walked some steps around the tree, and returned to where I waited, also now standing.

"Are you going to save us?"

I nodded.

"But how? Can you stop those giant stones from falling? Can you stop the seas from rising and swallowing the cities?"

"No. I cannot do anything like that. I am no god, Ritha. But perhaps I can save the people."

"Let me tell you another story." I continued. "Several thousand years before I was born, there existed a group of people whom God had selected as His. They had many adventures, fleeing from hunger and enemies, until they came to a land of riches, food, and honey. That land was called Kemet."

"Kemet." She repeated. "Alright, go on."

"They arrived there, and one of this people, Joseph, who had been elected by the king to a position of authority, gave the newcomers land, and the possibility to live in Kemet. These people are called in my time Jews, though I imagine that's not how they called themselves. They prospered in Kemet, they multiplied until they were as many as the people from Kemet, so these ones started fearing them. The Jews were enslaved by the king of Kemet, and they suffered much abuse, and death."

"Couldn't they escape?"

"No, the land of Kemet is surrounded by desert, totally devoid of water. And the king had lots of soldiers who would have killed them."

"You are saying many things, Andrew, that I cannot comprehend. I do not understand what you call a king, and I do not understand the term soldier."

"Don't you have a ruler, in this city?" I asked, amazed myself at what her question implied.

"Our city is ruled by the community of elders and some higher priests. Together they decide what is best for the citizens. If there's need for a new water distribution system, they talk to those who have expertise working with channels, and it gets done. Are you saying that in that land, only one person ruled? Only one person decided what was good or bad for the people? He must have been a god, or incredibly wise and good."

"No." I countered. "No, sadly that was not how they were. Throughout the centuries, civilizations have been ruled by kings, pharaohs, governors, dictators who were neither good, wise or gods. In fact, our history is plagued by terrible battles and murderous events started by those in power."

"And you want us to be saved so we would live in that kind of world? I don't think any of my people would agree to it."

"Ritha, in many ways you are right. Mine is not a civilization to be proud of, nevertheless there are good things in that world. I do not understand the reason God has asked me to save you, but I do His bidding. He is much much wiser than either you or I could imagine, He must have a reason for this."

"Alright," she said. "So what happened to those Jews in the land of Kemet?"

"Ah, yes! We were talking about them. It is told in the Sacred Book that God heard their cries of suffering and decided to save them from their slavery. Slavery is when a person is deprived of all liberty or power of decision on their lives. God elected a man and talked to him so he would help the Jews escape from Kemet. They did, they followed after this man, who was called Moses, traveling across the desert, crossing the waters of the sea. God fed them and cared for them, until they reached a land that He had promised their forebear many years before."

Sent Back

"So God saved them?"

"Yes."

"And that's what you are supposed to do?"

I stood there, frozen. Was I then, to be a Moses to these people? How could I? The mere thought of comparing myself to him made me ashamed. Had I understood the Mesiah's words correctly?

"Andrew?" She insisted. "Are you to be like that man to us?"

Again I saw the multitude in a long serpent-like crowd, walking, walking towards the mountains far away. I saw ships, and boats crowding the sea, on the way to the land where the Sun sets. Was it to be only the people of Kumari Kandam who would be saved? What about all those who lived in the cities by the sea or in other continents or islands. Was it only this people whom I had to save? Why them? Why only them? And most of all, why me, why me?

CHAPTER XXIII

How many cities, I wondered, made up this civilization? Were all in Kumari Kandam? What about the southeast lands, Sri Lanka, Eastern India? I was sure there must be cities akin to this one all around. Was I supposed to save them all?

If I was, it would be an Exodus like never before. And where to? To northern India? Towards the Himalayas? Or even farther? But where? Moses new he was leading his people to the land God had promised Abraham. Naturally he didn't know the coordinates, or anything about it, but he had faith, and trusted.

Should I just, like him, trust?

One way or the other, I thought my first step would be to test the waters with the Community of Elders. I had to get their help and approval if I was to do anything.

"Ritha," I said, "Do you think the Elders will believe me, as you have?"

"Many are they, from different origins and professions. I think many will accept your words, more so because we've known for a long time you were to come, and we should expect you. However, even in that aspect there were those that mocked the prophesies, you met one, the priest who came to our house."

"Yes, I imagine he would not believe any of it. Are there many like him?"

"I don't know, Andrew. My family is not very important, and we rarely had the opportunity to meet with the Elders. Are you afraid?"

I considered the question and took minutes to analyze my feelings. On one side, I knew that if the Mesiah had set me that task, I was due to fulfill it. All my life, I thought, had been a preparation for this moment. From another viewpoint, how many prophets had been massacred following the word of the Lord?

"I don't think I am afraid, Ritha, but the enormity of the task is overwhelming. Just think about it. Thousands upon thousands of your people moving, following me! Me! I mean, who am I to guide all of you to safety?"

"You are Andrew son of Osiris, descendant of Sir Ferdinand Thomas

Sent Back

Whittaker, Esq., the one we were told to expect. Surely the majority will recognize you and listen to you"

"Ritha, how many cities that you know make up your country? How many people make part of your civilization? Do you know?"

"I do not, Andrew. I can tell you this city where we live has many thousands of inhabitants, and I know there are hundreds and hundreds of cities spread all over Kumari Kandam, and many more farther inland near the five rivers land."

"The Punjab, yes." I commented absorbed in the numbers. Then I saw her expression, full of wonder and questioning. "They call it the Punjab in my time, how do you call it?"

"The Punjab." She replied, smiling. "I just wondered how you knew."

Not willing to engage in any more explanation about past and future nomenclature, I continued to ask about the Elders.

"When could I talk to the Elders? Do you think we could manage that?"

"Not on our own. How could we? But maybe the high priest Kashyapa would help us. He belongs to the council, you know?"

As luck would have it, the priest whom I had antagonized was the only one who could give us access to the council. Oh well, did I have faith, or not.

"Let's find him." I said, taking Ritha's hand in my own and walking back to the temple.

"The first thing you need to do, Andrew, is to convince Kashyapa of what's going to happen. If you manage that, I think half of our need to convince the council will be done."

"Is he so important in the council, then?" I asked.

"He is important, many people take his decisions as if coming from God himself. But as you know, he is very stubborn and proud. To admit you know something he doesn't, and that would put you in a position of authority, will be difficult, to say the least."

"Well, I imagine Moses convincing the pharaoh, had much more trouble than we can face with him, I hope."

We had entered the temple, and Ritha was guiding me through hallways and halls crowded with images. There were statues of several gods, carved in wood and stone. Many were, I thought, gilded, because I didn't think they were cast in gold. Others were garishly painted in brilliant colors, Indra, of course, with his almost bare body of a deep blue.

During all our walk through the temple, we had met no other priest, student, or servant but now we came to a huge hall and there we found a large group of priests, who were standing there, talking among themselves with muted voices.

As soon as we entered the room, they all, as a man, turned toward us. One of them, apparently of some importance, approached us. He bowed slightly, and spoke, without addressing Ritha or me in particular.

"How do you dare to come to this inner sanctum? You know well nobody is allowed here but the priests!"

Ritha bowed low, and without facing the priest, but with her face turned somewhat sideways, replied.

"Dire news have made us come here, and I beg your pardon for this violation of the temple's rules, but the high priest needs to be informed without delay."

"What can you know that we don't? How dare you think there's something you know that he doesn't?" He replied, also without looking at her, but staring high above her head.

"This is Andrew, son of Osiris, descendant of Sir Ferdinand Thomas Whittaker, Esq., the one we were told to expect. He brings to us the word of God." She said.

The man turned now to face me, a frown of disdain on his face.

"You are Andrew?"

I nodded, waiting.

"And you pretend to have news from God that we don't have? That's inadmissible!"

I smiled.

"Why would you have been told to expect me if it weren't for something important? High priest Kashyapa has already realized I am the envoy. Why don't you?"

The other priests had slowly come towards where we stood with the first priest and were surrounding us in a semicircle. I heard exclamations and mutters among them. One of them, surreptitiously, walked toward a large door in the farther wall of the hall and, without knocking, went in.

I suspected he had decided Kashyapa needed to know what was going on, and as I thought, several minutes after he emerged from the door, followed by the other priest.

The group parted, bowing with respect, and left a corridor through which the high priest walked towards me.

"What is this?" He asked, all his proud mien returned. "Why come you to the sacred hall?"

Now it was that I faced him directly, looking into his eyes and locking them with mine.

"There appears to be some doubt, Kashyapa, between your followers. Apparently, the prophesy about my coming has no importance, as you are supposed to know everything." I said, somewhat sarcastically.

I saw how he constrained himself from a violent reply, and after taking a deep breath, he turned to the group.

Sent Back

"Return to your tasks." He ordered. Nothing more, no comment, no explanation. His power among these people was complete.

We waited for a few minutes until all had exited the hall, and then he turned to Ritha.

"Why are you here, woman?"

"She is here," I interposed, "because I have selected her to be my helper, and you will do well if you respect her as such."

I knew he had to control himself not to answer me with one of his usual responses, but he still remembered what had happened before.

"As you wish." He said and gesturing for us to follow walked toward the door from where he had exited.

"Come in. In this place we can talk privately and is much more comfortable."

We entered. This room must be his private quarters. There was a low table full of scrolls, two candles and one of those lamps I had seen in the library. In a corner, a mat with some rugs showed where he slept.

Well, at least he was not like one of those priests nowadays that propound humility and frugality and yet at home live like kings.

He guided us to another corner, where several cushions were spread around another table, circular in form.

"Sit." He said, doing so himself.

I managed to sit in the cushion more or less gracefully while admiring the ease with which he, a man much older than I, sat gathering his robe around him.

We kept a few minutes of silence, and then he asked: "So what is this of such import that you have dared to come to these rooms forbidden to all but the priests of this temple?"

Ritha bowed.

"Which your permission, high priest Kashyapa, Andrew needs your help to convince the council."

"My help?" He wondered, brows raised in amazement or perhaps disdain. "The mighty Andrew needs my help?" He mocked.

I stood up. Only standing did I feel comfortable to explain what was to come.

"Your help, yes. What I am going to tell you will appear to be a myth, a story for children, a lie; but I am telling you it is the truth, as it happened and I have learnt."

"Al right, speak." He said, accommodating himself better in the cushions, and giving a quick glance to Ritha, who nodded.

"Before I came to this place, and to this time, I was far away, in a time many centuries into your future. In that place, I met the descendants of your civilization. They were the survivors of a terrible cataclysm that destroyed all the cities of the world and killed the majority of their inhabitants. From them, and from the history of my present, I know what happened."

"And what was that?" He asked, still mocking.

Ritha interposed.

"Huge rocks are flying through the skies, and they will hit our land and the lands of many other cities far from us."

"Lies."

"I said that was what you would think. So because of it, because of your lack of trust and faith, I will share my memories with you." I stopped, amazed at myself.

What was I going to do? I was not the elder Yudhishtra, I did not know how to read minds, or transfer my thoughts. And yet I had said it, and knew that, somehow, I would do it.

I went before Kashyapa and sitting, with more ease now, placed my hands on each side of his head.

At first he tried to shake me off, but then, the kind of trance I had endured in Arinjay's village began, and he remained still, trembling a little now and then.

I don't know how long it took. There were no windows there to check the time of day, nor was there any time measuring device. I found none of those in the time I was there. Then, when my memories were exhausted, just as my physical strength was, I let my arms fall.

We remained still for a long while, and then tears poured from Kashyapa's eyes. He cried, silently, but I could see the pain I had caused with my memories. Well, I was sorry, but it was what I needed to do to gain his trust and help.

"Is all that true? All that you made me see and experience?"

"Those were my memories, priest. I cannot manipulate my memories, nor the process by which I shared them with you, anymore than you can stop the Sun from rising. Yes, it's true, all of it."

"That is terrible, terrible!" He muttered. "How could the survivors live after losing everything?"

"Their pain never stopped, even though they created a new life, and formed new families and at the end, a new civilization with majestic buildings. And that pain lives still in me because I am their descendant and I inherited them."

He gazed at me with amazement and, perhaps, admiration.

"What do you want me to do? Is there a way to avoid the catastrophe? To save our people?"

"That's why I am here. That's why God sent me here. Now you know why I need you to convince the council of elders. We must leave. You must abandon your houses and temples, your images and constructions, your cities, and follow me to the North and West. Hundreds and hundreds of miles into the land near the mountains, away from the ocean that will destroy and cover all the cities, all the lands in this world."

He wrung his hands, in a paroxysm of agony.

"Leave this? Leave my city where I was born, where my parents and their parents were born and grew, and married? Where I dedicated myself to the service of Sri Indra? How? Why can't He stop the cataclysm? Where is His power if he's going to let his people be destroyed?"

I didn't answer. I had the same questions, but I knew that everything that happened was by God's will, and that He had a reason, difficult to fathom, yes, but a reason for what would happen.

"I do not know, Kashyapa, but the fact that He sent me here must mean something. The cities will be destroyed, and nobody will know about them for millennia upon millennia, but some day, far into the future, I promise you that your history will be known, and somehow your cities will once again be visible and admired. Isn't saving your people more important than the roads and monuments and houses and temples?"

Startled he looked at me with denial, but then, bowing his head, he nodded.

"Yes. The people are the ones we have to save. If we save them, the cities will again be born; but the knowledge, the libraries! How can we save the libraries?" He exclaimed in the cusp of pain.

"I suppose you can carry the most important treaties and writings with you. I know your library contains millions of scrolls, and it will be impossible to save them all. But at least some will be, which would not happen if you stay here until the cataclysm happens."

He nodded, and I could see he was already giving orders in his mind, selecting the most precious books, loading them into carts and bags.

"Yes." He exclaimed and stood up. "Come Andrew, Ritha. Let's gather the council."

And then, as an afterthought, he asked me.

"Can you do this, this sharing of your memories with them?"

"I doubt it, Kashyapa. You saw how it left me, so tired, so exhausted I could barely lift my arms. Let's hope there's no need for me to try it again."

"We'll see." He said, visibly not satisfied with my answer. "We'll see. Come now, let us go."

But we hadn't realized how time had passed, it had been evening when Ritha and I finally spoke with the high priest. It was now nearly midnight, and the priest's attendants were asleep in their posts.

"I think we will have to postpone the meeting with the council." Said Kashyapa.

I nodded. I was realizing now how tired I was after all I had been doing that day. Truly the day seemed to have had thirty hours instead of twenty-four and I thought that maybe in this time, the world revolved more slowly than in my time. However it was, we would need to find a place to rest, Ritha and I, as the priest was already in his quarters.

Apparently he had been following my train of thoughts, because he went to one to the attendants and spoke in a low voice. In a few minutes, places to sleep had been prepared, with cushions and a type of blankets that, even though light, provided good protection against the cool breeze of the night.

Food was brought to us, and we ate in silence. I do not know what it was, but I enjoyed it, as it was tasty and soft to the palate. We drank some tea, Ritha and I, but I saw the attendant pouring some liquid in the high priest's cup.

Kashyapa stood, and with the cup in his hands, bowed almost to the ground, he sang some verses at the time he spilt some of the liquid on the floor. Then, he drank what was left.

With a gesture, he indicated to the attendant to fill it again, and once done, Kashyapa approached me. He offered the cup.

"It's soma, the sacred drink." He said. "It will help you prepare for the morrow."

I bowed as I accepted the cup, and with a lot of apprehension, imitated his previous actions, spilling, trying to remember his invocation and failing miserably and then drinking.

It had a sweet pungent taste, perhaps it had milk in it, and I waited for any reaction of my body, but all seemed well.

The attendant approached with a piece of embroider tissue and gathered the spilt liquid, retrieving it and placing it before one image by the walls.

"Let us sleep, and maybe the gods will bring us dreams to help for what lies ahead." The high priest said.

CHAPTER XXIV

I settled down, thinking it would be difficult for me to sleep in this situation and with the impending confrontation with the council of elders, but I fell asleep immediately, maybe it was the effect of the soma, maybe exhaustion after all I had been through in the last days.

As I lay in a deep sleep, again the Son of God came before me.

"I'll show the path on which you must set them. Come with me."

I was aloft and alone, at hundreds of feet above the ground, and I started moving. I saw below me the city, with its tall buildings and temples, the streets, both broad and narrow, the small houses and shops. I flew over it, like those dreams everyone has had of flying, and soon I was leaving the city boundaries, and crossing over cultivated fields. To my left I could see the coastline, and it was weird, because I knew it was night, and still everything was illumined by a silver light. I twisted my head and yes, there it was a gigantic full moon.

I still flew, and passed over several hamlets, isolated homes and cities, not as large as Dwarka, but large indeed. Then, I realized I was passing over the Indus River delta, and still to the north by west I flew. Where was I going? Were the people I was supposed to save travel this way? Somehow I knew that yes, that was one of the ways. I will not detail each place over which I flew, suffice it to say that I understood they were to border the Arabian Peninsula, reach the entrance to the Red Sea and follow north, to the Nile River Delta.

Had I been walking, I would had stopped that very instant. What? This huge population, this gigantic exodus would arrive on the same place where thousands of years after Moses guided his people in the famous Exodus?

Not only that, no not only that. They would be going to the place where the survivors of the cataclysm and their descendants, those I had known and grown to love would go. They would go there because I told them; they would go there because Thoth advised it so. How was all this going to change the path of history? Would the two groups of survivors meet?

Then, another thought hit me. Did these have anything to do with the hate priest Ay had for me? Was this the damage I had done to his family?

But how?

Somehow, my flight stopped, and I felt a presence coming before me. I couldn't see a person, just a brilliant light emanating from something bigger than me.

"This is one of the paths selected to protect the ancient civilization, and yes, in the future, Ay's world will have something to do with them. That is not of your concern. Come now, the other path must be followed tonight, too."

I shrugged. What was I to do? I was not master of myself.

We went back, suddenly we were again over the Indus River delta.

"From here the paths diverge, and while one goes west and north, the other would go north and east. Through what will be called the Persian Gulf, they will go, seeking the rivers that had poured from Eden. Up the Euphrates, to the confluence of Sajur River and then further north and to the east, to find the Anatolian plateau. They will be founding the basis for the Sumer and Babylonian civilizations."

We had been going that way, as the light explained, and I had seen below me a huge plain that would become the Persian Gulf, and from it to the Euphrates River, and its confluence with Sajur.

"Are they...?" I stuttered because another crazy idea had come into my head.

The light stopped, making me stop to. And waited. I knew it waited for my question.

"Are they... are they, perhaps, the ones who will build Göbekli Tepe?"

"They will be the seed which will grow to create the place you thus call, yes."

I was flabbergasted. Was Göbekli Tepe then related to the ancient Indus civilization? How crazy was this development! Nobody would believe me. Well, nobody would believe anything of all I had been experiencing, so what mattered something even crazier. I nodded.

"Alright, so these are two paths for them to go. Is that it?"

"No, another and perhaps more difficult path will be offered for those cities further inland. To the foothills of the Himalayas they should go, crossing the scorched lands through narrow passages, and through mountain passes and vales farther into the high mountains, until they reach what in your times is known as the Tibetan Plateau. You should make it clear, however, they are never to cross the mountains farther north, into the lands below."

"But how will they be able to survive in the Himalayas, those mountains are incredibly high, scarce pastures and places to grow food; I also imagine the temperatures over there will be extremely low."

"Yours is to show where, and nothing more. Do you think He would save them just to go into extinction? He has plans."

Sent Back

I was ashamed, and bowed my head
Then the presence continued.

"After you've spoken to the council, you will request messengers to be sent to all the cities and those inland, and by the Indus, Saraswathi and Ganges rivers. The message will say: '*God has seen the wickedness of your civilization, and how your self-importance and ego has grown, abandoning His teachings. Now, all you consider important, all you construed and created; everything of which you are proud of will be destroyed to show you what is truly important. Abandon everything you covet, leave cities and towns, because they will be submerged by the raging seas, and seek the mountains, seek higher ground or you will all perish.*'"

And I found myself in the temple, among cushions and untidy blankets, awake, my heart pounding as if I had run several miles. So this was what I had to tell the council. Would they believe me?

The presence was gone, and I fell into a deep, dreamless sleep

I shouldn't have doubted.

Sun shining on my face woke me up. I looked around, all were still sleeping and when I say all, I refer only to Ritha and Kashyapa, as the attendants had all left during the night.

Only that ray of sunlight had fallen on my face, only on me, you must admire my luck, after spending most of the night wandering around the globe, my sleep had been cut short. Before I went to wake up the other two, the doors to the chamber opened and some attendants came in, bringing what seemed to be breakfast.

Kashyapa sat on his mattress rapidly, and Ritha yawned and stretched, also sitting up.

"Andrew? You are already up?" She said, stating the obvious.

"Yes, just a while before you. You slept well?"

"I did, I must have been very tired." She said smiling.

We three approached the low table where breakfast had been laid, steaming tea, and some small pastries, still hot.

After Kashyapa had performed his morning rites, and we were shown to a place where we could do some ablutions and take care of other matters, we went back again, and sat around the table.

"Now is the time ripe to go meet the council." Kashyapa said. "I will have someone go to them and announce us."

We set out in the carriage that had previously brought me here, so many years ago as it seemed, though it had been only yesterday.

It took only a little time to reach a large building that must have been ancient. Again the walls were decorated with statues of gods and animals, plants and flowers and all dark with the passage of time.

We entered a large room where, seated around in a semicircle, the council awaited.

Once again, I repeat, I shouldn't have doubted, but there was a previous happening. Mosses, too, had doubted of his ability to convince not only his people, but the Pharaoh. He had tried to shake off this responsibility, only to be shown he must comply.

I went, I faced the council and told them all I had been told to. I explained about the coming cataclysm, about the rising of the seas, the earthquakes and volcanoes. I told them they had to leave their city, their cities, because if not they would all succumb to the wrath of God.

It was no good.

They contended that theirs was the city of god, of Indra. That he would protect them and not permit anything happening to them. They doubted every word I had uttered, and even questioned Kashyapa's part on it.

They had been ready to leave when before them appeared an image. It was the city, Dwarka, the city where we were, but it was under the sea. We could see fish, and debris, and algae flowing in and out and above the high towers. The whole city wavered, as some strong current pushed against it.

The council members gasped, there were cries of consternation. Others, probably those more set on denying what was coming, spoke with authority.

"Stop this magic!" Some cried, and others were saying:

"This trickery will avail you nothing, young man!"

The image changed. Huge waves as high as four to six hundred meters seemed to come towards us, and they ducked, hiding behind each other. And then another, and another, image after image was shown before their eyes, the meteorite impact, the incredible explosion, the volcanoes suddenly becoming active and spewing lava kilometers into the atmosphere.

Then all stopped.

Moses had had his staff, and then the plagues. I had had the images of what would happen; it was enough.

Some time later, when they had all recovered from the terrific images, they came and bowed before us.

"We are sorry we doubted you." Said the oldest of the group, addressing Kashyapa. "Tell us what needs to be done."

"Is not me who is in charge here, but Andrew. He is the one God has sent to alert and save us." Said the high priest.

They muttered, but the images had done what my words had not, and soon they accepted me, and listened.

Hour after hour we spent, coordinating the groups, the property that should be saved, the libraries. They questioned the directions they were told to take, contradicting each step, but always at the end accepting.

Boats would be requisitioned, to carry the ones going to the west, to go past the Arabic Peninsula, into the Red Sea and north to where the

Sent Back

Nile's delta would be after the conflagration. Naturally these were not the names they used, but I knew what they meant, and it was all right.

However, when all was getting organized, when guides and protection had been assigned to the different groups, when the messengers to inland cities had been sent; it was time to transmit God's message.

'God has seen the wickedness of your civilization, and how your self-importance and ego has grown, abandoning His teachings. Now, all you consider important, all you construed and created; everything of which you are proud of will be destroyed to show you what is truly important. Abandon everything you covet, leave cities and towns, because they will be submerged by the raging seas, and seek the mountains, seek higher ground or you will all perish.

Now this raised a storm. The complaints, the angry comments, even insults addressed to me were many and loud. I had expected it and had been amazed when I had told Ritha about her "wicked civilization" and she hadn't argue back. The council, however, was arguing.

Kashyapa finally got them to calm down.

"Pay attention to the words, feel them in your souls. Aren't the words that Andrew has transmitted to us true? Think about them."

There were mutterings, and angry denials, but again Kashyapa stopped them.

"Aren't we proud of our cities, of our temples and homes? Don't we think the images of our gods are the most perfect and sanctified? What about our personal properties, our jewels? We have indeed become wicked, we have lost the path to God and instead follow the path to our pride. Don't you see it?"

Silence followed his words.

I knew how difficult it was to accept ones' failures, imagine accepting all their civilization was now catalogued as wicked by the only One who could judge them.

I felt a pall of sadness and depression fall on the assembly, and I knew that was not the way to go.

"God has shown you his judgement, but He has also shown you His love and mercy. Don't you see? He could have let you all perish under the sea, in the earthquakes and terrible disasters, instead, He chose to save you. Why is He doing this? I am not the one to interpret God's will or motives, but I can tell you that by the mere fact of giving you the possibility to be saved, He's showing His love for you."

They had now lifted their faces to me, and I could see hope coming back to their hearts.

"Just as in the distant future He will elect a small group of people to become a great nation, to be His people, in the same way I believe He has selected you this time. So be hopeful and let us try to understand His words and act accordingly. Will you now consider saving your jewels, your possessions?"

I saw them shaking their heads, 'No'.

"The statues? The temples' properties?"

Again shaking the head, 'No'.

"That is right, you must save your lives, your hearts, your beliefs and even maybe the Sacred Word you have protected for centuries, nothing more than that. He will provide."

I realized there had been a turn in their hearts, a new hope imbued them and a sense of pride, of being elected by their God to survive. I felt a tug at my arm and turned. Ritha was beside me, her face lighted with devotion and hope.

"You spoke well, Andrew. I now understand well why we were told to expect you."

"It is no merit of mine, Ritha, you should know that." I said.

"I know, but still the Word came to us through you. What now?"

"I don't know. I don't know if I am supposed to go with all of you or not; I don't know if I should go with the ones going to the West, or East or all the way North towards the mountains."

"I'm sure somehow you will be told." She said

,

CHAPTER XXV

The days passed swiftly, and I was involved in the Council decisions, as if I knew so much about their cities, traveling possibilities and resources. But I tried to help as much as possible, and sometimes the answers to their questions came as if dictated by a higher power, which I assumed it was.

I learned how their seaworthy transportations had been recalled, and now waited, moored in the port. There were large ships, the likes of which I had never imagined they had in what we called 'prehistory'; barges also, large and small, even boats which could carry at most four persons. All were there, and I was told there were many more out there, farther south and west, which they hadn't been able to contact. Messengers were sent to cities and towns where they were supposed to go to, and the council was hopeful they could still return on time.

Other messengers had already left in the evening after the meeting, on their way to the farther inland cities, those in my time were called Dholavira, Mehrgarh, Harappa and Lothal. A group was sent towards the Ganges River, to alert the cities and towns in the eastern regions.

In the meantime, I had gone back to what I called the library, to offer help in the preparation of the scrolls and manuscripts the priests had decided to save. I understood, by their orders and work, they had decided to send two groups, one with the ones leaving towards the west and the Nile River, though they didn't call it like that, another would go with those following the land route to the Near East, the Euphrates River and farther east.

I understood. They wanted to be sure something survived the cataclysm, at least the most precious of their sacred texts.

I helped, amazed at the amount of information that would be lost, because I knew well nothing of this would survive. There had never been found any scroll, any writing from this time. It pained me to see them working with such hope to select those they would carry, and those that were left behind; it seemed to me like parents trying to decide which child they would save. An impossible decision.

I had been invited to stay at Ritha's house, considering the work in the library was going on day and night, and nobody could sleep there. Not that

I thought I could get any sleep, but it was worth trying, and her family had been supportive of me.

They to, were selecting what they would take in this other version of the Exodus, an exodus I hoped would be more organized than the one the Hebrews had when leaving Egypt following Mosses.

Ritha was with them like a watchdog, reminding her relatives what was important to save. No jewels, no artifacts, no furniture; only that which would be really necessary to survive, warm clothes, blankets, the most necessary kitchen utensils and provisions, and those effects that related to their worship and history, history of their family that would need to be passed on to their descendants when they reached such a distant land.

They obeyed her; somehow her leadership had been accepted as they knew how great her association with me was.

Some days, the Council of Elders would meet again, and we would be recalled to clear doubts, take decisions, or simply confirm their efforts were pointed in the right direction. Kashyapa had taken an important role in the Council, and all his previous pride and lust for power had evaporated as a drop of water in the desert.

I was happy for this development, because I knew not how long was I supposed to remain here. Would I go with them? Was that what the Son of God intended for me? If yes, then with which group? West? East? North?

And how would my knowledge of what was to come, of history's development affect their future?

Ritha's family believed I would go with them, and as they saw the tightening bond between me and herself, one day, the grandmother, Nivedita, came to me.

It was not an unusual happening. Many times she had come to consult with me regarding importance of things to take, or to settle disputes among the family. This time, however, I realized something different brought her.

After the usual greetings, salutations, bowing and the sort, she sat before me.

"Andrew, Ferdinand Thomas Whittaker's descendant, Osiris' son, the time has come when I need to ask of you an important question."

I bowed my head in acknowledgement and with a gesture asked her to proceed.

"All this time we have followed your decisions, realizing you have brought to us word of God's plans to save us. Now I want to know if, in those plans…" She stopped and I saw she had blushed.

"Please continue, why do you hesitate?"

She appeared to regain her composure, and taking a deep breath, like one takes before submerging under water, she continued.

"In those plans, in your plans; what place does my granddaughter, Aashritha, Mahendra's daughter have?"

Sent Back

I looked at her, both intrigued and amused. What was the old woman asking? Was it, perhaps, something like 'what are your intentions towards my daughter' question a father asks of his daughter's boyfriend?

I pondered the answer. I had, myself, several questions. What were God's designs towards me? Would I remain in this time, travel with this civilization in their exodus to other lands? With which group was I intended to go? And if not, would I be sent back to my own time and land? And then, considering Ritha, was it right for me to take her as my wife in these conditions? I liked her, I liked her a lot, and had grown to depend on her for almost everything. She was beautiful, intelligent, and well mannered, and yes, my heart did beat faster whenever I saw her. But to become one? The gulf of time and history, was it too deep to surmount? Or was nothing of this important in the merging of our souls?

I knew I had no time to ponder the questions. She needed an answer now and would not allow me time to think about it.

So, in a jump of faith, considering something would prevent me from taking a wrong decision, I replied.

"Nivedita, a long path awaits us, a path where I know not the one God will set for me. I was brought here by His designs to save your world. He brought me to Aashritha and your family. I have grown to admire her, and though I don't think I can call this love as it is considered in my world, I know I could not be happy without her by my side."

She looked at me with a half-smile, twisting her had to the side, in a gesture that reminded me of a bird analyzing the worm it's planning to eat.

"Less than that is considered worthwhile in the joining of man and woman in my world, Andrew. So, will you join my granddaughter? Will you be her protector and defender? Will you be the father of her children?" She insisted.

Wow, that was a lot to consider. I had never thought of becoming a husband, much less a father to anyone. Would I? Could I?

Instead I asked.

"Nivedita, I wish to be truthful to you, but you are asking me about my desires and intentions. Which are Aashritha's own desires? Should you be making plans for her without her knowledge? Perhaps she doesn't like me in that way, maybe she has another person in her mind and heart."

"No. No she hasn't. She has been waiting for you since she was a small child. She told you, I know, that in her and myself the ability to talk with the gods is great, sometimes, we also see. She saw you, many years ago, much before you came to us; she saw you and since then she has waited for you. I, too, don't know if that is what you understand by love, but I am convinced she would not be happy with any other man, none that I or her father would have selected for her."

I thought about it.

"I will give you my definitive answer after I have talked to her about this, but I can tell you now, if what you say is true, if becoming my wife, my partner is what she truly wants, then yes, we will be joined."

"That's all I wanted to hear, Andrew. Let me know once you are satisfied of her response."

She stood, and as I did, too, she bowed slightly and left the room.

And I was alone, feeling that the weight of the whole city lay on my shoulders. What a responsibility I was taking! Was it right for me? Would I accept living in this time for the rest of my life? Living through the terrible cataclysm I had foreseen and knew from history would really happen? Or would I be returned to my world, leaving her behind.

The mere thought made my heart hurt. Thinking of her, alone, abandoned, looking at the sky that would bring destruction to her world and thinking that her world had already crashed with my abandonment was terrible.

In the silence of my room, in the innermost place inside me, I prayed to that God I had read about and learned to love with my beloved uncle. I prayed to the God of Moses and Abraham and Jacob and David.

"Do not let me take a path that would bring pain to her. Please guide me and let me know which is Your wish."

I heard no answer. No bright light, nor the presence of the Messiah. Naturally, what I was requesting was nothing compared to the destruction of civilization, a mere bagatelle.

Through all my life, however, I had been guided to the present situation, so I knew somehow, He would guide me again.

I went out of the room, in search of her.

CHAPTER XXVI

She was outside. A cart that would later be pulled by bullocks stood near the door, and she was overseeing how the most basic and heavy objects were placed.

She turned to me when I called, and now that I was aware of what was going on, and not deep in the consideration of catastrophic events, I saw how her face lighted at my call.

"Ritha, would you walk with me? Will you show me more of your city before we have to leave it?"

A cloud passed over her face, and I realized she was trying not to cry at those words.

I berated myself. I couldn't have been more brutal, I thought. This was not a great beginning for what I needed to talk about with her. Angry at myself I forged ahead.

"Wait! Andrew, why do you invite me and now leave me behind? Stop!"

I did, waiting for her.

"I'm sorry Ritha, I was angry at myself for causing you pain."

"Pain?" She repeated, not understanding.

"Reminding you about this, that your beloved city will be abandoned and destroyed."

"Yes. It causes me pain, but I must contemplate it otherwise, because the gods have willed to save us. The cities will disappear, but my people will survive. That's what I keep bringing up to mind, so as not to be ungrateful to the gods."

I looked at her in admiration. While many others were wringing their hands and crying over losing their properties and riches, she kept thinking of the important thing, the survival of her people.

"Where do you want to go?" She asked me, brushing aside the previous conversation.

"Anywhere you would like to share with me."

So we walked along the streets, already becoming littered with discarded items people had decided not to take. We walked under the trees, and through beautiful verdant parks, full of flowers and animals. And I saw how she caressed the trees and the bushes and even bent over to caress the grass. A bird came fluttering over us, and she lifted her hand, offering a perch for it. The little thing alighted on her finger, and for less than a minute rested there, looking at us.

"They, too, will be destroyed?" She asked, her eyes again full of tears.

"I think so, but I know many will survive, because my world is full of them." I replied.

"That's good to know, there's more hope, then." She said and walked briskly out of the park.

We continued walking and soon we were in front of a huge building. It was nothing like I had seen before. It had no statues or images on the walls, which were bare and tall of two floors, but without windows. The only opening was a large porch, where tens of columns, evenly spaced, sustained the roof. A beautiful stair lead to several doors, all now opened. I looked intently at the steps, they were made of marble, beautifully carved and set.

"What is this place?" I asked. "I never saw anything like it in your city."

"The city's baths." She answered. "No, you wouldn't have seen anything like it as there's only one. Come, I'll show you." She took my hand into hers and pulled.

Up the beautiful stairway we went, and through the doors. There was no need for windows, I realized, when there was no roof. Well, not really a lack of roof but there was a great opening, squarish and in the center of the building as I could see. Then my eyes, adapting, saw. In the center, just under the opening, a very large pool glittered under the slanting rays of the sun. It was huge. Not even an Olympic pool in my time would compare to it. How much water it contained, I couldn't even guess.

Ritha smiled looking at my astonishment, and again pulled at my hand.

We walked to a side of the pool and there I saw small openings, like doors without doors. She pushed me to look inside of one.

"Here is where we take off our clothes before going to the pool." She said I word I couldn't understand, but I imagined it was 'pool'. "And where we return to get dressed after."

"But it's huge!" I exclaimed. "How…? How…?"

"How what, Andrew?"

"I mean, the construction is really awesome, yet the temples I've seen are even more magnificent. But how can you have this supply of water? It's a feat of engineering, even in my world!"

I saw her pride, and I understood her well enough.

"Well, Andrew," she asked. "Do you care to go in?"

"In? Like, in there?" I asked. "Can we? Is it allowed?"

"Naturally it is. In any other day it would be crowded, children and young people playing water games, older ones just enjoying the water and swimming. Everyone is busy now. In special days, it is forbidden to all except those who are participating in a sacred ceremony." A fleeting cloud passed over her face, but she rapidly chased it away.

"Come, you take that one, take all your clothes off. I will take this one here." She explained gesturing.

Take my clothes off? All of them? Be naked in front of her? Was this an accepted custom? I blushed, and rapidly entered the small alcove.

I disrobed myself, laying my tunic and pants and the other small dressings on the stone bench at one side. But I couldn't bring myself to take off the loincloth. I really couldn't.

I hesitated in going out. What would she think?

She was outside, waiting. She smiled at my not-naked condition. She wasn't naked, either. A short tunic of some almost transparent material hung from her shoulders, but it did nothing to hide her body. This was going to be really difficult.

She took my arm and we walked to the edge of the pool. There were some steps, and I realized that, though extremely wide and large, it was not too deep. We walked in and the coolness of the water embraced us. That was good, the substitute for a cold shower I truly needed.

But I think she had noticed, because she had a mischievous smile and a queer glint in her eyes. I separated from her, and swam away. How nice. It had been such a long time I had enjoyed a good swim, in all this traveling through time, that I lost myself in it and almost forgot her.

A splash brought me to the moment, and another drenched me. Ah well, if she wanted to play war, we would play war.

We splashed at each other, trying each time to catch the other one inattentive. She was good at this, soon I was forced to retreat and grant her victory.

She laughed.

"Do you do this frequently?" I asked.

"What?"

"This, the water war or however you call it." I insisted.

"I would come here with my siblings and cousins, and many friends, yes. And we would have terrible battles." She smiled remembering. "We haven't done that in quite some time, though."

I didn't want to ask the reason, as I suspected it was around the time I appeared that everything had changed.

I was quite relaxed now, and tired, so I dared to go out of the pool and sit on the raised platform besides it, she followed.

I avoided looking at her, her beautiful body was something I couldn't afford at this moment to look at, not if I didn't want to disgrace myself.

"Ritha, let's get dressed and go out, I have something I need to talk with you about."

"Why can't we stay here and talk, Andrew?"

I realized that for her, body nakedness was natural, and not the tabu it had become during the dark ages of the world. But I would not be able to approach the subject in these conditions.

"Please!" I insisted, with such a voice I was reminded of a puppy asking for something.

"Alright." She answered, standing and going back to her room, while I went to mine.

A while later, and after we had left the building behind, we reached another park. These one had incredibly large trees, some so big I thought not even ten men could surround them. The leaves were dark green, the branches low and straight and the shadow they gave was complete.

She saw me staring.

"Do you like it? It's a sacred tree, a sacred fig."

I nodded; I knew about them. I also knew that, thousands of years into the future, a prince called Sidhartha would attain enlightenment under one, leading millions in the path to a new philosophy of life, many would say religion.

"We can sit here, if you like." She added, pointing to a bench near one tree, so there we went, and sat.

Now that we were here, the immensity of what I was to broach hit me. What was I doing? Was I going to propose to a woman that had lived tens of thousands of years before my time? I shook my head. That was not the issue to consider now. I had given my word to the matriarch and had to act in accordance with it.

"Ritha", I said, turning to face her. "We are going to set out now, or in a few days, in a trip that will take us to places we have never been to, and to face perhaps many dangers and difficulties. I don't know what God wants of me. Maybe He wants me to go back to my world, maybe He wants me to remain with you and your people, or maybe He is going to send me somewhere, or to some other time."

I could see emotions fleetingly passing over her face. Surprise, fear, hope; all went one after the other.

"Do you understand me?" I asked.

She nodded.

"I have learnt to love your people, your city, your family. I have felt that I was not a stranger, but someone welcomed and even, perhaps, cherished."

"Yes."

"I would hope the One who brought me, will let me stay with all of you, but I don't know His plans for me."

"Continue."

"As I said, we are going in a perilous journey, and if I am to remain in this time, I would like to have someone by my side that would help me, took care of me, taught me all the things I would need to know to survive."

Now she realized where I was going, and her face became dark with flush. She bowed her head, and again nodded.

"Ritha," I said again, taking her hand. "I don't know if I will remain with you forever, so it's selfish of me to ask this of you, but I will. Would you be that someone? Would you like me to be your friend, companion and mate?"

Her hand was trembling in mine, as if by some miracle that little bird that had previously alighted on hers was now trapped in mine.

I had asked, and she had replied. No need to dwell on it. We had spent some time there, under the tree, sharing ideas and hopes, even plans. We refused to think our lives could well not be destined to be lived together, we refused to consider I could be taken away, at that moment we though only about the present and the fact that, somehow, we had been brought together.

The darkness, that had somehow increased without us being aware of it, now reached totality.

"It's so late!" She exclaimed. "Come, we need to get home before they send a search out for us!"

"They would?" I asked, as I knew not this would be done when a young woman was out and about during the night. It hadn't happened when I called from her in the Temple, but maybe this was because the High Priest had called for her.

We left the park and the fig tree, walking briskly and through short cuts and hidden back streets, we reached her house way faster than it had taken us to walk away.

Nivedita was at the door, with a lamp and searching the streets with anxious glances.

"You are back, that's good." She said with a look I couldn't help but understand. I nodded and she smiled, satisfied.

"Come, come. Your father is waiting."

CHAPTER XXVII

Nivedita still kept her eyes fixed on mine. Indubitably she waited for a confirmation or perhaps denial of her proposal.

"We've spoken and she's willing." I said. No need for more.

The old woman's face lit with pleasure, and she embraced Ritha. No word was spoken then until Nivedita, grasping both our hands in hers, took us through the door.

"It is time, then, to talk to my son." She said.

Again the doubts surged, overwhelming me with fear. Was I doing the correct thing? And again I let myself surf the wave, knowing that, if I was not meant to be Ritha's husband, something would prevent it.

The matriarch left us in the same room I had previously stood, just at the beginning of my trip to Kumari Kandam. I suspected she had gone to talk with Ritha's parents. My worries must have shown on my face because she pressed my hand and whispered, 'all will be alright, do not fear' before leaving me alone."

Easy for her to say.

The curtain before the door opening moved, and Nivedita, Mahendra and his wife came before us.

"It is our custom, Andrew, descendant of Sir Ferdinand Thomas Whittaker, Esq., that the father of the man requests the daughter for his son. You are alone here, not a single member of your family is present. It is not acceptable, so I ask you, is anyone among us who could function as your father in the ceremony?" Said the man.

I was taken aback, and now, I thought, the complications start.

"I don't..." I hesitated and then, an idea came to my mind. "Maybe the high priest Kashyapa would do that for me."

This possibility amazed them, as they looked at each other with questioning glances. I didn't blame them, the last time Kashyapa had been there he had been pretty rough, even belligerent, and in their eyes he had been disrespectful of me. They couldn't know the change that had occurred some time ago.

"If he is amenable, yes, I don't know why not." Replied Mahendra, but I could see his doubts. "Will you address him today?"

I thought it seemed Ritha's family were pressed for time, and, though I

Sent Back

didn't understand the reason for this I had taken a decision and given my word to the matriarch.

"Yes, I will go now."

Nivedita nodded and took my hand in hers.

With a slight pressure of my hand as a goodbye, I left and set my steps towards the library, where I was confident I would find Kashyapa.

It took me a while, as there were no carriages or any other type of transportation, and I had to walk all the way, but I managed it and soon was in one of the great halls.

Kashyapa was there, and after the usual greeting ceremony I presented the situation to him.

He stood there, looking at me with eyes wide open in amazement.

"Do I understand you correctly, Andrew? Are you asking me to act in your behalf as your father for a marriage ceremony?"

I nodded.

"To Aashritha?"

I nodded again.

"Is this wise? Do you know if you are going to stay the rest of your life here, in this time, with us? Have you considered that in any moment God might decide to take you to another time and place?"

"I have considered it, Kashyapa, and if this is not the will of God, I am sure something will happen to prevent it. I hope it's not your negative that will do this." I added, with a look at the same time admonishing and pleading.

He smiled. A smile in that severe face, almost always set in a frown, was intense.

"I will comply to your wishes." And bowed his head.

"Would you come now? They are waiting."

"Why the rush?" He asked then, suspicious and I knew he thought I had done what I shouldn't.

"Nothing untoward happened, but I think her parents want her married before our trip begins."

"Yes, that could be it and it makes sense. Alright, let's go. How did you come here? Did you bring a carriage?"

"No!" I exclaimed. "They are all being fitted for our trip."

"Yes, naturally, I understand. Well, let's go then."

It took more time now, as the priest, older and with a less active life than me, was slower. At last we reached the house and entered.

A table had been laid in the room, with some delicacies they had prepared at the last moment, some fruits and a beautiful jar, filled to the top with a liquid I surmised was soma.

Kashyapa greeted and blessed them while they stood with a bowed head in his presence. I had not dared to go to Ritha, not knowing if that would be correct. Apparently, I was right, because Nivedita gestured for me to leave and simultaneously she took Ritha's hand and took her to the other alcove.

I do not know what Kashyapa and Mahendra said. In reality, I was not sure the priest would act in my behalf as I desired, and though I knew I should trust him, I still became very anxious, and walked from side to side of the outer room.

Then, the curtain was lifted and the priest made signs for me to enter.

"This is my son, Andrew, who is descendant of Sir Ferdinand Thomas Whittaker, Esq., Osiris son on whose behalf I have requested your daughter Aashritha for wife." He proclaimed.

"And we agree." Replied Mahendra. "In the name of my daughter Aashritha, we agree. She will become your son's wife, and the mother of his children."

"Let's partake of this meal, which the gods have provided, to bless this day." He added.

I felt a shiver run down my back, the hairs on my nape stood on end. What? Was the Son coming to me again, perhaps to prevent this? But no, it was just nerves, and the exhilaration of the ceremony.

I wondered why was Ritha not there, but I suspected that was how it would be until the marriage rites had been performed.

I realized Kashyapa was reluctant to sit at table with them, but he had taken his position conscientiously, and sat. For some minutes we shared, and then Mahendra lifted the soma bottle, offering it to the priest.

"It is for you to bless and perform the rite, high priest."

Kashyapa accepted the flask and poured some of it on the cups set before Mahendra, me and himself. The rite concluded,

Mahendra then stepped forward and offered his hand to Kashyapa and then to me. The deal was sealed.

Nivedita appeared again, alone.

"Who will take care of selecting a day of good augury for the marriage? Will you, high priest?" She asked.

"I will, yes, I will study the heavens and learn which day will be most propitious for the rite." He paused, and then continued. "I must now leave, many things are underway that require my supervision, and now this responsibility…" With a gesture of his hand, and a bow not addressed to anyone in particular, he left the room.

"You must understand, Andrew, that now you must not stay in the same house as your bride to be." Said Nivedita. "In other situation, you would naturally wait for the day at your father's house. You have not this option, so I spoke with my cousin three times removed, who lives nearby and he is willing to accept you in his house for the necessary time. He lives alone with his wife, as their children are grown and have their own families

Sent Back

now. I believe you will be comfortable with them."

I nodded. I had been nodding a lot lately and felt silly about it. But then, what could I possibly do?

The matriarch had taken me to her cousin's house, and I have been offered a room where I felt quite comfortable. Something, however, made me leave the place and walk again towards the library. It was already very dark, a night without moon, and the streetlights offered only a bit of glow to discern the road.

I was nearing the library when I saw a figure coming toward me, in fact, rushing, almost running. I gasped as I realized it was Kashyapa, and the man was really running.

He stopped as he saw me, and leaned, hands of his knees, gasping for air.

"Andrew!" he said when he had apparently recovered. "Andrew, I have dire news!"

My heart stopped and couldn't even ask.

"Andrew, doom is nearer than we thought. Look!" And he pointed to a place in the sky.

There, sketched in that black canvas, among thousands of dots large and small, a large arrow was pointing to us, and I knew it was one of the meteorites that would eventually crash upon the Earth.

The end had begun.

I stood there, gaping. My mind had gone completely blank with only a thought that kept running, repeating itself time and again.

'But I thought we had more time, I thought we had more time!'

Kashyapa shook me, and I'd say there was more rage than concern in his attitude.

"You said we had time!" He cried, like an echo of my own mind. "You said we still had time! What are we to do now?"

Slowly I looked down at my arm, where his hand still gripped me, and softly pried it away.

"I told you what I thought I knew, I didn't invent anything, nor told you lies. What is the need to make us prepare to leave the cities, why would I have been shown the paths to take, if our salvation was not intended? Something is wrong here."

He bowed his head, shaking it slowly.

"The gods have doomed us. There's nothing we can do, this is the end." He said, and turned to go back to the library, I don't know what he thought he could do there. I saw him leave, a broken man weighed with the destruction of his world.

I remained there, watching the apparently immovable star.

229

Which was this one? Which among all supposed to have struck the Earth was this one? And where would it fall? Perhaps we still had time, perhaps it would crash far away from us, on the other side of the world. And though this thought implied I was wishing catastrophe on another cities, it gave me some surcease from the pain I was feeling.

I decided to return and ask Nivedita and Mahendra to come to talk to me.

I arrived there to find they were already outside; all the family was, including Ritha. She ran toward me, her eyes full of tears.

"Andrew, Andrew, what is this? How can it be? Are you wrong? Did you lie to us?"

Yes, prophets always accused of lying. There we went again.

"No, Ritha, no! How could I lie about something as terrible as this? I followed God's orders, I never would have come with anything like what he has ordered me to do!"

She was wringing her hands in desperation, and I understood she had barely paid attention to my words. I took her by the shoulders, how weak, how fragile they seemed now, and shook her. Mercifully she came back to her senses, quieting down expectantly.

"Listen!" I said, and this time I saw she was paying attention. "I do not know what this means, but I have faith. The Lord does not play tricks, and He said we were to leave and reach distant lands where we would be saved. Maybe… Maybe that's not the meteorite of doom, or maybe it would crash somewhere else, far from here. You understand?"

She nodded, drying her tears with a shacking hand.

"We must continue our plans, we still must leave this city, and all the cities of your civilization. The time has been cut short, but I think we can do it, if we do not give ourselves to desperation and despondency."

She nodded.

"Come now, let's talk to your people. I'm sure Nivedita will see it my way."

And there we went, all thought of proper customs before marriage gone into the wind because of the present danger.

Ritha's grandmother turned to look at us, as if she had sensed us before we approached, and she waited expectantly, without asking.

"I imagine you are all thinking that all I said was a lie, and that you are in truth condemned to death."

"You say it." She replied.

"But I don't believe it so. Why would God have sent me here to prepare you all to leave, if He intended not for you to be saved?"

She shrugged, and I knew she had thought of many reasons I would have lied to them.

"I did not lie, nor did I invent any of it. Please believe me. I think we still have hope, I think we can still manage and leave this place, leave the cities of the coast and follow the path the Son showed me to follow."

"What hope have you? Don't you see the messenger of the gods coming towards us?"

"It could be going somewhere else!" I exclaimed, despairing. If this was how Nivedita, who knew all about me and my coming to her time, reacted; how difficult would it be to convince the rest of the people?

"It could be aimed for another land, not here! Don't you see? We have at least to make an effort! Or are you just going to sit down and wait for death to come?"

These last words apparently made her come back to reality, to the up and doing character I knew she had.

"You may be right, Andrew. Yes, you may be right. We can try, at least, and if the gods decide our doom, we will face it following the path they set for us." She stood, pondering, hand stroking her chin.

"Did you talk to the priest? Does he know?" She said after a while of silence.

"He was the one who showed me, yes."

"What does he think, then?"

"I believe he's as shocked as all of us, believing doom is unavoidable."

She nodded, and I had this thought, that she had always known how weak the high priest really was.

"We need to talk to the council." She said, "I don't care how late it is, nor that Kashyapa has given up."

"I didn't say he had, Nivedita."

"No, but I read you well. He's given up. Right?"

"Well yes, perhaps." I replied reluctantly.

"So we need to act, you and I." She insisted.

"And I, grandmother. Have you forgotten me?" Ritha asked.

We turned to look at her. Yes, we had forgotten her, though it shamed me to realize it.

No words were needed, she understood all.

"If we are going to talk to the council, if Andrew has words to convince them that we should proceed, and not even proceed but speed up the preparations and go on our way as soon as possible, the members would have to be recalled, and I think that is going to be very difficult considering how scared everyone is now."

"How can we do it, Ritha?" I asked.

"I suspect we can convince some of our family and neighbors. If those convince their families and neighbors, hope will spread like wildfire. We will ask everyone to let the members of the council know we need to talk to them." She explained, and I was proud of her. She had recovered swiftly and was taking a role I always suspected she was born for. This was a woman to have by my side, and if our hope turned out to be right, I would be a lucky man to marry her.

We did as she had suggested, some were more reluctant than others to see there still was hope. We didn't lose time with them but continued talking to the neighbors and went farther out, into other streets and places of gathering.

As she had thought, hope spread among the majority and soon a message was passed down to us that the council members were gathered.

There we went, Ritha, Nivedita and I, to convince them.

When we arrived, I was amazed to see that Kashyapa had also arrived. His face was angry again, and I could sense his distrust.

I really don't know all we said, the two women and I, about what they thought was impending doom and my lies. I do remember lots of arguments, cries, elders standing and pounding on the table, some arguing between themselves. At last, somehow, maybe tired, they subsided and fell silent.

And now an unexpected ally spoke.

"I have listened to all of you." Kashyapa said. "I have listened to the two women and to Andrew and I have listened to you, elders. Listen to me now."

He stopped and looked at each member of the council, fixedly and for some seconds.

There was absolute, expectant silence among us. What would he say, on that everything would depend.

"It is at moments like this when we show who we really are. The gods have seen it fit to test us now. Are we going to show weakness? Are we going to show lack of faith? By their will this man came to us from a time so far away from us we can't even imagine it. And he came to prepare us for this and to help save us. I have doubted him, oh yes I have, more even tonight. But I remember what I saw in his mind, and I remember what he showed all of us that first time here. We all saw it." He stopped for a while, perhaps gathering his ideas, perhaps thinking what to say. As it was, I was feeling pretty proud of him now and looked at Nivedita with eyes that said "you see, he's not so weak at all'.

She smiled and shrugged.

"I say these ones are right. I say we have to finish getting ready and start our sojourn to the distant lands. If the gods will to destroy us then, we will be destroyed following their will. To sit here, meekly awaiting for destruction, that's not how we were raised to be." He sat down, total silence in the room.

Then, one by one, the elders rose, bowing with folded hands towards him.

"As you say, so will we do." They said in unison. And the elder of

Sent Back

them then spoke.

"There will be no sleep, no rest, until we are on our way. In two days we must be out of the cities. Let our decision be known." He bowed again and left.

Exhilarated, I grasped at Nivedita's and Ritha's hands.

"We've done it, Ritha. You were right!" And I almost kissed her then, only Nivedita's presence stopped me.

"Let us return home now." Said the old woman. "And, Andrew, I think our other plans should be expedited too. I want you married before we leave the city."

We blushed, but nodded acceptance of the matriarch's decision.

CHAPTER XXVIII

Kashyapa was there, with all his high priest attire. Mahendra and all his family, those who lived nearby and could come, all dressed in their best clothes. Nivedita, Ritha and her mother were missing, perhaps still dressing up my bride.

I stood by Kashyapa, anxious and excited. Maybe my marriage to her was in God's plans. I could only hope and wait, a red cord attached to my wrist for some reason I knew nothing about.

Then, following Nivedita, an apparition of veils and jewels, and little bells and glittering ribbons entered the room. A red semi-transparent veil covered her head and face and fell to below her shoulders. Her tunic seemed made of gold, so bright it was, and underneath pants and a bodice of the whitest cloth, hung tightly to her body. Her feet, in some type of slippers, looked even smaller than I knew they were.

She walked, hesitantly, to where we waited, and coming in front of her father bowed down, very low, and brushed with her right hand the top of his feet.

He lifted her, taking her by the shoulders and spoke:

"I am setting you free, free from the rules of Varuna, by which you were bonded to me and my family. I place you now, by the law of natural and moral order, in the hands of your husband. He will now be your family, and you two will become as one, as has been ordered since time begun by our gods, may they be blessed."

Kashyapa then took my hand with the red string attached and took Ritha's hand also in his. Mahendra brought a cup, and Kashyapa taking it, spilled it over our hands, he then tied the string to Ritha's wrist, so we were in this way, physically bonded together.

"With this water I washed from you any tie you ever had to other person, you are now free from all ties to family or friends. With this thread I bound you to each other, Andrew to Ritha, Ritha to Andrew. You are in each other's hands."

Then Nivedita, also covered in a veil, not red, but white, approached with another cup.

Kashyapa took it from her hands bowing and lifting it above his head.

"This is the sacred soma, that the gods enjoy."

Sent Back

He took a sip and lifted it again. Then turning to us, he gave me the cup, and I, though I knew not what to do, imitated him. I was going to return the cup to him but somehow I knew what to do next. I lifted Ritha's veil, and stood there thinking how beautiful she was.

A small cough brought me to my senses.

I retrieved the cup from Kashyapa and offered it to Ritha, bringing it to her lips. No, she wasn't supposed to take it herself, but only from my hands was she to drink the sacred soma. She did, and then I poured the remaining soma over our hands while Kashyapa intoned a long blessing in a chant I felt in the depth of my soul as something I had known before.

Mahendra then spoke to Ritha.

"This is now your husband, he will be the father of your children, he will sustain you and care for you all the moments of your life; when you are in pain, he will too, suffer; when you are happy, he will rejoice. You will help him, and respect him, as he will respect and help you. And when the time come for one of you to go to the gods, the remaining one will wait in hope, because at the end of time, you will be together again and forever."

He then kissed Ritha on her forehead and pushed her towards me. They were all waiting, and I realized in this time, as in mine, after the vows and rites, the groom was supposed to kiss the bride. I did.

After that, all was merriment and eating, and joy. For a little while, for a short while only, because the time was coming to leave and start our sojourn to the distant lands.

Days passed as weeks, and weeks passed as months. Above us, the spearhead of doom still showed its path, traveling across the sky.

How fast was it supposed to move? I did not know of the science of the cosmos, had no idea how long it would take for a visible comet to fall to earth.

Every night we went to sleep in the carriages, or in makeshift tents and beds on the ground, each night our last look was to the spearhead of doom, and it was our first sight in the morning. And every day we would say, 'it's still out there', and every night we would say, 'still has not fallen'.

We had taken little time to set out. I can't remember if there were five or ten days after our marriage when we set out. Because I had no properties, nor carriage or bullocks, we went with Ritha's family, and shared with them their provisions and tents and beds, as if she were still a part of them, which I believed she still was.

Before us, using all types of transportation, went a part of the city, behind us, another. As we passed by other towns, their inhabitants joined us, so as we walked farther and farther from Dwarka, the column of our exodus grew longer, and broader. Sometimes, when those who went ahead from us went through hills, I could see them as a great serpent, spreading, writhing over the land, and going, going, in a constant movement toward the promised land.

Had it been like this with Mosses? I kept thinking about him and trying to recall all the chapters of the Exodus. I remembered some, but so many things had happened that I believed my memory could not hold it all, and some had been lost

There had been dissent between the Israelites, that, I remembered, and complains of hunger and tiredness. I remember they had questioned Mosses, 'why have you brought us here, to the dessert to die! Best we had remained in the land of the Pharaoh, where we had food, and drink.'

That had not happened yet here. Maybe the daily threat that loomed over us kept everyone together in the aim for salvation. I was sure, however, that soon complains would start and I hoped we would be strong enough to counter it when they came.

We had already reached the Indus River Delta, and there had been much trouble to cross it. Thankfully, the elders had prepared for this, and had sent messengers so boats waited for us to help us cross. It was difficult to carry the carts and bullocks, very difficult, and many boats overturned and were lost. People were saved, and those in luck shared with those who had lost all. I was told that, as soon as the crossing was over, those boats would join with the group aiming for the west, towards the Nile.

Days became like a dream, we were only intent on walking, walking farther each day, and watching the skies. True, I had Ritha by my side and a deep enjoyment in my heart. We were married, joined, and nothing had stopped the ceremony, so I hoped this was a path that had been approved by God. I truly hoped so, because each day made me love her more, and each night...What's to tell. You must know, and if you don't, I'm sorry for you.

Sometimes she would ask me to tell her about my world, and I would tell her about my dear uncle, and I would describe his house, and the library, and the rooms full of boxes and curiosities. Or I would tell her about our cities, and the university where I had studied, what seemed in another life.

She also wanted to know about my meeting with our descendants, with those who had survived the cataclysm and had lived in the shore of the Sea of Reeds. And I would tell her about them, and she would cry for their pain at losing their civilization.

I could see she had bonded with them, and she understood well what they had experienced, experiencing some of it herself. To divert her from that pain I would talk about something else, like the dogs we had, or the games I had played as a child, and then she would laugh and be merry again. But I knew she was hurting inside, as all those with us were hurting. Some more, some less, but pain among us was current. At least, the cataclysm had

Sent Back

not come and maybe, maybe, we would reach safety in time.

We had been, I think, almost a month on the way when we reached the entrance to the Persian Gulf. How did I know this? There were no signs, no roads, and the few towns and hamlets we found along the way had been emptied. I knew, however, we were already there, and I felt relief, thinking the most dangerous part of the trail was passed.

CHAPTER XXIX

I have previously stated how we kept constantly looking up at the sky, and the messenger of doom and destruction, and now it hit me it seemed stationary. Shouldn't it had already hit the Earth?

As I also said before, I knew nothing about the cosmic sciences, only the basic required for my archaeological studies, but I thought it had been many days since it was first seen by Kashyapa, more than enough days for it to have crashed.

I didn't want to share my thoughts with anyone, not even with Ritha, and I wondered why nobody had thought about it already.

We were now crossing what in my future would be called 'Strait of Hormuz'. It was several meters above sea level, because the great meltdown had not yet happened, though I surmised it would not remain like this for long. This thought made me impatient, and I looked behind me to watch the slow plodding of the bullocks that carried this people's items.

"They are too slow." I heard a voice beside me, and turned to see Kashyapa there. "Too slow."

He looked at the sky where, even with the sun pounding on our heads, the meteor was very visible.

"It seems to me it's not moving." He added, and turned to face me. "What do you think, Andrew?"

"I was just thinking the same, Kashyapa. I have never been a witness to anything similar, but in truth it seems to be taking an inordinate length of time to strike. Not that I want it to, as you can imagine."

He nodded.

"Yes, nobody would want that. But I think we should somehow make them speed up, the bullocks are able to move faster, I now that. They are just being very gentle with them." He commented, turning to face the sky again.

I heard him muttering something, and only because my thoughts had drifted in the same direction did I understand him.

"God has seen the wickedness of your civilization, and how your self-importance and ego has grown, abandoning His teachings. Now, all you consider important, all you construed and created; everything of which you are proud of will be destroyed to show you what is truly important.

Sent Back

Abandon everything you covet, leave cities and towns, because they will be submerged by the raging seas, and seek the mountains, seek higher ground or you will all perish."

"Maybe we are not supposed to be loaded with all this stuff, carts, properties, bullocks. Maybe he wants us bereft of everything, with only our souls and bodies." He mused.

I stared. Truly, I had not thought about it in this way. Remembering what is written in the Bible: "And the children of Israel did according to the word of Moses: and they borrowed of the Egyptian jewels of silver, and jewels of gold, and raiment; And the Lord gave the people favor in the sight of the Egyptians, so that they lent unto them such things as they required. And they spoiled the Egyptians."

Had the knowledge of this words influenced the interpretation of the words the Mesiah had said? Wasn't it clear in His orders? We were to save what was truly important. That was not what we had done. We had wasted time selecting the most cherished property, wasted time loading carts, and beasts of burden to carry them, and we were now wasting precious time waiting for the beasts to carry that loaded. Our exodus was being delayed because of our covetousness, because of our love of possessions, because of our ego instead of saving our souls and the dedication to God.

We were supposed to be born anew to this life, and as a child is born naked, so, I thought, were we supposed to arrive to the new land.

Kashyapa had been silent, looking at me, and I had the queer feeling he had followed my train of thought as if reading my mind.

He nodded.

"Yes, Andrew, I agree." He said, and I knew I had surmised the truth, he had heard my thoughts, somehow. "We have to abandon everything, even our sacred writings, though it breaks my heart just to think about it."

"But how are we going to convince them, Kashyapa? How are we going to ask this new sacrifice of them, losing everything?"

"Do you think they'd rather lose their lives?"

I shook my head. No, but it would be terrible telling them.

Word was sent through the crowd for all the priests and elders to come. Kashyapa had elected a small hill by the path and waited there for those he had called to come. It wasn't fast, this new gathering, but it was not yet noon when all were there, awaiting expectantly to learn what Kashyapa wanted to say.

I was not there, so I don't know what he said. I imagine it went more or less as we had been considering. But I needed to talk to my family; I needed to tell Ritha and Nivedita and Mahendra of this new sacrifice.

"Abandon everything, Andrew?" Ritha exclaimed, and I saw the consternation of all those that surrounded me. It was not only them, many others had come and were listening to me, all those who had trod the path with us.

I only nodded.

"All?" She insisted.

"Everything. The time God has given us to reach the land where we will be safe is, I believe, reaching its end. We were not supposed to loose so much time selecting, collecting, loading and carrying all this property. We were to save our lives, our souls, and our devotion to only Him. Instead, we took care of material things which today are, and tomorrow are turned to dust."

"Lay not up for yourselves treasures upon earth where moth and rust doth corrupt and where thieves break through and seal, for where your treasure is, there will your heart be also, but lay up for yourselves treasures in heaven." I heard the voice of my granduncle reciting, as he had so many times in the past.

Yes, I had misunderstood, such is the power of the world.

"We are faced with a decision. Two paths are before us; in one is saving our lives and going to a new life naked of possessions, the other one is perishing for love of things. It's for you to decide, each one of you must make this decision, and act in accordance." I took Ritha's hand.

"Come now. Will you follow me?"

She lifted her head with pride, her face glowing with hope, decision and love.

"I will go with you, Andrew. Yes, I will follow you!"

I could see many were worried, considering my words. Apparently, these words had spread around us, and maybe the priests and elders were also explaining what was to be done.

I saw a movement; a wave of people leaving the long column, stepping to the side and walking, walking without properties, walking without loads, alone. And they walked faster, and as they passed along the long column, more people joined them.

I could see them ahead of me, and behind me, only people, people walking without bullocks, or any other beast of burden, carrying only their children and elders.

Thusly another day past. I realized the amount of people walking with us had been reduced, and imagined many had trusted their luck and keep carrying their properties, bullocks and beasts.

This made me very sorry, more so because I thought it was because of me, because I hadn't transmitted the word of God as I should have. I was full of guilt at that moment. Then, I heard a very loud sound, as when a bullet is shot, or a missile, but many times louder. The ground shook, the air became hot to breath, and dust or ash rose like a cloud, making it impossible to see.

"It has come." I thought. "It's here and I didn't save anyone. I didn't

Sent Back

save anyone, not even Ritha!"

We had all fallen to the ground, covering our heads with our hands, trying to breath that hot air full of dust and ash.

Then came the wind, so strong and fast I thought it would pull us from the ground and send us, twirling, into the sky and death.

I pulled at Ritha, and placed her under me, trying to make myself heavy to keep us from flying away. It could have been hours, but I knew it was not hours, but scarcely minutes that passed before it abated, sand and dust slowly fell to the ground and the air was now breathable.

People were standing, looking around, trying to find their families, their friends. I realized no one had been taken, we seemed to be all there. And now, there were more of us.

This had been the wake-up call for those who thought they could serve mammon and God. God or money, and this last development had made them decide.

From then on, after recovering from this ordeal, we went much faster.

I had surmised this had been but a precursor, a small meteorite that heralded the destruction to come. Probably just a few meters large stone that had exploded in the atmosphere; if not, I think we would have experienced tremors, shaking of the land, something more. It had been terrible, but at least it had demonstrated to the other group this was not a joke, and their lives were on the line.

Next day around noon when the atmosphere had cleared, I looked up at the heavens. searching for the Arrow of Doom, as it had been called.

It was much bigger now, much brighter than the moon which was barely visible now. I knew it was coming, and that we had very little time to reach our destiny.

God had provided, once we trusted Him completely, and now we walked by the sides of a large river which gave us drinking water and some food. We had made a stop, both to drink and to take some minutes of rest in the shade of the trees that bordered it.

It came then. The first one had been terrible, this one, however was many times worse. Now did the ground shake in truth, cracks were opened, and the river swelled with huge waves. People ran here and there, terrorized, while priests chanted in agony, invoking the help of those gods that were doing nothing for them. I kept searching the horizon, trying to see where the blast had come from and I saw there, far to the northwest, a giant mushroom cloud, as the ones I had seen of an atomic bomb. I knew what was to come, I knew the burning air, the force of a wave that would shatter us in less than seconds.

Suddenly, there was silence, absolute silence and I saw everyone around me like frozen in time, mist surrounded me and I couldn't see through it, even Ritha, which had been at that moment very close had disappeared.

"You have fulfilled your task now, my son. Your wandering through the ages is finished and you will now return to your own time. You have done well, and I am satisfied with you. I will guide them now, your time to rest is come."

I would have screamed if I could, but I felt as if cotton had been put inside my mouth, I was paralyzed.

What? Return to my time? Why? Why now? And what of my wife, what of Ritha and the people I had learned to love? The terror I felt was unendurable, Why?! What was happening?! Were they all dead?

The scream was in my head, in my mind and heart, but the lungs wouldn't work.

I was in a room, a room I had but forgotten, full of books. I was back in my uncle's library, and I was all alone. I crumpled like a discarded sheet of paper, and fell to the floor, crying.

Sent Back

CHAPTER XXX

I laid in bed for many days, barely able to move. A man, a man I was aware I had known very well before my traveling, took care of me. I couldn't remember his name, nor the one of a woman who fed me with the care of a mother.

A dog had come into the room, and had lain by my side day and night giving me its warmth and silent companionship.

My memory was slowly returning, though this life seemed foreign to me. I felt detached, as if nothing of this was real. However, I had remembered my companions' names. The man was Gregoire, the woman Ms. Urville. Little by little I was remembering, and now the pain from losing my uncle was afresh in my heart, in a depth of feeling made even greater by the memory of the one I had lost.

I would wake during the night, pillows wet with tears, my hands searching for the one that had been mine. I would then get up, and walk the house for hours, the poor dog, Sachmis, I now remembered, would follow me keeping me company.

I had not left the house since I had returned, had not gone to the university nor to my apartment there. I didn't care for any of that, and the only place outside the house I went to was the garden. I would sit by my uncle's mausoleum, or by the old cat's little grave, and remember and cry.

Somehow, it came into my awareness that the sky at night was different, the stars more visible. I had not realized, still subconsciously living in that very distant past, but indeed the stars seemed brighter, and I could very well see the Milky Way, something that due to the light pollution had been impossible before.

I asked Gregoire about it, but he looked at me worriedly, wondering if I was going to be 'strange' again, and said it had always been like that.

The house, too, seemed smaller. I thought I remembered more rooms than there were now, the kitchen and the living room were smaller, too.

Had my perspective changed after all I had visited, all I had seen? Or was there something else happening here.

I had wanted to check my laptop, but it was nowhere to be found, and I couldn't find the computer I used to have in the library. I was realizing many things differed from what I remembered. There was no telephone, nor could I find the I-phone either, nor was there a TV. In fact none of those technological advances I had grown up with were anywhere to be found.

I had stopped asking Gregoire about them, as he would give me the same look, wondering if I was becoming insane. Then, one day, I finally decided to leave the house and go to the city.

I went in search of the garage, and found only a stable with several horses, beautiful animals, but no cars. I refused to ask the man again, and swiftly saddled one and mounted. Sachmis the dog had approach the horse nonchalantly, who seemed friendly with her.

The door to the outside was opened by a young man, practically a boy I didn't recall having seen before, but I paid no attention to it now, amazed at what I saw.

This was definitely not the town I remembered. What was this? What had happened? Had God brought me to another world? To a parallel world? Had He mistakenly placed me somewhere different? I felt I was losing it, scared that I was really going crazy.

The horse neighed, pulling at the reins, and trotted down the road, following the dog who seemed to be the leader. It was a simple road, not made of asphalt nor concrete or any other material but of stones laid out like bricks on a wall. By the sides, flanking the road, I saw large fruit trees, some in flower, others already bearing fruits. Groups of flowering bushes were also set here and there, and I thought the neighbors must take care of them.

The horse's hooves clippity clopped on them, with a rhythmic sound that sedated me.

I looked around and saw that, where there had been buildings and houses of two or three floors, there were only rather small homes, none with more than a single floor. Yes. I had been misplaced, God had returned me to another world. Maybe the same time, yes, but not the same space.

As the horse continued its route, which I most definitely was not selecting, I looked around finding that for many blocks the neighborhood was the same, small homes with gardens. I also realized that children were playing with no fear, it was a weekday, and they were playing, both on the road and in the smaller or larger gardens before their houses. Were there no schools? Or was this a holiday?

I saw no cars, no trucks, I heard no planes, nor trains, and all-around people greeted me politely, and with kindness. They were cheerful, too, the greetings always expressed with a smile I tried to imitate but failed, still awed by the changes I was seen, but basically distraught by my loss.

I had tried to keep memories of Ritha in a closed compartment of my heart and mind, but I had not managed, and she kept appearing before me, in all manners of attitudes and with all types of expressions. Now, I kept remembering how she used to ask about the world of my time. If she were to be here, she would think I had been lying, all was so different to what I had told her.

We had reached an empty place, a large field on a small hill where there were no houses and no trees to obstruct the view of the horizon. Maybe this was what was called in previous times, the village commons. I looked, I strained my eyes to see farther away to where I knew was Downtown, with the huge buildings of many floors. I searched in vain for the towers of St Paul's Cathedral, the Shard, the Gherkin or the BT Tower. Not a single one of them could I find.

I returned home, pondering on the meaning of all this.

I have already said my laptop and computer were gone, so was the TV, and the phone. If I was to find some explanation for this weirdness, I would have to use what was available to me, books.

I entered the yard and taking care of the horse, brushing it so no sweat would remain, and taking all accoutrements, rein, and saddle off, I returned to the library.

It felt small, yes, but still there were there many books. I started my search, looking for books about history of this world where I had been misplaced.

What I found there was in a sense terrible, in the other, well, let me just tell you.

First, and what left me gasping in amazement, was that our exodus, the exodus from Kumari Kandam and all the cities in the surrounding areas was recorded in that book. Even I was talked about, but not by name, but as 'the Envoy'.

I learned, with pain, that what I had experienced at the end was truly a meteorite impact, a forerunner of those that in the end had destroyed that civilization, those people I had learned to love. It had struck in Syria, in the place now called Abu Hureyra, and the destruction had been terrible.

Our sojourn, the decision to abandon everything and practically run for salvation, the intervention of God in all this, all was reflected there.

This was definitely not in any history I had studied. Nothing like this had been written in the multiple books I had read during my career, or even those moment of leisure when less serious books came into my hands.

Amazed at the change, not only of history, but at the way the writers referred to God, with respect and veneration and not as it had become fashion in my world, with mockery and derision. What had happened here?

I continued reading, searching. People from the exodus had reached the neighborhood of Mount Ararat, and settled there, awaiting the cataclysm in caves or similar refuges. Others had continued north and had reached the Caucasus before the great floods.

I was very glad to learn a great part of the extremely ancient writings had survived. The Vedas were apparently all complete, as was the Ramayana and other writings I had not known about. So I surmised some priest or priests had held unto their precious cargo and survived.

Intrigued, I searched for the bible, the very large and decorated bible I remembered reading with my uncle. It was there, but significantly changed. There were no gold illustrations, in fact no illustrations at all. The writing was simple, yet elegant. What amazed me was that even then, it was still a very large book. I searched for the New Testament; it was different. Pages upon pages spoke of the Mesiah, and it was not only the four evangelists. It comprised those texts catalogued as 'heretical' or 'apocrypha', those that had been left out of the bible by the decision of the Catholic church.

Everything was different, and I could make no head or tails of it.

I continued investigating about that past I had been such a part of and found that the group which had left to go towards the Nile and where its Delta had been supposed to be had gotten there, too. What I didn't know or perhaps I had forgotten, was that the Mediterranean Sea level was much lower before the cataclysm. Some people from that group had remained in Egypt and others had traveled farther north, reaching what was to become Greece before the Mediterranean level rose due to the melting of ice caps.

So they had survived, I thought, reclining in the chair. All the suffering had been worthwhile, as they had been saved. Nothing was said, naturally, about my beloved, or her family, and yet I hoped, with all my heart, that she had survived both the cataclysm and my abandonment of her.

My heart constricted at the memory, and tears flooded to my eyes, I could even say this had become a ritual every time I let my mind go back to those times. Would I, could I ever again, feel love or happiness?

They had been saved; the ancient civilization had been saved though their cities had perished. Was this what had changed this world?

I thought about it, and the more I thought the more convinced I was that that was what had happened.

I kept on reading, searching for the worldwide events that should be reflected in any history book. Napoleon and his wars, Genghis Khan, the first and second world wars. I looked even for the most recent ones, the Gulf War, the war in Afghanistan, the Korean and Viet Nam wars; none were there.

What? A world without wars? Impossible, this couldn't really be. Mankind's greed, hate and selfishness were the source of all of those, and I was sure greed and selfishness were still there. Men, and women, naturally, could not have changed so much.

"Really?" I heard a soft voice in my mind. "Do you think the Power of the Word, the Power of the Lord and of the Sacrifice cannot do that?"

I shivered. Had I forgotten? Had I forgotten how He and His Son had guided me? How could I?

Sent Back

"All is possible with Him." Said the voice.

I was silent, ashamed. Yes, I had forgotten, perhaps the pain of my loss, perhaps the incredible change that had befallen me had made me forget.

I sat there, lost in thought, when Mrs. Urville came in unannounced.

"She's here, Andrew!" She exclaimed with such a happy face and voice I was angry at her.

"The Mistress is here, they are back!" She cried and scampered out.

I could hear voices in the entry hallway, and the cry of a child.

I ran to the door, Ritha was there, enveloped in shawls and carrying on her arms a baby, a baby boy, my son.

ABOUT THE AUTHOR

Hortensia de los Santos was born in Cuba in 1948. Her first novel, Caverna de Cristales Gigantes was published in 2010. After that came the first book of the Dreamworld of Maya Series, The Broken Veil, also published in Spanish in two volumes: A Través del Velo Rasgado and Tras el Velo Rasgado. These were followed by Powers of the Gods, A Drop of Blood and First Exodus.

She also wrote and published The Noumenon – Shadow of Distant Past and A Forgotten Love Story, this last one also published in Spanish with the title La Otra Historia.

Ms. De los Santos has done extensive studies in Comparative Religions and Ancient History, holds a Bachelor in Science and enjoys programming web pages and gardening.

She lives in Miami in company of her family.

Made in the USA
Columbia, SC
16 November 2022